JACQUI ROSE
THE STREETS

MACMILLAN

First published 2022 by Macmillan
an imprint of Pan Macmillan
The Smithson, 6 Briset Street, London EC1M 5NR
EU representative: Macmillan Publishers Ireland Ltd, 1st Floor,
The Liffey Trust Centre, 117–126 Sheriff Street Upper,
Dublin 1, D01 YC43
Associated companies throughout the world
www.panmacmillan.com

ISBN 978-1-5290-7652-3

1 3 5 7 9 8 6 4 2

A CIP catalogue record for this book is available from the British Library.

Map artwork by Hemesh Alles

Typeset in Plantin by Jouve (UK), Milton Keynes
Printed and bound by CPI Group (UK) Ltd, Croydon, CR0 4YY

To Wayne Brookes, editor extraordinaire.
Thank you for believing in me. It means the world. J x

Three may keep a secret, if two of them are dead . . .

Benjamin Franklin

TEN YEARS AGO

'Move it *now*! Come on . . . Martin, move yourself!'

Groggy, Jo Martin pushed herself up on her elbows in the single metal bed, feeling the springs of the stained mattress digging into the back of her thighs. She flicked a gaze at her alarm clock; it was only six a.m. From underneath her fringe she stared in bemusement at the screw standing in the doorway of her cell. 'Ain't you ever heard of good morning? Or better still, how about a little morning kiss . . . Oh that's right, I forgot – you don't swing my way, do you, officer? Though as I keep telling you, the offer's always here if you ever change your mind. Once you've tasted pussy, there ain't no turning back.'

She winked and Officer Barrow's cheeks flushed red. 'Move it, Martin. I haven't got time for your filthy mouth today.'

Noticing a dribble of egg yolk on the lapel of the officer's uniform, Jo licked her lips, tasting the sticky dry spit at the corner of her mouth, a side effect from the medication she'd been put on. She smirked. 'Fucking hell, someone's got out of the wrong side of bed, ain't they? Or have you found out that your old man has been playing away? Is that it? Has he been dipping his dick where he shouldn't?' Still smirking, Jo could hear the venom in her own voice.

She knew full well anything other than a *yes miss, no miss* would get right under the skin of Officer Barrow and no doubt there'd be consequences. There always was. But she didn't care, not anymore. Or rather, she *did* care, she cared so fucking much it was

3

untrue, but there was no way she was *ever* going to let a fat, spiteful, bitter bitch like Barrow ever know that.

Swinging her feet onto the cold floor, Jo glanced away from the officer, watching the rain dripping down the rusting bars of the window. Barrow had made her life a living hell for the past four years, ever since she'd arrived here at Granger Hall. For some reason she'd never quite worked out, the officer had made it her personal mission to try to fuck her over, break her: solitary confinement, keeping her banged up for days on end, turning a blind eye when the other women on the wing had added crushed-up bits of glass to her food. Once, she'd even found a used tampon mixed in with her plate of ravioli. Though, like she'd told a grinning Barrow at the time, the prison food was so bland, it probably had added to the taste.

Oh God yeah, she'd had it all, thanks to Barrow, who'd always reminded her of a hyena, waiting hungrily for a reaction. But she'd never given her one. *Never.* And so far, much to Barrow's fury, it hadn't broken her; she'd survived everything the officer had sent her way . . . *Just.*

She'd even managed to get through last summer, sharing a cell with some crazy mare who'd killed her father while he'd been watching football: twelve, deep bloody blows with an axe to the back of his skull. The killing hadn't been the problem; in fact Jo had actually enjoyed hearing how the man squealed like a pig when the axe split his head in half. She'd giggled about that for a long while afterwards. Truth be told, Jo wished she'd done the same thing to her own family . . . It was a shame she'd never taken the chance.

No, the problem had been, at least once a week when the temperatures soared well into the eighties and the heat had crept in through the window like it was looking for shade, the woman had dirty-protested, smearing her own shit all over the walls. And

Barrow, well, she'd made Jo sit there in the cell, surrounded by crap, hour after hour, the stench climbing into her nose and seeping into her pores . . . She'd felt like an animal. But that's what the public had wanted, hadn't they? Taking away her freedom hadn't been fucking enough for them. They'd wanted to strip her of everything . . . and they'd almost succeeded . . . *Almost.*

Four years ago, when some snotty journalist had found out she was serving her sentence in a cushy closed condition prison, after a series of public outcries, she'd been moved here, Granger Hall, a CAT-A jail where she'd been ever since.

Looking back, it'd seemed the whole country had wanted to know she was suffering. Somehow, she reckoned it had made them sleep better in their beds, knowing she was locked up with the *real* scum of society. They'd even discussed her on TV, on some breakfast chat show; tea and toast along with a slice of public opinion.

Everyone was out for her blood after reading what the newspapers had written about her. It had made her laugh what they'd said: vicious, heartless, wicked, depraved, nefarious (that one she'd had to look up). If she had it her way, all of them, all those people who ever judged her, would end up squealing like pigs, because they didn't know. They didn't know her and they certainly didn't know what had really happened that day. No one did, except for her . . . and *him.*

Quickly, Jo inhaled, feeling like her chest suddenly had a crushing weight on it. She wasn't going to go there, and she hurriedly shut down her thoughts. One thing she'd learnt not to do in a place like this was think too hard.

Turning back to stare directly into Officer Barrow's dark, shrew-like eyes, Jo shrugged. 'Then what's all the drama about, *officer*?'

'I'm not here to play games. For some reason the powers that be have been fooled by your lies.'

5

Jo scowled. 'What?'

'Seems like this is your lucky day . . . You're getting out of here . . . You must have done a good job on the parole board. What did you do, Martin? Cry? Apologize? Show them your social reports to let them know how bad you'd had it as a kid? Well, whatever you did, it worked . . . So well done, Martin, well done.' Officer Barrow began to clap slowly as a sneer scraped across her face. 'Oh, don't pretend you're shocked, Martin; life clearly doesn't mean life anymore, but we both know you should be locked up forever and burn in hell for what you did to those poor, innocent children.'

Internally, Jo flinched, but she knew the only expression Barrow would see was a stone-cold face. No emotion. Nothing. It was something she'd practised since she was a kid.

'But I thought you couldn't leave here without a parting gift,' Officer Barrow continued. 'It was the least I could do.'

'What you talking about?'

Officer Barrow stepped back and nodded to the side of her. Within seconds three inmates that Jo had never seen before stood at the door.

The sneer was still on Barrow's face. 'Nothing to say, Martin?'

Jo's heart raced, her gaze darting between the women. 'Yeah, actually I have . . . *Fuck you.*'

The officer's fury was evident. She turned to the three inmates, hatred spitting out of her. 'She's all yours, girls . . . Enjoy.'

The night bus trundled along and Jo leant her face against the dirty window, watching the world go by. The cool of the glass soothed her left eye, which was so swollen it refused to open. Her probation officer had offered to drive her to the flat which she'd be staying in for the next couple of weeks, but she'd refused. She needed to remember what it was like to walk along the pavements and get on a bus and taste the evening air.

Jo shifted in her seat to try to get comfortable. Jesus, she was hurting; she could hardly swallow from the cuts in her mouth, her ribcage felt like a dozen boots had trampled on her and she was bleeding quite heavily. Before she'd left the parole office, she'd even had to shove a handful of paper towels down her knickers, but she wasn't going to worry about it, *not this time*, because she'd won the lottery . . . She was *free*.

She laughed loudly at the thought and the bald-headed man opposite looked up from his book, staring at Jo inquisitively. She glared. 'You got a problem, mate?' Her words slurred out; her tongue was split and she winced from the razor-sharp sting which shot through her. Pale-faced, the man hurriedly shook his head and shifted his gaze back to his book, causing Jo to snort with laughter again.

No matter what Barrow had said, her release *had* come as a shock to her. Yes, she'd had all the interviews with doctors, social workers and the parole board, but her solicitor and everyone else involved had kept quiet about the outcome, not even telling her what was happening.

She supposed they hadn't wanted the papers and the public to get wind of the fact that she might walk free. They hadn't wanted anyone to fuck it up for her. And this time, even the courts had come through. They had granted her anonymity. An opportunity to start again, because as the social worker had apparently told the courts, she'd been born into a living hell and never really stood a chance.

Her solicitor had told her most people sentenced for the crimes the stupid, fat-face jury had found her guilty of would be locked up forever. And so there were only a few people, half a dozen in the country, maybe, who'd been granted lifelong anonymity. And now she was one of them.

She'd never felt special before, but she guessed she was.

She was important.

Jo giggled, delighted at that idea, but her joy quickly faded as she thought about *him*. What *he* would say if *he* knew she was free. What *he* would say about her being special.

Jo dug her fingernails into her palms as hard as she could, forcing herself to think of something else. She wasn't going to let *him* spoil today. This was a happy day.

She turned her thoughts back to her solicitor and what else he had said; only a small group of senior officials in the public protection unit at the Ministry of Justice, up to two probation officers and one police officer of commander level working the area of where she'd eventually choose to live, would know of her original identity. So the likes of that bitch Barrow would be kept in the dark.

There weren't any photos of her really, which was good. There were certainly none from her childhood; her family hadn't exactly been big on sentiment . . . Then Jo suddenly remembered, the newspapers *did* have one. It'd been on the front of all the papers. The photo had shown her being led out of a police van like a dog when she'd first been arrested. But she wasn't worried. It had been too grainy. Even she wouldn't recognize herself from it. And besides, it had been taken twelve years ago when she'd been only fourteen.

So, she could really make a go of this new life. Start again. She'd have a new name, she'd dye her hair and even her date of birth was going to be changed for her. She didn't have to be Jo Martin anymore. She could kill off her old life, all without getting any more blood on her hands, and no one would know who she was going to become. And when all the paperwork had been sorted, well, she knew exactly what she was going to do. She was going to go back to London, back to the Streets . . .

NOW

1

'I'd have got there faster if I was being driven in a fucking milk float,' Ned Reid growled as he sat irritated in the passenger seat of his blacked-out Range Rover as it cruised along Duke's Road.

Cookie Mackenzie cut a sideward glance at Ned, hoping it didn't look *too* obvious that she was trying to waste as much time as she possibly could.

They'd left their large townhouse in D'Arblay Street, Soho, over forty-five minutes ago and they were *still* only passing Midford Place, a journey which normally would've taken them fifteen minutes. But after finding out what Ned's plans were, she'd hurriedly texted ahead to give warning before making sure she turned up every street with roadworks and got stuck behind every lorry she saw.

'Put your foot on it, darlin, I ain't got all day.'

'It's cos it's Friday lunchtime, it's always busier. The traffic round here is a nightmare.'

Ned started drumming his fingers on the armrest. A habit which usually signalled the beginning of trouble. 'If I didn't know you better, Cooks, I'd say you were deliberately going slow. And if that *is* what you're doing, it ain't going to work, you know that? Not only that, you'll piss me off – and neither of us wants that, do we?'

Ignoring the underlying threat, Cookie saw the traffic lights ahead turn red at the junction of Euston Road. She breathed out a silent sigh of relief and glanced at the clock. She needed more time. 'That's ridiculous, babe, why would I want to go slow?' she scoffed.

'You know why.'

'I have no idea what you're on about.' Turning to him, Cookie watched Ned absent-mindedly rubbing the long knife scar that started at the corner of his mouth and finished at the top of his ear. The Glasgow smile. Not that anyone had been smiling or laughing when it had happened; even now, it was a subject off limits.

Ned's green eyes flashed at Cookie, his handsome face – paradoxically enhanced by the scar – darkened. 'Don't play innocent, sweetheart.'

Cookie shrugged, hoping her voice didn't betray what she was feeling as the knot in her stomach tightened. 'It's hardly my fault if everyone chooses to do roadworks today, is it? Maybe next time you should drive.'

Ned gave a quiet chuckle under his breath and immediately Cookie felt her shoulders stiffen. She spoke as calmly as she could. 'Look, Ned, I'm sorry, OK. I never . . .'

At that moment, a call came through, keeping Cookie from what she was going to say. Ned glanced at the car screen as the name popped up on the large display.

'It's Simon Draper.'

'I can fucking read,' Ned snarled again.

'You not going to answer it?'

'Do I look like I am?'

'Are you sure that's a good idea?' She knew what Simon Draper was like if Ned didn't jump at his beck and call. Not that Ned would ever admit that's how it was. He liked to think he was his own boss, untouchable, and to a point he was . . . until it came to Simon, a big-time drug dealer who'd earned his millions and his place as gangster number one through violence and sheer terror. There was a long history between Ned and Simon, some-thing Simon never let him forget.

Still stuck at the traffic lights, Ned locked eyes with her. Though Cookie tried to smile, she couldn't quite manage it. He turned and glanced out of the window. '*Fuck*,' he muttered, more to himself than her, then banged aggressively on the side of the door with his fist. 'Get out of the car, Cooks.'

'What?'

'You heard me: *get out.*'

Cookie's gaze darted around. 'Come on, Ned. It's raining, and besides, it'll take me ages to walk back, and Louboutins ain't exactly known to be the hiker's boot of choice, are they?'

He brought his face inches away from hers, until Cookie could smell the peppermint gum he'd eaten earlier. He traced his finger over her cheek. 'I ain't asking you to walk home, sweetheart. I want to swap sides. I reckon if I drive, we can get there in less than five minutes. In fact, you can fucking count on it, Cooks.'

At the rumble of menace in his voice, Cookie felt as if her heart was leaping into her throat. 'Don't be silly, I might as well get us there now.'

'Do I look like I'm the sort of guy to be *silly*?' Ned whispered.

It was Cookie's turn to lower her voice into a hush. 'No, of course not . . .' And with those words, she reached for the door handle.

Stepping out into the road, she looked up to the grey February skies, feeling the light drops of rain on her face. She took a deep breath to steady herself but suddenly jumped at the sound of the car behind them, beeping its horn.

Instinctively, she spun round to Ned, then glanced at the driver before drawing her eyes back. 'Leave it, yeah, Ned?' she said, her tone placating. 'Ned, please.'

Paying no attention to Cookie, Ned opened his arms wide, staring into the Ford Fiesta. He gave a lopsided grin and his voice was unnervingly menacing. 'If you've got something to say to me, mate, why don't you get out and we can have a little chat?'

Behind Ned's back, Cookie gave the tiniest shake of her head to the driver of the Fiesta. The man caught her eye and, maybe picking up her sense of concern, he took his hands off the horn, looking like he was visibly shrinking down into his seat.

Fleetingly, Cookie held her breath, but Ned soon turned his attention back to her. 'Get in the fucking car! I said, get in the fucking car!' Stomping to the driver's side, Ned roared his orders to Cookie and, knowing better than to argue when he was in this mood, she did as she was told. Over the years she'd learned to pick her battles.

Barely giving her the chance to put on her seat belt, Ned flicked the Range Rover out of automatic and into manual, ramming his foot down hard.

Barely missing the elderly cyclist dressed head to toe in reflective wear, Ned sped aggressively across the junction, heading along Hampstead Road. Then he took a sharp left, the car bouncing at sixty miles an hour over the speed bumps. He turned right into Cumberland Market and halfway along, in front of a run-down block of flats, he pulled up.

Glancing at the clock, he winked at Cookie. 'Two minutes, forty-three seconds. Not bad, eh? . . . Right then, I reckon it's showtime, don't you?'

'Ned . . .' But she trailed off, realizing there was nothing she could say that would make the slightest difference to what was about to happen . . .

Feeling the north-west wind cut through her, Cookie pulled up the collar of her brown suede jacket. She shivered. It was freezing, and this truly was the last place she wanted to be, but it was better that she was here. To leave Ned to deal with it on his own would be like letting lambs go to the slaughter.

As she made to follow him, a London cab drove past, zooming through a large muddy puddle and showering Cookie with black streaks of water. 'You're having a laugh, ain't you, mate? Do you know how much this jacket cost?' Getting some of her tension out, she shouted after the cab, knowing the driver couldn't hear but making her feel slightly better.

'Are you coming or what?' Ned spoke with his back to her as he made his way to the entrance of the flats.

'Oh, don't mind me, will you? It's all right for some cabbie to drench me designers' with stinking water, but anyone beeps the horn at you for causing a traffic jam and you're ready to string them up.'

Turning round, Ned waited, grinning at her. 'You love to exaggerate, babes. And if it makes you happy, I'll buy you some new gear. Take you shopping tomorrow, how about that? See, problem solved.'

She rolled her eyes at the same time as trying to take a sneaky look at her watch. 'What would make me happy is if we went back home. I don't even know why we had to come.' She sighed, hoping the warning text she'd sent earlier had got through.

Ned's grin turned into a wry smile. 'Why you looking so jumpy, Cooks? Is there something you want to tell me?' His eyes danced. He knew her too well, but her motto with Ned was always *deny till you die*. The irony certainly wasn't lost on Cookie.

Ignoring the cold water dripping down her legs, she scoffed. 'No, no, of course not.'

'There better not be. And let's pray for your sake that the look on your face, the one which screams to me that you ain't telling the truth, is only a figment of my imagination, eh, Cooks?'

He turned away again, but Cookie grabbed hold of his arm. Desperate. 'Ned, listen to me, no violence, OK? Promise?'

Pushing back her long, chestnut hair away from her face, he kissed Cookie on the cheek roughly, his three-day shadow scratching at her smooth skin. 'I promise . . . or I would if I was a fucking priest. Now are you coming with me or what?' He moved away from her but immediately she ran in front of him, blocking his way.

'They're just kids, Ned.'

He glared at her. 'This past year, since we came to Soho, I reckon you've become soft. What happened to the stony-faced cow you used to be?'

'Am I supposed to take that as a compliment?'

'Take it any way you want to.'

As was her habit when she was irritated but trying not to show it, Cookie chewed on the inside of her cheek. 'I ain't soft, Ned, you know that. I'm only saying they're kids.'

The rain began to get heavier and the icy winds whipped up. 'Well don't. Keep that beautiful mouth of yours closed.'

He spun away from her and, using his knuckle to avoid the dirt and lumps of dried chewing gum stuck to the intercom unit, he pressed every single buzzer.

There was no answer from any of the residents.

'Maybe they're not there,' Cookie said hopefully.

Frowning, Ned stared at her. 'What? The whole of the block ain't in? You wish.'

Trying a different tactic, Cookie cuddled up to him. 'Look, let's go home, shall we? I can run you a nice bath, light some candles, give you a massage and we can come back another day. What do you say?' She moved in towards Ned, kissing him sensually on the lips, but he drew away and continued to glare.

'I say, don't act like a fucking little whore, Cooks. I thought them days were behind you.'

Anger flashed through her, but she stayed calm. 'Who said romance was dead, eh?'

'Look, whether you like it or not, I ain't going anywhere until I get what I came for.'

'But—'

Before Cookie could get the rest of her sentence out, Ned grabbed her chin, squeezing her face hard between his hands. 'What did I tell you? You need to watch that mouth of yours. There's only so much I'll take.'

Cookie hit his arm away and glared back. 'Anyone tell you that you're a prize wanker sometimes?'

'Yeah, and they ended up taking a trip to A and E. What of it?'

At that exact moment, the entrance of the flats opened and a man, looking very stoned, stumbled out, allowing Ned and Cookie to dip inside.

2

The entrance hall stank. The concrete floor was strewn with rubbish, cigarette butt ends, discarded needles and empty flattened lager cans. A used nappy was rolled up in a ball on the bottom stair. Misspelt profanities were graffitied over the walls as well as a capitalized threat to kill someone called Davey. And by the lift, which had an OUT OF ORDER sign taped to it, there was a large pool of ageing vomit.

Cookie shuddered, but not because of the smell, although that was bad; it was the fact that these flats, this place, reminded her of how her life had been after . . . *No.* She immediately blocked that thought before it had a chance to fully form. Right now, she needed to focus on dealing with Ned; later, when she was alone, then maybe she'd allow herself to open that box in her head, no matter how painful.

So many times she'd desperately wanted to share those thoughts – the ones which woke her up in the middle of the night – with anyone who would listen. She wanted to scream out the truth. Tell everyone the reason why she was *really* here in Soho. But she couldn't. Not yet. Maybe never. Because who could she trust? There was no one.

Trying to ignore the images beginning to play in her mind, Cookie let out a long sigh as she traipsed up the stairs after Ned. Some things were best kept as secrets. In any case, there was no way, after all this time and everything she'd had to put up with, she was going to let *anything* spoil the moment she'd waited all these years for . . . 'It was number thirty-six, wasn't it? *Cooks?*' Ned shouted, his voice echoing around the dank stairwell as he made his way to the first landing.

Cookie shrugged. 'I'm not sure.' She could hear the lack of willingness in her voice.

Leaning over the banisters, Ned stared down, the vein in the middle of his forehead prominent. 'I won't ask you again: was it number thirty-fucking-six?'

Cookie gave Ned the tiniest of nods. 'Yeah, it was. But, Ned, *please* go easy.'

Ned Reid didn't bother replying.

Flat 36 was located at the end of a draughty corridor on the top floor of the small block of flats. Kicking a torn-open rubbish bag out of his way, Ned turned to Cookie and winked. Not bothering to knock, he raised his leg and smashed open the door with a hard kick.

'Ned!'

Paying no attention to her, Ned charged through the dilapidated bedsit, followed closely by Cookie. Once again, he raised his leg and kicked open the only door which was shut . . . The look on the young couple's faces were a mirror image of fear and shock.

Ned stared coldly at the naked, spotty, skinny youth who looked no older than eighteen and was midway through getting a blow job from a girl who was similar in age and also naked.

He smiled wildly, though it didn't meet his eyes. 'Hello, Zee, surprised to see me, darlin'?'

The girl let out a tiny whimper and Ned chuckled, his glare fixated on her. 'What's that? Oh, take him out of your mouth, will you, I can't hear what you're saying.' Then his stare swept up to the boy's. 'Sorry to spoil your fun, mate. You see, I'm here to collect her, so you'll have to finish yourself off when we've gone.'

But it was too late; the young boy trembled and Cookie watched his knees shake as he climaxed with a loud, humiliated groan.

Looking bored, Ned continued to stare at the youth, who by now was red-faced and sweaty, causing his acne to look inflamed.

'Feel better now, do we?' was all Ned said before he turned back to Zee – a pretty Asian girl – who was busy picking a long ginger pubic hair out of her teeth at the same time as wiping her mouth.

Crouching, Ned poked Zee hard in her chest, then, like he'd done with Cookie, he swept her long, black hair away from her face, holding it tightly and pulling her head back. 'I told you that you could fuck him, Zee, not fall in love. Now get dressed and say goodbye to your little mate, cos you won't be seeing him again.'

Zee's hollow brown eyes, which had dark circles underneath them like ink smudges, filled with tears. Then, much to Cookie's despair, Zee proceeded to purse her lips, looking defiant. 'I ain't going nowhere, Ned.'

Smirking and letting go of Zee's hair, Ned gave a small shake of his head and stood up. 'Is that right?'

'Yeah, it fucking well is.'

Seeing Ned's fist open and close, Cookie stepped forward. 'Ned, let me handle it, hey?'

He shoved her aside, though she knew better than to push back. All she could do now was watch and *hope* that Zee would keep her mouth shut.

'So where were we, Zee . . . Oh, that's right, you were telling me how you ain't coming back with me?' Ned's laughter unnerved even Cookie.

Zee, who didn't look as confident as she had before, got up as well, and Cookie thought how tiny she looked standing in front of Ned's six foot plus, muscular frame. He tilted his head to one side, slowly licking his lips, but remaining silent. This had the effect of causing Zee to start to talk. Her strong cockney accent mixed in with her slight lisp. 'I love him, Ned. So like I say, I ain't going nowhere with you. I don't care what you do. Stuart makes me happy, that ain't a crime, we're going to get married and start a family. And I know you took me in an' all, but I'm sick of the life. I ain't doing it no more.'

Casually looking at his nails, Ned sniffed. Then he grabbed her throat, squeezing it easily in one hand. 'Get dressed, Zee, and stop wasting my time.'

With her face turning red, Zee scratched at Ned's hand, trying to release his grip. She gasped her words as she struggled to breathe. 'No. Ain't you heard what I said? I *love* him, but then you wouldn't know what that is. And anyway, you ain't my dad, I can do what I like.'

'Ned, let go . . . Ned, please,' Cookie implored him.

'Shut your fucking mouth, Cooks – unless you want me to break her neck here and now.'

Cookie shrank back, watching Ned turn his attention to Zee again. 'No, I ain't your dad, it's even better than that . . . I *own* you, Zee, and until you pay me back everything that I've spent out on you over the past couple of years, you ain't going nowhere. Now get *fucking* dressed.'

'You heard her, mate. She don't want to come with you.' Stuart stood with his hand on his hips, his flaccid penis dribbling with saliva and the last drops of sperm.

Without bothering to look at Stuart, Ned pointed at Zee. 'You better tell your boyfriend to keep his mouth shut unless he wants me to slice that limp dick off and shove it down his throat.'

Cookie stepped in front of Ned and, not for the first time that day, she could feel her heart racing. 'Do what he says, Stuart. You don't want any trouble.' Her voice was soft and quiet, then she turned to Zee. 'You need to tell him that Ned's right . . . You know he is.'

Zee glanced at Cookie, then at her boyfriend. Stuart shook his head. 'Ned ain't right – we can do what we like.'

'I thought I told you to keep your mouth shut. Did you think I was joking?' Ned reached into his grey Savile Row handmade coat and casually pulled out a flick knife. A quick press of the button and the large jagged blade sprang out hungrily, then Ned lunged for the young man, who let out a high-pitched shriek as he was grabbed by the scruff of his neck before being dragged into another room.

'Please, Ned, please! No! No! I'm sorry, I'm sorry! I'll come with you. I'll come with you, but leave him alone . . . Ned, *please.*' Cookie held Zee back as her hysterical screams mixed in with Stuart's. They cut right through Cookie, and she tried to block them out, trying to remind herself yet again why she still was here as she winced at the sounds coming from the next room. Though why the hell she flinched, she didn't know. By now, after almost ten years, she should've been used to it.

Nose running and eyes streaming with tears, Zee buried her head into Cookie's shoulder. 'I fucking hate him, I hate him, Cooks!'

Cookie drew Zee away from her. 'Stop talking like that, under-stand? You're in enough trouble already.'

'How did you know where I was?'

'Did you really think that the other girls wouldn't tell Ned where you'd gone once he started putting the pressure on? Now get dressed – come on, I'll help you.' She passed Zee the pair of skinny off-white jeans which had been lying discarded on the floor.

Waiting for Zee – who hadn't stopped crying – to get ready, Cookie glanced around. Smoke-stained flowery green wallpaper was peeling off the walls, exposing large damp patches and electric wires. The threadbare carpet looked like it was crawling with dirt and bugs, and the tiny kitchenette and stove was filthy. But she guessed Zee was too loved up to notice and was looking through a very large pair of rose-tinted glasses.

When Zee had met Stuart – another runaway – last year in the arcade in Soho, the girl had seemed genuinely happy. She'd fallen in love and Ned had eventually let them see each other twice a week. But now Zee had blown it. There was no way, no way at all, Ned would ever let her see Stuart again.

'What were you playing at? I told you to get out of here. Didn't you get my text?' Cookie whispered.

Zee, looking absolutely terrified at the sudden silence after the screams, wiped her running nose on the back of her hand. She shook her head. 'No, the signal's shit here.'

'Let's go . . . *Now*.' Barking his order, Ned stalked out of the other room as Cookie glanced at his bloodstained hand, then, without saying anything, she grabbed Zee's jacket.

'Come on, you heard him.'

Wide-eyed, Zee looked at Cookie. 'We can't! What about Stuart? We've got to go and check on him. What if Ned's—'

'Leave him, Zee,' Cookie interrupted. 'It's for the best. And listen to me, you've got to stop crying; it'll only wind Ned up.'

Zee's gaze drifted towards the room Ned had left Stuart in. 'Do you think Stuart will get in touch with me?'

'Not if he's got any sense.' And with those words, Cookie wrapped the jacket tightly around the girl's shoulders, leading her out of the bedsit.

★

Hurrying after Ned, Cookie and Zee made their way outside to the car. It was raining hard now and the February chill bit through Cookie's clothes. As she was about to step into the car, Zee's phone buzzed. Her face, despite being puffy and red from crying, lit up, delighted.

'Tell me it ain't that wanker texting you already, Zee. Fuck me, I must be losing my touch. The way I left him, I'd be surprised if he even knew his name. He's got some front, I'll give him that . . . Pass me your phone.'

The phone wasn't forthcoming.

'I said, *pass me your fucking phone.*' Ned stretched out his hand and, reluctantly but quickly, Zee, visibly shaking, gave it to him.

Snatching it out of her hands, Ned glanced at the text, then he brought his eyes up slowly to smile at Zee; a dead, cold stare. 'Well, well, well. Shall I read it?'

You need to get out now! Ned and me are on our way. Cooks x

Ned turned to Cookie, putting the tips of his fingers under her chin, raising her head up. He kissed her slowly, then suddenly bit down on her bottom lip, drawing blood. Letting out a tiny squeal, Cookie pulled away, feeling the blood trickling down her chin as Ned glared at her with the same dead, cold stare. 'I'd say, when we get home, you and me need to have a little chat.'

3

It was well into the afternoon, and on the corner of Berwick Street, Lorni Duncan was sitting in the small Soho cafe opposite her son, hugging a warm cup of milky tea into her chest. She gazed out of the window, watching the rain lash down and the blue tarpaulins on the market stalls flap about in the wind like flags in a storm. People hurried by, looking like they all had somewhere important to go, and Lorni felt more invisible than ever. A homeless man sat huddled in his sleeping bag in the doorway of the Greek restaurant, and a cat dragged out a chicken bone from a discarded box of KFC.

She let out a long sigh, took another sip of tea and, exhausted, sank herself back against the orange plastic chair, counting the coins in front of her while mentally calculating whether she'd have enough money to buy herself another cuppa . . . £3.62; that was all she had. It was a joke. But then, that was exactly how her life felt at the moment; one big, sad joke. And right now she had no idea how she was going to get it back on track.

'Can I get you anything else, love? What about a nice bacon butty? You can't beat one on a day like this.'

Lorni gazed up at the elderly cafe owner, who'd begun to hum quietly to some country and western song which was playing on the radio. Even though the smell of old cooking oil sat in the air and the egg on toast the old man across from her was eating looked slimy and under cooked, Lorni's stomach still rumbled at the thought of a hot sandwich. It had been two days since she'd eaten.

'We're fine, thanks.'

'You sure, love? You both look like you could do with a bit of home-cooked.'

'No, it's fine. We only had our lunch a couple of hours ago,' she lied. 'Thanks anyway.'

Shrugging, the woman wandered off, and for some reason the reality of her situation hit Lorni harder. She inhaled, feeling a wave of sadness crash over her. If anyone had told her this was how her life was going to turn out, she wouldn't have believed them. But now all she wanted to do was close her eyes and not wake up for a very long time.

Hating feeling sorry for herself, she absent-mindedly touched her black eye. Things had to change. This time round it *had* to be different. She was determined to make things better, if not for herself, then for her son.

'Mum, can we go now?'

'Five more minutes, eh, sweetheart? We don't want to be standing around in the cold, do we? Look at that rain, we'll get drenched, and where we need to go is only a few minutes' walk from here. We're not supposed to meet the landlord until half past anyway. Then after that, we'll be able to settle into our new home. Exciting, isn't it?'

Her son gave an exaggerated shrug, his shoulders almost touching his ears while his brown eyes looked dull. 'It won't be like the last place, will it?'

Picking up the paper serviette in front of her, Lorni reached across the table and wiped away the chocolate doughnut crumbs from her son's mouth. 'Of course not, don't look so worried.'

'Promise?'

Lorni smiled as she gazed at him. His freckled face carried so much anguish, and once again the guilt she always felt began to wash over her. 'I promise, Jace.' Though she knew it was another lie. She couldn't possibly begin to promise that. For starters, she hadn't *actually* seen the place, though over a hurried exchange of text messages, she'd already agreed to take it. Then there was the price; as studio flats went, it was cheap, which could only mean one thing: it was a dive.

The number of the landlord she'd got from one of the few people she'd made friends with at the cash-in-hand job she'd picked up last month. He apparently liked to be called Max, but other than that and the fact she thought she'd detected a slight Irish accent, she didn't know anything else . . . Apart from she had no idea how she was *actually* going to pay the rent. All she had in the world was £150 for the deposit which Max had begrudgingly agreed to . . . plus £3.62, and she knew she was lucky she even had that.

Touching her black eye again, she cast her mind back to last night. To the landlord who'd thought it was OK to get handy with his fists after she'd told him she hadn't quite got enough money to pay the rent . . . again.

The place had been a shithole, not fit for anyone, let alone a child to live there. Every night mice had run onto their bed, the damp patch on the ceiling stank of mildew, and the heating only worked occasionally, but the landlord had still got nasty. He'd acted like she'd stolen his credit cards when she pleaded with him to wait a couple more weeks for his money . . .

'You mugging me off again, Lorni?'

'No, I'm just asking you to give me a little more time, that's all. Look, here's part of it. There's a hundred and fifty quid here. Things have been a bit tight lately.'

'I think that excuse has worn thin now. I want my rent, otherwise pack your fucking bag and get out.'

'Please, Sid, you can't do that. Give me some more time, I prom—'

'I already told you, I warned you last month, I ain't fucking Father Christmas, Lorni. There ain't a free sleigh ride around here.'

She felt the sting of tears but she refused to cry. There was no way she was going to give him the satisfaction. 'Then what am I supposed to do?'

'Not my problem. But, as I'm feeling charitable, I'll pack your bags for you.' Going across to the neatly folded pile of laundered clothes, Sid began to pick them up, flinging them out of the tiny bedsit door and onto the dirty landing.

'Get off my things! You've got no right!' With tears now streaming down her face, she grabbed his arm but he shook her off, hurling her across the room, sending her hard into a chest of drawers.

'Don't hurt my mum!'

'Jace, leave it!' Lorni stumbled to her feet, but not before Sid clutched hold of Jace, shaking him hard. 'And what are you going to do about it? Come on, you snotty little bastard, show me what you've got.'

Sid drew his fist back and punched Jace hard in his stomach before putting him in a headlock.

'Get your fucking hands off him! Get off him!' Desperate, Lorni snatched one of the kitchen knives off the draining board and pointed it at Sid. 'I said, get your fucking hands off him!'

But Sid only looked at her, a grin spreading across his face, showing off an almost toothless smile. 'You stupid little bitch.' Then she felt a hard crack at the side of her head where Sid's fist connected and a trickle of blood ran down her cheek.

The room spun and she struggled to stay standing, watching through a hazy blur as Sid began to undo his belt, his erection already showing, pushing against his cheap, nylon trousers. But then she saw the pain and fear on her son's face, the pale terror. And that's all that was needed. Seeing Jace doubled over in pain was like a bucket of ice *water to her. Her head immediately cleared and she grabbed hold of her son's hand, snatching her handbag off the side before running past Sid and out of the bedsit to safety . . .*

Snapping her mind away from the events of yesterday, Lorni sighed. They were safe – well, for now anyway. That's what she had to focus on. And at least last night they'd had somewhere warm to go, unlike other times. In fact it'd been fun. They'd gone to Heathrow airport and watched the planes. It was one of the few places where no one would bother to question them. A boy and his mum, what was there to be suspicious about?

She'd also got away with not giving Sid any of the overdue rent, which was how she had £150. With the exception of her handbag, they'd left everything they owned behind, though most of it was only cheap clothes from the market and a few books and magazines for Jace. So, she guessed, things could be worse . . . much worse.

Winking at Jace and hoping that he didn't pick up on her mood, Lorni tried to sound chirpy. 'Anyway, you remember what I've told you, sweetheart? You understand what you have to do?'

'Yeah, I know.'

'Look at me. This is important, Jace.'

His big brown eyes swept up to gaze at her and she felt that familiar rush of love and fierce protection which dictated every-thing she did. It was the reason she found herself in this situation in the first place.

'I know, Mum. You tell me *every* time we move.'

Guilt as usual slapped Lorni hard, triggering her to snap before she could stop herself. 'Don't say it like that. We just—'

'We just can't let anyone know our secrets,' Jace interrupted, looking back down to continue fiddling with the frayed edge of the worn plastic tablecloth as tears shone in his eyes.

'I'm sorry, but it will get better. And keeping secrets, well that ain't a bad thing, is it? It's like a game, ain't it? We don't want anyone to know our business, that's all.'

'Why?'

Lorni could feel herself shutting down. 'That's the way it is, baby.' She heard the coldness in her voice.

Jace stared at his mum. That's what she always told him. Ever since he could remember, she'd said the same thing, but he never knew why, he never understood *why* he wasn't allowed to tell anyone about his mum and why most of the time he didn't go to school.

The last time he'd been was about two years ago, or maybe three. He couldn't really remember, but he *did* remember the reason why he'd left. The teacher had started asking him questions. Where they'd lived, what his mum did for a job, what his mum's favourite colour was, if she knew how to drive a car? Lots and lots of questions.

They'd been nice questions, questions for his class project, and the teacher had asked everyone else the same thing. She'd even written out a list of the ones he didn't know the answer to. But when he'd shown his mum, she hadn't thought they were nice. She'd got upset and then angry and torn the list up. Then in the morning, they'd packed their things and moved away. He didn't even get the chance to say goodbye to his friends. That was the last time he'd been to school, the last time he'd had a friend.

'I'll get you another doughnut. We've got enough money. Would you like that? Jace, please don't get upset.'

Jace blinked away the tears and shook his head. He hated secrets, though he did know you could have nice secrets; presents and birthday surprises, but he didn't have those kind, not really, because he wasn't sure when his birthday was. This year his mum had woken him up with a birthday cake with ten candles on 12

January, but the year before, she'd sung him 'Happy Birthday' in May.

She was always changing something. Every time they left a flat and moved to another area, his mum changed something else, even the colour of her hair. Moving and secrets. The two things he hated. Though he was pleased he'd moved away from Sid.

He'd been frightened last night and now he had purple marks all over his stomach from where Sid had hurt him.

'Look, you and me, Jace, we're all right, ain't we? I love you, that's what matters, ain't it? And everyone has secrets. Maybe even you've got secrets. Have you, Jace?' She laughed loudly and smiled at him, and once again he shook his head. But she was right, he did. As much as he didn't like them, he did have secrets of his own. He'd decided he wasn't going to tell his mum about the marks all over his tummy, and he wasn't going to tell her about all the other times Sid had hurt him while she was out at work. It would've made her too sad. So he guessed, if they stopped his mum from crying, maybe secrets weren't a bad thing after all.

'Don't look so worried, Jace. I'm only joking. But adults have them all the time. I bet everyone walking past here has secrets, Jace. It won't only be us. Look, look at that woman over there.' She laughed again. 'I reckon she's full of them, don't you?'

4

Pearl Reid waddled past Birdie's cafe, scowling at the young boy and woman who were pointing at her as she made her way towards Berwick market. Rude little shits. What did they want, a fucking picture? She tutted and stepped off the pavement feeling the pain of her bunion shooting through her big toe.

Angrily, she pushed past a group of schoolkids and weaved through the market. As a kid she used to love this place, crossing the river from Bermondsey to come up to the market for the day, but it had changed over the years. Now only a couple of traditional fruit and vegetable stalls remained, the rest cooked and sold international food, the sort of grub which would never pass her lips; rollmop and eels was foreign enough for Pearl.

The area had once been an energetic part of the red-light district, but that had also changed as the council desperately tried to clean it up. They were on to a losing battle; as one brothel was shut down another one popped up. It was one thing to get rid of the fruit stalls, but sex was going nowhere.

As the rain started to fall with a vengeance, Pearl cursed her son. She'd no idea why Ned couldn't have sent the driver to pick her up from the nail salon like he always did. He knew she didn't walk anywhere, *especially* in the rain, but he'd ignored all her texts to send someone to collect her until twenty minutes ago, when she'd received an angry phone call from him. Winding herself up even more, Pearl replayed the phone call in her head:

'You really expect me to—'

'Walk. Yes, Mum, is that so hard for you to get your head around? And if you don't fucking like it – tough. You can stay where you are, for all I care. Set up frigging camp – at least that way you won't have to wait for your next appointment.'

'But, Ned—'

'No, I don't want to hear what you've got to say, though I'll tell you this for nothing: whether it's today or tomorrow or next fucking week, I will not be sending anyone to pick you up. Me name's Ned, not fucking Uber . . .'

Thinking about her son's words *and* his attitude made Pearl tut again, though it certainly wasn't helping the situation that she was drenched through as she hobbled around like a stray dog. And if getting home by herself wasn't bad enough, Ned had instructed her, without a please or thank you, to pick up some lingerie from Agent Provocateur for a couple of the girls who had a sex party to go to later.

The client – some City lawyer – had so many fetishes she could hardly keep up. If she remembered rightly, last month he'd wanted the girls to piss all over him. This time round he was going for walking the plank: seven-inch stripper heels treading all over his penis.

Not that she cared. She wasn't in the habit of passing judgement, never had been. The tosser paid good money, that was all that mattered. She wouldn't care if he wanted them to shove a hairbrush up his arse, as long as he paid. In fact, she'd do it for him if the money was right.

She cackled out loud at the thought, but then her forehead creased into a deep frown. Money or not, she didn't appreciate being treated like Ned's skivvy. When she did eventually get home, she was going to give him a piece of her mind. He wasn't too old to get a mouthful. What had got into him? Actually, she could probably guess. Cookie. It always started and ended with that snide bitch. Her son was a fool when it came to that little whore.

It was always Cookie who got under his skin, Cookie he wanted to keep like a china doll, yet it was Cookie he wanted to rough-fuck all night, waking the whole house up. And it was the same Cookie he loved like the very breath of him depended on it at the same time as hating her like he was a man possessed.

Ned just couldn't let her go. He certainly didn't get that trait from her; Pearl had never felt like that about any man in her life. She could drop any one of them without so much as a backward glance. In her book, the only place for a heart was served up on a plate with mash and gravy. She couldn't even say Ned was like his dad, mainly because she couldn't remember who his dad had been. Even at the time. It could have been one of many.

She had thought when Ned was born it would trigger her into remembering. But it didn't. The baby didn't remind her of any of the men she recalled sleeping with, though she supposed that wasn't surprising. Her and her sister Ivy – God rest her soul – had got through men like packets of fags. She'd made them pay, of course. Nothing in life was free, especially not a blow job.

'Oh for fuck's sake.' Seeing that the shop was closed, Pearl stopped in her tracks and ranted out loud. She was still ranting when she spotted the owner of Desires, the club round the corner, coming towards her carrying a large box of doughnuts. She didn't bother acknowledging him though; she had better things to do with her time than chat to the likes of him. Then, still muttering to herself, Pearl took another left towards the house.

By the time Pearl arrived in D'Arblay Street her feet felt like they were on fire and the sweat was running down her spine and pooling between her large buttock cheeks. But she smiled anyway, as she always did when she saw Ned's imposing eighteenth-century townhouse coming into view. She couldn't help it and she couldn't imagine a day when she would ever be tired of seeing it.

It was a world away from Bermondsey and the poky flat they'd started off in. They'd be still there if it wasn't for Ned being so brutal and business savvy. What more could a mother want from a son? He'd done well for himself. This beautiful home was all his, along with a number of other properties, a fair few bob in the bank, plus a booming business. She was proud of him, though it was a shame he wasn't so savvy when it came to his taste in women.

About to put the key in the front door, Pearl paused. She supposed there was a simple solution to the problem. As Ned clearly wasn't going to sort it, she would have to get rid of Cookie herself. After all, she'd given him long enough. Ten years, in fact. And she was sure Ned would thank her in the end, because as she'd always told him since he was a young boy, mothers know best.

5

Barney Kane had no idea what the time was as he stood outside his club in Soho. Though he reckoned, judging by how dark it was, it must have gone five. Still feeling breathless from hurrying back from the doughnut store, he lit up a longed-for cigarette and sighed contentedly.

Friday was always doughnut day, and it'd been his turn to get them, but by the looks of the box, soggy from rain, the girls would just have to make do with a cup of tea. He chuckled to himself, knowing how much they'd complain. Half the time no one would ever think they worked for him, rather the other way round. But then, Barney wouldn't want it any other way.

Suddenly catching sight of a black Range Rover with distinctive private number plates driving by, Barney raised his arm, waving madly. 'Cooks! Cooks!' He stepped further towards the edge of the pavement, but neither Cookie nor Ned looked in his direction.

As they sped past, he managed to catch a proper glimpse of Cookie. Her face was strained. She didn't look happy at all. In fact he'd go so far as to say she looked downright miserable. Maybe he'd give her a call later, though hopefully she'd nip down to the club before it opened, like she often did. But he guessed that would depend on Ned and whether he was willing to share her tonight.

Blowing out a mouthful of smoke, he shrugged and wondered as he often did why Cookie stayed with Ned. Like everyone in

Soho, she was wary of him. Fear, was that what kept her with him? Barney didn't think so; fear was part of it, but there was something else too, he just couldn't put his finger on what it was.

Barney's thoughts moved on from Cookie when the lorry which had been parked to the right of him pulled away, giving him a clear view of the other side of the road. Immediately he spotted a young woman with the build of a sparrow shuffling along, walking a few steps behind a short man with bad skin who was equally skinny.

Throwing the box of doughnuts on the rubbish bags outside the club, Barney took a last drag of his cigarette before throwing that down too. Then, not looking where he was going, he dashed across the road, narrowly avoiding an oncoming motorbike which swerved dangerously in the wet.

'*Look where you're going, wanker!*'

He didn't bother to shout back at the motorcyclist, preferring not to bring attention to himself.

Ignoring the rain soaking through his jumper, Barney hung back for a moment but quickly picked up his pace when he saw the woman scuttle down a flight of stone stairs to the basement of the empty building on the corner.

Pausing to make sure no one was watching, Barney flicked a hurried glance over his shoulder then rushed down the concrete steps to the basement in time to catch the bald-headed man handing over a small wrap to the woman.

'I don't think so, Pete. Tabby don't need your shit. Now fuck off.'

Standing underneath the scaffolding, both Pete and Tabby had a look of surprise on their faces. 'What's it got to do with you?' Hostility dripped from Pete as he squared up angrily to Barney.

'It's got everything to do with me, Pete. Now if I were you, I'd take yourself off . . . Tabby, give it him back.' Barney held Pete's stare. He'd known the guy for years, and he'd always been a low-life. Most of the time he dealt his shit in Leicester Square, but lately he was coming over to this side of Soho to sell his over-priced crack and heroin. A small-time dealer who thought he was Mr Big. What Barney hated most about Pete was that he cut his gear with everything from talc to household detergent, making people sick.

'Barney, go away for fuck's sake! Why are you always sticking your beak in where it's not wanted?' Tabby shrieked between nervously chewing on her dirty fingernails.

'Tabby, last time you got stuff from him, you ended up in hos-pital. That's not going to happen again.'

'If she wants to buy my stuff, she can.'

Holding onto the wrap of crack tightly, Tabby Young curled up her face. She was trembling and Barney wasn't sure if it was from the cold or because she was beginning to cluck. 'He's right, I can do what I want. Now piss off, Barney, will ya?'

Used to Tabby's outbursts, Barney didn't take offence. 'Dar-ling, you're my friend and I love you, and if you insist on taking that shit, you know Cora said she'd score you some. Now be a sweetheart and let's go.'

He put out his hand but Pete blocked it, stepping forward aggressively. 'We had a deal, me and her. She was the one who called me up. So I ain't leaving here empty-handed.'

'The deal's over. Anyway, we both know she ain't got no money. So you were going to rack it up on her tab, weren't you? Get her to work it off by sleeping with some scummy sleazeball. Well I don't think so; she isn't giving you anything, not anymore.'

Looking incensed, Pete hopped on the spot. 'You're bang out of order, Barney. I don't appreciate being ripped off. I think you're forgetting who I am.'

Barney snorted. 'Who you are? You're no one, Pete. That's what *I* think you're forgetting.'

'You should be careful what you say, cos it ain't only me you'll piss off if you carry on talking to me like that.'

'You're pathetic. You sound like a schoolkid. Here, have it back . . .' Barney snatched the wrap of crack out of Tabby's hand and threw it down on the ground at Pete's feet, then he grabbed hold of her hand, pulling her with him.

No sooner had Barney begun to lead Tabby back up the stairs than Pete grabbed hold of him, yanking him back.

'One of you needs to pay for my time. So, come on, Barney, what do you say? Who's going to pay me?'

'I think you've been smoking too much of that crack. Now get your fucking hands off me.'

'I asked you a question.'

Without answering, Barney turned to go again, but he felt a sudden sharp pain in his side. His knees went weak and he staggered, resting his hand against the wall. Tabby screamed. 'Barney! Barney!'

He glanced down at his jumper, where a dark spot of blood had begun to appear. He'd been stabbed. Wincing, he touched his side, but he stood up straight and spun round to see Pete smirking, holding a small blade.

'Oh, big mistake, sweetie,' was all Barney said before he slammed his fist hard into Pete's face, knocking loose his front teeth.

Pete's blood sprayed over the concrete wall and he sprawled on the ground. Then as quick as he could, and paying no attention to the pain in his side, Barney raised his foot. He paused for a moment, making sure he had full eye contact with Pete, then said, 'You want an answer? Here's your answer.' And with that he brought his foot down directly onto Pete's nose, grinding his heel as deep as he could into it. Even over the sound of the rain hammering on the scaffolding, Barney heard the crunch of cartilage as Pete's nose shattered, causing it to bubble with mucus and blood.

Breathing hard and placing his hand on his side, Barney nodded to Tabby. 'Come on, let's go.'

Sniffing and wiping the tears from her face, Tabby was shaking uncontrollably. 'You need to get that seen to, Barney, you need to get to a hospital. I'm sorry, I'm sorry!'

Barney doubted he was in as much pain as Pete, who was writhing on the ground and groaning in agony. He pulled up his jumper carefully and examined the wound; it was only a small nick. 'Look, it's fine. Stings like fuck, but I'll live. A double whisky will sort me out, and it's not your fault, Tabby. So no tears, OK?'

She nodded miserably.

'Come on, don't look so glum, it's my birthday tomorrow and I've got a party to sort out. I expect to see you there.' Ignoring the throbbing in his back, he smiled at her as they climbed back up the stone stairs and she smiled too, an almost toothless smile: the ravages of years of crack and heroin.

'You look freezing, why don't you come and get a coat from mine, then I want you to do something for me.'

She nodded enthusiastically. 'Anything.'

'Go and see if you can find out if Cookie's all right. There'll probably be some of Ned's girls at Gina's salon now, or some of his boys might be down at the arcade. But be discreet.'

Crossing the road back to the club, Tabby shrugged. 'When ain't I? But it'll cost you.'

Barney laughed loudly and pulled her into him. 'When doesn't it? But I ain't going to give you anything until you report back, otherwise you'll be high as a kite and I won't see you for a couple of days. Like I say, I want you at my party. It's going to be a big one.'

A police car came into sight and Barney instinctively spun round. Tabby laughed, her cackle warm. 'You going to tell me your secret?'

'What are you talking about?'

'The way you ducked from that cop car – or any cop car, come to think of it.'

Barney stared at Tabby, her straggly brown hair covering her blue eyes. Her skin grey from the lifestyle she led, but her warmth still shone out. He'd known her for almost the whole time he'd lived in Soho, which was coming on for the past ten years. A place he loved, where no one asked too many questions, which suited him.

He'd come across her one cold day in November, as he was putting the bins out. She was outside his door, curled up in a ball, exhausted and hungry. He'd given her a bite to eat, and after that she'd kept turning up in the mornings like a cat looking for food and shelter. That was how she'd got the nickname Tabby. The truth was he didn't recall what her real name was. Now, like Cora and Natalie, who worked for him at the club, Tabby was part of the family, however dysfunctional that family was.

'Anyone would think you've got something to hide, Barney.'

He winked at her. 'This is Soho, darling – who hasn't?'

6

'You're fucking disgusting! If you carry on eating like that, you'll end up six feet under like Aunt Ivy,' Ned growled as he stood in the large, lavish basement kitchen of his house. He stared at his mother, who was shovelling yet another cream cake into her mouth.

'Do me a favour. Your Aunt Ivy – God rest her soul – was fat. That's what put her under.' Pearl spluttered her words along with a large piece of cream cake which shot out of her mouth, landing on the expensive hand-carved oak table. She picked it up happily, popping it back into her mouth.

'And you're not? Have you looked in the mirror lately, Mum? Your arse is as big as a fucking hippo's. It's a good job the circus ain't coming to town, otherwise they might think you're the one that got away.'

'Oi, I'm not fat, you cheeky bastard . . . See this' – Pearl proceeded to grab hold of the rolls of fat that squeezed against the expensive silk shirt she'd picked up from Harrods last week – 'ain't you ever heard of love handles, darlin'? In all my time, I've never had any complaints. This is what men want, not a skinny pussy like the ones the whores you hang round with have. How is Cookie, by the way?' She roared with laughter, breaking wind at the same time.

'For fuck's sake, you're like a pig.'

'Oh come on, how can you object to your mother having a little bit of a nibble after that bleeding walk you made me go on? In case you've forgotten, I'll be turning the old five dozen next year, so I've got to keep me strength up. I ain't Bear Grylls, you know.'

'Do me a favour! It was almost in spitting distance.'

'Got to warm meself up though, ain't I?'

Ned scowled at her. 'You don't warm yourself up on three frigging cream cakes. Last time I heard, Greggs' buns weren't the official treatment for hypothermia.'

Taking another bite, then sucking the cream off her short stubby fingers, Pearl shook her head. 'What the fuck's got into you anyway? Oh, don't tell me.' She rolled her eyes. 'Whenever your boat race looks like that, it can only be one thing: Cookie. What's she done now?'

Ned felt himself bristle. He glared at his mother. No matter how expensive her clothes were – and they certainly were – somehow she made them look cheap. Barely five foot one and borderline obese, she always reminded him of one of those puffer fish: round and bloated. 'She ain't done nothing, so give it a rest before you do me head in. I don't need you chewing me ear off, I've had a shit day already.'

'Problem with you is you treat her like a fucking princess.'

Ned slammed his fist down on the table, causing the Siamese cat his mother had insisted on buying to scurry out of the room. 'You mean I treat *you* like a princess, while you treat me like a cunt.'

Looking disappointedly at the empty cream cake box, Pearl shrugged. 'You don't fool me, son.'

He stepped forward, leaning down into his mother's face. 'I've told you, it's got nothing to do with her. Now do like I asked you and take Zee back to Hanson Street with you. Stupid little bitch fucked me over, and I don't like that.'

'What are you talking about?'

'Zee. She thought it was OK to betray me, even though I was

the one who found her sleeping rough back when she was a scruffy little homeless kid and put a roof over her head, saw to it she ain't got nothing to worry about. And what do I get in return? Her trying to do a moonlight flit with that skinny runt of a boyfriend.'

Pearl sniffed loudly. 'Don't give me that, son. You don't give a fuck about Zee. Easy come, easy go. She's just another little whore to you.' Rocking forward on her chair, she pointed at Ned, her large breasts resting on the table. 'Come on, admit it: you've had another row with Cookie. Go on, I'm right, aren't I?' she smirked.

'Wind your neck in.'

Unperturbed, Pearl continued: 'I don't know how many times I've told you this, but only a fool falls in love with a whore then brings her under his roof.' She shook her head. 'All this grief for a good-looking face and a corker of a body. You're better off having a wank.'

'You've always been jealous of her.'

Pearl roared with laughter, which infuriated Ned even further. 'Jealous of that trollop! How could anyone be jealous of someone that's named after a packet of digestives?'

'For fuck's sake, *shut it*!'

'I'm only trying to look out for you. That's what mothers do.'

Grabbing the box of cigarettes which was hanging out of Pearl's Fendi bag, Ned pulled one out and lit it. Something he didn't normally do in the house. He liked the place to be clean, pristine, but his mother, as she so often did, was getting right under his skin. And as he wasn't about to, nor would he ever, lay a hand on her – not that he wasn't constantly tempted – nicotine was the next best thing. 'Well don't. Keep your fat beak out of my business.'

Ignoring him, Pearl took a sip of her coffee, which left a choco-late froth moustache on her lips. 'I don't know how many times

I've said it, but the way you run around after her, it's embarrassing. You need to have a long, hard look in the mirror, Son, think about what you're doing.'

Clenching his jaw, Ned ran his fingers through his thick head of black hair. He glanced down at his phone, which was beginning to buzz on the table. Shit. It was Simon Draper *again*. The last person he wanted to speak to. Ignoring it, he turned back to his mother. 'Oh don't worry, I know exactly what I'm doing.' He went to the cupboard and pulled out a small black leather cosh with tiny metal studs on it. 'Anyway, Cookie's waiting for me. I told her I needed a word.'

Pearl's eyes made their way to the cosh. 'I thought you said she ain't done anything.'

'I lied.'

In the beautifully decorated master bedroom, Pearl, having slipped quickly upstairs before Ned – who'd taken a call from one of his clients – stared at Cookie in disgust. 'Where the fuck do you get off, trying to help Zee do a runner?

'I wondered how long it would take you to get involved. Go away, Pearl.'

Pearl chuckled, coming further into the room. 'You think you're so special, don't you?' she snarled nastily. 'Think your shit smells better than ours, don't you?'

'I've got nothing to say to you.'

'No, but my son's going to have something to say to you in a minute, ain't he?' She walked up to Cookie. 'And do you know what I'm going to do? I'm going to be on the other side of that wall and listen to every moment of it.'

Cookie shook her head, not reacting. She stared down at Pearl. 'However you get your kicks, darlin'.'

Pearl reddened. 'You think you're so smart! Well one day you'll be laughing on the other side of your face.'

'I've said it the polite way, and now I'm saying fuck off, Pearl.'

'Get out, Mum.' Ned walked into the bedroom, making both women jump.

Glancing at Ned, then at the cosh in his hand, Pearl's face lit up and a slow smile appeared as she headed out of the door. 'That's my boy.' And as she walked away, the desire to get rid of Cookie was stronger than ever. She just needed to work out how.

With Pearl out of the way, Ned stood staring at Cookie, tapping the cosh against his leg. 'Take your robe off.'

Without speaking, Cookie untied her blue silk dressing gown, taking it off and dropping it to the floor. She stood naked to attention by the dresser. She knew the routine. The punishment. All she needed to do was keep reminding herself why she was still here. The reasons outweighed any sort of humiliation Ned could put her through, and as long as she remembered *that*, she would shut up and put up with his punishments . . . Besides, wasn't this what she deserved after what had happened? Wasn't this the least she deserved?

So for now she'd accept the life she had to lead. Only once she'd done what she set out to do would there come a day when her conscience would let her walk out of here and not look back. In the meantime she reminded herself of Ned's oft-repeated warning:

The only way you're leaving me, Cook, is if you kill me . . . or I kill you.

And she supposed she knew in her gut that when it came to that day, when she was ready to go, Ned would be right. But the question was, would it be the former or the latter option?

'Right then, shall we begin?' And with that, Ned pushed closed the bedroom door.

7

It was now dark and with the weather turning worse, around the corner in Livonia Street, Lorni Duncan stood huddled under the scaffolding with her son. They were cold and soaking wet, and Lorni could feel Jace shaking. He wore only a thin beige shirt and trousers and a blue summer rain jacket which she'd picked up from the charity store, but it was no protection from the cold.

They'd been waiting for over two hours for the landlord, who hadn't shown and his phone was turned off. It didn't even have voicemail so she could leave a message on it. She'd been tempted to leave and go back to the cafe, but if she missed him, then what would they do?

A small whimper broke Lorni's thoughts and she looked down at the top of her son's head and realized Jace was crying. He was clearly trying not to show it. She opened her mouth to say something, to comfort him, but snapped it closed. What could she say to a kid who was cold and hungry? And she was certain that the smell of nearby restaurants wafting through the air wasn't helping.

The only thing she could offer him were a couple of sample coffee biscuits she'd picked up from Heathrow airport last night and a packet of salted crisps she'd had in her bag for at least a fortnight. The food bank wasn't an option, not for them anyway. She couldn't risk – however slim the chance – of anyone spotting them.

The usual guilt began to gnaw away at Lorni, then the doubts she tried so hard to push out of her mind started to surface. Always the doubts. She didn't know any more if she was doing the right thing. At one time it'd been so clear, she'd known – or rather she *thought* she'd known – exactly what she had to do. She'd felt in control. But not anymore. Even if she wanted to go back, she couldn't. It was too late.

'Excuse me, love.'

Lorni jumped at the sound of a voice close behind her. She hadn't realized anyone was there. Turning around, she came face to face with a small, scruffy woman who looked almost as cold and wet as she did.

'You ain't got a spare fiver, love, have you?'

'Sorry,' Lorni answered curtly, shaking her head and wishing that she actually did.

Much to Lorni's exasperation, the woman continued to hold out her hand, her nails black with dirt. 'A couple of quid will do then. I only want to get myself a cuppa.'

'I've got no money. Sorry.'

Thinking she would finally go away once she realized she had nothing to give, Lorni was surprised to see the woman staring at Jace.

'He your kid, love?'

Instinctively, Lorni drew Jace even closer, her heart beating faster. 'Yeah.'

'I thought so, he looks like you. Handsome lad.'

Not feeling comfortable with the conversation, Lorni turned her back on the woman, hoping she'd get the hint.

'You waiting for someone?'

Wiping the rain off her forehead with the back of her hand, Lorni let out an irritated sigh. 'If you don't mind, I'm busy, OK? So find someone else to bother.'

'Stuck-up cow, I was only trying to be friendly – you should try it sometime.'

Tabby stomped. Who did that woman think she was? She would've given her more of a mouthful if it wasn't for the kid. Poor sod, he'd looked freezing. Some people shouldn't be allowed children, but she was sick of it, everyone thinking they were better than her, always looking down their noses. Barney and the other girls were the only people who treated her like she was a human being, and one day she'd show everyone that she wasn't what they thought she was. She'd show them all who they were messing with.

Hurt and angry, she marched down the alleyway by the side of the garages while she continued to ruminate about the woman.

'Hello, Tabby.'

Coming to an abrupt halt, Tabby looked up. She'd been so deep in thought she hadn't taken any notice of her surroundings.

'Pleased to see me, darlin'?'

It was Pete.

Even in the dim light of the alleyway, she could see dried blood sitting on top of a mass of red and purple bruises, the skin around his mouth all torn. His broken nose looked caved in and Tabby could make out the footprint of Barney's shoe on his forehead. It looked like he'd stepped off the set of a horror film.

It was obvious that he was on a crack high, so Tabby began to back away, but not before Pete grabbed her, digging his long fingernails into her arm. She squealed.

'I don't think so, Tabs.' He slammed her against the cold wet brick wall. His face was now so close to hers that she grimaced at the mess of it. 'Not as handsome as I was, eh? I know you still love me though.'

Chortling, he clutched her throat tightly. Fear rushed through her. She felt his other hand on her, grabbing at the top of her skirt, forcing his hand down it. 'It's payback time, darlin', but now you owe me double.' He sneered, a torn flap of skin on his lip moving as he spoke.

Tabby tried to pull away, but Pete's strength made it impossible for her to move.

'You're not going anywhere until I get some of what you owe me. Hear that?' He stopped talking, listened, then laughed, his eyes wide and wild. 'That's right, there's no Barney around to save you.'

'Fuck off, Pete.'

Taking his hand from her throat, Pete punched Tabby hard in the face. He let out a high-pitch giggle. 'How do you like that? We'll look like twins now.' Grabbing her hair, he twisted it in his hand, pulling it hard at the scalp. Then he dragged her down onto the cold, wet ground.

In pain and trying to scramble away, Tabby kicked out, but the crack high was giving Pete a strength he didn't usually have. She tasted the blood in her mouth and she felt like she was drowning in it. Coughing and sputtering, Tabby turned her head to the side while Pete straddled her, banging her head against the ground.

In the darkness and pouring rain, he grappled with his trousers, pulling out his erect penis before forcing Tabby's legs apart.

'Get off me! Get off me, you fucking bastard!'

'When I've finished with yer. Come on, Tabby, it's not like you ain't had it before from me. It's not like you don't put it around when you want a pipe.'

'*Get off!*' Tabby screamed, her voice mixing with the hammering rain.

Pete slammed his hand over her mouth. 'Scream again and I'll kill you.'

He began to pull her knickers to one side. Tabby was steeling herself for what came next when there was a sickening crunch and Pete toppled forward.

'Are . . . are you OK? I heard a scream.' Tabby stared up through the rain and saw the woman she'd asked for money standing over her, a brick in her hand. She was shaking and gazing in horror at Pete lying face first on the ground, his head oozing blood.

Quickly, Tabby kicked Pete off her and struggled to her feet. Looking down at his body, she shuddered at the thought of what might have happened, what *had been* about to happen. It wasn't the first time in her life that some guy had jumped on her; in fact it had happened on more than one occasion, especially when she'd been sleeping rough or passed out in some crack den. But that didn't make it any easier to deal with. Though she couldn't stop shaking, she managed to smile at her rescuer. 'Thanks, darling, you did me a proper good turn.'

Lorni was struggling to keep her breathing steady. What the hell had she done? She hadn't even stopped to think.

'Come on, we have to get out of here!' Tabby began to hurry off.

'Wait! What are we going to do? What if he's dead? We can't leave him here.'

'We can – we have to. I know him. Pete's bad fucking news. Six foot under is the best place for him.'

'But . . .' Lorni trailed off. She stared down at him.

'But what, love? You've just cracked a fella over the bleedin' head with a brick – do you want to explain that to the Old Bill? Cos I certainly don't. He ain't worth doing time for, sweetheart. Now if I were you, I'd get out of here before someone comes. Are you listening?'

Lorni glanced away. What was she even thinking? The woman was right. There was no way she could get involved in this. If the

man was dead then she'd be looking at years, and if he wasn't –
someone like her, they'd still bang her up. Then what about
Jace . . . Jace. Suddenly her mind began to panic. Jace . . . *Shit.*

Running out of the alleyway with Tabby behind her, Lorni suddenly froze. Her gaze darted up and down the road, but it was
empty. Jace had gone. Cold dread crept up her spine, her legs
began to tremble. 'Jace! Jace! Jace!' Her voice sat on the edge of
a scream. 'Jace, where are you? Jace!'

'You should be careful, leaving your kid around here.'

From the other side of the road, a man stepped out of the darkness, his face lit up only by the cigarette he was smoking. 'I saw
him on his own, so I thought I'd stand with him, but better here
under this archway than getting soaked in the rain over there. He
said you'd be back in a minute . . . And he was right. Here you
are.'

Lorni watched a small, patronizing smile spread across the
man's face. She lurched forward and grabbed hold of Jace's hand.
The shock, however short-lived, of thinking something had happened to her son triggered Lorni to explode with rage. 'What did
I tell you? What did I frigging say to you? What you doin', talking
to strangers?'

'I'm sorry, Mum. I . . . I . . .' Tears rolled down Jace's face.

'It's not his fault, I was the one who spoke to him.'

A mixture of embarrassment and anger soared through Lorni.
She glanced at the man, feeling defensive at the same time as
trying to push away the thought that there might be a dead man
lying in the alleyway around the corner. She needed to move, but
she didn't want to look suspicious; it felt like she had guilt written
all over her. 'Well, he knows better than to speak to people he
don't know.'

'You're talking to me.' The man winked. 'Anyway, no harm
done, though it's hardly the weather for a young kid to be out.'

Lorni pulled Jace towards her. 'I'll be the judge of that.'

He nodded slowly, staring at her intently. 'Cut yourself, have you?' His eyes dropped to Lorni's hand and she realized it was covered in blood. Immediately she put it behind her back and tried to stop herself from shaking as she felt her face reddening.

'Yeah . . .' She had no idea who this man was, but he made her feel uncomfortable, his green eyes piercing into her. 'Anyway, look, thank you, I appreciate it.'

'No problem. But be careful. And mind who you choose to hang around with – there's a lot of scumbags around here, ain't that right, *Tabby*?'

He glanced over Lorni's shoulder, sneering, and she was surprised to hear that he knew the woman she'd saved.

Looking as edgy as Lorni felt, Tabby gave a tight smile. 'Yes, Ned.'

'Right, well goodnight, ladies.' He ruffled Jace's mop of wet, auburn hair. 'Look after your mum, won't you?'

Ned turned and walked away, disappearing into the darkness.

'And you're the biggest scumbag of all,' Tabby muttered under her breath once he was out of earshot.

'Sorry, I missed that.'

Tabby shook her head at Lorni. 'Nothing . . . Come on, quick, let's get out of here.'

'But—'

'Unless you want to wait here for the Old Bill? No? Then come on. Oh, I'm Tabby by the way. Why don't you come to the club with me? My mate Barney, he'll know what to do.'

The next moment they were running through the rain, unaware that Ned Reid was watching from the shadows.

8

As Lorni and Jace were crossing Wardour Street with Tabby, Zee was standing nervously at the door of the first-floor bathroom in Ned and Cookie's house.

'Are you all right, Cookie? Is this my fault?' Zee trembled out her words in a whisper. 'Is this cos of the text you sent me, Cooks?'

Dressed in her pale blue lounge T-shirt and shorts, Cookie leant her weight against the grey solid marble sink. Closing her eyes, she exhaled, then she snapped them open and glanced at Zee, looking at her warmly, her breathing staggered. 'Sweetheart, don't worry. It's nothing.'

Crying, Zee shook her head. 'But it ain't nothing! Earlier Pearl sent me upstairs to see if Ned could take us home, and your bedroom door was ajar, and that's when I saw what he was doing to you. I saw him—'

'I think you better go downstairs, honey,' she interrupted, not wanting to hear what Zee had seen. 'You don't want Pearl finding you up here, do you?'

'Cooks, you're bleeding!'

Cookie looked down at her leg then grabbed one of the large peach towels from the glass shelf. She wiped the trickle of blood that was running down the inside of her thigh.

'What can I do?' Zee panicked. 'Are you in pain?'

'Just go,' Cookie answered gently. 'I don't want you to be in any more trouble.'

'Are you sure?'

Fighting back the tears which were so often hidden, Cookie nodded. 'And Zee, thank you. I'm sorry, darlin', that it didn't work out with Stuart the way you wanted it to.'

Zee turned to go, then stopped and looked back. 'Oh, by the way, Barney was asking about you. Apparently he sent Tabby to speak to some of the boys to try to find out if you were OK . . . Look, I'll see you later.'

With Zee gone, Cookie began to clean herself up. Too sore to use a tampon, she rolled up a bit of toilet paper, placing it in her knickers. Then she threw the towel in the linen basket, making sure everywhere was as neat as it possibly could be. Immaculate, the way Ned insisted it was.

She lifted her T-shirt, but pulled it down quickly when she saw Finn, Ned's cousin, standing behind her.

He tilted his head to one side, and Cookie thought as she often did how similar in looks Ned and Finn were, more like brothers than cousins.

'What's going on, Cooks?'

'Nothing.'

Finn walked in, his handsome face etched with concern. He reached out to lift Cookie's top. 'Let me see.' He began to pull her T-shirt up, but she held onto his hands. 'Leave it, it's nothing.'

Ignoring Cookie, Finn gently pushed her hands away and carefully lifted up her top. He flinched. 'Like all the other times which were nothing?'

Pulling her top back down, Cookie stepped away from Finn. 'Look, I'm fine.'

His handsome face darkened, then he let out an exasperated sigh and ran his fingers through his black hair. 'Why do you let him treat you like that? I can't remember a time when he ain't

55

treated you like this, and I've never understood why you don't just walk out of here.'

Cookie nervously threw a glance across to the door, then closed it carefully.

'This has nothing to do with you, so leave it,' she whispered. 'Understand?'

His blue eyes held hers. 'How can I? I hate seeing you like this.'

Unable to hold his stare any longer, Cookie shifted her gaze to the wall fountain Ned had commissioned last year after seeing one on TV. 'You don't know what you're talking about. Like I say, I'm fine.'

'How about I go and find Ned and speak to him?'

Finn headed for the door, but Cookie clutched his muscular arm. 'What the fuck do you think you're playing at, Finn? Don't you dare, you hear me!'

He pulled away, his face twisted in anger. 'Well someone has to tell him that this has to stop.'

'Tell him what, Finn? Whatever you think it is, this . . . this thing that Ned's supposed to have done, you've got it wrong.'

'Who are you trying to kid, Cookie: yourself or me? He's been doing stuff like this to you for years, whether you want to admit it to me or not. I'm not a fool. And I can't stand around and watch it anymore.'

'I'm warning you, Finn, don't,' she hissed. 'He'll kill you.'

Finn shook his head; a wry smile sat on his lips. 'I ain't scared of my cousin.'

Cookie covered her face with her hands. 'Why are we even talking like this? Leave it. This is stupid.'

He pulled her hands away from her face, staring intently. 'Look at me . . . I said look at me, Cooks. What's stupid is you always making excuses for him. When's it going to stop, eh? When are you finally going to tell him enough is enough?'

Anger surged through Cookie. Finn and Ned were alike in many ways: both could be arrogant and ruthless at times – the businesses they were in, they had to be. But unlike Ned, Finn knew how to care. She'd seen the way he treated the kids that came to work for them. In contrast to Pearl and Ned, he gave them respect, which always surprised her because, essentially, Pearl had been Finn's surrogate mother since he was eleven years old. Almost thirty years ago.

Finn had been brought up by her after his mother, Ivy, had died. He was the same age as Ned, so the two boys had grown up together with the tightest of bonds. Best friends and cousins, and Finn had been Ned's wingman ever since. But none of that made it OK for Finn to get involved in her business. He had no right.

She rubbed her temples; she could feel a headache coming on, it'd been a long day. 'Where do you get off, talking to me like this?'

Finn spat out his words: 'I care about you. And you know something? I don't need your permission to speak to Ned. I won't have him treating you like this. Not anymore.'

Incensed, Cookie pushed Finn in the chest. 'No! You're not going to spoil everything. I haven't stuck it out this long for you to mess it up now.' Instantly, she could see the puzzlement in Finn's face and immediately she regretted her words. She'd said too much.

'What are you talking about?'

'I said, leave it.'

'Finn! Finn!' Pearl screamed from downstairs. 'Where are you? Seeing as your cousin has pissed on out, I need you to drive me and Zee over to Hanson Street . . . Finn! For fuck's sake, are you going deaf, or aren't I speaking fucking English?'

Finn rolled his eyes and opened the door a crack, shouting back, 'OK, give me a minute.'

'What if I don't want to give you a fucking min—'

But he closed the door, leaning against it and shutting out Pearl's rambling. 'Talk to me, Cooks. What is going on? What did you mean about me, spoiling everything?' He grabbed her hand, not unkindly, then touched her face. 'Whatever it is, tell me how I can help you.'

'Oh yeah, that's right, I forgot, you're my knight in shining armour, ain't you?' She flicked his hand away scornfully.

A glimmer of hurt passed through Finn's eyes. 'You never let me in, do you? I've known you for the past ten years but some- times it's like we're still strangers.'

'Why are you doing this? What's got into you, Finn?' She raised her voice but quickly brought it down to a whisper again, remembering that Pearl wasn't too far away. 'For your informa- tion, there ain't anything to talk about. It's all good.'

Finn's expression twisted. 'All fucking good, is it?' He snatched at her top, lifting it up to expose the swollen welts of whip marks on her skin. 'Is this what you call *all good*?'

'Maybe I like rough sex. Maybe I'm into a bit of bondage. Has it occurred to you that's what it could be?'

She watched Finn bite down on his lip. His cheeks flushed red. 'Do I look like a fucking mug, Cooks? I know what he does to you. We all do.'

Cookie could feel herself trembling with anger. 'Stay out of my business . . . And in case you've forgotten, you may be Ned's cousin and best friend, but if he even got a whiff of this conversa- tion, you'd be pushing up daisies.'

'Do I look like I care?'

'I love Ned.' Cookie spoke firmly.

Finn laughed bitterly. 'No you don't. You can't love someone who treats you like this.'

'That's where you're wrong. And if he's that bad, why are you still here? Why are you still working for him, eh? Now, if you wouldn't mind, I'd like you to leave the bathroom before Ned comes back, otherwise we'll both end up at the bottom of the Thames. Go on, get out of here, Finn. Find somebody else to save.'

Without saying a word, Finn walked out of the bathroom.

9

'Oh my fucking God, what have you done?' Standing in his club, Desires, Barney stared in horror at Tabby's face, which was now mottled and swelling rapidly from where she'd been punched.

'Pete did it.' She shrugged miserably at the same time as giving a small smile to Cora and Natalie, who were busy setting up for the night.

'He can't go round treating you like that. I'll fucking kill him.'

'I think that horse has already bolted, Barney.'

Frowning and grabbing a shot glass from behind the bar, Barney poured a large measure of gin from the bottle on the side. He walked across to Tabby, handing her the drink. 'What's that mean?' he said as he steered her across to one of the large sofas, sitting her down gently.

Knocking the gin back in one and tasting the dry warm burn of juniper before she answered, Tabby lowered her voice, not wanting Natalie or Cora to hear. 'I think Pete's dead.'

'What?'

'You heard me, brown bread. Some bird did it . . . her.' Tabby pointed at Lorni, who stood on the stairs with Jace shivering next to her. 'She saved me. I could've been a goner if it weren't for her, Barn. Proper plucky bird she was, and there's me thinking she was a stuck-up cow looking down her nose at me. But she put Pete in his place, all right.'

Like Tabby, Barney lowered his voice. 'Are you kidding me?'

'No, straight up. He's in that alleyway off Livonia Street. You know where the junkies go and shoot up?'

As Barney fell into a troubled silence, Tabby called across to Lorni, 'Come say hello to my mate . . . That's all right, ain't it, Barn?'

Distracted, Barney nodded. 'Yeah, yeah, of course . . . Come on, sweetheart, you both look freezing. Come and get a drink,' he said, gesturing to her.

Lorni stayed where she was, her gaze darting around. Even though the place was empty there was certainly a party vibe to it; a myriad of large and small disco balls hung from the ceiling. Mirrors gave the room a sense of being even larger than it already was, and the sparkly grey walls matched the lush regency heart-shaped sofas and chairs that were dotted around. A huge light-up dance floor flashed away and an empty DJ booth stood at the back, near the private VIP glass cubicles. But no matter how inviting everything seemed, this was the last place she and Jace needed to be.

She was kicking herself. Why the hell hadn't she minded her own business and ignored Tabby's screams? She should've stayed where she was and waited for the landlord. But how could she have done? Tabby had sounded terrified and she knew only too well what it was like to be afraid.

'Lorni, *come on.*' Tabby was smiling but Lorni could see Barney was looking uneasy.

'I . . . I don't know. I think it's best if I go. I . . .' She trailed off. What was she supposed to say? What *could* she say when she'd smashed a man around the head? This was turning into a night-mare. She didn't know anything about these people but suddenly she was connected to them, which made her want to grab Jace and run.

'Sweetheart, don't worry – there aren't any CCTV cameras, if that's what you're worried about. Most of us around here are camera shy, if you know what I mean . . . Anyway, you look like you could do with a large gin.'

Lorni watched him closely. Although she didn't feel like smiling, she couldn't help herself as she noticed the flamboyant orange paisley silk shirt and tight white jeans he was wearing. 'Go and sit down, Jace. I need to talk to these people for a minute, OK?' she said quietly as they made their way down the stairs.

Looking cold and unhappy, he nodded and sat down on one of the large couches.

'So, how about that drink?' Barney repeated.

'I wouldn't say no to another one.' Tabby shook her glass.

'When do you ever, darling?' And not unkindly he rolled his eyes at Lorni but, feeling self-conscious, she put her hand up over the side of her black eye.

'Maybe you should wash your hand,' Barney whispered, frowning at the blood on her. 'And then we need to think,' he muttered, more to himself.

Tabby pulled a face. 'What about? Good riddance to him. I hope he rots. You should've seen him, Barn, he was giving it the big one. I'm just pleased you were able to give him a good kicking before he copped it. There he was, giving it the large one with your footprint on his head. Mug!' she cackled.

Barney's face drained of colour. 'What?'

'You proper printed it.'

Barney became animated, his pupils widening with concern. 'Shit. Fuck. Fuck. *Fuck*. We need to go and sort Pete out. Move him.'

Eyeing up the bottle of gin on the bar, Tabby sounded uninterested. 'Move him? What are you on about?'

Barney grabbed Tabby's arm, pulling her further away from Cora. 'Aren't you getting it? Pete was alive when I finished with him, but no one's going to believe that, are they, when I've left my fucking boot mark on his face. They'll come looking for me.'

Tabby giggled. 'This is like Soho's version of Cinderella. But then, that's Soho all over, ain't it? One big fucked up fairy tale.'

'How is this funny, Tabs?'

Her face dropped. 'Well, you've got to laugh, don't you?'

'No, no, you don't, but then you're the only one who comes out of this smelling of roses, aren't you? I'm in the frame and so is she, poor cow. She's only just met you, yet as usual you've dragged her into your shit. Maybe if you hadn't called Pete in the first place, none of this would've happened. If you'd stayed off that shit like you said you were going to, I could be looking forward to my birthday instead of looking forward to a ten stretch.'

For a couple of seconds Tabby didn't say anything, then she burst into tears. 'I'm sorry. I'm sorry.'

Barney shook his head and sighed. He put his arm around Tabby's shoulder and immediately she burrowed her face into his chest. 'No, I'm the one who should be sorry Tabs, I shouldn't have said that. Fucking hell, I don't mean it.'

She turned her head to the side and gazed up at him. 'Really? I couldn't bear it if I fell out with you, Barney. If it wasn't for you, no one would bother giving me the time of day. I've never had anyone treat me like you have, please don't be mad at me.'

'I love you, Tabs, that's all there is to it. We're in this together. But we do need to know if anyone's found him yet. Only, I can't go, and neither should you.' He turned to look at Lorni. 'And you can't go either . . . Natalie? Natalie, come here, darling.' He called across to one of the women who was busy wiping down the bar.

'What are you doing?' Panic shot through Lorni. 'You can't tell her. Don't forget I'm the one who hit him, and I've got my son to think of. I don't want anyone else knowing.'

'Unless we find out what's happening, we can't work out any

kind of plan. We can trust Nats, she'll keep her mouth shut – not like Cora, she's got a mouth on her bigger than the overdraft on this place. Look, it'll be fine. Besides, what choice have we got? It'll be a knock, but I'll keep the club closed tonight. Natalie can go and have a nosey, OK?'

Lorni gazed at Barney; she didn't know if it was her imagination, but he sounded frightened. Who could blame him, though; this was going from bad to worse. What had she got herself involved in? And it wasn't helping that she could still hear the thud of the brick when it made contact with Pete's head. Maybe she should take Jace and go, leave them to it. Slip into the night. She could use the money she'd been planning to give to the landlord for a train ticket and be halfway to Newcastle by the end of the night. But then what? Where would she go? More to the point, where would she take Jace? She couldn't spend a night on a bench with him, though she also knew she couldn't even try to get into a refuge. They'd ask too many questions. But could she trust these strangers? Put her future and Jace's in the hands of two people she'd known less than a couple of hours. 'What happens then?'

Barney paused before answering. 'I don't know. Let's wait and see.' Then he shrugged and gave her a wry smile. 'Welcome to Soho, darlin'.'

10

The twenty-minute wait seemed like an eternity to them all. Barney had turned the music on at one point but immediately turned it off again, the upbeat sounds of disco making them all feel worse. So they'd sat in silence just waiting . . . and waiting . . .

'Oh my God, what kept you?' Barney jumped up excitedly from the bar stool. His face was a picture of nerves as Natalie came running down the stairs of the club. Her slender face lit up, wet from rain.

'Well? Come on. My nerves won't stand the suspense.' He rushed over to her.

'Well nothing.' She smiled at him.

'What, the police ain't crawling over it yet?' Tabby asked.

Natalie Ellis shook her head, her short brown hair stuck to her forehead from the storm which was brewing up outside. 'No, I mean there ain't no one there. Pete wasn't there.'

Lorni stared at her. 'That can't be right. Maybe you looked in the wrong place. It's the alleyway—'

'I know Soho, sweetheart,' Natalie said, interrupting with another smile. 'I know exactly where it is.'

Tabby grinned at Barney. Childlike, she clapped her hands. 'Then that's good, ain't it? He's not dead. Sly bastard, I suppose I shouldn't be surprised. This is Pete we're talking about, after all.'

Barney didn't seem so happy; in fact, he seemed clearly

upset. 'No, not if he's got up and staggered off and collapsed somewhere. We'll be fucked.' He gave them a small shrug. '*I'll* be fucked.'

Natalie grabbed his hand and squeezed it. 'It's fine, it ain't happened yet. I'm sure he's just crawled off somewhere. He probably was knocked unconscious and, before we know it, he'll be back selling his shit. I'll get some of Ned's lot to ask around, if you like. They might have seen him.'

'Thanks, hon, but I think it's best if we leave it . . . Agree?'

Both Lorni and Tabby nodded.

'And Nats is right. Maybe it will be all right. Maybe he's cooking up some crack as we speak,' Barney said, not looking or sounding like he was convinced. 'So let's try to forget about it, eh. It's my birthday tomorrow and I'm not going to let a piece of scum like Pete spoil it.'

'Yeah, that's right. It'll be fine,' Tabby added.

Then they all fell into an uneasy silence again.

An hour later everyone was feeling better, though Lorni was certain that had more to do with the amount of booze they were all knocking back.

'What were you even doing there? Actually no, ignore me, you don't need to answer that, that's your business.' Barney held up his hand dramatically.

Lorni smiled, feeling the burn of the gin warming her up. Even under the circumstances, there was something about Barney she really liked. 'It's fine. I was waiting for the landlord.'

Topping up his glass with more bourbon, Barney frowned. 'Of where?'

'The flats in the corner. The one next to the empty garages.'

'Oh, Max's place. I wouldn't call them flats, exactly – the place is a dump. More like a rats' nest.'

'Even rats have sense, mate, they all moved out last week.'
Tabby giggled.

'Well, you've had a lucky escape.' Barney added.

Glancing across to Jace, who was happily tucking into his third
bag of crisps at the same time as playing a game on Natalie's
phone, Lorni sighed. 'Anywhere's better than nowhere, but he
didn't show up anyway, and then I guess I missed him when all
the stuff happened . . .'

She looked downcast and Barney touched her hand gently. 'I
doubt he would have shown. He was probably down at the book-
ies. If you ever need to find Max, that's where to look. So what
are you going to do for tonight?'

'How should I know?' she heard herself snap. She didn't want
to think about it. The gin had made her feel carefree and even
the company, given the circumstances, had made her feel something like normal, which she hadn't felt for a very long time.
Although she had Jace, most of the time the loneliness gnawed at
her. Besides, it was all right for them. They all had beds to go to
tonight, but now she was completely stuck. She felt the tears
prick at the back of her throat. 'Sorry, I didn't meant to bite your
head off. The gin must be getting to me.'

He tapped her hand in an understanding manner and glanced
at Jace, then back at Lorni. 'I tell you what, why don't you stay
here tonight? I've got a spare room. Nothing fancy, but it's clean
and tidy.'

Lorni shook her head. 'It's a lovely offer, Barney, but I don't
think it's a good idea.'

'Nonsense. Go and get your things. I'll come with you.'

'I haven't got anything. Only my bag,' Lorni said, feeling
embarrassed.

Barney fell silent and gave a quick glance to Natalie and Tabby, which didn't go unnoticed by Lorni. It made her feel worse than ever.

'Well, never mind. There's something to be said for travelling light. So go on, what do you say?'

'No. But thanks.'

Jace glanced up from his game, a hopeful look on his face. 'Please, Mum.'

Annoyed that her son had been listening, Lorni scowled but didn't speak unkindly. 'Hush, Jace. What have I told you about getting involved in adult talk?' She turned back to Barney. 'Thank you, but we'll be fine.'

Walking over to the bar and grabbing the chocolate bar off the side, Barney threw it over to Jace, whose face lit up. 'Fine where, darling? Pride won't keep you warm, and it certainly won't keep the boy warm either. Look, I'm not going to be sticking my nose into your business. I'm offering you a bed for the night, that's all. I appreciate what you've done for Tabby.'

Lorni chewed on her lip, catching a glimpse of her son, who looked pale and tired. At least he'd have a place to stay for the night. That was the main thing. They could have a wash and get some sleep. Peaceful sleep, without worrying that some creep of a landlord was going to let himself into their room and try it on with her. Like Sid had done. Then in the morning they could disappear. And as Barney had said, she could forget about Pete and keep on moving. 'I haven't got any money to pay you,' Lorni said, starting to come around to the idea.

'I'm not asking for money, but I do know how you can pay it off . . . Help me blow up those balloons for my party tomorrow. Seriously, if I blow up any more of those things, I think I'll probably get a fucking prolapse.'

Tabby cackled. 'I told you, you should have got one of them

machines. You're such a tight bastard. Don't want to spend your money.'

Barney winked. 'Why do I need a machine when I've got you, Tabby? So, is that a deal then?'

Lorni's smile spread across her face. 'That's a deal, and thank you.'

'No problem. Natalie, go and show her the room, will you, darling? There's a small en suite, so you can freshen up. And later on tonight, you can put your clothes through the wash and dryer.'

'That would be really good,' Lorni answered, noticing that she still had Pete's dried blood under her fingernails.

'Then straight back down: my party balloons won't blow up themselves you know, more's the fucking pity.'

They laughed and Lorni smiled at Jace, who smiled too, looking happier than she'd seen him for a long time. 'I'll be back in a minute, sweetheart.'

As Lorni followed Natalie through the staff door, Cookie sauntered down the stairs. She walked, straight and regally, putting on an air of self-assurance. Her wall of protection to make it look like everything was all right. Something she'd perfected over the years.

Getting a quick glimpse of the back of a woman with dyed-blond hair and a pixie haircut walking out of the room with Natalie, Cookie raised her eyebrows. 'Who was that and how come you're not open?'

'It's a long story, but that's my mate,' Tabby said proudly before Barney had a chance to speak.

'Should I ask?' Cookie said, as she winked at Tabby, who she was fond of. Barney finding her curled up outside his club was probably the best thing that had ever happened to her. At least here she was among people who cared for her.

'Believe me, you don't want to know.' Barney grinned, waving the idea away. 'Tell me about you?'

'I'm good. You know, the usual. Zee told me you were looking for me.'

'I saw you earlier with Ned; you didn't look too clever. I wanted to check in.' He beamed at her.

'Thanks, Barn, but . . .' Cookie suddenly stopped as she caught sight of a young boy sitting by the bar. She stared at him and stepped back, holding onto the side to keep her steady. 'I . . . I . . .'

Barney frowned. 'You all right, darlin? What's the matter?'

'I've just remembered I've got somewhere I need to be . . . Sorry.' Secrets she'd harboured and kept hidden away suddenly flooded in, and Cookie turned and hurried up the stairs and out into the freezing February night.

11

It was edging towards midnight, and Pearl stood in the large dining room of Ned's house sneering at Cookie. 'So you're hitting the bottle now I see. But then that's what skanky little bitches like you do, ain't it?'

Propping herself up on the walnut sideboard, Cookie knocked back the sixth glass of whisky. 'Leave me alone, will you?'

Pearl waddled over to her, the tight Chanel trouser suit she wore bursting at the seams. 'I ain't going to leave you alone, cos this ain't right.'

Cookie laughed scornfully. 'What ain't right, Pearl? Me having a drink in me own home?'

As she did so often, Pearl tutted. 'Ned won't like this.'

Unsteadily, Cookie gazed at Pearl. 'I have news for you. Your son don't like anything I do, so what difference will it make?' she slurred, clinging to the back of one of the dining room chairs for support.

Looking furious, Pearl prodded Cookie. Unable to hold her balance from all the whisky she'd consumed, she stumbled back into the wall. 'You wait until I tell him.'

'Do what you like, Pearl, but first do me a favour, will you . . . Fuck off out of my face.'

Enraged and certainly not used to Cookie being so direct, Pearl shrieked, 'I always said you were nothing but trouble. You ain't nothing but a gutter whore.'

'Is that right, Pearl? Then if that's what I am, what are you? You can't stand it that your precious boy wants me. You're so fucking jealous.' She waved the bottle in the air, no longer caring what Pearl thought or what Ned would think when he eventually heard about it. Nothing mattered. All she could think about was that boy in Barney's club. Who was he? His brown eyes. His freckles. Bringing back so many memories. 'This is my house, so I can fucking do what I like. And if I want to drink myself into a stupor, then I will – and I'll enjoy every fucking moment of it.'

The fury which rushed through Pearl was clear on her face. 'No, this is my son's house, not yours. That pussy of yours might have kept him sweet at one time, but it's well worn out now. I'm going to make sure he sees you for what you are and then, madam, you'll be laters.'

'Why don't you give it a rest, eh, Pearl? Don't you ever get bored of sayin' the same thing over and over again? You've been trying to break me and Ned up for years, and if it hasn't worked by now, I don't think it's going to, do you?'

'Oh, believe you me, if it takes me till my dying breath, I'm going to make sure that my son kicks you out of here.'

The women faced each other, and in the back of Cookie's mind she knew what she was doing meant she was going to be punished by Ned.

'What's going on?'

The women turned towards the door. It was Finn.

Wiping away the tears which never usually ran, Cookie poured herself another glass and knocked it back in one. 'Oh, here's the cavalry. I suppose you'll have something to say, won't you, Finn . . . Don't look like that – a girl can have a drink, can't she?'

'I found her like this. Two sheets to the fucking wind! Back to her old ways, I reckon. I'm surprised she ain't lying on her back with some punter.'

'Don't talk about her like that,' Finn snapped.

'What's got up your arse? Don't you remember what she was like when Ned first found her? She was a mess, and she's gone back to her old ways.'

'That's bullshit and you know it.' Cookie threw a hard stare at Pearl.

Finn walked over to Cookie and took the bottle gently out of her hand. He stared into her eyes, pushing back the hair from her face. 'You all right, Cooks?' he whispered, his handsome face full of concern.

'Of course she's fucking all right. I'd be all right if I'd necked a bottle of Ned's best whisky.'

'Will you *shut* the fuck up, Pearl!'

At that moment, Pearl Reid looked like someone had punched her in the stomach. She stared at Finn, wide-eyed. 'I beg your pardon.'

Finn threw her a cutting stare. 'You heard me.'

Pearl blustered. 'Finn Reid, if your mother heard you speaking to me like—'

'Then it'd be a miracle, wouldn't it?' Finn cut in. 'Given the fact she's been buried in Whitechapel cemetery for the past thirty years. Now if you ain't got anything good to say, leave. Go downstairs to the kitchen and I'll drive you home later.'

'Wait till our Ned finds out about this.' And without another word, Pearl waddled out of the dining room, muttering furiously to herself and breaking wind as she went.

Finn turned back to Cookie. 'Let me take you to bed.'

Wiping her runny nose with the back of her hand, Cookie looked at him through glazed eyes. 'Oh yeah, you'd like that, wouldn't you? You and me while Ned's back is turned. Well let me tell you something, pretty boy. I might have been a whore once, and maybe that's what I still am – and I ain't ashamed of it. But it still doesn't mean you can snap your fingers and fuck me when you want.'

Looking amused, he offered her his black shirt sleeve, letting her use that instead of her hand. His smile twinkled as he said, 'You've got the mouth of a sailor when you're pissed, ain't you? But for your information, I'm not talking about sleeping with you. I want to make sure you're OK, that's all. I think maybe you should sleep it off. Sometimes things don't look so bad in the morning.'

'This will. This ain't going away. What I've done, nothing will change.'

Glancing up at the door and making sure it was properly closed, Finn gently placed his hands on her shoulders and looked into her eyes. 'Cooks, please tell me what's going on. I hate seeing you this way. This ain't like you.'

There was a long pause before Cookie opened her mouth, but almost immediately she shut it again and shook her head, turning away from Finn. 'I can't. Trust me, I can't.' And to the surprise of both of them, she leant on Finn and began to cry. Deep wracking sobs.

Gently he stroked her hair. 'Cooks, listen to me, I have to drive Pearl back in a minute, but you need to go and lie down. OK? And maybe tomorrow you'll be able to tell me what's going on.' And at that point, Finn scooped her up into his arms and carried her upstairs to bed.

Hours later, well into the early morning, Cookie curled up in a tight ball on the bed listening to the rain. Long-suppressed memories had been awakened and she buried her face in the pillow, crying herself to sleep.

12

'It's only me – Finn. Are you decent?'

'Apparently never.'

Early the next morning, Finn opened the door and walked into Cookie and Ned's bedroom. 'I brought you a drink. Green tea. Apparently, it's good for hangovers – well, that's what Natalie told me, so blame her if it don't work.'

Gratefully, she attempted a smile though she felt like hell. 'Fancy turning around and coming back with a large glass of red? Hair of the dog?' she said, shrugging. 'But thank you. I appreciate it.' Tears threatened to fall.

He sat next to her on the edge of the bed. 'Cookie, listen, whatever's going on, let me help you.'

'Finn, I told you: leave it. *Please.*' She pulled the tie on her silk dressing gown tighter, then gently touched his hand. 'I don't feel great and I don't want to talk about it.'

He handed her the tea. 'OK, I promise . . . I won't say anything.' Then he reached out and gently lifted her chin, wiping away the tears. 'I hate to see you like this. If you tell me—'

'You promised.'

'I know I did but, Jesus, I can't just sit here and pretend everything's all right. Whatever it is, let me help you, let me—'

'*Stop.*' She stared at him, feeling the warmth from his eyes. 'You better go before Ned finds you here.'

Finn nodded, irritation written on his face. '*Fine.* Fine.' He stood up, clenching his jaw. 'Fuck's sake.' Then he turned on his heel, kicking the chair and slamming the door on his way out.

'Get up. Get the fuck up.' Ned stood naked apart from a pair of Calvins above Cookie. His naturally muscular body flexed with tension. 'Look at the state of you. What the fuck is wrong with you, Cooks? And I want to know when you took up drinking again. You look a mess, by the way. Go clean yourself up.'

Still feeling under the influence from last night and having fallen back to sleep after talking to Finn earlier, Cookie sat up and was hit by a headache pounding behind her eyes. She pulled her knees into her chest, wrapping herself in the emerald green silk sheets. The grey velvet curtains were still drawn, though a crack of morning light managed to make its way through the tiny gap at the top.

'You ain't got nothing to say? Though clearly you did last night.'

Cookie stared at Ned and sighed, though her mind was on something else. She still couldn't get the boy out of her mind. Those eyes. They were so like . . . But she stopped herself, feeling like she was unable to breathe. 'For your information, Ned, I ain't taken up drinking *again*. I fancied a tipple, that's all. Who told you?'

'I had a phone call from Mum last night. I had a bit of business to attend to, otherwise I would've come home there and then. Count yourself fucking lucky I didn't. But don't worry, darlin', she gave me the whole low-down on what happened.'

'Good old Pearl,' Cookie sneered sarcastically.

Ned leapt forward onto to the bed and gripped her face with his hand. He glared at her, then pulled back her head, stretching her neck tight before biting down on it. 'Why you doing this to me?' His other hand began to move up her body, roughly caressing her as he spoke. 'You keep pushing my buttons, Cooks. Why? Why do you always want me to be angry with you?'

'Ned, please, I need to go and see Barney. It's his birthday.'

'You ain't going anywhere, not yet anyway.'

'Ned *don't.*'

Letting go of her hair, he stared into her face. 'That beauty of yours will get you into trouble. You get in my head. You play with me too much, Cooks.'

'I ain't doing anything to you, Ned.'

He reached across and opened the top drawer of the black leather and gold nightstand. 'Don't play the innocent, you know exactly how to get to me. I don't know what's going on in that skull of yours, but you make me feel like you don't want me any-more . . . Is that it, Cooks? Don't you want me?'

Wide-eyed, she watched Ned remove a silk bag from the drawer. 'Of course, I want you. I love you, don't I?' She tried to keep her voice steady. She knew what he was like, he fed off any kind of uncertainty.

'You better, Cooks, cos we both know what will happen if you think you're *ever* going to leave me.' He pulled out a black rope from the bag, along with an oval-shaped silver-handled cat-o'-nine-tails.

Rubbing it against the side of her face, Ned whispered breathing heavily. 'Wasn't yesterday's punishment enough? What will it take for you to learn your lesson? You clearly need to be reminded again . . . Lie back.'

'Ned.'

'*I said, lie back!*' he bellowed, pulling off her knickers and kneeling between her legs. 'Open your legs wide . . . That's it.'

Ned continued to kneel over her, stroking the oval handle of the cat-o'-nine-tails up her leg. He bent down and kissed her inner thigh, then he flipped her over.

Once she was lying face down, he tied her hands and ankles to the bed then leaned over her, sinking his teeth into her neck again. Cookie whimpered and pulled against the ropes, feeling his erection pushing against her back as he whispered in her ear. 'You know the rules, Cooks. If you struggle, I'll only have to tie you up tighter. And if you make any kind of noise, I'll have to gag you, baby, and you know how much you hate that gag. Now tell me you love me again, and this time make it sound like you mean it.'

Downstairs in the kitchen, Finn and Pearl sat at the table, with Finn trying to ignore the fact Pearl was busy gorging herself on another six slices of toast oozing with butter.

'You should have seen that cow from the hairdressers – thought she was the dogs bollocks, she did, but I told her what for. I fucking said to her, if she wants to—'

'What are they doing up there?' Finn slammed his fist on the table, unable to take Pearl's chatter or the fact that Ned had stormed upstairs over half an hour ago. 'He's been ages. Ned said we were going to look at a couple of blocks of flats over in Southwark.'

Pearl sat back in the Louis XVI velvet and wooden chair Ned had paid a small fortune for. She eyed Finn suspiciously. 'I already told you, he needs to have a little chat with her.' She winked. 'You know, teach her a lesson. Cheeky fucking cow, the way she spoke—'

'What do you mean, "teach her a lesson"?' Finn's face darkened and he clenched his jaw. 'Actually, don't bother telling me. He never changes, does he?' He leapt to his feet, his chair scraping loudly against the black marble floor.

'Where you going?' Pearl asked as she crunched into a thick slice of toast.

'Where I should have gone a long time ago.'

Pearl, who never moved faster than snail's pace if she could help it, jumped up and rushed to the door, blocking Finn's way with her large frame. 'You ain't going anywhere, Finn Reid.' As she wagged her finger at him, the rolls of fat under her arm flapped back and forth.

Finn bit down on his lip, tempted to push his auntie clean out of the way, but like Ned, he could never lay a hand on Pearl. 'I should have put a stop to this a long time ago. It ain't right.'

At that moment it would've been hard for Pearl to get any more scorn on her face. 'Ain't right?' she hissed, glaring at him. 'What goes on between a man and his woman is their business. Anyway, what's this about Finn? First last night and then today, you're sticking up for that trollop a bit too much for my liking. If you ask me, her days here are numbered.'

Her chin jutted out as she appraised him. 'If I didn't know better, I'd say you had a soft spot for her. And if that's true, I don't think that would go down well with Ned, do you?' There was threat in her tone.

Finn looked down at Pearl and over her shoulder in the direction of the staircase. He backed away and grabbed his navy jacket, knowing that if he did anything now, if he lost it, it would only make things worse . . . especially for Cookie. 'Don't talk fucking crap, Pearl. Me, have a soft spot for Cookie? Do me a favour. I don't like Ned keeping me waiting: he's bang out of order. He wants me to give up my Saturday morning and show up for work, then leaves me hanging – *that's* what's not right. That's what I'm talking about. You need to rein in that imagination of yours. Look, tell Ned I'll see him later.'

He strode out of the front door, slamming it behind him, hoping he'd been able to pull it off without making Pearl more suspicious. Because as much as he wasn't scared of his cousin, he knew there was only one way it could end . . .

13

Finn walked through the kitchen door, his face breaking into a smile at the sight in front of him. He was relieved to see her looking OK, though he knew Cookie was good at hiding how much Ned hurt her. But at the back of his mind, he always expected the worst. 'What are you doing?'

Cookie jumped. 'Jesus, you gave me a fright.' Turning to face him, she grinned. 'I'm baking a cake. Problem?'

Finn's laughter rang out, filling the room with warmth. He was dressed casually in jeans and a cashmere Ralph Lauren sweater. A light of mischief danced in his eyes as he came face to face with her. 'Now of all the things I'd thought I'd see, I never imagined I'd come in here and find you playing the domestic goddess.'

She grinned and continued to stir the cake mixture. 'You'd be surprised. Now I ain't saying I'm Nigella, but I know the difference between me flaky and me filo.' She giggled, then shrugged. 'It was one of the things they taught us how to do when I was in care. Teach you how to cook, make sure you can look after yourself when they chuck you out on your ear at sixteen.' With no bitterness, she laughed again and continued to stir.

Finn leaned over her and peered into the bowl, then gave her a sideward glance. 'So what's the occasion? Oh, don't tell me.' He rolled his eyes. 'It's for one of the clients who's got some sort of food fetish and likes to have their bollocks smeared in chocolate?'

'That was very specific – you sure you're not talking about

yourself?' She winked at him cheekily and reached for more flour. 'Actually, I'm making a birthday cake.'

'For Barney?'

'No – Zee told me it was one of the girl's birthdays as well. Alice. So I thought it would be nice to do something for her.'

'Playing mummy?'

For the briefest of moments, Cookie bristled, but she quickly regained her composure, giving a tight smile which seemed to go unnoticed by Finn. 'Something like that.'

He dipped his finger in. 'Not bad.'

She slapped his hand with the wooden spoon. 'Don't put your mucky hands in there.'

'I'll have you know my hands are clean.'

'Since when?'

'Funny.' He flicked a bit of flour at her and in return she threw a handful back.

'Oh it's like that is it?' Covered in flour, he snatched the spoon, which was dripping with cake mixture, and pointed it at her. 'Apologize, or the lady gets it.' He waved the spoon towards her.

'Don't you dare! Don't you dare throw that at me!'

'Then apologize.'

'Never.'

Cookie's giggles were infectious and Finn, laughing just as much, took one step closer to her, hovering the spoon nearer to her face. 'Apologize.' He moved it over her head. 'You know I'll do it.'

'OK, OK, OK.' She grabbed his arm, the hand holding the spoon, and for a moment he held her stare, looking straight into her eyes, inches away from her. 'Cooks, I—'

'Well, this is fucking cosy.' Pearl's rough voice cut into the conversation and Finn leapt away from Cookie. Flustered, Cookie wiped her hands on the tea towel and began busying herself with tidying up.

Pearl sniffed and shuffled in, a pair of fox-fur slippers on her feet, bringing a tense atmosphere to the room. She prodded Cookie in the back. 'What's all this?'

Her cheeks bright red, Cookie turned to face Pearl. 'Nothing.' She wiped the flour from her hands onto her jeans. 'I'm . . . I'm making a cake for one of the girls. I thought she'd like it.'

Pearl stared into the bowl in disgust. 'Ain't you heard of Mr Kipling?'

Cookie sighed and turned away to carry on tidying up. 'I thought it'd be nicer.'

Pearl eyed them both suspiciously. 'There's no end to your talents, is there?' she said nastily. 'Who'd have thought, eh? Street hooker to cordon bleu chef!'

'For fuck's sake, turn it in Pearl, she's only baking a cake,' Finn snapped.

Pearl glared at Cookie. 'Yeah, or as I like to call it, *une tarte.*'

It was almost midday and Soho was buzzing, packed with Saturday shoppers and tourists. The bells of St Patrick's in the main square rang out and the incessant drilling from the roadworks in Old Compton Street could be heard even inside Barney's club, where Natalie and Cora were singing 'Happy Birthday' for the fifth time.

'. . . *to yoooooooooo!*' They burst into laughter, jumping up and hugging Barney round the neck and smothering him with kisses.

'Has anyone ever told you two cats that you can't sing?'

'I should take offence at that, Barn.' Natalie grinned, her blue eyes twinkling.

Cora winked. 'Yeah, too right – bang out of order, but then I suppose you are officially a grumpy old man now.'

'Forty-five isn't old,' Barney protested.

'It ain't, but you aren't forty-five, Barn.' They all laughed but even though Barney was having fun, he was trying his hardest not to think any more about Pete. He hadn't been able to sleep, and judging by the sound of pacing up and down from the spare room, neither had Lorni.

Not wanting to bring himself down, Barney snapped himself out of thoughts about last night.

'Thanks, girls, I really appreciate you making an effort for me. Hopefully the party tonight will be a good one. And you know, I couldn't think of a better way to spend it than with you guys.'

Cora Webster pulled a face. Her long blond hair was plaited and tied up in a high ponytail, ready for Barney's Diva Queen party later that evening. 'Yeah, yeah, turn it in with the sentimentals. You're only saying that cos you ain't had any better offers. What you need is a fella. When are we going to find you a nice man, Barn?'

'Never. *Ever* . . . But if we're talking about a nasty man, a downright bad man, consider me interested.'

'Soho's full of those, Barn,' Natalie chipped in as she waved at Cookie, who was walking down the stairs dressed in dark denim jeans and a simple white sweater which matched her Gucci sneakers.

'Then send him my way, will you? There's been something of a drought lately, I can tell you.'

Catching sight of Cookie, Barney trotted up to her. 'You OK, Cooks? You looked terrible yesterday; I was worried about you. Though you don't look too clever today either.' He gave her a kiss on both cheeks.

'I ate something bad, I think. Anyway, happy birthday, old man.'

Barney turned dramatically to Natalie and Cora. 'Why does everyone keep saying that?'

'Here, I got you something.' She passed him a small, beautifully wrapped present. Barney's face lit up, but Cookie seemed distracted, her gaze darting around in search of the boy she'd seen last night.

'Ain't you going to wait to open it until later, Barn? When everyone comes around?' Natalie asked.

'Later. You joking? Fuck that. I'm going to milk this birthday for all it's worth.' Delighted, he squeezed Cookie round the waist, forcing her to breathe deeply to prevent herself from flinching at the pain of her bruised skin.

'You shouldn't have done, but if you hadn't . . .' Barney trailed off and pursed his lips, looking Cookie up and down in mock outrage. Then, giggling like an over-exuberant child, he proceeded to rip off the gold wrapping paper. Inside was a blue box which he slowly opened. 'Oh my God, that's beautiful! Cooks, seriously, this must've cost you a fortune. But I'm not complaining,' he trilled, flinging the wrapping aside and putting on the green-faced Breitling watch. 'I love it! What do you think?'

'It looks good – and you deserve it. Thanks for being a good friend to me, Barn.'

Something in her tone of voice made Barney's expression turn serious. 'You OK, Cooks? You don't seem yourself.'

'Like I say, it was something I ate,' Cookie replied, working hard to force a smile. For some reason she felt on edge, uncomfortable. She couldn't even blame it on Ned. What happened earlier was nothing new, a scene that had played out many times over the years. So many times that she'd got used to it. 'I'm fine though, I'm sure I'll feel better soon.'

At that moment the door of the staff room opened.

'Oh look at you two, you certainly seem refreshed after a good night's sleep. Hey, Cooks, this is Lorni and Jace, they're my birthday guests . . . Lorni, this is Cookie, one of my besties.'

'Hi, nice to meet you.' Lorni gave a shy smile. 'Say hello to the lady, Jace . . . Jace, speak up.' She pushed him gently forward. 'Sorry, he gets a bit shy when he meets new people. Go on then . . .'

'Hello.' Jace's face went red, embarrassed at the way his mum was talking about him.

It felt to Cookie like she'd frozen. Even though she wanted to, she couldn't tear her eyes away from the boy. She knew she needed to say something, she could feel everyone looking at her strangely, but the words wouldn't come out.

'Cooks? Cooks?' Barney's voice echoed somewhere in the back of her head. '*Cookie!*'

'Sorry . . . Sorry.' Shaking her head as if trying to clear the fog, Cookie smiled at everybody, though she avoided looking at Jace. 'Wow. God, I spaced out there, didn't I? I had a drink last night and I haven't had a drink for a while; I must be getting old.' She winked. 'But not as old as some.' The tension was broken and they laughed and began chattering amongst themselves, though as Cookie went to talk to Natalie, Barney touched her arm gently. 'I thought you said it was something you ate?'

She bristled, locked eyes with him and shrugged. 'Same difference, ain't it?' And not wanting any more questions, she moved hurriedly towards Natalie.

An hour later the club was ready for the party. Dazzling LED transparent balloons, along with the blush and peach ones everyone had taken it in turns to blow up, lined the room. Columns of white roses filled the walls, pale pink dip-dyed drapes laced with fairy lights hung from the ceiling, and four-foot-high light-up letters that spelled out BARNEY took centre stage. Exhausted, everyone was sitting around enjoying a well-earned drink.

Although Cookie was tempted, she decided it was probably

better if she stuck to lemonade, at least for now. Her thoughts were all over place as it was, without adding alcohol to the mix. She was thankful Jace had gone upstairs, because she didn't think she would've been able cope with being in the same room as him.

She was dying to ask Natalie about Lorni – where she'd come from, who she was – but with the woman still within earshot, it would have to wait.

'Have you read this?' Barney stared at the newspaper he'd been reading for the past twenty minutes.

'Obviously not, cos you've had your nose stuck well into it while we've all been grafting.' Tabby grinned and munched on a bag of crisps while hugging a glass of gin. 'What is it? It's not one of those horoscopes again, is it? You love those things – maybe we should all have our tarot cards read?'

'My mum used to read the tea leaves; we ought to do that. Though I guess it's hardly going to be the same with a bag of PG tips, is it?' Cora added with a wink.

Barney seemed oblivious to the happy banter. 'No, it's about that Jo Martin,' he said. 'Remember her? The one who killed those two kids . . . and whatever else she did to them.'

He tutted and the room fell silent. 'It's an article about some of Britain's worst crimes. Apparently, it's been ten years since she was released from prison. Can you believe it was that long ago?' He looked up. 'I don't even know why they let her out . . . And it was all done underhand, wasn't it? No one knew she'd been freed; it only came out a year later.' He glanced back down at the paper. 'Look, it says here they gave her lifelong anonymity. But she's had to move around a few times, cos people have found out who she is.'

Barney paused to lean across to the bar and grab a bag of salted peanuts. He opened them and threw a handful into his mouth, then continued to talk while chewing away noisily. 'Fucking bang out of order, if you ask me. I know everyone has their secrets, but I don't reckon it should be allowed. I mean, she can live with someone, make friends, marry, have kids, get a job, and all without having to tell anyone who she is. And there was never a photo of her, was there? Of her dad, but not her . . . Look at her dad, he looks evil, doesn't he?' Barney held the newspaper up so they could see the large black-and-white photo of Colin Martin. 'But it's fucked up that the law lets her pretend she's someone else . . . Imagine that – she could be anyone, anywhere.'

He shrugged and sounded like he was talking to himself as he went on: 'But then I guess you never really know someone, do you? Not really. Not what goes on in people's heads and behind closed doors . . . I'm not surprised people try to expose her. You wouldn't want that monster living next door to you, would you? What she did to those poor kids – picked them up and well, you know . . . She was working with her dad, wasn't she? Sick bastards, the pair of 'em. Yeah, it's all coming back to me now, I remember when it happened, I was—' He broke off and gave everyone a tight smile. 'Anyway, I hope that piece of scum is rotting in hell somewhere, don't you? More to the point, I hope they find her and expose her. String her up. The likes of her shouldn't be able to hide.'

There was a murmur of agreement, then Barney continued reading the article in silence and everybody else stayed in their own thoughts.

'I'm going to the bathroom.'

'Sure, honey,' Barney muttered, without looking up to see who was speaking.

14

In the tiny staff bathroom, she stared into the mirror, holding onto the sink, listening to the others chattering away. She felt sick, seeing her dad in a photo like that: smiling out as if his eyes were taunting her. Like he knew where she was and what her life had become. She'd tried so hard to get away from it all, and even though she hadn't been Jo Martin for ten years, not since she'd walked out of the probation office that sunny March day with a new name, new age, new life, a new history. Inside, right there at the core, underneath the smile, she was still Jo and she hated it. She'd wanted Jo to die when she assumed her new identity, but she was imprisoned by her, by the past, by the memories. She longed to forget, but how could she forget when those pigs out there thought it was all right to talk about her like that? They didn't know her. They didn't know what *really* happened that day. No one did. Only *him*. Yet they judged her like they knew. *A piece of scum*, that's what Barney had said. *String her up*. Well, they were all pigs and they deserved to squeal like pigs . . . That's what *he*, her dad, always said to her, wasn't it? That she was a pig – and God, he'd made her squeal like one, over and over and over again.

Shaking, she took a deep breath and continued to look in the mirror. If only she could believe what everyone else believed. Embrace the name that everyone called her. Enjoy the smiles that everyone gave her, the banter, the trust they showed in her. But it wasn't real, was it? They only liked the shell of her, not the person inside. Because if they knew, really knew her secrets, knew who she was, they wouldn't be smiling. In the meantime, all she could do was be careful, make sure no one found out who she truly was.

She touched her face, watching her reflection in the mirror as she twisted her cheek in her fingers until it was red. Somehow she had to stop thinking of herself as Jo, she *had* to stop, put that mask back on and pretend, even to herself. The problem was, she saw Jo when she looked in the mirror. Not the hair, not even the face – time changed faces – but the eyes were the same. No matter what she did, there was Jo staring back at her, reminding her what she'd done. There was no escape and there was certainly no escape from *him*. He was always there in her head, speaking to her, telling her she was nothing but an ugly, worthless piece of shit.

Angrily, she picked up the chair and smashed it against the mirror, which shattered into tiny pieces. A moment later she heard a voice. 'Fucking hell, what's going on in there? You having a fight with the lav?'

Rushing to the door, she called back, 'No, it's nothing, Barney. It's fine, just the mirror broke – I think there must've been a crack in it. Sorry . . . That'll be seven years bad luck for me then.'

'And a twenty-quid bill.'

She laughed back, a hollow empty laugh, and began to pick up the pieces of glass. But she stopped and, pulling up a sleeve, she began to make tiny cuts at the top of her inner arm. She winced at the pain, but it made her feel better, it had *always* made her feel better, even back when she was a kid. And she thought back to the first time she could remember doing it, all those years ago, twenty-eight years ago to be exact. She'd been eight years old . . .

'Jo, Jo, you little shit . . . come here.' Cold terror ran through Jo as she felt the box she slept in being slid out from underneath her dad's bed.

In the tight space, she curled up in a ball, reaching into the pocket of her grubby pyjama top. It was still there; the small stuffed elephant toy she'd found by the bins in the backyard when she'd been scavenging for food. She'd hidden it from her dad, knowing she'd get into trouble for keeping it. She wasn't allowed things of her own, she knew that, but the small raggedy elephant kept her company, especially at night when she was made to sleep under the bed, listening to all the strange screams and noises.

'Jo, what have you been up to?' The box, made out of an old brown wardrobe, was opened. Her dad stood over her, swaying and smelling of the whisky he liked to drink. The whites of his eyes were tinged with the same colour as his tobacco-stained fingers and tiny red veins, reminding Jo of spider's legs, ran through them. Jo could see a slight trace of dried vomit on his chin. She guessed it was from where he'd thrown up, wiped his mouth and then started drinking again as if there was no time to waste.

'I said, what have you been doing?'

'Nothing, Daddy.' Jo was never sure why her dad always asked her that question. He knew she was in the box. He'd put there yesterday, and there wasn't any room to do anything but lie as still and quiet as she could.

He stared at her and it made her curl up tighter into a ball. Then she watched him sniff the air and screw his face up in disgust. She knew she smelt today. She'd tried so hard not to go to the toilet in the box, but her tummy had been hurting, twisting and bubbling though she'd been too afraid to call out and ask to be let out. So she'd struggled to hold it in as long as she could, hoping that morning would soon come. But it hadn't worked and now her legs were all wet and covered in brown.

'You're like a dog,' he snarled at her. 'A disgusting dog. And if you're going to act like one, Jo, then as I always tell you, I'll treat you like one.'

'No, Daddy, please.' But Jo knew her words were wasted as her dad grabbed her roughly, dragging her out of the box. 'You're a filthy fucker. A dirty pig.' And pulling her by her pyjamas, he tugged her along while she tried frantically to keep up with her father's long strides. She knew she shouldn't cry; she'd learnt that her tears only made him angrier, but by the time they got down the stairs, she couldn't help it.

He flung her to the floor at the feet of a man she'd never seen before. Her knee caught something sharp and through her tears Jo glanced down. It was a pull-top from one of her dad's beer cans. She wrapped her fingers around it, holding it in her hand while the tall wiry man stood up swaying in time with her drunken Dad. The smell of alcohol from the man made her feel sick. Jo knew exactly what was to come.

'She's all yours, mate, but first she needs to eat.' Her dad marched through to the kitchen and a moment later he returned with the dog food bowl. He threw it on the floor then sank back into the faded grey armchair. 'Eat it, Jo . . . Eat it. Now!'

Eight-year-old Jo Martin knew better than to hesitate. She knelt, trembling, bending her head over the bowl. As she started to eat, the rattle of the man's belt buckle being undone made her wet herself in fear. The feeling of being tugged towards him made her vomit, and the laughter from her dad made her die that little bit more inside. But then, without knowing why, and making sure they didn't see her do it, Jo pushed the pull-top into her palm, digging the metal deep into her flesh. She felt the warmth of a trickle of blood, and for Jo it seemed to silence the screams of terror in her head, allowing her to distract herself from what was about to happen . . .

15

Finn lay on the bed, getting a blow job from one of the toms he knew from the sauna in Euston. He'd thought it might make him feel better, but it hadn't and that pissed him off no end. And the reason? His mind was on Cookie . . . Cookie and Ned. 'Watch your teeth, love. I'm not in the mood to fuck a cheese grater.' His tone wasn't unkind, more exasperated. Annoyed.

He lay back and sighed and stared at the ceiling of the large building in Hanson Street, one of the many properties Ned owned. It was also where he happened to live, and the place Ned housed the runaways who worked for him.

It had been Ned's idea to house them here, and he supposed it was the perfect cover, a stone's throw from the University of Westminster where throngs of students lived and studied. No one would be suspicious at the sight of teenagers going in and out of a building in this area, especially as the place was always so well kept.

His cousin had a thing for cleanliness. He insisted on the windows being cleaned on a weekly basis, the stone steps outside the tall five-storey Georgian building scrubbed and immaculate. In fact the whole building had been restored to perfection, like his place in Soho. And whenever anyone moved in, Ned made sure he read them the riot act: no trouble, no parties, certainly no drugs, no anything really. By eight o'clock each evening the place was quiet, and to Finn the silence felt strange, considering there were twenty kids or more living in the building. The most he ever heard was the hum of televisions and whispered chatter, and it was Pearl – who sometimes stayed overnight – who made sure it stayed that way. Finn found it difficult to pull up kids wanting to have fun. But here, it wasn't him that called the shots. It was Ned, and basically it came down to one thing: Ned had rules and none of the kids dared break them.

'What the fuck's got into you, Finn? I'm getting jaw ache here. The amount of action coming out of your dick right now makes the Sahara Desert look like the Niagara Falls. I thought you said my blow jobs would make even Nelson's column come.'

He laughed and stroked her hair. 'They do, Mo, I'm sorry, it's—'

Cookie walked in, bringing an end to the rest of Finn's sentence. She rolled her eyes as she looked at the woman she half recognized hovering over Finn's penis. 'Sorry, don't mind me.' Then she turned and, for some reason, a streak of jealousy shot through her. Angry with herself, she marched out of the room.

'Cookie, wait! Cookie . . . *Fuck, fuck, fuck.*'

'We can if you want,' Mo said, teasing him. ''Cos it's a shame to waste it. Such a thing of beauty.' She giggled and licked her lips as she stared at Finn's large, erect penis. 'You should see some of the dicks I have to suck normally. Seriously, it would put you off your tea.'

Even though he didn't feel like it, Finn couldn't help but laugh. He kissed the top of her head. 'That's why I love you, Mo . . . I'll see you soon.'

She winked. 'I hope so, baby.'

Then Finn scrambled off the bed, pulling on his jeans, and headed for the door while stumbling and struggling to put on his trainers.

Still pulling on his hoodie, he sprinted down the stone stairwell after Cookie.

'Cookie, listen to me,' he said as he caught up with her.

'What is it, Finn? What do you want?' She tried to sound casual, like she didn't care, but she had a feeling her voice betrayed her.

'Back there, I know it sounds like a fucking cliché, but Mo, well she don't mean nothing to me. I mean, I like her as a mate, but she's a hooker, that's all.'

Cookie rolled her tongue across her teeth, tasting the tiniest residue of the lip gloss she was wearing. 'I know what she is. Same as I was.'

She turned to go, not wanting to feel the way she was, not wanting to look at Finn or think of him in a way she knew would only cause trouble.

'Cookie, listen—' He jumped in front of her.

'You don't need to explain anything to me. What you get up to is nothing to do with me. I really don't care.'

Finn stared at her. His eyes drilled into hers. 'But I *want* you to care, though.'

Cookie lowered her voice. 'You need to stop this, Finn. I don't know what's got into you, but this isn't OK . . . What if I told Ned?'

He tilted his head to one side. 'But I know you won't.'

Annoyed at his arrogance, Cookie began to edge away. 'That's where you're wrong, Finn, because if you continue talking like this, you'll give me no choice.' She dipped round him, walking slowly down the stairs, but then she came to a stop, not quite turning fully to look at him. Against her better judgement, she asked, 'Why now?' Her voice was quiet. 'Why say this to me now, Finn, after all these years?'

'Because I can't keep pretending.'

'And Ned? What about him? He's your cousin, Finn, though

you're more like brothers. Don't that bother you? Have you even thought about that?'

His expression hardened and he grabbed her arm. 'Of course I've thought about that. I've thought long and hard about it, but let's face it, Cooks: he don't deserve you. He treats people like shit. And as for you, he thinks he owns you, Cooks. Like he thinks he owns all these kids who live here. What has he ever done for you, apart from treat you like crap, or like his sex toy?'

Cookie's cheeks reddened. 'That's none of your damn business. Besides, you know exactly what Ned did for me. He cleaned me up when I had nowhere else to go; he sorted me out. And now we're together.'

Finn stepped closer to her, so close she could almost feel the heat of his body. 'And *you* know that was never about you. He cleaned you up for himself. He does it with everyone, with all the kids, but the difference is, he decided to keep you.'

Cookie bristled with stubbornness. 'That's the business we're in. If you don't like it, then you need to get out. And as for the kids, well, if they weren't here, they'd be on the streets or with some scummy pimp who'd treat them nowhere near as good as the way we do.'

Finn let out a bitter laugh which echoed around the stairwell. 'You don't believe that any more than I do. Come off it, Cooks, look around you, open your eyes. Just cos it's covered in gold don't mean underneath it ain't murky. We ain't any better than those penny pimps.'

'That's not true,' Cookie snapped but she couldn't look Finn in the eye.

'We both know it is. We pick them up, clean them up and fuck them up . . . I want out, Cooks, and I know you do too. This isn't you, I know it.'

Cookie stared at him. She could feel her hands shaking and she clasped them together, not wanting Finn to see. 'You don't know anything about me, otherwise you wouldn't be saying this.'

'Come away with me, Cooks . . . Let's start again somewhere. You and me.'

Cookie hissed through her teeth, 'You've got to leave this alone, you understand? I've already told you, don't mess this up for me.'

'You keep saying this, but mess what up? I don't get it.' Finn frowned and shook his head.

'There are some things you don't understand. Now back off, Finn.'

Finn suddenly moved in to kiss her and, just for a moment . . . the smallest of moments, Cookie didn't move. A split second later, she pushed him away, slapping him hard around the face. 'What the fuck do you think you're doing?'

'I'm sorry, OK. I'm sorry but I can't help the way I feel. Fucking hell, Cooks, you're the first thing I think about when I wake up and the last thing I think about at night. And upstairs with Mo just now, you know what that is? That's me trying to get you out of my head, to try to fuck you out of my head.'

'Oh please, do me a favour; why don't you try playing Scrabble instead.'

He flushed with annoyance. 'This ain't funny. Don't you get it? I don't want anyone but you.'

'No. I don't want to hear it.' She pointed at him. 'This conversation is now closed.' Then Cookie spun around and walked away, her heart racing, her thoughts a whirl of confusion. What she didn't see was Pearl Reid staring down from the top of the stairs . . .

Pearl smiled to herself, delighted. From what she'd just seen, Cookie was playing right into her hands. Before too long she was sure she would get rid of that smug little bitch.

★

On the next landing down at the end of the corridor, Cookie walked into one of the bedrooms, where she was greeted by Zee and two young boys who looked no older than eighteen. She'd never actually asked any of the kids how old they were. She'd made it her business *not* to get involved. It made it easier to distance herself.

The kids came from all over the country. Runaways who couldn't or wouldn't stay in their foster homes, care homes or family homes. Kids that thought being a runaway was a better deal than the one they already had. That thought caught Cookie and she took a deep breath, focusing her attention instead on why she was there.

'You ready, guys? We'll be late if we don't hurry.' Her voice was warm. She glanced around, checking nothing was out of place before they left. Not for her. She didn't care, but Pearl was sure to come in after they'd gone and then report back to Ned. The last thing she wanted was kids getting into trouble, given the mood Ned was in at the moment.

Picking up a pair of shorts, a jumper and jeans from the floor, Cookie set about folding them in the pastel grey room which Zee had called her bedroom for the past couple of years.

Everything in it had been bought by Ned, and he'd made sure it all matched to the point of obsession. The Chantilly Pebble Grey furniture coordinated with the wooden handmade bed. The delicate silk curtains bore an identical pattern to the bedspread and the Queen Anne chair in the corner.

'It's not that weirdo, is it? The really fat one that likes us to call him Daddy?' The boy, tanned skin and short black curly hair, rolled his eyes.

'Yeah, then watches us all make out before he bangs us. Yuk!' Zee added, sticking out her tongue.

Cookie sighed. 'Sorry guys, I'm afraid it is.'

'I can't stand him, he's proper rough.' The other boy – the shortest of the three kids – pulled a face as he spoke.

'Ain't they all?' Zee said matter-of-factly.

The kids all groaned and for the first time ever, Cookie couldn't look at them. It felt like the wall she'd worked hard on building was starting to crumble. Brick by brick. The moment she'd seen that boy in the club last night, everything had begun to unravel in her head.

'Come on, for God's sake, and stop complaining. No one asked you to do this, did they? Your choice. You can always move out and doss in a bus shelter,' she snapped – something else she'd never done before, but her hatred for herself in that moment washed over her like a tidal wave and she couldn't stop herself lashing out.

The kids glanced at each other, looking upset.

'Sorry, Cookie,' Zee said, sounding like a scolded child.

Her shame at hurting them stopped her saying anything else aside from a quick mumble. 'Come on, we can't keep him waiting.'

16

They drove in silence, the kids in the back and Finn driving while Cookie stared out of the window watching London go by. They cut over Tottenham Court Road and through Covent Garden, the Saturday afternoon shoppers out in their droves. Past the Royal Opera House and towards Waterloo Bridge, crossing the Thames – the London Eye taking pride of place – as if they were tourists, a regular family on a day trip. But there was nothing regular about what they were about to do.

They weaved through the traffic, taking short cuts through Wandsworth and onwards to Wimbledon, the silence between them speaking louder than anything Cookie could say.

Finn's words rang in her head: *Just cos it's covered in gold don't mean underneath it ain't murky. We ain't any better than those penny pimps.* The words she'd tried to avoid thinking about over the years, even though her conscience had always pricked at her. But now? Now everything was changing.

Deep in thought, she jumped at the sound of her mobile ringing and pulled her phone out of her bag. It was Ned.

Flicking a glance at Finn, who didn't take his eyes off the road, she answered, knowing that Ned didn't like to be kept waiting.

'Hey Ned, how's it going, baby?' She kept her voice light and peeked again at Finn. She knew straight away he was avoiding catching her eye.

Ned boomed down the phone: *'How the fuck do you think I'm doing after this morning? You wind me up, Cooks, and you know that.*

And as if what you did ain't bad enough, I've got Simon Draper calling me all the time – and I certainly don't want to speak to that cunt. Then on top of everything I have to deal with a phone call from the client, asking me where the fuck you are . . . Why ain't you there already? I hope them fucking kids aren't being a pain in the arse, cos if they are, they'll get what for. And what the fuck is Finn playing at? He knows what time you needed to be there. Tell him he needs to pull his finger out.'

He fired out the words and although Cookie didn't have him on speaker, the Range Rover was quiet enough for everyone to hear. Feeling embarrassed, an emotion she didn't normally do, Cookie leant her forehead on the window glass so that her face was turned away from the others and kept her voice low. 'This ain't Finn's fault, Ned. Or the kids'. We got a bit delayed.'

'Delayed? Are you having a laugh? You ain't fucking Southeastern railways, you—'

The phone was snatched out of her hand by Finn, leaning across from the driver's side. He clicked it off while giving a quick glance at the road before taking the next turning.

'What do you think you're doing?' Cookie stared at him.

'You don't need to listen to someone talking to you like that.'

Angrily she grabbed for the mobile, but Finn held it away. 'Well, thanks a lot.' Her voice dripped with sarcasm. 'That will go down well with Ned.'

'Tell him your battery went, OK? And if he's got a problem, he can take it up with me.'

Cookie didn't say anything for a few seconds then she nodded, leaned back in the seat, closed her eyes and tried to think of nothing but nothingness.

Twenty minutes later, Finn pulled up outside a set of large black gates on a secluded road not far from the Wimbledon tennis club.

The camera fixed onto the post pointed at them and the gates open smoothly.

As they headed along the tree-lined driveway, Cookie could feel the strained mood between her and the kids. She wanted to say something, but she couldn't quite bring herself to. Her weakness, she knew that, but guilt had a strange way of silencing her.

Pulling up outside the large detached mansion, complete with freshly painted white Corinthian columns and set within an acre or so of well-kept gardens, Finn threw a glance at Cookie. 'You OK?' His gaze was tender.

Taking the opportunity to direct her frustration on someone else, Cookie mustered up as much hostility as she could. 'Why wouldn't I be?' Then she opened the door of the Range Rover and stepped out into the rain.

Inside the house, the lounge was as Cookie remembered it: expensive and minimalist. Glass ceilings and walls, marble flooring and a six-foot-high bronze sculpture that didn't look like anything in particular. There was also a shiny red grand piano, which she suspected had never been played. Everything here seemed for show.

'Nice to see you again, darlin'. You're welcome to join us, if you fancy.' The client, Brian, who was small and extremely fat, dressed in a black kimono with over-tanned skin and a very obvious hair transplant, leered at her. He was around fifty, and Cookie had no doubt he was one of life's habitual Viagra poppers – not that he'd ever admit it – and she inwardly shivered at the idea of him touching her.

Making an effort to keep a smile on her face – he was after all one of Ned's clients who paid good money for the services he got – Cookie shook her head. 'Thanks, Brian, but I'm only here as a chaperone.'

'Are you sure I can't tempt you? I'll make it worth your while.' He licked his lips.

'It's an attractive offer, Bri, but I'll let you enjoy the pleasures of these three.' Her words instantly made Cookie feel like there was a sharp pain running through her. Her breath snagged at the back of her throat, her stomach knotted, and she looked away from the kids, not wanting to catch their eye. But a moment later she forced herself to watch as Brian began to fumble his fat lardy fingers between the tallest boy's legs. The kid's expression was frozen, resigned to what was about to take place.

Cookie's whole body stiffened and her gaze moved apprehensively across to Zee. Although she had been working for them a couple of years and was used to guys like Brian, the girl's eyes were dead, the only emotion in them was sadness.

Brian's lecherous smirk began to grow as he let out a very loud groan. 'Oh yeah, I think this is going to be a good afternoon. I know you're going to show Daddy a good time . . .' He nuzzled his pudgy face into the neck of Craig, the smaller of the two teenagers, and gruffly whispered. 'You going to put your tongue in Daddy's arse, the way he likes it?'

Cookie watched as Brian moaned at the thought, then her gaze dropped to his erect, stumpy penis, undesirably poking through the black kimono he wore.

'Enough.' Her voice was loud and seemed to startle not only Brian but the kids too.

'You what?' Brian snarled, his vibe broken.

Cookie blinked rapidly as if coming out of a daze, then glared at him. 'That's enough. No more.'

From the look on Brian's face, it took him a few seconds to comprehend what was happening. 'What the fuck do you think you're playing at?'

Giving a small, almost an apologetic smile to the kids, she

stepped closer to Brian. Her voice was as steely as her eyes. 'That's exactly what I've been asking myself, Brian: *what the hell am I doing*? And as we agree on that, you'll understand when I tell you, this is over . . . Come on, kids, let's go.' She paused to give a withering look to his penis. 'Oh and Brian, you might want to put that away.'

Visibly shaking, Brian clenched his teeth. 'You can't do this. It's not over until I say it's over.'

Cookie laughed. 'I don't know who told you that, Bri, but I can do exactly as I like.'

'You fucking bitch.'

Amused, she winked at him. 'And I wear that badge with pride . . . Kids, *now*, let's go.'

As Cookie whirled round, Brian pulled her back and slapped her hard across the face. Anger surged through her and she thrust her head forward, slamming it into the bridge of his nose. 'Don't you ever fucking put your hands on me! Do you understand?' Cookie panted out her words at the same time as Brian, shrieking like an animal, lunged at her, his nose bleeding profusely.

She staggered back under his weight, but the next moment she heard Zee's voice: 'Get off her! Get off her, you fat cunt!'

Then the two boys, Matthew and Craig, joined in, throwing wild punches at Brian. 'You fucking bastard, leave her alone.'

'Don't you touch her!'

Cookie felt a sharp tug as Brian put his full weight into yanking her hair, but she twisted around, trying to break his hold. She managed to slam her elbow into his mouth, but he caught her viciously in the stomach with his knee, prompting her to fight back even harder until eventually, with the help from Zee and the boys, she fought Brian off and sent him sprawling across the floor, kimono over arse.

Cookie stood over him, gazing down in disgust at the exposed ripples of flabby flesh. Although his nose was still bleeding and the skin on his forehead was split, she was in no doubt that it was his ego that hurt most. 'We're going to go now, Brian, but let me tell you this: if I ever see your sorry face again or hear about you wanting to fuck about with teenagers, I'll make sure you get what a nasty little man like you *really* deserves.'

17

Outside in the car, Finn was waiting. He looked surprised to see Cookie hurrying towards him with Zee and the boys, all three of them animated and chattering away.

'How come you've finished so early? Not that I ain't pleased to see you all.' He winked at the kids as they clambered in the back seat, looking relieved.

'Let's just say we didn't quite see eye to eye with Brian.' Cookie shrugged while putting on her seat belt.

He looked at her, puzzled, then frowned, touching her chin and turning her head slowly to the side. 'What's that mark on your face?'

'Like I say, me and Brian, we had a difference of opinion.'

'I'll fucking kill him.' Finn reached for the car door handle, but Cookie managed to snatch hold of the bottom of his jacket, pulling him back in. 'Finn, *no*, leave it.'

'But—'

'I said, *no*,' she cut him off, then gave him a warm smile. 'I appreciate the gesture, but I don't want you to go wading in. You don't need to – it's sorted. So *please*, for my sake, leave it.'

The struggle within Finn showed on his face. 'For fuck's sake, how do you expect me to do nothing? No one should put their hands on you. *No one*. I can't let him get away with it.'

'He didn't – I had my three musketeers.' She swivelled around in the passenger seat and grinned at Zee and the boys. 'Thank you for what you . . .' Unexpectedly, her emotions began to get the better of Cookie and she found herself having to take a deep breath and start again. 'What you did back there, being my corner like that, I don't reckon, in fact I *know* I don't deserve your support, but I'm truly grateful . . . Anyway,' Cookie said, feeling exposed and wanting to change the subject, 'who fancies going to McDonald's? Finn's treat, of course.' She laughed.

Their faces lit up and they cheered, reminding Cookie just how young they were. How vulnerable. Shame ripped through her.

'What about Ned, Cooks? He won't like it. He told us we had to make sure we kept this geezer sweet,' Matthew said, looking scared as he stared at Brian's front door as if expecting him to appear at any minute.

She paused before answering, trying to push Ned out of her mind because she knew *exactly* what he would think *and* do. 'Don't you worry about Ned, OK?' Cookie replied, trying to keep her voice chirpy. 'I'll sort it. I won't let anything happen to you . . . *We* won't, will we Finn?'

'Of course not, mate. You got my word, Matt.' Finn gave a small acknowledging nod to Matthew.

Cookie leaned over and squeezed Matthew's hand. 'I swear, honey, it'll be all right. Trust me, yeah? What do you reckon?'

'I reckon a double cheeseburger with double large fries,' Zee giggled, lightening the mood.

Matthew playfully nudged Zee, roaring with laughter.

'Right then, Mackie D's here we come.'

Finn set off. As they drove out of the gates and away from Brian's, Cookie – not wanting anyone to notice her unease – turned to gaze out of the window, watching Wimbledon go by. For once there was only one thing on her mind: Ned. What the hell was she going to say to him?

★

They sat in the car, parked up by Riverside Walk near Vauxhall Bridge, watching the boats go by. The rain hammered on the roof and mostly they sat in silence. 'Were your eyes bigger than your belly, Craig?' Cookie gestured towards Craig's half-eaten Big Mac and chips.

He shrugged, his face flushing red under his splodge of freckles. 'Sorry.'

Placing her Sprite in the cup holder, Cookie leaned over and tapped his knee gently. 'I don't care if you don't want it . . . Look at me . . . Craig, I said look at me. What's going on?'

Craig drew his gaze slowly up to meet Cookie's. 'It's just . . .' He gave a sideward glance at Zee, who nodded encouragement. 'It's just, while you and Finn were getting the food, we were talking and, well, when Ned finds out what we did to Brian, he'll proper hurt us.'

'I won't let that happen, Craig.' Cookie sounded adamant.

He pushed his ginger hair out of his eyes. 'But you ain't about all the time. And then after Ned's done what he's going to do to us, well, he won't want us around no more . . . and . . .' Craig's voice broke. He swiped away the tears and began to shake, then broke down sobbing, covering his face, unable to get his words out.

'Craig . . .' was all Cookie could manage to whisper. She looked at Zee and Matthew and realized they were crying too.

'The thing is, we can't do it, Cooks. Not again. Please don't make us,' Zee mumbled so quietly Cookie struggled to hear.

'Do what, Zee?' Cookie asked, trying desperately to put that wall back up in her mind, the one that protected her from feeling, the one that other people's pain bounced off of. But it had already crumbled away. 'Talk to me, baby.'

'We can't go back to the streets. Not again. I know what we do ain't exactly the stuff you read about in fairy tales, but at least we've got a roof over our head and food and stuff.'

Matthew nodded. 'Yeah, and when it's fucking cold we ain't having to bang ourselves up with smack or something to keep ourselves warm, or worry about going to sleep cos our stuff's going to be nicked, or stress about some nonce jumping us.' He glanced at Craig, whose tears were dripping through the gaps in his fingers. 'Craig's scared, Cooks – we all are. But last time it did his head in, being homeless. Starting from the time he was booted out of home at fourteen until Ned took him in a couple of years later, he was proper abused out there. Ned's place is home to us, it's safe, and now we don't know what we're going to do . . .' He trailed off.

No one said anything – the only noise was from Craig, weeping.

'I . . . I . . . Sorry . . . Sorry . . .' Cookie jumped out of the car and ran across to the railings. Below her she could see the dark, swirling waters of the Thames. The sound of the rain covered the noise of her vomiting.

She felt a hand on her back. 'I ain't going to say, are you OK? I just didn't want you to be on your own.' Finn handed her a McDonald's napkin.

Wiping her mouth with it, she shook her head, chewing on the corner of her lip. 'Safe? Did you hear what Matthew said? Jesus Christ, Finn, how desperate do you have to be to think the place which is farming you out to the likes of Brian is safe?' She stared intently into his eyes, but it was herself she was seeing and the things she'd done. 'It's me who's done this to Craig and Matthew and Zee, and to all the others. I just closed my eyes to it all.'

Pulling up the collar on his navy Cad & the Dandy overcoat, Finn watched a tug sailing under the bridge. He was quiet for a moment. 'You ain't to blame, Cooks. When Ned picked you up, you were a vulnerable homeless kid just like them. It's Ned and me and Pearl who the finger should be pointed at.'

'Don't make excuses for me. Yeah, I have me reasons for being here, but that doesn't excuse what I've done to these kids. It's not OK and it never was.' She took a deep breath to stop herself from crying. 'You were right, I am a penny pimp – only worse, cos I should know better, Finn. I've been there. And it's true what Matthew said: Ned *will* throw them out without a second thought. It's so fucked up, cos when they want to run, he brings them back, and when they want to stay, he's happy to force them out. The worst thing is, they would've known that when they went at it with Brian, but they piled in anyway. They did that for me.'

'Cos you've always treated them well, Cooks.'

She felt a mixture of sadness for them and anger directed at herself. 'I might've talked to them with respect, given them the time of day, but apart from that I'm no different to Ned. I'll tell you something, though, I won't chuck them out when they've got nowhere else to go. But I don't know how to help them.'

'Look, I've got an idea. They can stay in the house over in Harrow for now. My mate's place, the one I told you about. I'm keeping an eye on it while he's banged up. That would work.'

'Won't he mind?'

He gave a small smile. 'No. He'll be pleased it's not standing empty. Plus, he's still got another eight years to go, so I don't think they'll be outstaying their welcome anytime soon. Ned doesn't know where the house is; he won't even suspect. They'll be properly safe there as long as we keep our mouths shut, and they can stay as long as they like. Zee can even have that drippy boyfriend of hers, Stuart, come and stay. It makes no odds to me, and I'll sort them out with cash until they get a job or something. They'll be looked after.'

'You'd do that, even though Ned's your cousin?'

Finn gave a half-smile. 'I think it's a bit late to be thinking of that now, don't you?'

'But why? Why do you want to help them?'

He shrugged. 'I told you already, I ain't got the stomach for this anymore. Truth is, I've never really had the stomach for it, but I still did it. Things have to change, though. And let's not forget, putting those kids up in a house is the easy part. It ain't a biggie. The hard part will come when we have to deal with Ned. The thing is, he may be my cousin, but the minute we ain't brothers in arms no more, he'll be as happy to put a knife in my back as he was to share a glass of whisky with me.'

'Don't say that.'

'You know that's what he'll want to do to me . . . Look, come on, let's go back to the car; you're soaking and we can tell them the good news . . . And Cooks, I told you that you had a heart.'

She smiled at him, but as she did the image of Jace came rushing into her head . . .

18

Cookie heard Ned's breathing before she saw him in the dark hallway of their house. She switched on the light. He stood facing her.

'Where've you been?' he growled.

'Ned. Shit. Ned, I . . . I didn't realize you'd be in already.' Her heart raced. Her head full of the kids. Full of Brian . . . Full of Finn.

He eyed her suspiciously. 'That wasn't what I asked you. I said, where have you been?'

Taking off her wet coat and walking past him, feigning confidence, she tried to ignore the knot in her stomach. 'You know where.'

He clicked his fingers. 'What's with the attitude?'

Cookie swallowed. 'I'm just saying.'

'There it is again.' He raised his voice and stormed over to her. 'Are you looking to wind me up, cos you're doing a good job of it! And after what you've done.'

'I take it you've been speaking to Brian?'

'Brian? Why the fuck would I want to speak to that cunt? Anyway, my phone's been off.'

It threw her for a moment. 'Oh . . . I . . .' She trailed off, thinking fast. 'I thought he might have called, because we ended up being well late . . . sorry.'

Cookie stared into Ned's eyes, trying to work out the best way of calming him. She knew from years of painful experience that when he was like this, he was looking for one thing only: another fight. 'Look, I'm sorry if I've pissed you off somehow . . . I tell you what, why don't I get changed and we can get ready for the party, maybe have something to eat before? What do you say?'

'You think it's that easy? A bit of medium rare and everything'll be OK again?'

'I don't even know what I'm supposed to have done.'

'You got a short fucking memory, ain't you? Wasn't it the other day you were helping Zee? Is that what you're going to try to do, run off? Run off like a little bitch?'

'No, I ain't going to do that to you.'

'Well you better not, cos I've told you enough times what'll happen if you try to leave me . . . No matter where you go, I'll find you. If it takes me the rest of my life, I'll find you. And when I do, I'll kill you . . . But you know that already, don't you?' He stroked her face gently.

Her voice was small. 'Yes.'

'So, are you going to apologize? You made a mug of me with Zee.'

A flash of anger shot through her, and before she could stop herself she snapped, 'I already said I'm sorry, didn't I? You made sure of that.'

Ned sneered, his face inches away from hers. 'What the fuck's that supposed to mean?'

Even though Cookie knew it was not in her best interest to answer, she did. 'I'm only saying. There's no doubt you got an apology out of me, and then some.' Tears pricked in her eyes.

Ned licked his lips. His green eyes blazing, he slammed her head against the wall. She squealed and he held her ponytail so tight she reached up to try to drag his hands off. 'When is it going to sink into that thick brain of yours: getting sassy with me don't pay. Think on, darlin.'

He let go of her hair and began to turn away but almost immediately, he spun back and grabbed hold of her throat. 'Did you
just roll your fucking eyes at me?'

Cookie gave the tiniest of head shakes.

'*Don't* fucking lie to me.' He dropped his grip. 'And *don't* push
me too far, Cooks, cos you'll regret it if you do.'

Jace sat on the bed swinging his legs as he watched his mum go
through the letters in her bag. They were the only things she ever
bothered taking with her when they left the different places they
stayed in. It was odd, because she was happy to leave everything
else behind, even the comic books he really liked. He wondered
again what the letters said. He knew they must be important
because anytime he'd ever tried to look at them, she told him off,
snatching them away, telling him he'd get his dirty fingers on
them, even when his hands were clean.

He wasn't a brilliant reader, though he reckoned he would be
if he could still go to school, but when he'd managed to get a peek
at them, he'd seen most of the letters were from a *so-lic-i-tor*,
whatever that was. Old letters mainly, from a long time ago when
he was a baby. But his mum kept them like they were treasures.
She was always looking at them when she thought he was asleep,
but he didn't know why she did that because they always made
her upset.

He let out a long sigh and kicked the bed with the back of his
heels. Secrets, there were always secrets.

'You OK, Jace? What you thinking?'

'Nothing.' He wasn't going to tell her; she'd only get cross, so
he quickly thought of something else: 'I like it here. I like Barney.
Can we stay?'

Lorni's smile melted away. 'We can't, I've already told you that
Barney won't let us stay for nothing and I ain't got any money to

give him.' Her tone softened. 'Don't worry though, it'll be fine . . .
I love you.'

As Jace opened his mouth to reply, Barney, looking rosy and
sweaty, popped his head around the door with a small knock as
an afterthought. 'Only me.'

Lorni scrabbled hurriedly for the letters, shoving them into her
bag. 'Hi, Barney, everything all right?' She was trying to sound
relaxed, but her voice was too high, too fast and too breathless to
come across anything like normal. It didn't help that she felt herself blushing, as if she'd been caught doing something she
shouldn't – which in a way she supposed she had.

'I was going to ask you the same question.' Holding a glass of
champagne and looking glassy-eyed, Barney was staring at the
letters, which were still sticking out of Lorni's bag.

An awkward silence followed before Lorni, growing more
paranoid by the minute, broke it. 'How's your birthday going?
Your watch looks good, by the way. Proper classy.' Her blue eyes
twinkled.

Looking delighted, Barney shook his wrist, jangling the gold
strap. 'I love it and I'm telling you, any mugger who thinks they're
going to come within an inch of this, they better fucking think
again. I'd rather they take my eyes first.' He laughed and grinned
at Jace, then gestured with his head to Lorni. 'Can I have a quick
word, sweetheart?'

'Of course . . . Jace, I'll be back in a moment, OK?'

Jace nodded, watching his mum walk out with Barney. He
hated that his mum kept so many things a secret from him, so he
tiptoed across to the door, hoping to listen to what his mum and
Barney were saying . . .

On the other side of the door, Barney, dressed head to toe
in white – shirt, trousers and loafers – leant against the wall. 'I

wanted to give you an update about Pete. As you know, I wasn't going to start asking around, didn't want to bring the devil to the door, but someone came by a minute ago, looking for him. Apparently, no one's seen him. It's like he's disappeared from the face of the earth,' Barney said. 'Pete's good at that. He'll often go AWOL, then a few weeks later he'll turn up selling his shit like nothing's happened.'

'So you reckon we're in the clear?' There was a tone in Lorni's voice, as if she wanted it to be a statement rather than a question.

'As clear as we can be, considering the guy got hit on the back of the head with a brick . . . Only joking! Look, I've been as worried as you have, but until there's a knock on the door, I think we should try to get on with things, don't you? I want to get back to how things were.'

Lorni gave a small nod. 'I understand. Look, me and Jace, we can go right now if you like. It won't take us long, cos we ain't got any stuff to take with us, apart from them few bits of clothing Natalie gave us.'

Barney took a gulp of champagne. 'You're going?'

Lorni tilted her head to look at him. 'Yeah, of course, we've already outstayed our welcome.'

He waved his hands round dramatically. 'Sweetheart, you've been here all of twenty-four hours. I've had one-night stands who've lasted longer. What's the rush?'

'I'm not a charity case, Barney. I like to pay my way, but I don't have the money to do that. And to tell you the truth, I'd rather leave on a good note. There's been too many times people have chucked us out cos they think I'm taking the piss. I don't want that, not with you.'

For a moment the only sound was the Bees Gees medley booming out from the party downstairs, while Barney gazed at

Lorni, beads of sweat glistening on his forehead. 'Look around you, Lorni. This place, the reason it works, the reason I love it, is because of the people here. Natalie, Cora, Tabby, Cooks – they're all part of my family. Yes, we're all messed up in our own way, but without them it's only bricks and mortar. It means nothing.'

Lorni frowned. 'I'm not following you.'

'A few years ago I found Tabby curled up outside my door. She was there one morning. I didn't know anything about her, where she'd come from, what her story was – and in a way, I still don't. But none of that matters because now I couldn't think of being without her.'

'She's lucky to have you.'

'The feeling's mutual, babe. She's trouble, but she's my trouble. I dunno, life throws us what we need sometimes. I'm a big believer in that. And that goes for you too. You come along, give Pete a cosy clump across the head . . . Well, to me that's a pretty good initiation into our oddball family. And if you feel bad about not paying, there's lots of things around here you can do until you find a job. As I said before, I'm not going to start asking questions and stick my nose into your business. Same thing goes for every-one here. I don't know anything about the girls' past. They only tell me what they want to. The past stays in the past and that's the way we all like it.'

Lorni nodded.

'So the room's yours as long as you want it. Besides, it's my birthday and you staying here shall be my birthday wish, so you can't say no.'

Lorni took a deep breath. She was usually too proud to take handouts – not that many had come her way – but tonight she was tired. She'd looked over her shoulder for so long, moving on whenever questions were starting to be asked. Always running. Going here, going there, forever trying to make ends meet.

Scrimping and scraping to get by and put a roof over their heads. At least this way she'd have a base for the time being. Maybe she could get some money behind her, set them up for the next move. And she had Jace to think about. He was and always would be her first priority, and she couldn't take him out in the cold again, trying to find a room for them with nothing more than a few quid in her pocket.

'It's only for now though, until I get a job,' she said, rushing her words partly through embarrassment and partly in case she changed her mind. 'Cos I ain't someone who leeches, I ain't—'

'. . . Lorni, I get it,' Barney cut her off, laughing. He raised his glass, moving in time with the music, which had been cranked up even louder. 'Here's to you.'

'No, here's to you, Barney . . . and thank you, I won't forget this. If there's anything I can do for you, you only have to ask.'

'Well, let's start off by you owing me a dance. Come on, I can hear Streisand playing and, let me tell you, that woman waits for no one.' He turned and hurried down the hallway but came to a sudden stop by the door. 'You'll find everyone welcoming here, Lorni. But be careful, yeah?'

Lorni seemed taken aback. 'Of what?'

'Of Ned Reid. Do yourself a favour, sweetheart, and stay well away from him.'

19

Downstairs, Barney's party was packed and in full swing. The free drinks were flowing. Bare-chested, spray-tanned waiters in tight spangled hot pants walked round with canapés on silver trays. Beautiful drag queens kitted out in feather showgirl outfits sashayed about handing out glasses of pink champagne, and the disco beats were banging. In the midst of it all, Pearl Reid sat scowling in the corner with Cookie and Finn, who looked handsome in black shirt and black jeans.

Crossing and uncrossing her legs, Cookie – now wearing a figure-hugging Rasario red satin dress – tried not to look as tense as she felt, though in the end she gave up and had a glass of champagne.

She thought about Ned and wondered how long it would take Brian to contact him. It felt like a ticking time bomb. Ned's phone had been turned off earlier, but no doubt he would've switched back on by now, and there were probably dozens of messages from Brian on his voicemail.

Anxiety gnawed at her. She glanced at Finn but caught Pearl glaring at her. Deciding it was probably better to make small talk, she leaned over the table to be heard. 'So how come you're here tonight, Pearl? We've been living in Soho for well over a year now, not to mention how many years we've been coming up for work, but this must be the first time you've stepped foot in Desires. A late night out – that's not like you.'

'Well, it's a shame the same can't be said for you, knocking back the booze.'

Used to the old bag getting the knife in at every opportunity, Cookie kept her cool as Pearl went on: 'And why would I want to spend my time and my money in a poof's bar? This ain't my idea of a good time. Look at the place, it's heaving with them! They might be a friend of Dorothy's, but I certainly ain't.'

Cookie shook her head. 'You are so bang out of order! And if that's the way you feel, why are you here?'

'Well, I wouldn't have to be if it wasn't for you. Let's face it, someone has to keep an eye on you while Ned's not about. Once a trollop, always a trollop.'

'Careful you don't cut yourself on that tongue of yours, Pearl. And to be clear, I ain't knocking back anything and I'm certainly not on the booze. Those days, as you know full well, are long gone. So don't feel you need to keep an eye on me.'

Pearl pouted. 'I ain't talking about the booze.' She spoke quietly enough for Finn not to be able to hear, giving Cookie a sly, knowing smile. 'The cosy little number you've got going is soon to be over, mark my words. Then that smug look on your face will be wiped off good an' proper.'

'What are you on about, you stupid cow?'

'You'll see.'

The tension between them was palpable.

'Look, why don't I go and get us some of them snacks that are going round, I'm hungry,' Finn said, picking up on the tension and trying to defuse it. 'Pearl, you fancy some nibbles?'

'I'd rather eat shit.'

'Sometimes, Pearl, sometimes . . .' was all Finn said before heading off in search of food.

Cookie waited until he was gone then said, 'Pearl, I asked you a question, what are you talking about? Oi, don't ignore me, I—'

119

'Hey.' Lorni sauntered over, interrupting the conversation. 'Sorry, but Barney sent me across to see if you ladies need anything.'

Cookie gave her the quickest of glances and a tight smile. 'No, I'm fine, thanks, Lorni.'

Nothing else was said between the women and Lorni, feeling awkward, glanced at Pearl then hurried away.

'Bunch of fucking freaks in this place,' Pearl muttered as she watched Lorni go.

'I take it you're including yourself in that statement,' Cookie snapped.

'*What the fuck has been going on?*' Through the crowd of people, Ned's voice boomed out, putting a stop to the conversation between Cookie and Pearl. She watched him as he pushed past a waiter, glaring at her, making his way to where she was sitting.

'Ned . . .' She sat up straight, her heart beginning to pound. 'Ned,' she repeated as he got to the table.

'Don't fucking Ned me, darlin'.' His face was twisted up in rage.

'Ned, I can explain.'

Not caring there were people around, Ned bent down and grabbed her face, bringing it towards his. 'Explain? You seriously think there's anything you can say after I've had to listen to Brian telling me that you and them fucking kids kicked the shit out of him?' She tried to push his hands off her face, but he only squeezed harder. 'And why didn't you tell me when I saw you earlier? Did you conveniently forget? Well, what you got to say for yourself?'

'I can't do it anymore.'

'What the fuck are you going on about?'

Finally managing to yank his hand off her face, Cookie unleashed the anger rushing through her. 'I said, *I can't do it anymore.*' Through gritted teeth she fought back tears. 'I can't take kids to people like Brian. I won't, I can't – I can't do it to them. It's wrong and I'm through with it, Ned.'

'You've clearly swallowed something to come out with this crap. The only thing they have to do is open their legs or their fucking arse.'

She slapped her hand on the table, accidentally knocking her glass of champagne over. 'And that's why I won't do it anymore.'

'You'll do as I fucking say. And while we're at it, seeing as I'll need to deal with Zee and the other two useless cunts, we're going to have to get some more kids. Send the crew out and see what they can sniff out.' He winked, amused.

'They've gone!' Cookie spat out her words. 'Yeah, that's right, Ned: they've fucked off, and I don't blame them.'

Under the flashing disco lights and glitter balls, Ned's eyes darkened. 'Fucked off *where?*' he growled dangerously. 'Come on, Cooks, where? You obviously know more than you're saying, and I reckon it's in your best interest if you tell me, don't you?'

She heard the threat again but she shook her head defiantly. 'I've no idea. All I know is, after we left Brian, we stopped for some petrol and I got out as well to get some bits from the shop. When we came back to the car, they'd legged it.'

'You're lying.'

'I ain't. Come off it, Ned. If you were them, wouldn't you? They were so terrified of what you'd do to them, they did a runner.'

Ned stared at her, cracking his knuckles one by one, then chuckled. 'Right, OK, babe, so that's the jackanory – now I want the truth.' He bent down to her again.

'Leave her alone, Ned.'

'Fuck off.' He clicked his fingers and pointed to Natalie

without bothering turning around to look at her. 'This is between me and Cookie. Now if you want to make it worse for her, be my guest and continue sticking your cunt into my business.'

'Natalie, it's OK.' Cookie gave her an anxious but grateful smile.

'It's not OK. You're a bully,' Tabby said, touching Ned's arm.

This time he did turn around. His eyes blazed. 'If you *ever* touch me again, I'll fucking bury you! So take your junkie self and fuck off out of my sight before you start to piss me right off.'

'You ain't got any right to talk to me like that.'

'Ain't you gone yet, Tabby? You're like the shit on my shoe; you stink, and nobody wants you.'

'You heard what my son said. Now do one. Both of you,' Pearl snarled.

Natalie glared at her for a moment then, without saying anything else, turned away, pulling Tabby with her. They went over to join Cora, who was standing by the bar.

'What's all this?' Barney stumbled across to the table looking somewhat the worse for wear. 'Is there a problem?'

'It's fine, Barney, it's good. Really. Me and Ned, we're just having a chat.' Cookie smiled, not wanting the situation to escalate. She knew what Ned was like; once that switch had gone in his head there was no turning back.

This time Ned spun round. 'You heard the lady . . .' He stopped and laughed again. 'What am I thinking? I'm giving her too much credit, ain't I? So let me change that: you heard the *whore*. She's fine. Now fuck off.'

'You're way out of line, Ned. Why not let Cookie enjoy my birthday instead of doing this?' Barney said, his words slurred.

Ned stepped towards Barney. Although they both stood well above six foot, Ned seemed to bear down on him. 'Are you having a fucking bubble, Barney? You seriously telling me what I should be doing with me own missus?'

'Enough, all right?' Finn, having come back from trying to find food, stepped in. 'This ain't the time and it certainly ain't the place, Ned. Understand?' he snarled.

Ned angrily clasped his lips together and slowly turned his head towards Finn. 'Are you really doing what I think you're doing?'

Not backing down, Finn shrugged. 'That all depends what you think.'

'I think my own flesh and blood is mugging me off in front of all these people. I thought you would've known better than that.'

Taking his time to answer, Finn picked up the shot of Wild Turkey bourbon one of the waiters had left for him earlier. He knocked it back and slammed the glass on the table, then gave Ned a bemused smile. 'Maybe you need telling.'

The only thing that stood between the cousins was the table. Ned, with nothing but hostility in his eyes, placed his hands on it, leaning forwards towards Finn. 'I'd be careful if I was you. That's all I have to say.' He drew away, turning his attention to Cookie. '*You*, get fucking home now.'

'Don't speak to her like that.'

'It's OK, Finn, leave it, yeah?' Cookie sounded breathless as she spoke, her nervousness coming out in her voice. 'Ned, let's go, shall we?' She touched his arm gently, but he hit it away, knocking her into Barney. He stared coldly at Finn. 'Who the fuck do you think you're talking to?'

Finn's face was taut with the same anger which was rushing through Ned.

'Back off, Ned,' he said, starting to turn away, but the next moment Ned flipped over the table, sending drinks and champagne glasses flying and shattering everywhere, then lunged at his cousin, taking Finn by surprise.

123

'Ned, *no*!' Cookie yelled as Finn staggered backwards, the first punch landing on his mouth. Spitting out blood, Finn snarled and charged Ned, wrapping his arms around him and sending himself and Ned sprawling backwards, slamming them both onto the ground.

'Don't! No! Ned, don't!' The urgency in Cookie's voice rose above the music as she watched Ned pick up a broken glass and swipe it towards Finn, who managed to roll out of the way in the nick of time. But with the other hand, Ned caught hold of Finn, pulling him back and giving Ned the chance to scramble up and slam his body on top of him, resting the jagged glass on Finn's cheek.

He pressed it down into Finn's flesh just enough to draw a spot of blood. 'It's a good job there are witnesses around, otherwise I might have cut you up a bit to remind you of your manners. So maybe it's a good thing we ain't on our own – after all, you are family, and who wants to slice up their own flesh and blood up, eh? But let this serve as a lesson,' Ned, panting out his words, lay on top of Finn, so close his nose rested on his cousin's.

Sitting up, Ned threw the broken glass to one side, then got to his feet and dusted down his clothes before giving Finn a hard boot to the ribs. He stared down at his cousin.

'Right. I'll see you back in the house then, won't I? And we can put this behind us, *for now* anyway . . .' He spun round to glare at Cookie, pulling her into him. He stroked her hair and Cookie could feel Finn's eyes on them. 'I reckon I need to take you home, don't you? You know why,' he whispered hoarsely into her ear, and Cookie did everything she could not to shrink from his touch. 'Tell me, Cooks. Say it, say you love me.'

'Ned, do we have to do this here,' she whispered back. Although she knew the music made it too loud for the others to hear her, it felt like everyone was listening.

Staring into her face now, Ned held onto Cookie's hair, though not quite hard enough for it to hurt. '*Say it* and *mean* it.'

'I love you.'

He laughed and let her go. His green eyes narrowing, he leaned in and said, 'You see, Cooks, that wasn't hard, was it?' He nodded to Pearl. Come on, Mum, for fuck's sake, get a move on, I want to get out of here.'

The three of them started making their way towards the exit, but Ned came to a halt in front of Barney and, using his hands as if they were cymbals, he slapped Barney simultaneously on both cheeks, leaving bright red marks. 'Happy birthday, mate.' Then he winked, grabbed Cookie's hand, and tugged her roughly along behind him.

In the bathroom of the Reids' house, Ned gripped Cookie hard and smacked her across the face. She yelped, feeling the blood from her nose trickle into her mouth. 'You think it's all right to embarrass me? You think that I want my missus making me look like a cunt in front of those lowlifes? Do you? It's bad enough my own cousin doing it, but you—'

He pushed her, her back banging hard against the sink as he slapped her again. 'And all that shit with Brian – you've lost your fucking mind.'

'Get off me, Ned! Get the fuck off me!' she yelled at him, trying to defend herself. Without thinking, her hand shot out, catching his face.

Immediately realizing what she'd done, she froze and stared at Ned. 'I'm sorry. I'm so sorry . . . Ned, I didn't mean to do that.' She began to shake.

Without applying any pressure, Ned placed his clenched fist on Cookie's nose, holding his hand still. 'One. I'll allow you that one. But next time you touch my face like that, I'll break that pretty little nose of yours. Understand me?'

She nodded. It was the only response Cookie could manage without retching as Ned undid his zip, pulling out his erect penis.

Fifteen minutes later Cookie lay on the floor in a small pool of blood, in too much pain to move. Ned finished buttoning up his pale pink shirt then looked down at her, crouched and bent over to kiss her gently. 'Why don't you have a nice relaxing day tomorrow, hey? You look tired. Go for a massage or something and I'll book us a table at that Japanese restaurant in Mayfair.' He stood and walked towards the door. 'And Cookie . . .' He winked at her. 'I love you.'

20

Cleveland Row was always quiet on a Sunday, apart from the occasional car turning into the Prince of Wales' residence, Clarence House. Ned Reid made his way along the pavement and prowled into the reception hall of an exclusive apartment block bought for cash by Simon Draper, prick extraordinaire.

He'd been trying to avoid speaking to or seeing Simon, and he would've succeeded if it hadn't been for his frigging mother answering his phone last night without checking to see who it was. Now there was no avoiding it. Simon had summoned him.

He'd thought this week couldn't get any worse. First he'd had to put up with the shit from Zee and her muggy boyfriend, Stuart; then all the stuff with Brian, and the kids doing a runner; his mother had been chewing his ear about any old crap; Finn had fucked him right off. And then of course there was Cookie. Sweet fucking Cookie . . . *Bitch*.

He could smell her on him now. He'd made sure he'd punished her for the shit she'd pulled at Barney's place last night, but for some reason she never seemed to learn her lesson. Everything about Cookie got under his skin. It was almost as if she wound him up on purpose. Wanting to be punished just so she could fuck him right off. And when he did punish her – like last night – she always had a look in her eye, taunting him . . . Seeing how far he would go. Sooner or later she was going to make a mistake and push him too far . . .

Fuck, she was the last person he wanted to think about,

especially now he had to deal with Simon. What he really wanted to do was track down Craig, Matthew and Zee – those ungrateful fuckers owed him – but he didn't have time to go scouting for them now, which meant they might be well away. Oh yeah, a bad fucking week, and getting worse by the minute.

With that in mind, Ned stalked across to where the concierge was waiting by the gold mirrored elevator, his footsteps echoing on the marble floor. Now he had to come up with an excuse for why he'd been ignoring Simon's calls over the past few days. At first it was purely because he didn't want to speak to him; the guy was an irritating cunt at the best of times, but now – now things had got very tricky. The only thing he could do was front it out.

'Good morning, Mr Reid. Mr Draper's waiting for you in the penthouse apartment, sir.'

'Did I fucking ask you that?' Irritated at having his train of thought derailed, Ned's words slapped the concierge into an uneasy silence.

On arrival at the penthouse apartment moments later, the doors of the elevator glided smoothly open.

'All right, Ned. How's it going? Thanks for coming, mate.'

'You hardly gave me a choice, did you?' Stepping straight into the opulent drawing room, which was furnished floor to ceiling in Ralph Lauren, Ned glared at Simon. 'So come on, tell me what the fuck you want that you couldn't say on the phone.'

'That's what I love about you, Ned, always the gentleman, ain't you? Anyway, where are my fucking manners?' Simon sauntered across the room. Although he was older than Ned by at least fifteen years, he still looked good for his age. He took care of himself. A silver fox, dripping with money. But as Ned thought every time he saw him, it only made Simon a bigger cunt than when he'd been shit-arse broke.

With his eyes fixed on Ned, Simon took a seat by the tinted

windows which looked out over London's skyline. On the floor at his feet, two young women – who Ned thought looked Mediterranean – sat naked apart from the long black wigs they wore.

'Before we get down to the important things, I thought we could relax a bit. Never do business on an empty stomach, that's what I say.' He reached across and took a glass plate off the coffee table. Chopped-up lines of cocaine sat neatly on it. Taking a silver monogrammed toot out of his pocket, Simon hungrily snorted up the fattest line. When he'd done, he pinched the end of his nose for a moment then sniffed loudly, his eyes glazing over. 'That's good shit. I tried it on my dick the other day; it left me with a hard-on for ages.' He laughed loudly. 'Here, have some.' He offered the plate to Ned.

Ned had walked over to where Simon was sitting, but he remained standing. 'No thanks, not really my poison, plus it's a bit too early for me to start snorting up the old oats and barley. I prefer something with a bit more sustenance for me Sunday brunch.'

A sneer spread across Simon's face. 'I *said*, have some.'

Ned glared at Simon, who was holding the plate out shakily to him. Every part of Ned wanted to show the bastard what he did to people, no matter how rich and powerful they were, when they showed him a lack of respect. But he knew what would happen. He knew what he was like and, once he started – well, he just wouldn't be able to stop. Then it would get too messy. Too many people would get involved. Nothing good would come out of killing Simon Draper . . . not yet anyway.

'I ain't your cunt, Simon, so don't start fucking me off. I'm here cos you called me, nothing else.'

The plate was still held in the air. Simon's face darkened. 'You know, in Japan it's considered bad manners to refuse a gift.'

'Well then it's a good fucking job I don't like flying, ain't it? Now what is it you want?'

Shrugging, Simon leaned over the cocaine again, taking another fat line and sounding to Ned like he was snorting it as far down the back of his throat as he possibly could. Finally he placed the plate on the side and nodded to one of the girls, who instantly knelt in front of him and proceeded to undo his button flies to give him a blow job. He winked at Ned, grinning inanely. 'Then perhaps I can interest you in a hors d'oeuvre?' He pointed to the other girl, who licked her lips seductively at Ned.

'Let's get on with business, shall we?'

'All in good time, Ned, all in good time . . . Most importantly, how's my nephew? How's Pete? I ain't seen or heard from him in a while, which I suppose ain't a bad thing. Only time I do hear is when he's after money.' Simon laughed, but his eyes told a different story. 'The thing is, me and Pete, we'd arranged to meet the other day, but he didn't show. Now that's odd, cos Pete knows not to be so fucking disrespectful to me – he knows I wouldn't like that – so I was wondering if you could shed any light on it.'

Ned shrugged. 'He could be anywhere. My bet is he's on the pipe, lost in some fucking crack haze. So no, I ain't seen him.' He ended the sentence with another shrug.

'You sure?'

'Am I *sure*? Do I look like a cunt? Of course I'm fucking sure: I ain't seen him,' Ned snarled, his eyes fixed on the young woman working hard on Simon's semi-erect penis. 'He'll come crawling out of whatever gutter he's in.'

'Well he better. He's on your patch, Ned – which, may I remind you, is only your patch cos, out of the goodness of my heart, I let you have it. But it does mean you have to look out for people, even if the person in question is a muggy cunt like Pete. We look out for our own, don't we? And it'll be you who'll have to answer for it if anything's happened to him.'

'Whatever. I ain't here for small talk, Si, so if that's all, I'll be getting off,' Ned grumbled impatiently.

Simon let out a small groan as the woman continued to pleasure him. He rested his head back on the couch, pushing the large cushions out of the way. 'Has anyone ever told you, you're shit company? Fuck me, I'd get more entertainment out of a fucking corpse . . . But no, it ain't everything. Here's the thing; as you know, I've got a lot of clients I need to keep sweet. I've got this big deal about to happen. It's worth a ton of money to me, but this guy has certain tastes and I need you to help me out. I'm sure that won't be a problem, will it, Ned.'

It sounded to Ned more like a threat than a request, but he continued to listen in silence.

'So this client, although he's married to the female of the species, like I say, he's got certain tastes – which is where you come in. I need you to get someone to keep him company while he's over here.'

Irritated, Ned rubbed his chin. He had no idea why Simon had to drag him over to his apartment to tell him this. Since he'd started his business, he'd been supplying Simon with the goods. Soho was a magnet for runaways and Ned's business thrived on them. He gave them a fair deal and the rules were simple. He'd house them, keep them safe and clean, feed and clothe them. He even gave them 10 per cent of the money they earned for him, on the understanding they didn't tell him anything about themselves. The less he knew the better. And if they were picked up by the Old Bill, they'd keep their mouth shut. Otherwise, when he caught up with them, he'd shut it for them, permanently if necessary. And then there was the final rule, the one Zee had broken: no one walked away from him until they were no longer needed or until they'd paid back every single penny he'd spent on them. If they tried to run, he wouldn't rest until he'd found them, and there would be consequences. Always.

'And that's it? You pulled me over here to ask me that. Why the fuck couldn't you say this on the phone, Si? You usually do, and right away I send someone over. That marching powder you're taking is addling your fucking brain.'

'I ain't finished yet. The geezer, he likes his boys young.'

Ned shrugged. 'So, I got loads of boys who work for me.'

'No, you ain't following me. I'm not talking about your sixteen-, seventeen-, eighteen-year-old kids. I'm talking younger.'

Ned bristled. 'I ain't a fucking nonce, Si. You know that. I don't deal in that kind of shit. The answer's *no.*'

Simon clicked his fingers and pushed the young woman off him, tucked his penis back into his trousers and leaned forward, pointing. 'In case you've forgotten, Ned, you don't call the shots.'

'I do with this.' Ned's voice rumbled dangerously. 'The best I can do is send one of the boys who looks younger than he is. He can have one of them. Otherwise you sort this out yourself. I ain't getting involved. I didn't think even you would sink so low.'

'I don't appreciate your fucking tone, Ned. Remember who you're talking to. First off, I ain't a nonce either, and there are certain things I won't get involved with, regardless of the money.'

Ned shook his head. He seriously doubted that, but he stayed silent nevertheless.

'This geezer, well, it ain't as bad as it sounds. All he wants to is to have some company. No touching and certainly no fucking. He just wants to look. You know, to admire the boy.'

'And somehow that makes him less of a sick bastard, does it? I'll say it again, the answer's, no. You want it, you sort it out.'

'I need to keep this client happy, and you need to keep me

happy. And as for me shopping around for a kid, I don't think that would do my reputation any good.'

'Your reputation? Reputation for what, being a cunt?'

Incensed, Simon stood up. He walked across to Ned, who was by the elevator. 'You might still be a street dog, but the people I mix with know me as a businessman, a gentleman – something you wouldn't have a clue about, eh, Ned.'

'Let me tell you something, Simon. You may have a closet full of handmade whistles and flutes and a roller parked outside on standby, and a gold seat for your khazi, but you ain't any more of a fucking gentleman than my mother's a lady. You came from the streets like we all did.'

Simon's jaw tensed and he licked his lips slowly. A shadow passed across his hazel eyes. 'How is Cookie? Fuckable as ever, is she?'

Ned closed his fists and stared down at his loafers, breathing deeply, then spoke slowly, his voice low and streaked with mean. 'It ain't going to work, Si. You ain't going to get to me, no matter what you say.'

Laughing nastily, Simon tapped Ned on the back. 'That's not what I see. I see a geezer who's barely keeping it together.'

Ned pressed the button for the lift. The wait seemed like an eternity. He swallowed hard, clenching and unclenching his fists.

'I was just thinking about the last time I fucked her. How long ago was that, Ned? A few years ago, wasn't it. But I can still remember that tight pussy of hers.'

Ned's breathing got louder and deeper.

'It's a shame she ain't for sale anymore, but that's what happens when some jumped-up pimp like you falls in love with one of their whores. All that sharing goes out of the window. But if she goes back on the market again for some reason, send her my way, won't you. It would be a shame not to have that pussy sitting on my face again.'

The lift doors opened and Ned, his fists still clenched and his stomach now in knots, stepped inside.

'Goodbye, Ned. And think about what I've said. This deal's worth a lot to me, which means it *should* matter a lot to you. You know I don't like anyone saying no to me, don't you?' Everything about his words spelt a threat. 'Oh, and get Pete to call me ASAP – I want a word.' He winked. 'And don't forget to send Cookie my love.'

As the lift door closed, Ned Reid decided the sooner Simon Draper was a dead man the better for everyone. In the meantime he had two very big problems.

Pulling his mobile from his jacket, he stepped out of the lift and pressed call. 'Mum, it's me. Meet me this evening at the flat in Seaford Street. We've got trouble.'

21

In the breakfast room of the Reid house, Pearl frowned. She clicked off the phone and stared at Cookie. 'That was your other half, in case you were wondering.'

'I wasn't.'

Scooping her boiled egg into her mouth, Pearl spoke, wagging her spoon at Cookie, as was her habit. 'No, I didn't think you would be. You've got your mind on other things, ain't you?'

Cookie sat on the opposite side of the table. She'd been doing her best to ignore Pearl, who'd come downstairs for brunch looking even more self-satisfied than usual. No doubt she'd heard Ned dish out his *punishment* last night.

Usually when Ned did what he did to her she managed to keep it to herself, but last night he had clearly wanted to make her scream. And she had, despite all her best efforts not to. She suspected that hearing her make a noise when she usually didn't, had thrilled, aroused and angered Ned all at the same time. And now she was sore and it felt almost too painful to sit down.

She was thankful that Finn had decided to go back to the house in Hanson Street. Aside from the fact that it was probably safer for him right now, Ned would view his show of defiance last night as unfinished business. There were always consequences, and somehow she had to try to defuse the situation as best as she could before things got out of control.

Mainly she'd been pleased Finn hadn't been around to hear her screams. For some reason the thought of him listening to her being punished by Ned would've been humiliating, which was strange because why would she care what Finn did or didn't think about her?

She glanced at Pearl and was grateful to see that she'd got her nose stuck back into the newspaper. Taking a final sip of her coffee, Cookie got up, sliding her chair back. Every part of her ached as she slowly walked across to the sink.

'I knew her, you know.'

Hearing Pearl beginning to talk again, Cookie rolled her eyes and let out the tiniest of sighs. The last thing she needed this morning was the old bag chattering away and getting as many sly digs in as she could, but knowing it would make life easier if she appeared to be making an effort to join in, she asked, 'Knew who, Pearl?'

Pearl tapped the article in the newspaper she was reading. 'Jo Martin . . . I was in prison with her.'

Cookie froze, her body going rigid as fear gripped her, Pearl's words feeling like they were chilling her to the very bone. She held onto the side of the sink. 'You . . . you were in prison with her?'

Pearl let out a nasty chuckle. 'I only saw her once though, so I wouldn't recognize her if she shat on me.' She shrugged. 'But then again, maybe I would . . .' She spun around in her chair to glare at Cookie, who immediately turned to head for the door.

'I know,' Pearl said loudly, causing Cookie to stop in her tracks as if she was playing musical statues. Then Pearl got up and shuffled across the room to her, putting her finger in her face. 'I know.'

Fear crept into Cookie's chest, but in that moment she was too afraid to ask what Pearl was talking about. 'Don't play the innocent and don't look so shocked – you should know that secrets never stay hidden forever.' And with those words, Pearl walked out.

'You all right?'

Jumping at the sound of the voice behind her, Cookie turned to see Finn standing in the grand hallway of the house. Her mind was preoccupied with what Pearl had said, what game she was playing, if it was a game, but seeing Finn standing there caused her stomach to flip. She surprised herself at how pleased she was to see him. 'You shouldn't be here,' she said, her reply certainly not reflecting her thoughts.

He took a step towards her. 'Why not? You heard what Ned said last night: apparently we can put this behind us, *for now.*' His striking features lit up as he let out a chuckle.

'It's not funny, Finn. You know what Ned's like. He ain't going to let this go.'

He shrugged. 'Ned doesn't bother me. After all, he can only kill me once.'

In the quiet hallway, the only sounds the light hum of traffic outside and the mesmeric tick of the eighteenth-century grandfather clock Ned had paid a small fortune for, Cookie shook her head angrily. 'How can you think any of this is a joke? You can't come here and wind him up. He'll see it as a liberty. Don't play with fire, Finn – someone's going to get hurt.' She reached up and gently touched the split corner of his lip where Ned had punched him last night. 'It looks sore.'

Staring at Cookie, Finn placed his hand on top of hers, locking his fingers between hers. Cookie held her breath and neither of them moved. In that instant it felt to her that no one else existed apart from Finn.

A loud car horn broke the spell and prompted Finn to speak. 'I wanted to let you know that the kids are doing well. They were playing Xbox all last night and ordering pizza. I don't think they're missing Brian.' He gave her a wry smile. 'I needed to see you.'

His words broke the moment and served as a reality check to Cookie. She pulled her hand away from under his, wrapping her arms around herself as if in self-preservation. 'Don't, *please.*' She couldn't look at him; not that she didn't want to, but she didn't need things to be any more complicated than they already were.

'What do you want me to do, Cooks, turn off my feelings?' he whispered gruffly, no doubt aware Pearl was somewhere in the house.

'Actually, yeah, cos nothing can come of it. I've got to think about Ned.' It was almost like she could taste the bitterness of his name as she said it. She looked down and absent-mindedly followed the pattern on the carefully restored Georgian floor tiles with her gaze. 'I'd like you to go.'

'Then I'll call you, OK?'

'I don't think that's a good idea.'

'At least a text then?'

'No, nothing.'

'It doesn't have to be like this.' He sounded disappointed. 'Cookie . . . Cookie, look at me, babe.'

Apprehensively, her gaze crept up to his face. 'It does.'

It was Finn's turn to shake his head. Without saying anything, he moved towards the large grey front door.

His hand resting on the crystal doorknob, he stopped without turning round. 'Did he hurt you? Last night. Did he hurt you?'

Cookie didn't say anything. Still facing away from her, Finn nodded slowly. 'That tells me all I need to know.' And with that, Finn Reid strode angrily out of the front door, slamming it behind him.

★

Not wanting to stay in the house, which felt oppressive with only her thoughts and Pearl for company, Cookie grabbed her beige cashmere trench coat and made her way through Soho.

The air was sharp but the February sun had decided to make an appearance, bringing with it crowds of Sunday tourists. The bells of St Anne's and St Patrick's churches rang out, and unexpectedly Cookie felt a wave of emotion hit her. Her heart began pounding against her chest, and images she didn't want in her mind whirled unstoppably. With each passing year the battle in her head seemed to get greater until sometimes it felt like she couldn't keep on fighting. Though she knew giving up wasn't an option . . . *not yet.*

She exhaled, trying to steady her breathing again. Rather than standing there, wallowing in self-pity, Cookie quickened her stride and turned right, squeezing past a large group of excited French school kids.

'Hey, Cooks! Cooks!'

In front of her, Cookie saw the girls from the club as well as Lorni – who she still didn't know anything about – sitting outside the Greek coffee shop. She waved back and held her smile although her heart wasn't really in it. The last thing she wanted was to fend off questions about last night, but she walked across to join them anyway.

'We're playing posh today, Cooks. Fuck Barney's instant coffee,' Cora laughed, holding out her pinkie finger. 'We're having capper-fucking-chino. You going to join us? I've got the worst hangover. Barney's still dead to the world – well, I hope not. Though, saying that, a corpse would look healthier than he did when we left him. We had to put him to bed this morning, he was proper hanging. I think he drank his weight in Sambuca.' She grinned and lit the cigarette which was sitting in the corner of her mouth, inhaling gratefully.

'You all right, Cooks?' Natalie pulled up a metal chair for Cookie, tapping the seat. 'Was Ned all right when you got home? He was a proper fucking bastard last night.'

Cora winked. 'When ain't he?'

Tabby, who until now had been resting her head on the table, sat up slowly. She stank of booze and still wore the same clothes as she had last night. Her mascara had run and now it looked as if she had ink smudges under her eyes. 'I ain't partied like that for a long time. I swear I can't remember anything past the first drink. Fuck me, I thought crack was bad, but those Alabama slammers done me in.' She cackled, then immediately sank back into her chair, rubbing her temples. They all laughed apart from Cookie, who sat in silence.

Natalie frowned. 'You're worrying me, Cooks. I know there was all that shit with Ned, but there's always shit with him. Are you sure you're all right? I dunno, you seem really quiet, like you've got something on your mind.'

Cookie, feeling self-conscious, picked up the menu. 'Oh I think I probably drank too much champagne last night. I'm fine – and thanks for standing up to Ned like that. You too, Tabby. I'm sorry for what Ned said about you, but you don't have to worry about me. I mean, who hasn't got something on their mind?'

22

Twenty minutes later the sun was still out in Old Compton Street. Sitting listening to the other girls chattering away at the table, she took a sip of her coffee. She was tired from last night but, given everything that had occurred, it had been good to see how many people cared for Barney, wanting to give him a great birthday party.

Stifling a yawn, she glanced across to the next table at a couple reading the newspaper together. Immediately her blood ran cold and her stomach knotted as she saw the centre page headline of the Sunday tabloid:

JO MARTIN – THE STORY OF A CHILD KILLER

Anger twisted up inside her. There was no getting away from it, was there? Didn't they understand she wasn't Jo anymore, *not really*? She was just one of the girls now, Barney had officially made her part of his family, taken her under his wing like he had with the others. She was like them now, wasn't she? That's how she needed people to see her. She needed to feel like she was no longer Jo. So why couldn't they leave her alone? Why couldn't they stop writing their pathetic crime specials and leave what happened that day in the past? Because the more they wrote about her, the more determined the public – those squealing, judging pigs – would be to work out where she was and what her name was now. Then, like always, they'd find out, and like always she'd have to move on. Leave another life to find a new one.

Suddenly dizzy, she clutched the edge of the metal table. She could feel herself shaking. Everything in her wanted to get up and ram the newspaper down that couple's throat. Make them choke on the dirty lies they were reading about her. Make them gag, while their eyes begged her to stop. Oh yeah, if she could, right now, right here, she'd make them squeal like her dad had made her squeal when he thought she was telling lies.

'Jesus, you all right, you look a bit peaky? Oh my God you're well shaking. Oh my God, she's having to hold onto the table! That's a proper hangover you've got there. What you need is some hair of the dog. Maybe we should all go back to Barney's and start again on the cocktails. Can you imagine! I think I'd be sick if I even smelt any booze now. Happy days, eh?'

They all laughed, and she pulled her gaze away from the couple and joined in with the banter. *Happy days. He* used to say that to her when she was growing up. She could even remember where she was the first time she heard him say it, and she remembered exactly what *he* was doing. And as she sat at the table taking another sip of her coffee, the other girls' chatter faded into a distant murmur as the memory took her away from Old Compton Street and back to her tenth birthday . . .

Jo didn't know how long she would be in the box this time but now she preferred it to being alone in the house with her dad. Being with him frightened her so much more than being in her box.

Even though over the past few years she'd got used to it, often it felt to Jo as if she'd been in the box for days on end. At times her dad would pull it from under the bed then use it to rest things on rather than letting her out. Last week, he'd put his tray of food on it while he'd relaxed and watched the small television in the bedroom. She'd been able to see the bottom of the dirty metal tray through the gaps of the old wardrobe he'd made the box out of. And when Jo had smelt the food, it'd made her mouth water, thinking of how nice it would be to eat. But in a way she hadn't minded; she'd learnt that, when she had no food in her tummy, it stopped her making a mess in her box.

At least now she always had her stuffed elephant with her. Ever since she'd found him a couple of years ago near the bins, all scruffy and smelly from being in the rubbish, he'd made Jo feel better. Though it had taken her a while to decide what to call him, in the end she'd settled on Grey, because that was the colour of him. She didn't really know any other names apart from her own, and the ones that her dad called her on days when he was angry, which was most days. She didn't like those names and she certainly hadn't wanted to call Grey any of them. She loved Grey and never wanted him to feel sad like her.

From under her dad's bed, Jo watched him through the splintered crack of her box while he sat slumped by the open bathroom door, drinking from a bottle that always seemed to be in his hand. She'd often thought he held onto his bottles of drink in much the same way as she held on to Grey. Today he was drinking even more than he normally did and getting more and more angry, shouting at things that weren't even there. He'd even thrown the lamp against the wall and it had shattered into tiny pieces, landing on the metal bed above her, sounding to Jo like hailstones were falling from the sky into the room.

'Jo! Jo! Jo! Jo! Jo!' her dad started to shout her name, but she knew better than to answer. She kissed Grey and held him tight, hugging him to her, then she put her finger to her lips and whispered to the elephant: 'Sshhhh, Grey, we've got to keep quiet. We can't make a noise.'

A sudden slam of a door from downstairs made Jo jump. The next moment she heard footsteps, then another door opened and closed as someone else came into the bedroom.

'Where've you fucking been? Fucking other men, no doubt.'

Jo began to tremble at her dad's slurred shouting. With her hands shaking, she covered Grey's big ears, worried he might be frightened.

Trying to see who it was her dad was shouting at, Jo pushed her eye against the crack, feeling the wood scratch against her face. She could make out the woman with the long brown hair; Jo didn't really know her, but Dad had told her a few times that the woman was her mum.

'I thought I'd get Jo a birthday cake.' She swayed on her feet and it dawned on Jo that everyone who came into the house seemed to sway on their feet. 'Give me some of that.' The woman snatched the bottle and took a long drink.

'Bet you forgot to get candles, didn't you?'

'Of course I didn't forget to buy some fucking candles. What do you take me for? I got nine pink candles.' She slurred her words and Jo could see dribble coming from the woman's mouth.

For some reason her dad's face began to turn red and Jo watched as he used the door frame to lean against and slide himself up onto his feet. His head wobbled from side to side and he pointed at the woman, though he couldn't keep still enough to point straight. To Jo it looked as if his hand was bobbing about in the breeze.

'What did you fucking say?'

'I said I got some candles. Nine candles.'

Her dad burped loudly and wiped his mouth with the back of his tattooed arm. 'She's ten, you stupid cunt. You needed ten candles, not nine. You always fuck everything up, don't you?'

Jo covered Grey's eyes, but she watched as the woman dropped the bottle onto the floor when Dad lunged at her. Then he dragged her into the bathroom and began to run the bath. Checking to make sure Grey wasn't peeking, Jo continued to watch as her dad threw the woman into the water, gripping her by her hair, pushing her under while her legs kicked out. And all the time Jo was glad that Grey couldn't see what was going on.

Her 'mum' tried to sit up but Dad pushed her back down. He pushed again and again, and it seemed to Jo like every push got harder, angrier. Then Jo sat very still as her dad dragged the woman out and over the side of the bath, sending her body tumbling onto the hard floor, reminding Jo of a wet fish falling out of a fisherman's net like the ones she'd seen when she'd watched television through the cracks of her box.

There was silence. The woman had stopped kicking and Jo, still not letting Grey see, watched her dad stagger out of the room. Now she and Grey were left alone with the woman, who lay on the bathroom floor, staring. Although the woman's eyes were wide open, they didn't move and her eyelids didn't blink, they just kept looking at her and Grey.

It seemed like a long time before Jo's dad came back into the room. He went straight into the bathroom, wrapping her 'mum' up in the black bin bags he'd brought with him, something else she didn't want Grey to see.

As her dad dragged the woman past the box, he stopped and bent down and knocked lightly on the side. Jo slipped Grey behind her back; she didn't want him anywhere near her dad.

'Ten candles, not fucking nine, that's right, ain't it, Jo? We told her, didn't we? And who needed her anyway? Not us, not when we've got each other. Ten years old today. My big girl. Happy Days, Jo, happy fucking days . . .'

Snapping herself out of the memory and back to the safety of the here and now of Old Compton Street, she felt the sweat dripping down her back. Out of sight under the table, she dug the end of the teaspoon into her palm in an effort to lock out the memories of that day. Then she took a deep breath and, so well practised at pretending everything was fine, she smiled at the others and began to get up.

'Come on, girls, it's freezing out here. Maybe the hair of the dog at Barney's ain't such a bad idea after all . . . Happy days.'

As she watched the others laugh and get to their feet, she resolved to make certain that they would never find out who she was. No one must know, ever. She would do anything to stop that happening . . . anything at all.

23

In a maisonette on a rundown estate in Seaford Street, one of several ex-council properties he had bought up over the years, Ned sat staring at his mother, his face twisted in a sneer. 'Why do you always have to be so fucking coarse? Where's your manners?'

Pearl, still red faced from climbing up the stairs, was busy spitting sunflower seed husks onto the bare wooden floor. 'For fuck's sake, no one would believe you were born in a lav on the Bermondsey Road! The way you talk, anyone would think you had the crown jewels stuffed up your fucking arse.'

Irritated but determined not to rise to the bait and answer her, Ned stalked across to the door opposite, unlocking it and walking in.

The room had a small bathroom off it, but it was empty apart from a single metal bed. On it, unconscious and looking very much the worse for wear, was Pete Draper, nephew of Simon.

'He ain't looking good, is he?' Ned spoke to his mum as she came into the room.

'What do you expect? This place is hardly St Thomas's, is it, and what do I know about giving him the old Nightingale treatment? Do I look like an angel of mercy? Fucking hell.'

'Shut up and let me think,' Ned snapped. Pete's face was deathly white and, from what he could see, his breathing was shallow.

'I don't know why you didn't leave the little weasel to rot in that alleyway. You should've left him where he was.'

Feeling the stress beginning to creep up on him, Ned massaged the back of his neck. 'Didn't I just tell you to shut the fuck up? Like I told you: it seemed like a good idea at the time. I was desperate. What could I do? I could hardly leave him to die, and I couldn't take him to hospital, cos either way Simon would've been all over it. He thinks I'm Pete's fucking keeper, and somehow he's got it into his mind that if anything happens to this cunt, it's on my head. And you know what that means.'

'What are you going to do about it? Simon's a fucking nutter. Last time you went up against him, you were lucky to get out alive. He might have come from the streets, but he's got a lot of people backing him now, son. One wrong move and he'll snuff you out – he'll snuff us all out, Ned. Regardless how big a cunt Pete is, he's family to Simon. And family and loyalty mean everything to that bastard,' Pearl said, finally taking the situation seriously.

Ned ran his fingers along the scar that ran from the edge of his mouth to the top of his ear. Like the Reids, Simon was originally from Bermondsey, which was why Ned had backed him when he'd gone up against some of the most powerful faces in London. The turf wars that followed had been messy; a lot of bodies had been chopped up and scattered all over Essex and Kent. Somehow, against all odds, Simon, being street smarter and more ruthless than the rest, had come out on top.

In return for his loyalty, Simon had given Ned a few districts to run, Soho being one of them. He'd made Ned rich and powerful, but there was a price to be paid. When Ned wanted to go his own way, truly be his own boss, Simon had told him that wasn't an option. He would consider it a betrayal, a breaking of loyalty and bonds. Either Ned backed down and did as he was told or

Simon would regard him as the enemy. And everyone knew what happened to Simon's enemies.

To make sure there was no doubt what he'd do if Ned tried to walk away, Simon had arranged a beating for Ned which lasted three days and nearly ended his life – though Simon had ordered his men not to go that far. He'd wanted it to serve as a reminder of who was the boss, who called the shots . . . and it had. So Ned understood there was no walking away from Simon – which was fucking ironic, given the trouble Ned had been having with Zee and Cookie. And if Pete were to die, Simon would make sure that Ned was only six feet behind.

'We need Pete to wake up and walk out of here. He can say what he likes – most of the time he's on crack or some other shit, so Simon won't want to hear any of his jackanorys – the main thing is that we get him walking and talking and back in Soho. All Simon cares about is making sure that he's alive.'

Pearl sniffed loudly. 'Well it don't look like he's going to wake up in a hurry. You read about that shit, don't you? You know, where they have an injury and then they end up brain dead.'

'How is this helping? That's the last thing I need to hear. Pete has to get up sharpish.'

'And what about when he does wake up? It's hardly going to be clever for us two to be standing over him. You say Simon only wants to know he's all right, but I think us playing Annie Wilkes crosses the line, don't you?'

'Annie Wilkes? What the fuck are you on about now?

'*Misery* – ain't you seen the film?'

'Look, if you've got nothing helpful to say, keep it zipped.' He rolled his eyes, but he could see the truth in the rest of what his mother had said. 'We'll keep checking on him, but the moment there's any sign of life and I know he's getting better, I'll get one of my men to move him – someone Pete don't know, someone there's no chance of him setting eyes on again. Dump him in some crack den somewhere. He'll be in seventh heaven.' He sighed and glanced at his watch. 'Right, we better go – and do me a favour, Mum, keep that big fucking mouth of yours closed. I don't want Finn finding out about Pete. Understand? We tell no one.'

As Ned shut and locked the door, Pete opened his eyes. It had been relatively easy to keep them closed and lie absolutely still. He felt like death; cold sweat drenched his body, while his hair was caked to the pillow with dried blood. He didn't have any memory of how he got here; the last thing he remembered was Barney and Tabby mugging him off. After that, it was all a blank.

Or at least it had been, until he eavesdropped on Ned and Pearl. Now he knew they were involved in whatever had happened to him, he was determined to make sure they didn't get away with it. Or rather, Uncle Simon would make sure. Now all he had to do was work out how to escape. And when he did, it would be Ned's blood caked on the floor . . .

24

Tuesday morning brought nothing but rain and grey skies. Stepping out of the shower, Cookie wrapped herself in her favourite white towelling robe. Looking in the mirror, she could see the faint bags under her eyes, a giveaway from the sleepless nights she'd been having. At least Ned hadn't come home for the past couple of nights, which had given her some peace. Trying to keep Ned happy, accepting all his punishments without complaint, was becoming increasingly difficult.

Pulling her robe to the side to examine her inner thigh, Cookie examined the mottled bruises left by Saturday's punishment. They'd heal, like all the other times, but Ned was getting more relentless, more obsessive, more sexually aggressive than ever. And there were times when she genuinely worried if he'd go too far and end up killing her; aside from the beatings, she feared choking on the gags he stuffed down her throat, or the ropes he used in the autoerotic asphyxiation games he insisted on making her play. And unless she wanted to walk away – which she couldn't, right now – there was nothing she could do to stop Ned. Her only hope was to stay alive long enough to do what she'd set out to.

As she began to brush her freshly washed hair, Cookie's mobile vibrated. She glanced at it and, seeing it was a text from Finn, she snatched it up before anyone could see, even though she knew Ned wasn't about and Pearl had gone to the hairdressers.

For a moment she held the phone against her chest, breathing deeply and annoyed that she could feel her heart beginning to race. Cookie swiped open the message . . .

Hey, it's me checking in. Everything all right?

Cookie stared at the message. On any other occasion, Finn texting her would've been no big deal, an everyday occurrence, but since the fight with Ned, and knowing the way Finn felt about her, his texts could land them both in trouble. He was playing with fire. After all, there was no way he could know if Ned or Pearl were about; either of them could've picked up her phone. And she'd told him on Sunday *not* to contact her. No calls, no texts. Nothing. Irritated at the fact he hadn't listen, Cookie replied:

Why wouldn't it be?

Within moments the reply pinged back in:

You on your own?

She decided the best thing to do was ignore him, so she put the phone in her pocket and made her way out of the luxurious en suite bathroom. But by the time she'd reached the door, her phone was vibrating again.

???

Again she ignored it.

Shall we meet? I want to see you.

Frowning, she was tempted to text back and let him know what she thought of him being so bloody stupid, especially after she'd told him nothing could happen between them. She couldn't believe that he'd be so blatant: risking her safety by sending texts about meeting. Finn was one of the few people that really understood what Ned would do to her if he ever suspected her of even looking at another man, let alone his cousin.

Turning off her mobile, Cookie wearily sat on her bed watching the rain out of her window. In deep thought, she wondered again what the hell Finn was playing at.

'What are you doing with my phone?' Accusingly, Finn stood in the doorway staring at Pearl as she scrambled to put his mobile back into his jacket pocket, which was hanging on the chair.

Dressed in a marl grey sweater and jog pants, Finn walked into the kitchen of the Hanson Street property, drying his hair with a small blue towel. He strode over, snatching the phone away from Pearl. 'Well, come on, what was so interesting about me phone?'

She sniffed. 'Nothing.'

'Pearl, people don't have someone's phone in their hand for nothing, do they?'

'Well I'm certainly not looking to see if you've been sending dick picks, am I? Just checking the time, that's all. Ain't a crime, is it?'

'There's a clock on the wall.' He pointed to the clock, regarding her suspiciously.

'Fuck me, not everyone has eyes like a bleedin' hawk. That dickory dock may as well be invisible when it comes to me old mince pies.'

'It's massive, Pearl. If Big Ben ever breaks down, they'll know where to come. And lay off the "old mince pies" shit; if there was fifty fucking quid on the ground, you'd spot it from a mile away.'

'Excuse me for wanting to know the time. Maybe you shouldn't have given me your passcode if you're so precious about your phone.'

'It was in my pocket, not on the table. Has no one ever told you that it's fucking rude to take things without asking?'

'I'd say that was your speciality, wouldn't you?'

Sitting down, Finn stared at Pearl. 'What's that supposed to mean? Come to think of it, why are you even here? Since we've been living in this place, you've never once come and sat down for breakfast with me before. After what happened with me and Ned the other night, I'm surprised you're here at all.'

She leant over and tapped him on the hand. 'Aren't I allowed to be concerned about me nephew?'

He stared at her. 'You're up to something, aren't you?'

Slurping her milky tea, Pearl shrugged. She didn't say anything. She hadn't actually planned to text Cookie using Finn's phone. The truth was she'd come to speak to Finn about Zee and the boys. Like Ned, she was furious that they thought they could do a runner. But while her son was too preoccupied with Simon Draper and Pete to do anything about it, she wasn't prepared to let the little bastards off the hook. When Finn's phone had started ringing in his pocket while he was in the shower, it had given her an idea.

It'd been easy because Finn had used the same pin code since he'd first had a phone: his mother's date of birth – God rest Ivy's soul. Although Cookie had played smart, holding back and not responding to the texts in a way that would incriminate her, Pearl was determined to persist until she had proof to show Ned. Then finally she'd have the pleasure of waving goodbye to that trollop.

25

So far the week had passed quietly, although that didn't stop Cookie worrying. She hadn't seen much of Ned, which had suited her fine, though each time she'd seen his mother, Pearl had chuckled nastily at her. It was clear that Pearl thought she had something over her, and not knowing exactly what that might be was making Cookie feel very uneasy.

And as Cookie sat in the club on Thursday evening, she tried to push Pearl and Ned out of her mind. But now she was here, every instinct she had was telling her she shouldn't have come. She should've stayed away because she knew it was on Thursday nights that Finn came into the club for a drink.

Her life was messy enough already – something else she'd told herself on several occasions – without adding Finn to her problems. She couldn't; it was too dangerous and she *had* to keep focused on the bigger picture, her plan. Yet she was still here and Finn was a bad idea waiting to happen. So why then had she convinced herself that the only reason she was popping down the club tonight was to see Barney and the girls? In truth, Cookie knew the answer; it didn't take a genius to work it out. As much as she didn't want to admit it, and even though she was mad at him for sending her those texts the other day, she was missing him. It was as simple as that.

For years she'd kept her emotions locked away, unable to feel anything, not *allowing* herself to feel anything other than pain. Unhappiness. Guilt. Which was what made it possible to be with

Ned. Now Finn had triggered something in her, feelings she hadn't even known she had, feelings she thought she wasn't capable of, and it scared her and made her feel vulnerable. And Cookie understood full well that vulnerable was the last thing she could afford to be. Yet here she was, sitting in the club and hoping to see Finn, to speak to him, even though she would never let him know how she felt.

Sitting on the bar stool next to Lorni while Natalie and Barney busied themselves getting the club ready for opening time, Cookie sighed. 'So tell me about yourself: what's the story?' she said, wanting to fill the silence as much as seizing the opportunity to see if she could find out more about Lorni now that she had her on her own.

She was wary of strangers and she wasn't quite sure why Barney had decided to give Lorni a home. When she'd asked, he'd been evasive, which automatically made her suspicious and gave her even more of an incentive to find out more about her.

Lorni didn't answer immediately but raised a glass and took a sip of orange juice. It didn't go unnoticed by Cookie that Lorni's hand was shaking. As she put the glass down, she gave Cookie a sideward glance; though she was smiling, the smile didn't reach her eyes.

'Sorry to disappoint you, Cookie, but I ain't got a story – not one that's worth telling, anyway.'

Cookie smiled back but it was forced. 'How about you try me?' She could hear her voice was cold but she didn't care; there was something about Lorni that didn't sit well with her. 'You never know, I might find it fascinating.'

Lorni bristled and her gaze darted towards Barney. 'Like I say, nothing to tell . . . Maybe I should give Barney some help; I wouldn't want him to think I was taking the piss.'

Raising her eyebrows, Cookie cupped her hands around the

half-drunk glass of rosé d'Anjou Barney had insisted on pouring for her earlier. 'Are you?'

Lorni frowned. 'Am I what?'

'Are you taking the piss? I mean, as you can see, Barney's a soft touch; he'd take anyone in if he thought they needed help, and of course that's admirable, but it also opens him up to people taking advantage.'

'I think Barney is old enough to know what he's doing, don't you?'

'You make it sound like you know him, but you've been around less than a week.' Cookie tilted her head to one side, her long hair falling over her shoulders. 'Yet here you are, feet under the table, telling me about my mate.'

Lorni didn't say anything though her cheeks flushed. 'I'm not sure what your problem is. If you don't like me being here, maybe you should take that up with Barney. We've already had a chat about things and, not meaning to be rude, it isn't your business.'

'Maybe not, but I'm not keen on strangers,' Cookie replied, deciding that she liked Lorni less and less with every word which was coming out of her mouth.

'Funny, cos that's exactly how I feel about bitches.' Lorni got up to go but Cookie placed her hand on the woman's arm, preventing her from leaving.

'You've got a lot of front for someone who's just popped up. I'd be careful if I was you: we're a close bunch and no one likes a bad attitude.'

Lorni looked down at Cookie's hand on top of her arm. 'I haven't got a bad attitude. I won't be pushed around by people, not anymore.'

Icily, Cookie grinned. 'So there is a story.'

'I've already told you,' Lorni said, trying to pull her arm away.

'There isn't. I wonder, did you give Tabby this much grief? Did you make her tell you her story too?'

'You leave Tabby out of it, OK? We all love Tabby, and Tabby's different.'

The atmosphere between them was charged with hostility. 'Look, Cookie, I don't want to argue and I certainly don't want trouble. I'm here trying to get myself sorted and keep my head down. It's only temporary, then me and Jace can move on.'

'So why didn't you go to a refuge? If you've got nowhere to stay, that would have made more sense, wouldn't it?'

'Most of them are full.'

Cookie took a small sip of wine. 'Come off it, Lorni, that can't be it. You've got a kid, they're not goin' to turn you away. They'd find a bed for you both somehow, even if it's not in the area.'

'Well maybe not all of us want people getting involved in their business.' Clearly annoyed, Lorni pulled free of Cookie's grip. 'And from the bits and pieces I've had about *you*, I would've thought you of all people would've understood that. So back off and don't try to ruin anything for me and my son. We like it here, and I won't let someone like you spoil it.' At which point Lorni moved across to join Natalie and Barney.

Fuming, and tempted to go across and drag her back, Cookie took a deep breath. She had to give it to Lorni, the girl had front. It was obvious to anyone she had something to hide, but then, hadn't they all. It was true that she hadn't asked Tabby about her story, or the others, come to think of it. So why Lorni? Why all the questions for her? Maybe it was because she was certain Lorni was lying. Or maybe it was because of Jace . . . Cookie stopped her thoughts, forcing her attention elsewhere.

Her mind began to drift back to Finn. One thing that had surprised her was that Ned wasn't gunning for Finn, which was unlike him. What was going on? As long as she'd known Ned, he'd never let anything go. Yet the few times she'd seen him over the last couple of days, Ned hadn't mentioned Finn or the kids, or even Brian for that matter. In fact, Ned had seemed completely distracted. She'd even go so far as to say he seemed worried.

Mid-thought, Cookie's chest went tight and she found herself having to rub it to take away the sudden ache as she watched Jace walk into the club. He smiled shyly at her.

'Hello.' Cookie barely managed a whisper.

'Have you see my mum?'

Again she found herself struggling to speak. She clasped her hands together, forced the words out: 'She's over there, helping Barney.'

'Thank you.' He smiled again and Cookie stared into his brown eyes. *Those eyes.* The next moment, Cookie ran out of the club and into the bathroom to be sick.

An hour later, Lorni was back upstairs with Jace, while Barney, Natalie, Cora and Cookie sat chatting in the club, drinking Barney's instant coffee and sharing a packet of KitKat that Cora had bought earlier.

'You don't know anything about her, Barney. You sure it's a good idea having her staying here like this? And what's the story about . . .' she swallowed, settling her breathing as she tried to make it sound like casual interest, '. . . the boy? What's going on there?' Rather than meet his gaze, she focused on her coffee, blowing gently to cool it down.

'I never asked and I'm not going to. That's the way it is around here, you should know that. Anyway, what did you say to her? She looked upset.'

Cookie shrugged, unwilling to let Barney know what they

talked about. 'I ain't said anything. Maybe Nats upset her.' Cookie winked at Natalie, teasing.

'Not guilty, your honour.' Natalie laughed but then turned serious. 'Cookie's right though, Barney, maybe you shouldn't adopt the first stranger that comes along. I know she helped with all that stuff with Pete . . .' Natalie trailed off, looking awkward. 'Sorry, Barn. My big mouth, eh? That's usually Cora's job.'

'Pete? What about him?' Cookie looked surprised. Her glance darted between them. 'Am I missing something here?'

Barney gave Cookie a tight smile. 'Nothing worth talking about . . . Anyway, you two can talk. I mean, I don't know anything about you guys, not really. All I know is you're here. Tabby's an enigma, so is Cora. Let's face it, all you girls are. But I still love you and want you about. We don't always have to bring out the old curriculum vitae to be mates, do we?' He winked at them. 'So why don't you try and give Lorni a squeeze?'

Cookie pulled a face. 'It's OK, thanks . . . And while we're talking about it, the same could be said about you, Barney. What's your secret?'

He roared with laughter, but the way he did, Cookie wondered if it was only her imagination or if it really sounded too loud and too forced.

'Well, if you spill the beans, maybe I might think about telling all. Go on, who's going to go first?' Barney said. 'Cora, you want to tell us what dark secrets you've got in your closet?'

'The only thing I've got in my closet is fucking dirty underwear from where me old man dumped it, cos he couldn't be bothered to bung his kegs in the washing machine. And on that note, I'm going . . . I'll see you tomorrow, guys.'

They blew Cora kisses as she walked out.

'It could be worse,' Barney said, turning the page of the magazine he'd left lying on the bar. 'You could be hiding a dead body under the floorboards. I tell you, this true crime mag will give you nightmares. There's some sick people in this world . . . Did you know that Jo Martin and her dad had *two* bodies under the floorboards? One of them was her mum, apparently. Wrapped up in bin bags . . . It says here, they think Jo helped her dad kill her mum. Can you imagine that? And the other body was Jo's baby – they think it was stillborn, but who knows with those two. When they did a DNA test on it, they found out her dad was the father.'

Cookie's voice was tight and it felt like her heart had missed a beat. 'Why do you keep going on about it?'

Still flicking through the pages, Barney shrugged. 'You know I like my true crime stories, and the Martin case is in all these mags at the moment. I already told you, it's the tenth anniversary of her release from prison, and the tenth anniversary of when her dad hung himself. Say what you like, it's a good read.'

'Jesus Christ, two kids died, Barney – we ain't talking about some neighbour cutting down next-door's hedge. And those magazines sensationalize everything. They make people's suffering into entertainment.'

'I can't understand why you want to read all that stuff,' Natalie agreed. 'It's people's lives, Barn.'

Ignoring them, Barney continued: 'Look here, there's a photo of one of the kids they killed.' He held the magazine up to show Cookie and Natalie. 'He's a sweetie, isn't he? Well, he *was* a sweetie.'

'What did I tell you?' Cookie snapped, pulling the magazine out of his hands and throwing it on the counter. She wiped her face, feeling the sweat prick at her forehead. 'I don't want to see it.'

'Barney, you can be a fucking idiot sometimes.' Natalie got up. 'I'm going to put the dishwasher on, OK? And Barney, maybe think about what you're doing. Not everybody wants to hear it. It ain't something people want to go to bed thinking about . . . I'll see you later, Cooks. Love you, babe.'

Cookie began to get her things together, hurriedly gathering her stuff. She grabbed her bag and coat and started heading for the exit of the club.

'I'm sorry, OK?' Barney apologized, running after her.

'Whatever.'

Getting in front of her to block her way, Barney opened his arms wide. 'What's going on, Cooks?'

Close to tears, Cookie licked her dry lips. 'I don't need this, all right? I've got enough shit with Ned, without you being a fucking prick.'

'Excuse me?'

Cookie could feel her temper rising and she shook her head. 'You heard me, Barn. You're a fucking prick. I love you, but you need to stop, OK.'

Barney's expression hardened. 'If you've got a problem with me, you better come out and say it.'

'I think you're forgetting who you're talking to. I don't have to say anything. Now get the fuck out of my way.'

'Wait,' Barney sounded as upset as he looked. 'What's brought this on? I'm confused.'

As Cookie headed for the stairs she nodded. 'Yeah, I gathered that. I'll see you around.'

'Oh no you fucking don't! You are not going to have a hissy fit and walk out on me without explaining,' he barked after her.

She turned round, walking backwards as she went up the stairs. Her laugh sounded pitiful and she could feel the tears stinging her eyes. 'Sorry, you must have me mixed up with your other half. Last time I checked, we weren't swinging the same way.' The she spun around and ran the rest of the way up.

'No way, no fucking way!' Taking two steps at a time and looking visibly upset, Barney chased after her, catching up in the foyer, he grabbed her arm. 'Start talking. *Now . . .*'

26

'Get your fucking hands off me.'

In the elaborate gold decor of the foyer, Barney stared at Cookie. 'You sound like Ned.'

'Funny that, I wonder why. Now I'll say it again: get your fucking hands off me or you're going to regret it.'

Clearly bemused, Barney shook his head. 'Haven't you heard a word I've been saying? You're my friend, Cooks. Whatever's going on, I want to know.'

'Don't push it, Barney, you may be my mate but everything has a sell-by date,' she hissed, but he continued to hold onto her. 'If you don't let go of me, Barn, it ain't only me you're going to have to worry about.'

'Really?' There was a mixture of shock and anger in Barney's voice. 'You're really going to threaten me with Ned?'

'If you let me go like I'm asking you to,' Cookie yelled, burning with anger, 'I won't have to, will I?'

'Now I'm really worried, because for you to say that, I know there's something wrong.'

Cookie started to pull harder, desperately wanting to get away. She felt trapped and the pain she always tried to hold back rushed through her veins. With the other hand she wiped away her tears. 'Let me go. *Please.*'

'Then tell me.'

'There's nothing to tell; now *fuck* off!'

At the same time she tugged her arm, she kicked Barney hard on the ankle.

'Jesus Christ. Fuck's sake, that hurt!' he yowled and staggered back, taking Cookie with him as he began to tumble to the floor, but she managed to stay on her feet, pulling her hand away just in time to save herself from falling.

Her rose gold locket bracelet broke off her wrist and fell by the side of Barney's leg. Immediately, Cookie scrambled onto the floor grabbing at the locket, the heart-shaped charm lying snapped open on the ground.

Barney reached to pass it.

'Leave it! Don't touch it! Don't you fucking touch it!' Cookie's scream was loud and aggressive and Barney's face wore an expression of shock, but ignoring what Cookie had said, he reached out to pick up the locket.

'No!'

Barney stared at the bracelet, his mouth gaping open. 'What the fuck is this?'

'I told you not to touch it, I told you not to touch it!' Cookie grabbed for the locket, but Barney turned his body around, putting his arm in the air, preventing Cookie being able to grab it.

'Give it me! You've got no fucking right! I swear to God, Barney . . .'

He batted her away and stared again at the locket, then he jumped up, running down the stairs and into the club.

'Barney! Barney!'

Cookie chased him, watching as he ran to the bar, grabbing the magazine he'd been reading to flick through it again. For a moment he didn't move, only stared, then he tapped one of the pages, looking down at it. 'There. There.' His face was unusually pale and he lifted his eyes to glare at Cookie. 'You going to explain this?'

Walking forward slowly, Cookie stood in front of him. She held out her hand, which was shaking. 'Give me my bracelet.'

He shook his head furiously. 'No. Not until you tell me about *this.*'

'I don't know what you're talking about. Hand it over, Barney.'

Now it was Barney's turn to shout. 'No? Really? You don't know what I'm talking about?' He grabbed the magazine, shaking it, holding it up in the air and banging the page he'd been looking at. 'Jo Martin. That story. The photo of the kid in your locket is the *same* as the photo in here. The boy that was murdered.' Wide-eyed, he backed away from her, shaking his head in disbelief. 'What are you? *Who are you*?' He looked again at the bracelet charm, carefully cranking the rose gold heart open even more. 'Oh my God . . . That's a lock of hair in there.'

Cookie lunged so fast that this time she was able to grab the bracelet from Barney. Face red and breathless, she pointed at him. 'If you tell anyone about this. I will make sure Ned buries you. He won't even ask why; he'll be happy to do it.'

'I thought I knew you, but you're one of those sick people, aren't you?'

'Shut up, Barney.'

'You hear about it all the time. Killers that take trophies from their victims, they like to take the trophies out and look at them, it helps them relive the crime . . . You're Jo Martin, aren't you?'

Hearing Barney's words, Cookie turned and ran.

Cookie ran through the darkness of Soho, charging through the puddles as the rain lashed down. She could hear Barney calling her, chasing her, wanting answers, but there were none she wanted to give.

Still running, she turned into Charing Cross Road, and all the while Barney's voice continued to cut through the wind. As she ran, she looked for a cab, but the rain was so heavy they were either full or they sped past, spraying her with muddy water.

Cookie wasn't thinking about where she was running or where she was going; all she knew was that she had to get away from Barney.

'*Wait! Stop! Cookie! Stop!*'

Hoping to lose him, Cookie darted through the traffic on the Strand and turned into Villiers Avenue. Within minutes the air turned colder and Cookie realized she had reached the embankment, and there were no longer any buildings to block the chill February wind bouncing off the river.

Panting, she slowed down, not knowing, not caring how long she'd been running. She glanced over her shoulder, hoping that she'd finally lost Barney. There was no one in sight, and a thick mist was beginning to drift off the Thames.

Exhausted and relieved that Barney appeared to have given up the chase, Cookie made her way up the stairs of Jubilee Bridge. Her whole body felt weary, as if she was carrying a bag of stones on her back.

She leaned over the railings, looking down into the water, the icy air welcoming, a distraction from her thoughts. Then she put her hands over her face. 'Oh God.' She heard her voice and felt her warm breath against her fingers, once again the feeling of nausea hit her. She breathed deeply and slowly, then exhaled just as slowly, hoping it would pass.

'I want the truth.'

She jumped and Cookie swirled around.

Standing on the bridge, soaking wet, his expression drawn, was Barney.

'Leave me alone, Barney.' She tried to sound firm but her voice wavered. 'You hear me?'

Barney looked around. 'No, why should I? There's no one here apart from you and me, and you're going to start talking.'

'Get out of my face,' Cookie yelled, trying to push past him.

High up over the Thames with the storm raging, Barney shouted back at her: 'I said *tell me*, tell me who the fuck you are. You at least owe me that.'

'You know who I am.'

Visibly upset, Barney shook his head. 'I thought I did. I thought I knew my mate. You know, the one that I love. All these years, we've always been there for each other.'

Tears of anger, of frustration, of hurt began to prick at her eyes. Angrily she wiped them away, along with the rain. 'And nothing's changed, unless of course you carry on with this crap.'

'It's not crap though, is it? I can tell. No one runs the frigging length of Soho and hikes it down to the river if they've nothing to hide.'

Barney's face was red, part from the freezing wind and part from anger. 'Come on, stop playing games. You're Jo Martin, aren't you?'

Backing away, Cookie felt a pain in her chest. 'You have no idea what you're talking about.'

'Oh I do. I think this is one big charade. Ms Cookie Mackenzie, Little Miss Perfect. It's all bullshit, isn't it?'

She shook her head in bemusement and she tasted the rain-drops on her lips. 'Little Miss Perfect?' she screamed at him, her usual cool demeanour broken. 'Are you fucking kidding me? You don't have a clue. Nothing about my life is perfect. *Nothing.*' Cookie held onto her head.

'The truth stings, does it? That poor boy, what you did to him.'

'You've got to stop this, you've got to stop!' Her voice edged on the hysterical as she pointed at Barney.

'When did you get the lock of hair? When he was alive? Or when you killed him? When he screamed, is that when?'

'Shut up!' Cookie wrapped her arms around herself, her voice breathless as if she were in pain. 'Stop. Stop it!'

'Why should I?'

'Because . . .'

'Because what?'

'Because . . . because he was my son. That photo in the locket is my son, Parker. Parker was murdered by Jo Martin.' She dropped to her knees at Barney's feet, weeping. 'He was my son, Barney, he was my son and they killed him . . . They killed him. He was three years old and they killed him.'

'Oh my God. Oh my God.' Barney dropped to his knees as well, sitting next to Cookie on the cold iron bridge. 'I'm so sorry, Cookie, I'm so sorry.' He held her, wrapping his arms around her, rocking her as she wept. And through her tears, through the most unbearable pain, Cookie managed to whisper.

'I will find her, Barney. I will find Jo Martin. And when I do, I'm going to kill her.'

27

Lorni, meanwhile, was hurrying along the back alleyways of the West End with Jace in tow. She'd been in every cafe and club, but no one was hiring, or rather no one wanted to hire for cash in hand. And now she was broke. There was no way she was going to sponge off Barney. The way Cookie had treated her had made her feel like dirt. And she had no idea what the woman's problem was: she'd hardly spoken to Cookie since she'd moved into Barney's spare room, yet she was sticking her nose into Lorni's business like she was the Queen of Soho. Though in Lorni's mind, Cookie wasn't any queen, she was an out-and-out bitch.

'Mum, can we get a cab?' Jace tugged on her hand. 'I'm cold.'

'No, sweetheart, we ain't got the money.'

'We never have the money.'

Lorni stopped in her tracks and stared at her son. 'What's that supposed to mean?'

'Nothing.' Jace looked down. His face crumbled as he huddled, shivering.

'That's not a proper answer.'

'We never have anything.'

Guilty and upset, Lorni crouched next to her son in the pouring rain and lifted his chin, wiping the tears from his eyes. 'Is that what you think?'

Jace nodded.

'I know it's hard, darlin', but Mummy's trying. I know we ain't got much, but we've got each other, ain't we? You and me, that's all we need, isn't it?'

'I guess.'

'Aren't you happy, Jace?' Lorni asked, not really wanting to hear the answer, though of course she knew it. Sometimes it seemed she spent all her time trying to ignore what was right in front of her. It was obvious her son struggled to cope with moving from one place to another, constantly being cold and hungry. It was no life for a kid.

He looked up at her and Lorni had to look away, the sadness in his eyes shining out too brightly as they stood under the street-lights of London. 'I don't want to move from Barney's. Can we stay there, *please*?'

Grateful that Jace hadn't answered the question, Lorni drew her son into a hug. 'I hope so, but I'm finding it really difficult to get a job, and we won't be able to stay if we can't pay our way. Barney's been real good by feeding us and not charging us rent, but he won't be able to do that forever, will he? He ain't family.'

Jace shrugged. 'I wish we had family.'

Lorni bristled. 'Well, we ain't. My family's dead, you know that already.' She closed then opened her eyes quickly. 'I'm sorry, Jace, I shouldn't have snapped at you.'

Before Jace could answer, a horn sounded. They both turned.

'Fancy a lift? I thought it was you.' It was Ned, leaning out of his blacked-out Bentley Bentayga 4x4, one of the several cars he owed.

'We're fine, thanks.' Lorni's voice was clipped.

'The boy's freezing. Maybe I should ask him . . . Fancy a lift, mate?' Ned winked.

Looking up at his mum, then back at Ned, Jace shrugged again.

'You've got a good kid there, loyal to his mum, I like that. Keeps his mouth shut even when he's freezing his nuts off.'

'I don't need you to tell me that.'

Ned laughed then stepped out into the pouring rain. He flicked up the collar of his jacket and opened the back passenger door. Playfully he bowed, pretending to tip an imaginary hat while he held the door open to them. 'Where to, ma'am, sir? Your carriage awaits.'

'Mum, *please*.' Jace glanced at his mum hopefully.

Standing straight, Ned smiled at Lorni. 'Come on, darlin', you heard the kid. It's late and it's cold, so why don't you park your pride in the rain and hop in.'

Without answering Lorni gave a nod to Jace, who jumped happily in the back, followed by a reluctant Lorni.

Thick black stitched leather seats and chrome greeted them. 'Wow, this is cool.'

'It's only a car, Jace,' Lorni whispered. 'As long as it gets you from A to B, that's all that matters.'

Ned looked at Lorni in the driver's mirror and smiled. 'So where to?'

'Desires.'

Ned raised his eyebrows. 'I didn't know you were staying there.'

'Well why would you?'

Instead of answering, Ned took his eyes off the road and turned to look at Jace as he stopped at the junction for the red lights. 'If you lift that armrest up, there's a drinks cooler there. Help yourself, but maybe leave the gin for your mum. I think there should be a Coke for you.'

As Jace began to lift the armrest up, Lorni slammed it back down. She directed her words at Ned. 'Thank you, but we're fine. You've done more than enough by giving us a lift.'

'Suit yourself,' Ned said, setting off again at speed.

In the warmth of the car, lit up by the low, soft lighting of the dashboard, they fell into silence. For the next couple of minutes, the only sound was the rain. Lorni stared out of the window at the downpour. As much as it was clear the guy was an arrogant arsehole, she was pleased that he'd persuaded her to get a lift back to Barney's. Not that she particularly wanted Barney to see her with Ned. She didn't know what had gone on the other night in the club – she'd gone upstairs before it had all kicked off, beating a quick exit around the time he arrived to join the rest of his family. But she'd heard Natalie and Cora talking about Ned causing a ruck shortly after. Though, when they realized she'd been listening, they'd taken their conversation over the other side of the room. She'd also heard Barney and Tabby calling Ned all the names under the sun, but she'd been excluded from that chat as well.

All in all, from what she'd pieced together about Ned, Barney's advice on avoiding him was probably justified.

'So what's your story?'

Lorni let out a quiet chuckle. 'Why is it everyone keeps asking me that?'

Ned rolled his tongue in his mouth before answering. 'I want to know a bit more about the person I've got in me back seat, that's all.'

'Well, what's your story? After all, you're the one driving me, and the only thing I know about you is that you like to cause trouble in nightclubs.'

Pulling up outside Desires, Ned nodded. 'Touché.'

'Anyway, thanks for the lift,' Lorni said, opening the car door.

'See you, mate. Look after your mum, won't you?'

Jace nodded enthusiastically. 'I will . . . And I like your car, by the way.'

Ned laughed and winked. 'Maybe next time you can have a drive of it.'

Jace giggled. 'Yes please!'

As Jace and Lorni walked away, the car phone rang. Sighing, Ned pressed answer from the leather steering wheel. 'Simon, what can I do for you?'

'Well I ain't fucking phoning you to drop me bollocks in your mouth, am I? If I wanted tea-bagging, you'd be the last cunt I'd come to. Which reminds me, how is Cookie?'

Ned clutched onto the steering wheel then spoke through clenched teeth. 'What do you want?'

'I want to know if you've clapped eyes on that nephew of mine – and if not, why the fuck not? I've also had that client on me tail again, about his "special requirements". Wants to make sure I've lined up a boy for him.' Simon's voice filled the Bentley.

'Told you, I've got loads of boys he can have.'

'And as I told you, I'm not looking for some teenager.'

Ned rubbed his face as if it were wet with sweat. 'Like I said last time you asked, I ain't a nonce.'

'For fuck's sake, Ned, put away the Mother Theresa act, will ya? The geezer wants to look, not touch. You've heard of a whisky dick, right? Well he's probably got a dole dick – it don't work and the only way he can get off is by using his goggles. So no, I ain't asking you to be a fucking nonce. I'm asking you to sort out a kid for me – and soon, Ned. Cos next time I won't be asking, I'll be fucking telling.'

The call went dead and for a moment or two Ned sat seething in his car, then his mind began to tick over as Jace stopped in the doorway of Desires and turned to wave goodbye to him.

Half an hour later, Finn sat in the club with Tabby and Natalie, who was working behind the bar. He was disappointed not to see

Cookie here. Even though she'd asked him not to contact her, he'd hoped that he might bump into her or – and perhaps it was arrogant of him to think this – she might have shown up knowing that he always dipped his head into Barney's place on a Thursday night.

'So how's Cookie been?' Finn took a sip of bourbon and looked around the club, which was surprisingly busy for a rainy Thursday night.

'Is that you asking or is that you *asking*?' Natalie grinned as she leaned on the bar.

'I'm not following.'

'Come off it, Finn, you ain't fooling me. I know you've liked her for a while. And you fighting Ned over her honour the other night proved it.'

Knocking back the Wild Turkey bourbon, Finn slammed the glass on the bar. 'Give me another one, will ya . . . And if you must know, I wasn't fighting for her honour. I didn't like the way me cousin was treating her, that's all.'

Pushing Finn's glass against the optic dispenser, Natalie laughed as she poured him a double bourbon. 'If you say so.'

'I think it would be a good thing if you and Cookie were together. She deserves to be happy,' Tabby chipped in. 'You two would make a great couple. Nats is right, anyone can see you really like her.'

'Don't say shit like that.' Finn brought his voice down. 'If anyone heard, whether it's true or not – which it ain't by the way – Cookie could come to harm.'

'I won't say anything, I promise,' Tabby said defensively. 'She's me mate.'

'I've already told you, there ain't anything between us, she's as good as me sister-in-law. So change the tune, will you, cos when you're on that shit you like to take, you'll end up talking all sorts of crap and it'll bring a whole fucking heap of trouble to my door and Cookie's.'

Upset, Tabby blinked away the tears then got off the bar stool, walking away through the crowd without saying another word.

'Tabs . . . Tabby . . . Tabby, come back, babes!' Natalie called after her, but she didn't turn around. 'What's wrong with you? There was no need to say that to her,' she snarled at Finn. 'She was only trying to be nice, so don't come in here and treat her like she's nothing. She gets enough of that shit from your cousin.'

Taken aback, Finn nodded. 'Yeah, OK, I was out of order. When I see her next, I'll apologize. No harm done?'

'Hold on . . .' Natalie went over to serve someone at the other end of the bar while Finn wondered if he should bother sticking around in the club. The longer he waited, the worse he felt. Each minute seemed like it was a reminder that Cookie wasn't coming.

Each time he thought he was getting closer to her, she backed even further away from him.

'Does she know you like her?' Natalie returned from serving another customer. 'And don't start all that denial shit – I ain't going to say anything.'

Finn hesitated. One of the rules in his world was to keep his mouth shut, go to the grave with tight lips, but he needed to speak to someone and Cookie had always told him that Natalie was someone she trusted. Someone who was in her corner. Taking a deep breath, knowing that admitting the way he felt to anyone could be, *would be* dangerous if it got back to Ned, Finn slowly nodded. 'Yeah, I've told her.' Spinning his glass of bourbon around in his hands, he gave a tiny shrug. 'I ain't told Cooks that I love her, but I do. Which is mad, cos I've never thought about having a relationship. Fucking someone and getting a blow job was enough of a commitment for me.'

'If you ever write a love poem, maybe leave that line out of it,' Natalie laughed.

He laughed back. 'I know it sounds stupid, and it don't feel too clever either. I can't think of anything else but her. It's doing me nut in.'

'You got it bad then.'

He took the last sip of bourbon and shrugged. 'This is all new to me. I've never loved anyone in the whole of me life, apart from me mum. But a woman? Never.'

'Does she feel the same way?' Natalie asked, taking his glass without him asking and refilling it again. She smiled. 'On the house . . . But don't tell Barney.'

'Cheers . . . Look, you swear this ain't going to go further? Even you discussing it with Cookie, well, it can't happen.'

'Of course.' Natalie spoke with warmth. 'I want the best for her, I need you to believe that. I really do.'

'I don't get it, Nats. I don't understand her. I can see she feels the same way, but she keeps holding back. It's like she's got a wall up. And I know she don't want this life anymore, she's admitted that. I don't either. So there's nothing keeping her here, and she ain't happy. I can't get me head around why she won't give me a chance.'

'How much do you know about her?'

'I've known her ten years.'

'And before that?'

Frowning, he looked down in his glass. 'I don't know much. Actually, I don't know anything.'

'So maybe that's your answer. We all have a past, and that can shape the here and now. What's going on with Cookie, it ain't personal.'

'Has she said something?'

'No.'

'Then how can you be so sure it ain't me.'

'Call it intuition . . . And Finn, if you love her like you say you do, then you need to have patience. Give her time and I'm sure it'll work out.'

'Maybe it won't. Maybe she and Ned have something after all.'

'She don't love Ned!' Natalie scoffed. 'She doesn't even like him.'

Finn stared into Natalie's eyes. 'Then answer me this. Why does she stay? Why does she stay with Ned?'

28

'I stay with Ned cos I have to.' Cookie sat across from Barney in a small late-night cafe on the south side of the river. Her eyes were sore from crying and her nose was blocked. She and Barney were holding hands, Cookie clinging onto him as if she were drowning, needing his love and strength for her to be able to open the box of secrets in her head, where the memories, the images, the sound of Parker's voice were so vivid. And sharing her story was one of the hardest things she'd ever done. Saying it out loud felt like she was back there again.

'You keep saying this, sweetheart, but I still don't get why.'

Cookie looked around. The windows were steamed up and the smell of hamburgers, coffee and wet clothes lingered in the air. A young couple sat in the corner, both looking the worse for wear, and an old man with his cap pulled down over his eyes lounged back on his chair, fast asleep.

She leaned in, bringing both her body and her voice down. 'Ned will kill me. No matter where I go, he'll track me down and kill me. And I accept that.'

'Cooks, you can't—'

'No, Barney, please listen, you need to understand. When I met Ned, I was working as a hooker, but before that I'd been homeless like the kids who work for us. That's how I started, but I was working for someone else. There are a lot of Neds in this world. I was seventeen and in care and . . .' she took a deep breath '. . . and Parker had just been murdered. I couldn't cope, Barn. So I ran. Started drinking, selling myself, I wanted to die . . . I might as well have been dead. I was like the living dead. I worked for different pimps, then Ned came along at the right time.'

'That don't mean you owe him.'

Cookie gave a wry smile. 'I don't mean it like that. He certainly wasn't my prince. But he did come along ten years ago. The same time I found out that Jo had been released. The public didn't know right off, but the *victims'* families did. Well, not straight away – six months after she was let out, I was informed. From time to time I checked in with my victim liaison officer and she told me then. Funny thing is, that's what gave me life. It made me want to live again, Barn: hearing Jo Martin had been let out.'

He squeezed her hand lovingly. 'I don't understand.'

'Up until then, I never had any reason to go on. I was drinking to excess, taking coke, anything I could get my hands on. It didn't matter, I was waiting to die. But at the same time, it was weird, Barn, cos I felt like the pain I was going through was what I deserved. It feels a bit like that with Ned.' She shrugged, glancing to the side at the old man who'd begun to start snoring loudly. She smiled and turned back to look at Barney. 'Anyway, although Ned still pimped me out, I was getting better, stronger. I was determined to get well. Now there was a reason: revenge. I know it's an old classic, Barn, but it was like a drug, *it is* like a drug to me. When Jo was inside there was nothing I could do to get at her. But now she was out . . .'

Cookie trailed off as Barney nodded, looking like he was beginning to understand.

'Can I get you anything else?' The waiter, who looked as bored as he sounded, stood above them chewing gum and wearing a dirty white tabard.

'Yeah, we'll have another two coffees please,' Barney replied while Cookie waited for the waiter to leave before continuing.

'So Ned, well, he started to get feelings for me – although, as you know, they're fucked-up feelings. He got really possessive, jealous, which hardly makes sense when he's sending me out to screw his clients. But in the end he couldn't handle that. He moved me into his house, much to Pearl's disgust, got me properly cleaned up and stopped pimping me out. Then came all his rules . . . and his promises: he'll kill me if I leave him. And by then it was too late to turn back the clock. I was trapped. But as I said, I accept that I'll probably die by Ned's hands, I ain't scared of that.'

'Jesus, Cookie, can't you hear what you're saying?'

She gave a small smile. 'I ain't saying I'm going without a fight. I'm not feeling sorry for myself and I certainly don't feel like a victim to it . . . to him. But I dunno, over the years I've come to think of it as my destiny. But what I am scared about, and what I can't accept, is that I might die before I find Jo Martin.'

'Cooks, no, sweetheart. No, no, no. Your thinking is all wrong. This is so messed up.'

She nodded, heavy teardrops landing on the plastic tablecloth. 'I know.' She spoke in a hoarse whisper, struggling to get her words out. 'I ain't so far gone that I don't know that, but what else can I do? I can't leave Ned, cos I know he'll follow through on his threat. And, Barn, I can't let Jo Martin get away with it. Parker was three years old. Jo and her dad tried to dispose of his body in the fire – to cover up the crimes, I guess – and he was so badly burned, they wouldn't let me go and see him. I couldn't kiss him goodbye. And I think he's out there somewhere as an angel, wondering why Mummy didn't kiss him goodnight.'

'Cookie . . .' Barney's eyes filled with tears.

'The lock of hair was from when he was born. But that's the only thing I've got left of him. Well, that and the photo in the locket which I took a month before he was killed. But what gets me through each day is thinking about Jo. Every lash Ned gives me, every sick game he wants to play out on me, I can live with it – *just* – because of Jo.'

'Listen to me, Cookie: Jo and her dad killed your son, but what you're doing, the way you're living, they're killing you as well. You've got to get out, Cooks. This can't go on, sweetheart.'

'I don't have a choice. The one thing I can't carry on doing, is being a penny pimp, as Finn puts it. I had a wall up, I couldn't feel anything, turned a blind eye to what I was doing with the kids, but when I saw Jace . . .'

'Jace?' Puzzled, Barney tilted his head.

'Yeah.' Without letting go of Barney's hand, Cookie bent her head to the side to wipe away her tears on the top of her shoulder. 'Jace, he reminds me of Parker.' She laughed softly. Sadly. 'Parker had these big brown eyes, with them cow lashes, like Jace. And the same freckles. You know, like he's been splattered with paint on his nose. When I saw Jace, my wall came tumbling down. That was it. I knew I had to stop. I ain't doing it no more, Barn. I mean, what would Parker think of his mummy, hey? Who'd want a mummy taking kids to guys like Brian?'

'Well, I'm proud of you, Cooks, and I love you.'

'Don't.' She shook her head. 'Don't be nice to me, Barn, I'm trying to hold it together and I won't be able to if you're nice to me. You know I never planned on this life. It ain't what I wanted . . . When I was a kid, I wanted to be a farmer. Can you fucking imagine? It's all I can do to go near Pearl's cat, let alone a bleedin' cow. Then I wanted to be a postman. Me, a postman, Barn, in me Louboutins?'

They both snorted with laughter, then Cookie fell quiet. 'Then I wanted to be a mummy. That's what made me happy, Barn. It felt right. Me and Park made the perfect pair. I thought I was good at it.' She shook her head. 'Good at it? I got him killed, that's how good I was at it.' The tears came again and Barney stood up, leaning over the table to kiss Cookie on the top of her head.

'What happened that day, Cooks? The day Parker went missing . . . No, I shouldn't have asked that, I'm sorry.' He sat back down on his chair.

'It's OK.' She took a deep breath and once again looked around the cafe. Then she closed her eyes, wondering if she could really go back there. That was the door in her head she hadn't been able to open.

She exhaled and chewed on her lip and she felt Barney squeeze her hand again. 'I'll try to tell you, if I can . . . I'd just turned seventeen – I had Parker when I was fourteen, the same age as Jo was when she killed him. The father was some boy I hung around with. He was in the same care home as me. Then, when I had Parker, I moved to a care home for kids with babies. Me and Parker stayed there for a couple of years. It was all supervised and I had my own social worker. She was lovely, really helpful, and she thought I'd be able to manage on me own. Independent living. So she arranged for me and Parker to get a studio flat. I was so happy. I hated that care home and I couldn't wait till I moved out. I got the keys the day after my seventeenth birthday. One month later, Parker was dead.'

'Oh my God.'

'That day, nothing seemed different. Parker loved this one place with swings we always went to. And that was my mistake. Taking him to the same place every Tuesday at the same time. The police said Jo and her dad had been watching us for a while.'

'None of this is your fault.'

She turned away, unable to look at Barney. 'But it is, because while they were watching Parker, I wasn't watching him.'

'Cookie, you don't have to do this.'

'No, I do. I'm ready to tell you now . . .'

29

'I was seventeen and I remember what happened like it was yesterday . . .'

'Come on, I thought you wanted to play on the swings? I know some snails that move faster than you, Parker.' Cookie walked backwards, watching and smiling as Parker crouched down for what seemed like the twentieth time.

The playground they went to was only ten minutes' walk from the flat, but it had taken over half an hour – as it always did – to get there. Nevertheless, Cookie couldn't think of anything she'd be rather doing. 'Come on, Park, I'll turn into an old lady before we're there.'

Parker giggled, though he seemed more interested in looking at the wet leaves on the ground. 'Look, it's a bug, Mummy.'

Smiling at his lisp, which she found so endearing, Cookie bent down to see exactly what creepy crawly her son was looking at now. 'Oh, it's like the hungry caterpillar, ain't it? You think it's going to eat us up?'

Parker burst into laughter and it was so infectious, Cookie couldn't help but laugh along with him. Stroking his hair, she looked into her son's face as he held the caterpillar in his hand. Sometimes she couldn't quite believe how much in love she was with him. It had been like that from the very moment the bossy midwife had placed him in her arms.

Having her own place with Parker, being able to tuck him up at night and wake up in the mornings with him jumping up and down on the bed, was happiness she hadn't thought someone like her would ever have. Life couldn't get any better.

'Can I keep it, Mummy? Can I take him home?'

Hating anything that had more than four legs, Cookie pulled a face. 'Maybe it'd be better if it stayed here, darlin', with its family. We don't want to take it away from its Mummy, do we? His mummy might be upset. We wouldn't want her to be sad, would we?'

Parker stared at the caterpillar crawling on his blue mitten and looked thoughtful for a moment. 'No.'

She winked at him. 'Good boy.'

Planting a kiss on the caterpillar before Cookie could stop him, Parker gently placed it back on the leaf. 'Can we go to the swings now?'

'Finally!' she laughed.

'Oi. Oi, Mary Poppins!'

Cookie looked towards the playground railings. She grinned. 'All right. What's happening?' she shouted in response. They'd been her friends at the last care home she'd been in before she'd had Parker. Though she hadn't seen them for well over two years, they'd chatted on the phone.

'Not a lot . . . You must be Parker,' a gangly boy with a shaved head shouted warmly to him. 'Hiya, mate.'

'Hello,' Parker mumbled shyly, then tugged on Cookie's sleeve. 'Swings, please.'

She smiled, ruffling his hair once again. 'You go on ahead, baby and I'll come and join you in a minute. Mummy will be right there. OK?'

'OK.' Looking delighted, he skipped off, twirling and spinning around as Cookie walked over to her friends.

She glanced over her shoulder at Parker, who'd clearly changed his mind about the swings and instead was busy going down the small slide the wrong way.

Over the next half hour, Cookie chatted away, keeping an eye on Parker, who seemed to be delighting in hiding either in the mini tree-house or in the bright green plastic dragon tunnel, frantically talking away to imaginary friends.

Eventually, Cookie sighed, speaking in an upbeat manner to her friends. 'Anyway, I better go, guys. Text me about that party at Adam's, yeah? I ain't been out for ages.'

'Yeah, cos you ain't allowed to go raving now you're a mumma. You need to hang up that thought, girl. From now on the only Es you'll be dropping are the ones on Alphabet Street!'

She pulled a face. 'Very funny, just text me.'

Happily she walked away towards the dragon tube. 'Parker. Parker.' She bent down and peered inside but it was empty. Then she looked around, trying to work out where he was hiding.

'Come on, baby, let's go home, it's getting cold.' Absent-mindedly she began to scratch off the sparkly varnish Parker had painted on her nails a couple of nights ago.

She walked past the treehouse and stood on the edge of the small copse where they often pretended they were going on a bear hunt or tracking the Gruffalo – like the characters in two of his favourite books. Cookie frowned because she'd told him so many times not to go into the woods on his own. Although she knew that was exactly where he'd be. He'd probably followed some butterfly or some other yukky insect which she hated and he seemed so fascinated by.

She shivered, wishing she'd brought her coat. It was May but felt like March, and all she really wanted to do was go back home and cuddle up with Parker watching TV.

She walked amongst the trees, poking around every bush, waiting for Parker to jump out on her as he always did when they were playing monsters.

'Parker, come on now.' Cookie tried to keep the irritation from her voice. 'Mummy's getting cold. We can play when we get home if you like.'

Reaching the end of the copse, she turned and again began to search behind and under every bush, her irritation growing, though she wouldn't be cross with Parker when she eventually found him; she loved the fact that he was a happy boy, always playing games and giggling.

A branch cracked underfoot and Cookie didn't know whether it was the twilight drawing in or the fact that the utter silence in the woods made her feel uneasy, but a cold disquiet began to rise in her.

Running now and trying to tell herself all was well, she called to her son: 'Parker! Parker! Please come out.'

Hearing her own breathing getting heavier, she pushed through a thicket, but she tripped over the gnarled roots of a tree, tumbling forward onto the cold earth. Her teeth bit down into her lips and Cookie tasted blood as she landed hard. Her hands torn by the rough ground, her heart pounding in her chest. A wave of sickness crushed down on her as she scrambled forward on her knees, trying to stop the panic, the fear, the terror rushing through her. In front of her was Parker's shoe. 'No, no, no. Please, please God no.' Cookie jumped to her feet. She ran back through the woods holding the shoe. 'Parker! Parker! Parker!' She spun round, looking in every direction, but the play area was empty. 'Please, baby, you're scaring Mummy now. Parker, please. Baby, where are you?'

By the gates of one of the entrances to the playground, Cookie spotted a lady and she sprinted across. Her words tumbled out. 'Please, have you seen a little boy, he's three. He's got brown hair and he's wearing a red jacket.'

'Sorry, love.'

'No, you must have seen him. He's only little. This height. He's got freckles.'

'I'm sorry, love, no.'

Cookie reached out and clutched her arm, fear and desperation overwhelming her. 'You got to think,' she screamed. 'Think, fucking think! He was here, he was here only a few minutes ago.'

The woman – who looked terrified – tried to back away, but Cookie's grip was too firm. The sound of a car engine made her turn, releasing her grip on the woman, and instinctively she started to run towards the road, to the entrance on the other side of the playground.

Ahead of her she saw an old grey Ford Fiesta, thick with dirt and rust, beginning to move off at speed, chugging out dark black fumes. She stood in the middle of the road and was about to turn away when her legs buckled. In the rear window, tears streaked down his face, was Parker.

Her scream sounded like it came from someone else. Hysterically she began to chase the battered car, watching Parker's hand banging on the rear window with someone sitting next to him who Cookie could only see the back of. 'Parker! Parker! Come back! Where are you taking him! Parker! Parker!'

Parker was staring at her as she ran, mouthing the word 'Mummy'. His eyes wide and fearful.

'Parker!'

The next moment Parker was pushed down onto the seat by the person next to him.

'Parker! No! No!'

He was gone.

Cookie continued to run but the car was getting further and further away . . .

The number plate – she knew she had to get the registration, but when she looked, the plate was covered in thick mud. Impossible to read.

Hands shaking, Cookie pulled out her phone. 'No, fuck, no. No please no!' The battery was dead. She looked around: no houses, no cars, no people. And as the Ford Fiesta disappeared into the distance, Cookie stumbled down the road, blinded by terror, calling for help. 'Please, someone help me. Help me. Please, help me.' But the silence screamed back at her. Shaking uncontrollably, not noticing she'd wet herself, Cookie dropped to her knees in the middle of the deserted road, screaming. 'Parker! Parker! Parker . . .'

30

Cookie blinked away her tears and tried to catch her breath and lock away the memory of the horror of that day. Barney swiped away his own tears with one hand and held her hand in the other. The two of them sat in silence for a moment. The couple and the old man had left, and they were the only ones in the cafe.

With the coffee now cold in front of her, Cookie eventually said, 'I can't even feel Parker around me. From that day on, I never have. I want to, but when I think of him, I don't think of his giggle, which could make the grumpiest bastard laugh. I don't picture his face – God, Barn, he was beautiful. No, I think of what they described in court on the first day. I think of his charred body and I think of him crying for me. That's what haunts me. That's my ghost. And killing Jo Martin will bring some sort of peace . . . and justice.'

'Do you even know what she looks like?'

'I went to court once. I wanted to see her. I wanted to see him too. I wanted to see the last faces my son would've seen, but she was hidden behind a screen and throughout the trial she never gave any testimony. She never said a word.'

'What about her dad, what was he like?'

'He was smiling, grinning at the details about Parker and about the other boy. It was as if he was reliving what he did, getting off on it. I couldn't go again. That night I packed my bags and left. That's when I ended up homeless. I felt guilty about not going back to court though, like I felt guilty about not going to his funeral. But I couldn't. I just couldn't do it.'

Barney looked thoughtful. 'Does Ned know about this?'

'No, and he doesn't suspect anything. He thought I wanted to move to Soho because of how nice he did up the house.' She rolled her eyes. 'I think part of him really believes that I love him.'

'And don't you?' Barney looked at her, unconvinced. 'Because I know what you've said, but it always feels like there's something between you two.'

'I did love him. Well, I thought I did. I was a mess, but when you've been with a bloke like Ned, it gets complicated. He gets in your head. But I do know a habit ain't the same as love, Barn. But believe me, when it comes to Ned, I'm ready to break that habit now.'

'So why did you move to Soho?'

'You were right, what you said on the bridge earlier. About Jo being in Soho. That's what I found out. I've been looking for years, and there have been loads of false leads, but the Soho one seemed like there might be something in it.'

'Who told you? Where did you get the information from?'

'The dark web . . . Because of the game me and Ned are in. You come across lots of scumbags in that line of work, and about seven, eight years ago this client, he was talking about stuff he'd seen on the net. Turned my stomach, but he also talked about these groups who track down people – paedophile hunters, among other things. It got me thinking. Then one day when I was feeling desperate, I got onto the dark web, reached out to one particular group. Told them my story, or part of it, and after a lot of back and forth, we met and they agreed to help me find Jo.'

'You pay them, I take it?' Barney asked.

'A lot of money. That's another reason why being with Ned helps. I couldn't afford it, not even close. The last property he sold, most of the profits he made went to them. Not that Ned cares or notices. He thinks I spend thousands on designer bags and couture. Pearl's the one I have to watch out for. She's the suspicious one when it comes to money. Safeguarding her life-style, no doubt.'

'You're playing a dangerous game with these people.'

Feeling a headache beginning to come on, Cookie let go of Barney's hands, rubbing her temples. 'I know. Once you start going down that rabbit hole, you realize there are lot of damaged people about. You hear a lot of messed-up stuff. Do yourself a favour, Barney, and never go there.'

'So you've been following leads all this time?'

'Yeah.'

'But Jo could be anywhere. OK, you've heard that she's in Soho, but a lot of people live there, and she could be anyone. Even if she was there, she might have left already. You could be paying out and chasing these false leads for the rest of your life. These people supplying you with leads, you don't know anything about them. They could be ripping you off, feeding on your grief, all their leads could be a pack of lies, and you wouldn't know.'

'What choice have I got? And don't ask me to leave it and try to move on, cos I can't.' Cookie's voice was firm.

Once again Barney fell silent. He took a swig of the coffee but finding it stone cold, he pulled a face. 'Jesus Christ.' He swallowed it down, pushed the mug to the side and stared intently at Cookie. 'Maybe I can help you.'

'That's really kind of you, Barney, but after we leave here, I don't want to discuss this again. This is it. And you swear this won't go further?'

'You have my word, but I don't mean *talking* about it. I mean . . .' Barney stopped and took a deep breath, giving her a tight smile. 'What I mean is that I hate the idea of you getting mugged off by this group so . . .' He stopped again.

'What is it, Barney?' Cookie asked, puzzled.

He leant over the table, picking up her hands in his and squeezing them. 'I would never have said anything, but I love you, Cooks, and sometimes other people's stuff is bigger than your own.'

Turning her head, Cookie gave him a sideward glance. 'I love you too, Barney, but I have no idea what you're talking about.'

'Maybe I can help, doll, with the Jo Martin stuff.' He spoke slowly, and Cookie noticed how anxious he looked. '*Perhaps* – and this isn't a guarantee, in actual fact more than likely nothing will come of it. But maybe I can help with getting the name for you. And I'm not saying that I think what you're doing is the right thing, but I can't sit back and see you chasing shadows. Breaks my heart, Cooks.'

She shuffled in her seat. 'When you say *name* . . .' It was almost as if Cookie daren't speak the words. She felt a cold sweat breaking out on the back of her neck.

'The name Jo's using now,' Barney said, filling in the blanks.

Cookie rubbed her chest, struggling to get her breath. 'You . . . you could get me that?'

'I can try.'

'How?' Impatient and panicked, Cookie raised her voice. 'Barney, *how*?' Then, aware the waiter was looking over at her curiously, she brought it down to a whisper. 'Sorry, I . . .' She trailed off, her mind racing.

'I have a friend. I haven't spoken to him for over ten years, but we were really close at one time – there was no falling out, life just got in the way.' He shrugged. 'But if he can help, I know he will . . . He owes me.'

'Who is he?'

'And this is the part I wouldn't have said, but maybe secrets aren't supposed to be hidden forever, hey?' He gave her a wry smile. 'He's in the serious organized crime unit. It also deals with witness protection and anonymity orders. They try to make out there's only a handful of officials who know the given name of the people with the orders, but that's bullshit. If Jo's in the area, all the guys in that unit will unofficially know the name she's using.'

Cookie stared at Barney. She felt her shoulders stiffen and she drew back from him, sitting upright in the hard, plastic chair. 'And how do you know this guy?' Her pleasant tone had changed and a cold wariness sat in its place.

'I worked with him . . . Don't look at me like that, Cooks.'

She shook her head and hissed, 'Are you telling me you're Old Bill?'

'Cookie—'

'I asked you a *fucking* question.' She stood up so quickly her chair flipped onto its side, and this time Cookie didn't care the waiter was watching.

'It's not what you think it is.'

She slammed her fist on the table. 'You still haven't fucking answered. Are you Old Bill?'

'Yes. Well, no, I—'

'All this time,' she shouted, anger flashing through her. 'You've been lying to me, you've been lying to all of us.'

'I want you to listen before you judge me.'

'I don't *want* to listen to anything you've got to say. What were you doing, eh, Barn? I take it your name is Barney? Were you building a dossier? Taking notes on everything I've told you? Everything that you know goes on in Soho? Was that it?' She stopped then stepped forward. 'Jesus, I've just told you that I'm going to kill Jo.'

'Cookie, you've got this all wrong.'

'I ain't got anything wrong. What, should I expect a knock on my door any minute now? Am I going to be pulled in?'

'For fuck's sake. I was offering to get you Jo's given name. Think about it, what does that say?' Barney stood up as well. He raised his voice. 'Maybe you'll learn something if you listen instead of jumping to conclusions.'

'You're Old Bill, what else is there to say? How could you lie to me like this? You were my mate and you've betrayed me. I loved you, Barney, but in my world you and me don't mix.' Real pain seeped from Cookie.

Just as hurt, Barney snapped, 'What is your world, Cooks? Cos all I see is a broken woman who's lost. Someone who thinks they're in control, thinks they know what they're doing, but that couldn't be further from the truth.'

Scorn poured out of her. 'The truth? Don't you give me that. You're the one who misrepresented themselves, not me. That was you . . . Does anyone else know? Does Cora know, does Natalie?'

'No, no one. Only you. But you can't say anything, Cooks. I've built my life in Soho, I—'

'I'll say what I like, when I like,' Cookie cut in.

'Don't forget I know something about you too now, and I only told you about myself so I could help you.'

Cookie stepped in close to Barney, inches away. 'Are you threatening me?'

'No, I'm only saying we both know things about each other that we wouldn't want to be made public.'

'Be careful, Barney, cos if for one minute I think you're going to breathe a word of what I've told you, you'll be buried along with my secret.'

31

'Where the fuck is she? Look at the fucking time. You reckon she goes out of her way to mug me off?' It was less of a question and more of statement as Ned prowled round the monochrome kitchen at the property in Hanson Street.

His jealously was eating away at him. He didn't need this shit. He had enough to think about without going home to find Cookie wasn't there. Nowhere to be fucking seen. He'd waited for ages and in the end he'd felt like he was going crazy, wondering, thinking, imagining. And it certainly wasn't helping that he had a picture in his mind of Cookie sitting on Simon's face when he'd whored her out to him. So he'd jumped in his car, driven over to see his mum, hoping that would calm him down.

But it hadn't helped. It was now almost three thirty in the morning. She wasn't answering her phone. Nothing. She was a wind-up. A fucking *whore* . . . He shook his head and laughed quietly to himself. A truer word was never spoken. You could take the hooker off the corner, but you couldn't take the hooker out of the girl. Wasn't that what his mum had always told him?

Anger rushed through him and he threw the glass of water he'd been drinking across the other side of the room. It smashed against the cabinets, tiny fragments of glass showering down.

'I liked that fucking glass. Don't come here and take all your agg out on the bleedin' crockery. I told you, you should've kept a closer eye on her. But oh no, you don't want to listen to what your old mum has to say, do you? Who knows what she gets up

194

to when your back's turned?' Pearl sniffed haughtily. 'Don't you think, Finn?' She threw a look at her nephew, who'd also been woken up by Ned's ranting.

'Don't fucking start, Mum,' Ned growled. 'I don't need to hear your *shit*.' Emphasizing the last word, he bent over the long, thick line of cocaine he'd cut up a moment ago, noisily snorting it up a fifty-pound note.

He pinched his nostrils, squeezed his eyes at the burn, swallowed as it hit the back of his throat, numbing it slightly, then waited for the buzz to hit his veins. '*Fuck. Holy fuck!*' he exhaled.

Indifferent, Pearl tutted. 'I thought that wasn't your poison no more.'

Ned wiped the droplets of sweat from his forehead and shook his head, trying to clear it. 'It is tonight, cos I've got a whore for a fucking girlfriend and a cunt like Simon on me back. We've all got a limit and right now, this is mine.'

Taking a sip from the cold bottle of Budweiser he'd popped open on the edge of the black marble table, Finn, like Pearl, seemed indifferent to Ned. He yawned widely. 'He's always a cunt, so what's the big deal this time?' Finn asked. 'But then, I told you that you should never have got involved with him.'

'Have you been taking tips off *her*?' Ned raged, pointing a finger at Pearl. 'Talking fucking crap that won't help anyone?' Raging, he bent over the cocaine again, holding one nostril while he snorted up the remains of the couple of grams he'd bought from a Chinese dealer.

'Then what's this about?'

Standing up straight and feeling better now the cocaine was taking the sting out of his mood, Ned slurred. 'Simon wants a boy.'

'What?'

He stared at his cousin. 'He wants a boy for some client that's worth some proper dollars.'

Finn looked back at him, confused. 'Why's he coming to you? You ain't a nonce – you've never dabbled in that shit. He knows that.' Finn paused, took a sip of Bud, studied his cousin for a minute. 'There's no way you're thinking about it, are you?'

Feeling specks of cocaine trickling back down his nose and not wanting to waste any, Ned took a mighty sniff. 'No. Fuck's sake, what do you take me for? I'm only telling you that's what he's saying. But he don't seem happy that I ain't jumping through hoops to sort it. Plus there's all the shit with Pete.'

'Pete?'

Even with the coke running through his system, Ned knew better than to divulge what was going on there. He brushed it off: 'Something and nothing. Main thing is, I've got to work out what I'm going to do about this boy.'

Finn yawned again. 'Nothing, I hope.'

Irritated, Ned snapped. 'I already told you I won't, but I've still got Simon on my back, ain't I? So what I thought is, maybe you—'

'I'm out.' Finn cut in before Ned could finish. 'I won't have anything to do with this game, not anymore, and I certainly don't want anything to do with Simon. I've served my years and I can't do it. I was going to wait to tell you, but now seems like the perfect time. I'm out.'

Ned couldn't look any more surprised if he'd tried. He began to pace round the kitchen, staring at Finn the whole time. 'I say when you're out.'

Finn smirked. 'I ain't the apprentice and you ain't my keeper.'

Striding over to where Finn was sitting, Ned loomed over him. 'You're blood – there is no getting out. Not without a body bag.'

'That coke's getting to your head, mate,' Finn spat out the

words. 'You've always been a prize wanker when you're on the oats and barley. Do yourself a favour and knock it on the head . . . You're a joke.' He stood up to go, but Ned pushed him back down on the white leather kitchen chair.

'Is that right? Look around you, Finn.' Ned stabbed a finger into Finn's chest. 'If it wasn't for me and Mum, where would you be? We took you in when you were a kid, and now you owe us.'

'I owe you fuck all, and I ain't going to do this now. If you want to talk, Cuz, then do it when you're not buzzing off your tits.'

'No, we'll talk *now* . . . Do you really think you'll be able to walk away from your family and everything we've built? Throw it all back in our faces?'

'I don't think, I *know*. I'm through with it, I've got to be able to live with myself, and pimping them kids out makes it pretty tough.'

Ned licked his lips, sticky from taking the cocaine. 'Sounds to me like you're talking fluent bullshit. When did you turn into such a pussy?'

Finn chuckled as Ned leaned over him. 'Not wanting to be a penny pimp ain't being a pussy. But if I stayed around here with you, I'd probably say that would make me one.'

'Is that right?' Ned turned round to go but immediately spun back, pulling out a small handgun from the inside of his jacket. Before Finn could dive out of the way, Ned flicked off the safety latch. He pushed the gun against his cousin's face, digging it and rubbing it against Finn's cheek. Then he moved to push the nozzle hard onto Finn's lips, breaking his skin open as he did.

Ned's face was red, fizzing with anger. 'You still saying the same thing now? What was that? I can't hear you.' He laughed as Finn stayed completely still. Then Finn moved his eyes up to look at his cousin and spoke slowly, mumbling through lips which were pouring with blood and pressed tight together by the gun. 'You're not going to kill me.'

'Really? You think I won't?'

Ned flicked his wrist to the side, aiming the gun at the kitchen cabinets, shooting holes in them.

'For fuck's sake, you silly cunt, you want the Old Bill to come storming in?' Pearl rushed up to Ned and smacked him hard across the face. 'Put that thing away – and you can stop snorting that shit as well. If you can't handle Charlie, don't fucking take it. I love you, son, but I ain't being banged up for you again.'

Ned glared at Pearl but he didn't say anything. A moment later he threw the gun on the table and marched out.

Wiping his face, Finn took a moment to recover his senses. He wasn't sure what to say or think; he certainly hadn't been as confident as he'd sounded that Ned wouldn't have pulled the trigger, especially after all the coke he'd been sniffing.

He was conscious of Pearl staring at him, but then he felt his phone begin to vibrate. He slipped it out of his pocket and frowned when he saw it was Cookie. It was unlike her to call and therefore clearly important. He needed to talk to her anyway, let her know what mood Ned was in. 'I've got to go.'

Grabbing the tea towel to staunch the bleeding from his lips, he rushed towards the door.

'Your lover trying to get in touch with you, is she?'

'What are you talking about? Ned's right, you can chat fucking shit sometimes – well, most of the time actually . . . I'll see you later.'

'Cookie.'

Finn stopped and with blood staining his chin, he slowly turned round. 'What did you say?'

Pearl grinned. 'Was that Cookie? Oh, you two are as bad as each other at playing the fucking innocent.'

He pointed at Pearl. 'Reel it in. As usual you've got it all wrong.'

She waddled forward. There was a nasty sneer on her face and a twinkle in her eye. 'I'm trying to decide when to tell Ned. Tomorrow, you reckon? Day after? Or perhaps the mood he's in, how about I tell him now . . . *Ned!*' She hollered, and immediately Finn ran across to her, slamming his hand over her mouth. She bit down on it and burst into a high-pitch cackle as he let go, his fingers now bleeding. 'You're a fucking animal.' He blew on his hand to take away the throb.

'How long have you been banging her? Come on, you can tell me. How long have you been scoffing that fat pussy of hers?' She laughed again, just as nastily.

'Shut the fuck up. You hear me?'

'I've rumbled you, ain't I? Now if you don't want your brain splattered all over the wall, maybe you should think about helping my Ned with Simon. However much I loved your mother – God rest her soul – I ain't going to let anything happen to my Ned, so you better do what's right, otherwise I'll be opening my mouth.'

Finn narrowed his eyes to glare at her. 'No you won't, and you'll have to do better than that, Pearl. He won't believe you.'

'When it comes to Cookie, Ned will believe anything – you know that. I could even tell Ned that old queen Barney's been shagging her and he'd believe me. Ain't you seen the way he's riddled with jealously? Burns through him like fucking acid when it comes to that tart.'

Finn dabbed his lips and winced at the sting. 'But even though nothing has happened and it's all a pack of lies, he'll still kill her if you open your mouth. Is that really what you want?'

She shrugged. 'And you. He'll kill you as well . . . But maybe you should've both thought about that.'

'I don't care about me. But *her* – that's different. I have never laid a finger on you, Pearl, or any woman. But if you insist on doing this, so help me, you'll be the one who's looking over their shoulder, cos I'll make sure that you meet your maker before we do. So don't push me. I may not be Ned, but that don't mean I haven't been brought up by the best. So yeah, I might not lay me on hands on you, Pearl, but I'll get someone to shut you up permanently if you even think about playing your nasty games . . .' He opened the door, throwing the bloodstained tea towel on the table. 'So if you want to live to your next birthday, think on before you mess with our lives.'

32

The early morning February sun had broken through the clouds, rising above Soho, leaving a hazy brightness. And in the chill of Friday morning, Ned – with his phone on speaker – marched along, trying to get a word in edgeways.

'If you'll just listen, Simon, I've already . . . Simon, for fuck's sake, can—' Then the call was cut off by Simon, leaving Ned fuming as he walked past the Turkish deli in Berwick Market.

Flicking the cigarette he'd only half smoked into the gutter, Ned contemplated calling Simon back. He was sick of the smarmy cunt thinking he could bawl him out then put the phone down. But, however tempting, Ned knew it wouldn't be a smart move, especially when he still didn't know how he was going to get out of complying with Simon's request. Although, the way Simon was turning the screw, it was less of a request and more of a demand.

'*Fuck!*' Ned didn't want to think about that now. He was too tired after having spent the last couple of hours coming down from the coke, which made him feel like shit, and being so full of agg that he'd had to fight the desire to go back to Hanson Street, find the gun and ram it down Finn's throat.

He'd spent most of yesterday evening driving round London searching for Cookie, and not having been able to find her made him want to do someone an injury. About an hour ago he'd hammered on Barney's door – she had been known to have a lock-in with Barney and the other girls in the past – but no one had stirred; the place had looked deserted. So he'd been left with no idea where else to look, and his imagination working overtime: picturing Cookie in bed with another man, Cookie being fucked by another man, Cookie with a hard cock down her throat. '*Shit.*' Ned spoke out loud again as he turned towards home. Sometimes being with Cookie was fucking torture.

The last week or so had been shit, and the only good news he'd had was when he'd got a couple of his men to pop in on Pete earlier. They'd found him awake. Too groggy to make sense, but all the same it was a start. Apparently Pete had looked terrified when his men walked in wearing Disney masks. Ned smiled at the thought. Hopefully they'd move him within a couple of days; once he knew for certain that Pete was going to make a full recovery, they could dump him in some crack hole. Then no one would be any the wiser and he'd have one less thing to worry about.

As he neared his townhouse, Ned slowed down. Standing outside his front door he could make out the shape of a woman. He quickened his pace thinking it was Cookie, but almost immediately he slowed. It was Lorni.

Seeing Ned walking down the road towards her, Lorni took a deep breath. She hadn't wanted to come; in fact, she'd walked away twice, but she was desperate. More to the point, her son was desperate – desperate to stay at Barney's, put down roots somewhere instead of running all the time. And right now, that was all that mattered. So, if that meant coming to see Ned, well, that's the way it had to be.

'Good morning.' She smiled at him, noticing how red his eyes were; she also noticed a few tiny flecks of white powder round the edge of one of his nostrils. 'Hard night?' she asked, guessing how he'd spent the last few hours.

Ned raised his eyebrows. 'What's that supposed to mean?'

Not wanting to alienate him before she'd even told him what she was there for, Lorni attempted to play the innocent. 'Nothing. Sorry, I thought you looked a bit tired, that's all.'

He stared at her.

'Anyway, I'm glad I caught you, Ned.'

'You didn't fucking catch me. This is my house and I'm about to go inside. It's hardly a storyline for *Line of Duty*, is it?'

'It's only a saying,' Lorni backpedalled, feeling humiliated at having to ingratiate herself with the likes of Ned. 'I know this is where you live. What I mean is, I'm glad I've seen you – well, I'm glad you're here.' She blushed, knowing how stupid she sounded.

'What are you, a welcome home party?' Angrily Ned started punching in the numbers for the electronic keypad.

He was even *more* arrogant than Lorni had initially thought, but regardless, she took another deep breath and tried again. 'You're not making this easy.'

The front door automatically sprang open and Ned turned to glare at her. 'I must be missing a trick, darlin', cos you've turned up on me doorstep talking all kinds of shit, yet I'm supposed to be making it easy?' A thought crossed Ned's mind. 'How the fuck did you get my address anyway?'

'As everyone keeps telling me, this is Soho. People talk,' Lorni said, although it had actually been Tabby who'd told her. 'Look, how about we start again?'

Ned gave her a bemused stare.

'*Please.*'

'I don't even know what you want.'

Lorni cleared her throat. 'I want a job.'

'Excuse me?'

'You heard. I want a job, I *need* one and, from what I've heard, you might be able to help.'

Rubbing his facial stubble, Ned brooded, his handsome looks

darkening. 'And what exactly have you heard?' He bent down to speak into Lorni's face. He oozed intimidation but she ignored it, focusing instead on what she'd come for.

'That you have businesses, lots of them.'

'Is that what they call it now?'

'So have you?' she shrugged, trying to look confident, though with Ned glaring into her face she felt anything but.

'I will say you have front. But I'll also say . . .' He paused and looked her up and down, then leaned towards her ear. She could feel his warm breath against her neck and she shivered, not quite sure as to what she was feeling. Then he whispered. 'You're too old.'

She pulled away, stepping back. 'What are you talking about?'

He roared with laughter, which infuriated her.

'You may be a pretty little thing, but you're, what – thirty?'

'For your information, I'm—' But she stopped, feeling even more uncomfortable. 'Look, it doesn't matter how old I am. If there ain't any jobs going, fine.'

'Mum!' The door of the Italian espresso bar a few doors along flew open and Jace came running out, waving to Lorni.

'Come on, slowcoach, I thought you'd bought up the whole shop,' she called back.

Panting and giggling, Jace scampered up to her. 'Look what I got.' He grinned widely as he showed Lorni the packet of Italian sweet almond biscuits and the San Pellegrino orange juice he'd bought.

'Well, make sure you say thank you to Natalie.' She turned to Ned. 'She gave him a couple of quid for helping her with piling up the crates,' Lorni muttered, not knowing why she felt the need to explain.

Ned nodded. 'I think we can do better than that, can't we,

mate?' He stuck a hand into his pocket and pulled out a roll of fifty-pound notes. Immediately, Lorni shook her head.

'It's fine, please don't. I want him to learn the value of money. That it doesn't come easy.'

Ned stared at Jace's cheap scruffy trainers. 'From what I see, the boy has probably learnt that lesson already . . . Here you go, Jace.' He peeled off a fifty-pound note, shoving it into Jace's hand. 'If you really want to learn a lesson, mate, try this: never *ever* listen to what women have to say – they all talk crap.'

'You're bang out of order.' She pulled Jace away and snatched the money out of his hand, throwing it on the ground.

As she stormed off, Ned glanced at his phone. Another text from Simon . . .

Sort it fucking out.

Ned let out a long sigh. What the fuck was he going to do? There seemed to be no way out of the situation unless he agreed to do what Simon wanted. He glanced up, watching Lorni and Jace for a moment as they strolled hand in hand along the pavement. His mind whirling, he called out after them: 'Wait! Lorn, hold on, darlin'!' He jogged up to them. 'Look, I'm sorry.' He gave a cloying smile while Lorni glared. 'You're right to be pissed off with me. I was being muggy. I shouldn't have done that.'

'Whatever.' She tutted and moved to go.

'No wait, please. I think I might have something for you.'

'I thought you said I was too old.'

He shrugged and grinned. 'For some things, yeah, *but* I've been looking for another cleaner. I've got one already, but the house is too big for her to manage on her own. If you want the job, it's yours, for cash . . . I tell you what, why don't you come in and we can talk business?'

Lorni nodded eagerly. 'Could you just give me ten minutes to take Jace back to Barney's, then I can come right back – I could start this afternoon, if you want.'

Ned gave a lopsided smile. He winked at Jace. 'Now why would I want the guest of honour not to join us?' And then Ned put his arm round Jace's shoulder and smiled to himself. Maybe things had a funny way of turning out right after all.

33

Cookie had been walking for hours. Her feet were throbbing and her clothes were drenched from the rain. Her head was a whirl of rushing thoughts and memories of Parker, her beautiful, beautiful boy.

The pull in her chest made it feel like her heart was about to stop. She was so tired, so tired of living without Parker by her side. She missed him. It was too hard. What she wouldn't do for one last moment with him. To hold his hand, to feel his arms around her neck as she carried him. And each day got harder instead of easier. Each day was one more day without him.

Every morning she struggled to keep going because she had no other choice. Like she'd told Barney, finding Jo gave her a reason to get up each day . . . She shook her head. She didn't want to think about Barney now, not on top of everything else. It hurt too much. She supposed that was another reason why she'd been wandering around for hours. She didn't want to go home, and usually when she felt like this she'd phone Barney, but now she couldn't even do that.

At one point she'd called Finn to come and pick her up. She'd been desperate to hear his voice, to see him. She'd even been planning to tell him what Barney had said. But he hadn't answered, which, thinking about it now, was a blessing. There was enough trouble, enough tension between everyone without involving Finn. She hadn't even begun to get her head around it all, or what she was going to do with the information.

And now there was a deep sense of betrayal inside her. She'd confided in Barney, he'd known everything, he knew even more now. But she'd loved him and she'd fallen for his bullshit, which made her so angry with herself.

After all this time, safeguarding herself against Ned, safeguarding against her memories and secrets, she'd let Barney in. Now she had to pray he kept his mouth shut about Parker . . . about Jo Martin . . . No, no, she didn't have the energy to go there; everything was too confusing.

Cold and exhausted, she turned right, pulling her mobile out to check the time. When the screen lit up, she noticed there was a voicemail. She pressed call and heard Finn's voice:

'Hey, it's me. I hope you're OK. I saw your call but I was with Pearl and Ned . . . Listen, I want to see you. I need to speak to you about something, give you a heads up, but not on the phone, yeah? So call me, anytime . . . And Cookie, I'm here for you.'

Momentarily, she closed her eyes, willing herself not to cry. There'd been too many tears and they didn't ever do her any good. So instead, Cookie took a long deep breath, clicked delete, and opened her front door.

Walking into the hallway, Cookie threw her wet coat and bag onto the Dutch velvet high-back winged chair in the corner. Then she dragged herself up the three polished wooden stairs. She came to a halt at the sound of voices, laughter, coming from the drawing room.

Opening the door, she stared in surprise to see Lorni, who appeared to have come over all girly and giggly, as Ned sat opposite her in front of the fire, recounting some tale or other.

'Sorry, disturbing you, am I?' Cookie snapped, then slammed out of the door but she was startled by someone coming out of the kitchen. 'Jace.'

He carried a large glass of lemonade. 'Ned told me it'd be all right,' he said, sounding and looking worried.

Cookie nodded and spoke at the same time. Her words rushed out. 'Yeah, yeah sure, of course, anything, baby. It's lovely to see you.'

As Jace went to open the door, Cookie skipped forward to help him. She smiled. 'These doors are heavy.'

'Thank you.'

Before Cookie fully opened it, she looked at him, the image of Parker coming into her thoughts. 'Jace, are . . . are you OK? I mean, if there's anything you want, just ask. Yeah?'

He smiled back as Ned walked out of the drawing room. He ruffled Jace's hair but stared at Cookie while he spoke. 'Thought I'd have to send a search party for you, Jace . . . Go on back in and join your mum – I need to speak to Cookie. She's been out all night, so I've got a bit of catching up to do.'

Jace hurried in. Once the door had swung to behind him, Ned grinned at Cookie. 'Well, well, well, the dirty stop-out returns. What were you doing, hon? Who were you fucking?'

'I don't need this, Ned. If you must know, I had a row with Barney, OK? We'd gone down to a bar he knew, by the river, and then he pissed me off. I ended up walking home. I should've called you, and I'm sorry. OK?' Then, baffled, she frowned. 'Anyway, more to the point, what's *she* doing here? What's Lorni doing in my house?' Cookie kept her voice low, not wanting Jace to hear her say anything negative about his mum.

Ned stepped closer to her. Putting his hand under her chin, he held it tightly, pushing her against the wall. 'Jealous?' He pressed his hard body into hers.

'Jealous?' She sounded incredulous and she wanted to laugh in his face, but she could see that Ned had been snorting: his eyes were wide and his pupils dilated. He also had a particular way of speaking when he'd been taking Charlie: slurred yet trying to sound like he was still in control. But ultimately the coke made him even more unpredictable than normal.

'No, I don't like her, and I don't trust her either. There's something about her I can't put my finger on. And to tell you the truth, I don't want strangers in my house,' she whispered.

'That's fucking ironic, cos it's you who feels like the stranger. You're hardly here.'

'Don't exaggerate.'

Ned slammed her head against the wall but she didn't react, knowing it would only make things worse. She felt his growing erection against her leg.

'Tell me you love me.'

Her voice a dull monotone, she whispered, 'I love you, Ned.'

He stroked her face. 'Show me,' he whispered back. 'Come on, I want you to show me.'

'Ned don't, there's a kid in there.'

Ned bit her neck then drew away. 'He has to learn about the birds and bees one day.'

'This ain't right.' She went to move away.

'What the fuck do you think you're doing?'

Without warning, he spun her round and scooped her hair to one side, exposing the nape of her neck. His breathing changed, becoming fast and shallow, and his teeth grazed her ear as he cupped her breasts roughly in his hands. 'Take your jeans off.'

'Ned—'

He pushed one side of her face against the wall. 'Just fucking do it. And if you don't want them to hear, you better keep your voice down and do as I say, understand?'

'OK . . . OK.' Cookie nodded, doing as she was told, desperately not wanting Jace and Lorni, who were only a few feet away, to hear.

Still facing the wall, Cookie stood in her shirt and underwear. She felt Ned pull her knickers to one side, then in the darkness of the hallway, she felt his penis enter her as he grabbed her round the throat with one hand, thrusting deeper, harder. 'You're mine, Cooks, no one else's. If you look at anyone else, if you ever try to leave me, you know what will happen, don't you?'

She nodded again.

'Then say it. Say it to me, Cooks, tell me what will happen.'

'You'll kill me.'

He moaned.

'Say it again.'

'You'll kill me.'

Moaning even louder and thrusting ever faster, he squeezed Cookie's neck harder causing her to gasp for air. 'That's right, baby, I'll break your fucking neck.' At which point, Ned began to climax.

34

It was seven p.m. and it had already been dark for a few hours. A drizzle of cold rain fell over central London where Pearl, standing in Gray's Inn Road dressed in her chinchilla fur coat, glared at Cookie through the open car window.

'Pearl, are you sure you want me to drop you off here?'

'I already said, didn't I? I won't be long, so don't go away.'

'I can't park in the bus lane. Look, I'll go and find somewhere I can pull up nearby and I'll wait for you.'

Not bothering answering, Pearl drew her face into a tight line.

'Fine, suit yourself. Call me on your mobile when you're finished,' Cookie said. 'I'll pick you up from wherever, OK?'

Pearl watched the car lights fading into the distance and she crossed the road. She hadn't wanted Cookie to drive her, but there'd been no one else so she'd sat in the back not speaking, just staring. The other thing she hadn't wanted was for Cookie to know where she was going; the less that little trollop knew the better.

She hurried along Sidmouth Street pressing her phone against her ear. 'Ned, it's me. I'm almost there.'

'Good, now do as I said; check on Pete. He should be fine, but the guys went back and gave him a good old mouthful of diazepam to keep him quiet, cos he was sounding a bit off. They didn't want him to start hammering on the windows or calling for help or any other stupid shit he might do. Though there's a difference between quiet and dead. So make sure he's still breathing, will you?'

'And if he ain't?' Pearl asked, not particularly bothered either way.

'Then call me. We'll have to dump him in an alleyway, make it look like he's overdosed – but that's the last thing I fucking need right now.'

'And being out in the freezing cold is the last thing I need! How come I have to do your dirty work? Couldn't you have sent the boys round?'

'They're busy. Now do as you're fucking told.'

The call cut off and Pearl, indignant, shoved her phone back in her pocket. Feeling the wind nipping at the back of her neck, she pulled up her fur collar.

Her thoughts drifted to Finn and the threat he'd made. She'd never seen him like that before. Ever since he was a kid, she'd thought of him as a bit of a wet weekend, although Ned reckoned he could pull it out of the bag when needed. But Finn still seemed a lightweight compared to her son, and she blamed her sister Ivy – God rest her soul – for that.

Ivy had spoiled him, wrapped him in cotton wool like he was a bleeding ornament, so it hadn't surprised her when he'd come to live with her and Ned that Finn had been the kid who cried at school when he got bullied, cried when his dog died, cried when his friend left, cried whenever anyone got hurt. The teachers called it sensitive; Pearl called it being a pussy.

So when he'd threatened her last night, she'd not only been shocked but she'd taken it more seriously than she might have done if it had been anyone else. Finn's threats certainly didn't come lightly.

Turning right into Seaford Street, Pearl frowned then stopped in her tracks and glanced over her shoulder. Her eyes darted around the darkness, the flickering broken lights throwing out strange shadows. She could've sworn she'd heard something behind her, but she couldn't see anything so she continued towards the estate.

Halfway along the deserted road, Pearl came to a halt again. That wasn't her imagination; she'd *definitely* heard a noise. Not only that, it felt like someone was following her. She spun round and by the wheelie bins a few yards behind, Pearl caught a glimpse of something moving.

Her heart beat faster, but she told herself it was probably some rat or stray cat rummaging in the rubbish, though her thoughts couldn't help flitting back to the threat Finn had made: *I'll get someone to shut you up permanently.*

Cursing her nephew for an ungrateful little bastard, she placed the blame firmly on Cookie. The little trollop had not only got under his skin but under his covers as well; Finn had been blinded by pussy, it was simple as that. Maybe, with Cookie's encouragement, Finn would go actually through with his promise to do away with her whether or not she opened her mouth to Ned. There was no telling.

Watching the wind pick up a clump of leaves and whirl them around in the gutter, Pearl shivered. Then, attempting to make herself feel better and to stop her imagination from running away with her, she told herself that she was being stupid; Finn wouldn't dare get anyone to lay a finger on her . . . Would he?

Taking a deep breath and pushing her nephew out of her mind, Pearl felt the drizzle turn into rain and picked up her pace, hurrying towards the small estate at the end of the road.

Inside the block, Pearl put her key in the door of the maisonette, all the while trying to shake off the feeling that someone was following her . . . watching her. The door creaked open and she was met by the smell of damp, but she was relieved to be in the safety of indoors.

Trudging up the staircase of the maisonette, Pearl heard the echo of her footsteps banging against the bare wooden floors. The door to the lounge was open, so she waddled across to the bedroom door where Pete was being kept.

She pressed her ear against it, but she couldn't hear anything. From what Ned had said, that wasn't surprising. One diazepam was enough to knock her out, so no doubt Pete would be away with the fairies.

She unlocked the door and began to walk across to where Pete lay spark out on the bed. But halfway there she stopped and listened . . . What was that? She took a step back towards the direction of the sound she'd heard . . . There it was again . . . She was sure she could hear the floorboards creaking . . . Someone was coming up the stairs.

Breathing heavily, Pearl hurried out of the bedroom and back into the lounge; her heart was hammering and a chill ran through her. 'Hello?' It came out as a whisper, and Pearl cleared her throat, hoping to sound more confident next time: 'Hello?'

There was no answer . . .

'Finn, Finn, is that you?' Pearl heard the fear in her voice. 'Finn? Finn?'

Unaccustomed to being frightened, Pearl's panic turned into anger. 'Listen, you little fuck, you don't bother me, and if—'

Pearl let out a gasp as the lights suddenly went out.

As she edged her way out of the lounge, she told herself that it was only the fuse box on the blink; after all, the flat was run down and in need of repair. Hearing nothing, she continued to creep along the small landing to the top of the stairs. She peered down, but it was too dark to see anything. 'Hello?' she called again, then jumped as a door slammed. This time there was no doubt that she'd heard footsteps. Too terrified to look around or listen before making her move, Pearl raced down the stairs and out of the door, running into the deserted road, hoping whoever it was wouldn't follow . . .

35

Panting, Pearl scuttled along the road. It wasn't until she came to the pub on the corner that she realized she'd forgotten her bag with her purse and phone in it. So she wouldn't be able to call Cookie to come and pick her up, and she had no idea where she'd gone to park. But there was no way Pearl was going back inside the flat to get it. No way at all.

As she glanced towards the block of flats, a sudden noise from the communal entrance had Pearl running faster than she'd ever run in her life. She darted along at such a speed she struggled to catch her breath, but she was determined not to give way completely to her panic. Trying not to think about her pounding heart, her dry mouth and the sick feeling rising in her stomach, she focused instead on Finn's parting words. Unable to keep up the pace, and thinking that she was going to be sick at any moment, Pearl came to a standstill, wheezing heavily and leaning against a wet brick wall to steady herself.

Even though she didn't have her bag, Pearl decided to hail a cab; she'd pay at the other end. There was no way she could walk any further with her bunions feeling like they were on fire. The only problem was, there *were* no taxis in sight; the roads were deserted. Cursing with each step, she hobbled up the road. The wet chinchilla fur coat was weighing her down, and if she hadn't paid nearly ten thousand quid for it, she might've dumped it in the nearest trash bin.

She could feel the sweat trickling down her back and she was wheezing so hard it turned into a coughing fit. As she spat out a large lump of phlegm, Pearl felt as if her lungs were on fire as well as her feet.

Ten minutes later and halfway up York Way in the freezing fog and rain, Pearl, still hoping to get a taxi, contemplated what she was going to say to Ned when she saw him. Certainly some choice words. Looking right to cross over, she froze. There was someone standing by the cycle rank. The figure was too far away for her to make out who it was and she couldn't tell if they were watching her, but as she hurried across the road she glanced over her shoulder and saw they were heading her way.

Moving as fast as she could, her breathing short and shallow with the effort, fear flashed through her. Feeling like she was going to collapse, she pressed her hand against her heart as a searing pain gripped her. Knowing there was no way she could outrun them, she looked left and right, trying to find a hiding place. It was then that she spotted the walkway running down the side of a building, leading to the canal.

At the bottom of the slope, after another quick glance around, Pearl picked up her pace along the rubbish-strewn canal path. She hurried under the bridge, feeling the squelching in her shoes from where the rain had seeped in.

'Hello, Pearl.'

The sound of the words behind her nearly knocked her over; her name being called made her freeze even though she wanted to run. *Move*. She had to move but she couldn't, and she was too scared to turn round; not that it would have made much difference, the fog was so thick that she could hardly see a few feet in front of her.

'Pearl?' The voice was muffled and she didn't answer.

Forcing herself to put one foot in front of the other in spite of the terror clutching at her, Pearl began to make her way along the canal again.

'Where are you going, Pearl?' It seemed like the voice was getting louder, or perhaps that was in her head. She wasn't sure anymore, it felt like her senses were letting her down. She was trapped like an animal, and her panic seemed to be making the pain in her chest worse.

'Don't go, Pearl, I'm over here.'

Pearl Reid had never felt fear like it, never known such an overwhelming sense of the inevitable. 'Whoever you are, just . . . just fucking stay away, you hear me?'

'That's not very nice . . . Hello, Pearl . . . Remember me?'

Pearl's face had a look of surprise as the figure came into sight. She took a step back, then composed herself, puffing out her chest. 'Who the fuck are you?'

'Take a closer look.'

It took a moment, then Pearl nodded. 'You were in the club, weren't you? At Barney's birthday party.'

'You can do better than that. Look again.'

Pearl studied the face, then stepped back, curling her lip into a sneer. 'Oh my God . . . Oh my fucking God . . . Well, well, well, look what the cat dragged in: Jo Martin . . . Hello, Jo, or should I call you by your new name, should I say hello—'

'Jo will do fine. After all, we're old acquaintances, ain't we?'

Pearl scoffed. 'To tell you the truth, Jo, I'm glad it's you that was creeping up on me. Who'd have thought it, eh? I take it that was you back in Seaford Street?'

'Who else would it be? Oh, don't tell me you've got other enemies. I can't believe that, Pearl.' The sarcasm dripped through her words. She winked. 'Bit lost for words, are you? Reckon I look different?' She twirled around, laughing. 'Ten years is a long time.'

'Oh I can see it now. Yeah . . . You've lost a bit of weight, changed your hair – nice colour, by the way. But you're still you – there's no changing that.' Pearl laughed nastily. 'I take it that poof Barney and his mates have no idea who you are . . . But I must say, I'm surprised *you* remember *me*.' Pearl shrugged. 'You only saw me once.'

'Thing is Pearl, you tend to remember the person who fucked you with a metal bar on the day you got out of prison. Funny that, who'd have thought it?'

Pearl narrowed her eyes and tilted her head. 'Ain't you worried about what I'm going to do now? I could bring your little world crashing down if I wanted to.'

Jo laughed. 'It did cross my mind. Soon as I'd seen you, I wondered if you'd put two and two together. I didn't know whether you'd clocked me, and I had to be sure. Then there was always the possibility you might come in again. That's why I thought we needed this little chat, so I can make sure my secret will be well kept.'

'That all depends on what it's worth.'

'Oh, I don't think you quite understand. You see, what you and your cronies did to me on that last day, I took it as a goodbye present. And even though my upbringing wasn't all it should be and I wasn't taught the best of manners, I do know that a present should always be reciprocated.'

The bridge they stood under dripped with water and a rat scurried past the two women; apart from the sound of the driving rain bouncing off the canal, there was silence. Then Pearl spoke:

'What are you on about?'

'Here's the thing. I can't have you ruining what I've got here – and I can guess what you're like. You'll open that big fat fucking mouth of yours and I'll have to move on again, go somewhere else. But for the first time in me life, I've found a place where I'm

220

happy, and I won't let you take that away from me.' She stepped closer to Pearl. Her words hissed out. 'So now I reckon it's time for me to give you your present. *I want to hear you squeal like a pig.*'

Pearl felt the first blow to her head and the trickle of blood on her face as she fell to the ground. She groaned in agony at the crack of her ribs from the kicks, and as the blows rained down, the rat scurrying over her body was the last thing Pearl saw.

36

Jo stared at Pearl lying still on the wet ground. She looked dead, just like her mother had done all those years ago. But she wasn't going to leave it to chance, so she booted her again, this time aiming for Pearl's head. Then she stopped and listened. Someone was coming.

She glanced around, then looked down at Pearl and saw a trickle of blood coming out of her ear. Putting one last kick in to be certain, Jo scrambled away, jogging along the canal and up the concrete stairs into York Way.

Making sure there was no one around, she glanced at the time. It was just gone eight thirty. Wanting to get back to Soho as soon as she could, she started to run across the road.

A car horn blared and through the fog a Fiesta sped towards her, screeching to a halt in front of her as she stood in the middle of the road. The driver, a man who looked to be in his fifties, stuck his head out of the window. 'Watch what you're doing, you stupid cow,' he yelled, glaring at her. But she stood transfixed, staring at the rusty Ford Fiesta. Almost identical to the one *he'd* owned. The one he'd driven her about in. The one he'd used on *that* day . . . She blinked, the memories flooding back until she could almost smell the dirty seats and taste her fear. It was like she was fourteen years old again . . .

Jo and Grey sat in the Ford Fiesta. It was cold, there was no heat and the windows were steamed up. She put her mouth over Grey's floppy ears, blowing on them, hoping to warm him up. He didn't like the cold.

He didn't like anything about being in the car, and he certainly didn't like being driven around for hours every day, looking and watching.

She wiped the window, staring out, but jumped back as her dad's face – so red, so distorted – suddenly appeared staring back at her. Then she watched him hurry around, clambering into the driver's seat. As usual, she slipped Grey into her pocket, not wanting her dad anywhere near him.

'They were there again. It's always at the same time at the same place. Every Tuesday without fail. She lets him wander about, she'll sit on the bench nattering away to someone or other while he'll be playing on the swings on his own or collecting bugs. As I walked past, I heard her call him. His name's Parker, apparently.' He winked at her and cackled, his mouth showing off the large gaps where his teeth once were. His watery yellow eyes were threaded with bloodshot veins and his skin was a mass of pockmarks.

Leaning across Jo, he opened up the glove pocket, pulled out a tatty notebook and pencil. As he flicked through the pages, he grinned at Jo. She could smell the alcohol; it was like his personal cologne. 'You see, Jo, I told you: they're here every Tuesday, they have been for the past two months, and I don't reckon anything is going to change anytime soon.'

He rolled down the window, the cold air rushing in as if it was looking for sanctuary. He stuck his head out, snorted, then spat out a gob of phlegm before closing the window again. 'So next week, you know what you have to do, don't you?'

Nervously, Jo's knees bounced up and down. She nibbled on the top of her thumb, pulling the already gnawed, peeling skin away with her teeth. 'I think I'll get caught.'

Immediately, her dad gripped her ponytail, pulling her head back. Then he let it go, tapping the notebook with his tobacco-stained fingers. 'I haven't sat here every fucking week for you to tell me that. You get caught, Jo, and you see what you get. You see what happens to you.'

He clenched his fist, putting it against her face and grinding his heavy knuckle into her cheek. 'You understand? You're fourteen, not fucking four.'

Jo shook with fear. She hated him, she really hated him. She'd even told Grey that she wished he was dead, and she knew Grey wanted him dead too. So many times she'd wanted to run away, to leave, but she was too scared to go, even with Grey. She was afraid if her dad caught her, she and Grey would end up under the floorboards, same as her baby.

And where would she go? She didn't know anyone, didn't have friends – apart from Grey – and her dad had often told her that no one would want her and most people in the world wouldn't be as kind as him. He was the only one who loved her.

The one time she had found the courage to go – the night the whole sky burned with fireworks – her dad was sleeping, having drunk himself into a stupor. Jo made it halfway down the garden path before she turned back, realizing Grey wasn't with her. She'd searched everywhere, and eventually she found him concealed behind the toilet where she remembered she'd helped him hide earlier when her dad had been raging and smashing holes in the kitchen wall with his baseball bat, as he so often did. But by the time Jo had dusted down Grey, it had been too late; her dad had woken. She'd never again been brave enough to try to run away.

'Are you listening to me, Jo?' He squeezed her knee, his lecherous smirk spreading across his face.

'Yes. Yes.'

He stroked her hair and Jo shivered; he made her feel sick. Sometimes she was even sick at the thought of him coming near her.

'Next Tuesday, Jo, you're going to go into that playground and bring that boy to me. It's time I met Parker properly.'

37

The next morning, walking out of the French patisserie in Greek Street carrying a warm baguette, Cookie stifled a yawn. She felt exhausted, and not only because she'd spent over three hours parked up behind St Pancras station the previous evening, waiting for Pearl to call and tell her where to pick her up.

Knowing Pearl, she'd probably found it amusing to leave her hanging around. That was her way of showing Cookie who was in charge. But by ten o clock she was through with it; she'd given up, driven home and gone to bed. No doubt she'd see her later, complete with a supercilious smile.

'Cooks . . . Cooks!'

Cookie put her head down and quickened her pace.

'Cookie, don't ignore me, doll . . . Cookie, don't fucking ignore me!'

'Go away, Barney.' Cookie pushed past a group of office workers and set off across the road.

'Cookie, we need to talk.'

'No, *you* need to talk. I, however, need to get on with my day.'

Barney ran in front of her. 'Ten minutes. Please, give me ten minutes, that's all I'm asking – you owe me that at least.'

Stopping in her tracks, Cookie whirled round. 'Owe *you*! Are you for real? I don't owe you anything.'

'We're friends, and friends hear each other out.'

Vehemently, Cookie shook her head. 'No, we're not, because—' She broke off and waited for the owner of the Turkish deli to pass, nodding to him in acknowledgement. 'You're Old Bill and you lied to me – two good reasons why we're not friends. I'm sure I can find a whole heap of other reasons if you give me a minute.'

'You can be such a bitch, you know that?'

'Excuse me?'

'You heard. Sometimes it feels like you want the whole world to revolve around you, Cooks, and you're not interested in anybody else's life.'

'And that's a problem because . . . ?' she trailed off and shrugged at the same time.

'It's a problem because I love you, and for you to drop me out of your life like that, well, it hurts.'

'I confided in you, Barney. Everyone around here has confided in you. You're the guy Tabby went to when she was trying to get off the crack, the guy Cora ran to when her old man was knocking her about. Natalie came to you when that arsehole of a landlord booted her out. Even Lorni – you took her and Jace in when you knew fuck all about them. But there's a reason why we all came to you; it's because we trusted you. Now it turns out you've been mugging us all off.'

'Maybe if you heard me out.'

Again Cookie shook her head. She stared at him noticing the puffy bags under his eyes. 'No, Barn, you know full well that Old Bill and our lives in Soho don't mix. None of our lives do. Tabby would run a mile. She'd also be gutted. She looks up to you, Barney. You're as near to family as she's ever had.'

'You don't have to tell them, especially as you don't even know the full story.'

'Oh, I think I do. Now leave me alone.'

Barney grabbed her arm. 'Don't do this to me. I thought that you'd—'

'Oi! What the fuck's going on?' Ned shouted out of his car

window, mounting the pavement and coming to a screeching halt in front of Barney, his Range Rover blocking the way. 'You think it's OK to put your hand on me missus?'

'Ned . . . Ned . . . leave it.' Cookie rushed round to Ned and reached through the window, touching his arm. 'It's nothing, OK? We were only talking. Ain't that right, Barn?' she called over to Barney, who nodded agreement.

'That's not what it looked like to me.' His stare darted over her face. 'And is that what you do when I'm not about, let people touch you?'

Cookie could see Ned was beginning to wind himself up. 'No, don't be stupid – this is Barney we're talking about.'

Beginning to reverse back into the road, Ned pointed at Barney. 'You and me need a conversation.' He glanced back at Cookie. 'I've got to go, I've just had a call from the hospital: Mum's been taken in.'

'What? When? Is she OK?'

Driving off at speed, Ned shouted his answer: 'I don't know more than that, I'll call you when I do.'

'Ned! Wait! Ned!'

But he drove off leaving Cookie and Barney standing in the street together.

'You talk about me lying?' Barney said, his face red. 'My heart bleeds for what you've been through, Cooks, it really does, but your whole life is a lie. You don't even see that you're lying to yourself about Ned. You're never going to leave him, you only tell yourself you are. You're as addicted to him as he is to you. You tell yourself the reason you're still with him is because of what happened to Parker, but you're using your son as an excuse.'

The slap to Barney's face was so hard, he almost lost his balance. Holding the side of his face, he fell back onto the window of the wine bar. 'Cookie . . .' he said, looking shocked. 'Cookie,

I'm sorry. I don't mean that, I was only lashing out cos I'm hurt. I should never have said that.'

Cookie's face was a mixture of anger and pain. 'It's a bit too late for apologies, cos you already have.'

In the corridors of University College Hospital, Ned pushed past the magazine trolley and strode purposely towards the critical care unit on the third floor. Not bothering with the lift, he stormed into the stairwell, taking the stairs two at a time.

He had no idea what had happened: a heart attack, a stroke? The only thing the woman on the phone – who he struggled to understand due to her heavy foreign accent – had told him was that Pearl was in a bad way and needed an operation.

Halfway between the second and third floor, his phone began to ring in his pocket. He didn't even bother looking, he knew who it would be: Simon. The guy had already called over twenty times this morning but, whatever he had to say, Ned didn't want to hear it. The truth was, he wasn't in the fucking mood.

He stepped out of the stairwell and into a corridor that reeked of bleach and antiseptic, then followed the signs to the ICU. He pressed the buzzer.

'Hello?' a female voice answered.

'I got a call, they said my mother's here. Pearl Reid,' Ned mumbled.

There was no reply but the double doors clicked open and Ned walked in, feeling his phone begin to ring again. This time he turned it off.

The young blonde nurse, barely in her twenties, smiled at Ned. He gave her a glare in return. 'You're looking for Pearl, right? She's your mum.'

'I know who she is, and I want to see her.'

Clearly not put off by his attitude, the nurse led him down the corridor and pointed. 'She's in bay three. She can talk, but she's in a lot of pain. We'll be taking her down to surgery in the next few minutes, so it's good you're here now. The doctor will be available if you—' Ned, not bothering to wait to hear the rest of what the nurse had to say, made his way to the far bed to where he could see his mum.

Machines and monitors surrounded the bed. Various tubes and multicoloured electric wires hung between the equipment and the wall. And Pearl lay with her eyes shut, her face bruised and swollen, breathing through an oxygen mask.

Ned stared at his mother, trying to take in what he was seeing. Pearl looked like she'd been in a car accident. The only movement he could see was her blood flowing through the countless tubes she was attached to and which fed into the plastic bottles hanging from the bed.

Ned curled his nose, the smell of iodine heavy in the air. 'Mum? Mum?'

It took a beat, but slowly Pearl opened her eyes. She croaked from behind her mask. 'Son?'

'What happened? Did you fall? No one's told me fuck all.'

Swallowing and looking like she was in pain, Pearl attempted a smile. She took a deep drag from the oxygen. 'I was attacked . . .'

Ned visibly flinched. His breathing became as ragged as Pearl's. 'What, someone attacked you? Tell me you're lying. Tell me this is a fucking wind-up.'

'No, son.'

He clenched his knuckles. 'So what? You got mugged, is that it? Some crackhead jumped you?'

'It ain't that . . .' Her eyes began to flicker.

'Take your time, OK?

'I *was* jumped, you're right, but not by some random lowlife.'

Ned turned away, trying to hold his temper in check. 'Jesus, don't tell me this was Draper? Did Simon do this to you? All cos I didn't sniff out some kid for him?' He spun back round to stare at her, noticing how swollen his mum's black eye was. 'For fuck's sake, tell me.'

He wiped the invisible sweat off his face, he squeezed his eyes open and shut, the pressure behind them building. He hissed through gritted teeth. 'Please, Mum, *tell me* – who did this to you?'

Pearl licked her dry, cracked torn lips. Then she turned her head to look directly at her son. 'Cookie.'

Ned blinked in astonishment. His gaze darted around, his mind whirled, thoughts not making sense while his heart pounded and cold perspiration prickled the back of his neck. 'Cookie? No, she wouldn't do this. You must've got it wrong. You and her might not get on so well, but this, nah. Maybe you've made a mistake, probably can't remember properly cos you were clumped?'

Pearl winced, clearly in agony, struggling to talk. 'I can remember all right. It was her.' She gasped, pulling a face, and her eyes closed. After a moment, she opened them again. Her voice even weaker and almost a whisper, she added, 'It was Cookie, as clear as you're standing there now.'

Ned stepped closer to her and leant over to try to hear her. 'It don't make sense though. Why would Cookie do it? She's got nothing to gain from hurting you.'

Pearl winced before she spoke again. 'That's where you're wrong . . . Cookie wanted to shut me up.' She paused, looking ever weaker. 'I went to the flat like you asked me, but then I couldn't get in contact with Cookie to pick me up. I began to walk; that's when I felt someone following me, so I took meself down the canal . . .' Looking exhausted from the sheer effort of talking to Ned, her eyes started to look heavy. 'That's where she jumped me. Did it with a smile on her face an' all . . . Some jogger found me – good job he did, otherwise I wouldn't be here now . . . I'm sorry, son.'

Still leaning over her, Ned held Pearl's gaze. 'Mum . . . Mum, try to stay awake . . . You still haven't told me why. Mum!' He shook her gently. 'Mum, please stay awake. Tell me why.'

'She's having an affair with Finn. It's been going on for a while . . . Ned . . . Ned, wait up, son.'

In agony and gulping for oxygen through her mask, Pearl watched Ned go. It was one thing knowing about Jo Martin, but it was something else putting Cookie in the frame. She didn't care about Jo, not really, especially when the outcome of telling Ned that her attacker was Cookie, and the reason why, would benefit her so much more.

And by the time she got home from the hospital, Cookie would be long gone. And if she didn't make it through the operation, if the good Lord took her, at least she'd have made good on her promise. *If it takes me until my dying breath, I'm going to make sure Ned kicks her out.* Finally that tart would get what was coming to her once and for all.

And as the nurses came to wheel her towards the lift, even though Pearl Reid's life was hanging in the balance, she couldn't help but smile.

38

Ned was almost blind with rage by the time he got home. Parked up outside his house and sitting behind the wheel of his car, he snorted up another line of coke, his mind full of what his mum had said, his hands itching to wrap round both Cookie's and Finn's necks and strangle every bit of life out of them.

Finn and Cookie, Cookie and Finn, naked and fucking. That's all he could think of; he didn't even have room to think, to worry about his mum having an operation to save her life. He felt consumed. All he could see was Cookie wrapped around Finn's cock. *'Whore! Fucking whore!'* Yelling, Ned slammed the steering wheel with his fists, then gripped it, knocking the remainder of the coke onto the floor of the car.

'Fuck. Fuck. Fuck.' His bellow filled the car and he thumped the steering wheel again.

'All right, mate?'

A knock on the window startled Ned and furiously he turned. Immediately he recognized the face: it was one of Simon Draper's goons, Mark.

'Having a moment, were we?' The man grinned, showing off his diamond-studded teeth.

Ned pressed one of the buttons on the driver's door, the window gliding down smoothly. 'What the fuck do you want?'

'Simon sent me to see you. He wants a word. He's wondering if you might be ignoring him – you know, seeing as he can't get through to you on the phone.'

Ned stared at Simon's henchman, one of many he had at his beck and call. He imagined himself doing some damage, maybe taking the geezer's head and smashing it on the side of the car, but knowing that Simon would be none too pleased – an understatement – instead Ned just sneered. 'I've been busy, *mate*. Personal stuff, illness in the family and all that.'

Mark shrugged, unimpressed. 'Turn it in, Ned, that's too much emotional talk for me. All I'm interested in is making sure you speak to Simon.'

Ned wiped his face with his hand, the cocaine in his bloodstream not enough to take away the edge this time, to take away the thoughts that his cousin had fucked his missus.

Images of Cookie rushed into his head again, and the deep betrayal cut through him once more. It felt like he was going crazy, another man touching her. But it wasn't just any other man, was it? *Finn*, his own flesh and blood – brothers in arms – had done the worst thing imaginable, and now there could be only one outcome for his cousin . . .

'Tell him I'll call him later. I'll catch up with Simon tonight.'

Mark gave a small shake of his head. 'No, the boss wants to see you *now*. He says it's urgent. So you better look a bit sharpish.'

Ned, not liking Mark's attitude one little bit, pressed the car's start button. As the engine purring into action, he began to close the window, but his door was flung open by Mark. 'Where the fuck do you think you're going? Get out now.'

'Are you having a bubble?' Ned growled. 'I got things to do – and that doesn't include having a cosy chat with Simon. So you need to go back and tell him that I'll call him when I can.'

Mark smirked. He looked around then pulled his long black coat back enough to show Ned the gun he was carrying. 'You can tell him yourself . . . Now, if you don't want your kneecaps blown off, Ned, best do the sensible thing: get out of the car and make your way across to mine without any fuss. It's right over there . . . Or you can be a silly cunt about this. It's your choice.'

Breathing heavily, Ned glanced around. Catching another glimpse of Mark's gun, he got out of his Range Rover, slammed the door and followed the guy, wondering what the fuck Simon wanted that was so urgent.

The lift took Ned and Mark directly into the penthouse apartment where Simon was standing waiting for them, smoking a cigar and dressed entirely in black. He opened his arms wide as Ned stepped out of the lift. 'There he is. There's the man of the moment.' He stepped towards Ned, a large grin on his face.

'Ned, what you doing to me, eh? I've never chased anyone as much as I've been chasing you; I'm like a fucking fly following a cow's arse . . . But you're here now, that's all that matters.' Simon smiled, then without warning smashed his ring-heavy knuckles into Ned's face, splitting open the corner of his mouth.

Ned staggered to the side, touching his face, the pain shooting down his body. Ned being Ned, he refused to show weakness; turning his head to the side, he winked at Simon. 'Greetings to you too, mate. Can't beat a Bermondsey welcome, can you?'

Panting, Simon wiped his hand on his trousers and smiled again. He chuckled, wagging his finger at Ned. 'I've always liked the fact that you've got a sense of humour. Usually I'm surrounded by miserable cunts, so you're like a breath of fresh air. I reckon that's what's kept you alive . . . *so far* . . . Anyway,' Simon went on, yawning and taking a large drag on his fat cigar, 'I wanted to check in on you, find out how everything stands. You see, I'm wondering if there's been any news on my nephew? It's not like Pete to go AWOL. I reckon something must have happened to him, don't you?'

Conscious of the blood trickling down his chin, Ned wiped it away with the back of his hand, then shrugged. 'I don't know.'

Simon furrowed his brow. 'Well for the life of me, I can't imagine what might've happened. Are you sure you ain't heard anything?'

Feeling the pulse in his jaw, Ned glared at Simon. 'I've already told you: I don't know.'

'Funny that.'

A door opened behind Simon, and Pete walked in. Ned felt the blood drain from his face.

'Hello, Ned.' Pete grinned. 'Surprised to see me?'

'I . . . I . . .' Ned had no words.

'You ain't so full of it now, are you?' Pete cackled, showing off his lack of teeth, the result of years of heroin and crack abuse. 'I reckon you would've been happy if I'd been a goner, wouldn't you?'

'It wasn't like that, mate. I wasn't the one who clumped you – it was me that found you. OK, looking back it wasn't the best decision, but I thought it would save some agg.' He turned to Simon. 'I didn't want there to be trouble between us,' Ned said, appealing to him. 'I knew that Pete being shitted up didn't look great. No harm done, but I swear on my life, I didn't knock him about.' Seeing the look on Simon's face, Ned didn't bother trying to say anything else.

'I'm not saying it was you – Pete can't actually remember what happened. But that doesn't alter the fact that you lied to me. That's never OK. I need to be able to trust you, Ned.'

'You can. I made a mistake. It won't happen again.'

'You're damn right it won't, cos I'm going to make sure of it. But first a little word of advice, Ned: if you ever keep anyone holed up in a room again, maybe tell your mum to lock the door when she runs out of the flat. By all accounts she got spooked when the lights went out and fucked off at the double. Not very clever . . . Cat got your tongue?' Simon walked across to Ned. He grabbed his hand. 'Come on, mate, you know I ain't keen on the old silent treatment. It's downright fucking rude in my books.' And taking his lit cigar and smiling, he ground it into Ned's hand.

Ned screamed in agony, whipping his hand under his armpit as the circle of skin burned and bubbled into a seeping mass of peeling raw flesh.

'That's better . . . Now I should really put you at the bottom of the Thames for what you did to Pete, but I like you, Ned, always have done.' He licked his lips. 'Though in all honesty, I do prefer your missus. You'll have to bring Cookie round for the evening soon, so I can have a bit of fun with her.' He shrugged. 'Though there's nothing stopping us having a *ménage à* three, as they say in Peckham.' He laughed and Ned had to dig deep not to rush at Simon, but if he wanted to get out alive, he knew he had no choice but to suck it up.

'See, after this, after what you did, there's gonna be no more messing around, Ned. You owe me even more than you did before. So from here on in, I won't be brushed off. I won't be taking no for an answer when it comes to you finding me a boy. I won't be humiliated in front of my client for you. He's asked for something and I am – or rather, *you* are – going to provide it. He's coming across in ten days, so you better have something for me by then, otherwise I will kill you. But first I will destroy everything you own. Then I will kill Pearl, I will Cookie – I'll fuck her first, of course, then kill her, very, very slowly . . . So, the games stop here. Understand?'

Simon nodded to Mark, who threw him the cricket bat which had been sitting on the walnut table. Simon turned to Pete. 'Fancy having a go, Pete?'

Pete grinned, shuffled forward and took the bat from Simon,

then he brought it back and swung it hard to smash Ned on the side of his head. Immediately Ned dropped to the floor, groaning. When Simon stepped forward and booted him in the face, Ned yelled in agony.

'I hope you're going to learn your lesson, Ned. Don't ever try to get one over on me again.'

Mark threw Simon the black monogrammed towel which was waiting on the chair. He crouched and pressed it against Ned's bruised and bloodied face.

'Stop being a fucking baby . . . And don't even think about trying anything stupid, otherwise I'll be feeding you your bollocks.'

39

The next day, Ned stood banging on the door of Barney's club. Cookie and Finn raged through his mind like a storm. The only thing he was feeling was unadulterated, burning hatred. Hatred for Simon, but most of all hatred for Finn. As for Cookie, well, he didn't even want to go there.

There was nothing he could do about Simon right now. He got that. Simon had too many men working for him to take the guy on. So if he wanted to still be breathing by the end of the year, he knew he had to find a boy for Simon. Simple as. And he would, he had to, but in the meantime, before this day was over, he hoped, *no*, he would *make sure* that Finn was cut up into tiny pieces and fed to his mother's cat.

As an image of Cookie and Finn came into his head, he hammered even harder. 'Open this fucking door, will you!'

Eventually it was opened by Cora, who looked nearly as bad as he felt. 'Jesus, Ned, what happened to your boat race?'

Ned glared. 'Same thing as probably what happened to yours. It's a fucking mess.' He stormed past Cora into the entrance of the club, down the stairs and gazed around. 'Has anyone seen Cookie?' He banged on the bar of the empty club. 'Barney! Barney! Where the fuck are you?'

'He's not here.'

A small voice sounded behind Ned. He whirled round and saw Jace standing there. Ned blinked; once, twice, thoughts rushing around. He had to find Cookie, find Finn, but this was too much of an opportunity to miss. 'Hello, mate. It's good to see you.'

'What did you do to your face?' Jace asked, staring intently at Ned's bruised face and black eyes.

'I was climbing a ladder, then like a silly twat, I fell off it . . . Where's your mum?'

'She's cleaning at yours. The other lady who cleans for you told Mum to meet her at your house at eight.' Jace gave Ned a shy smile.

'Yeah, I forgot. So that leaves you here on your own, does it?'

He shook his head. 'No, Cora and Tabby are here.'

'Those two dozy mares – you don't want to be hanging around them. How about you and me go and get a McDonald's? After the night I've just had, I could do with a bit of breakfast. See if I can actually open me mouth wide enough to get some grub down me.' He laughed. 'Oh shit, that hurt . . . Come on, get your gear, let's go.'

Jace shook his head. 'I'm not allowed.'

'A big man like you ain't allowed out? What's that about?'

Looking embarrassed, Jace shuffled from one foot to another. 'Mum gets worried.'

'But we know each other, don't we?'

'Yeah.'

Ned, playing it cool, shrugged. To him, kids were as gullible as women; you just had to play them right. He saw it all the time with the runaways, the homeless ones: they were all crying out for a bit of attention, a bit of care. He'd pick them up, take them in, and before long they'd be willing to take their draws off for any old punter. Seemed to him, Jace was no different. The kid only wanted to be liked. 'Well, that's a shame, Jace, we could've had a laugh. That would've been good. But suit yourself.' Ned shrugged and turned to go.

Jace watched Ned. He liked Ned. He was different to all the other men that he'd known. He was kind and he liked that he called him *mate*, like they were friends. He didn't have any friends, not since he'd stopped going to school and that was such a long time ago. But none of his friends at school had ever been as cool as Ned.

'Ned! Ned! Ned!'

'What is it, mate?' Ned turned.

'Can I come?'

Ned tilted his head. 'Ain't you worried about going against your mum?'

Jace's shoulders dropped. 'I guess.'

'Never mind, another time, eh . . . Unless – no, no, you won't do that.'

Wide-eyed with excitement, Jace asked, 'Do what? Do what, Ned?'

'Well, it would be nice for you to come with me, but I don't want you having your ear chewed off by your mum, so maybe, what I was thinking is, we could keep it a secret. It's only a little secret, ain't it? Two mates going for breakfast, that's all . . . What do you think? You any good at keeping secrets?'

Jace stared into Ned's eyes. He was good at keeping secrets; he always kept them for his mum, and he'd kept the secret of the landlord hurting him when his mum went out, so he *knew* he'd be good at keeping this one. And McDonald's wasn't even that far.

He smiled at Ned. 'Yeah, I can keep a secret.'

'Good on you, mate. Who knows, if you keep this one, you and me, well we may be able to go other places together without your mum knowing, what do you reckon? Would you like that?'

'That would be wicked,' Jace giggled.

'Good.' Ned put out his hand. 'Come on then, what are we waiting for?'

And Jace ran to Ned, holding his new-found friend's hand . . .

40

'Where've you been with him?' Natalie stood at the bottom of the stairs in the club, hands on hips, as Ned walked towards her with Jace in tow. 'Does Lorni know you took him out?'

Ned sneered. 'What are you, the bitch police?'

'Jace, why don't you go upstairs and I'll come and see you later, yeah?' She smiled at Jace, who was busy stuffing his face with a chocolate muffin.

Jace nodded. 'OK, see you later, Ned.'

Ned raised his hand. 'Yeah, see you later, mate.'

Natalie watched Jace go then she turned to Ned. 'What's going on?' Her eyes were dark and suspicious as she stared at Ned.

'The kid needs a break. Problem?'

'Don't fucking lie, Ned. You ain't some Mary Poppins, so what's the story? Are you trying to get your claws into him?'

Ned clicked his neck. 'Now I know you're not talking to me that way, are you, cos you wouldn't be stupid enough for that.' He began to step away.

'And you wouldn't be stupid enough to walk away when I'm talking to you.'

Ned turned slowly, his gaze trailing along the floor for a moment before he lifted his stare up to Natalie. 'Are you taking me on? You ain't, are you?' He laughed.

'I'll do what I have to do. Men like you make me sick.'

'Men like me? Now what sort of man is that?'

It was Natalie's turn to laugh. 'You don't need me to tell you, just look in the mirror, *mate*.'

Ned lunged for Natalie, slamming her against the mirrored column in the middle of the club. He pressed on her throat, squeezing her neck tightly. 'You're one mouthy bitch, ain't you?'

Gasping, Natalie spluttered her words: 'You'll have to do much better than that to scare me, Ned.'

'Yeah?'

'Oh yeah, believe it.'

He smashed her head against the column. 'Don't push me, Natalie, cos the mood I'm in, I will bury you, understand? Now we're going to have a little chat. Where's Cookie?'

'A million miles from here, hopefully.'

He smashed her head again, so hard this time it caused a crack. 'Let's try again, shall we? Where's Cookie?'

Natalie just stared at Ned, the tiniest smile on her face as the small cut on her head from the broken glass began to trickle with blood. 'I don't know, but I wouldn't tell you anyway. So do your worst.'

Ned could feel himself wanting to snap her neck but he resisted. *Just*. 'What about Finn? Cos I need to speak to him as well.' The snarl in his voice matched the hatred he felt. 'I need to speak to both of them.'

'Like I say, I don't know anything.'

Ned smirked then his hand drove between Natalie's legs, but immediately she screeched and began to fight back, head-butting Ned hard. 'Don't you fucking touch me, don't you *ever* touch me.'

Holding his nose and taken by surprise, Ned stumbled back. 'I'm going to kill you.'

'Leave her alone!' Tabby, who'd been in the staff kitchen, ran into the main club and leapt to Natalie's defence. She hit out at

Ned, but he pushed her off with ease, throwing her down onto the floor. 'You crazy bitch.' He raised his foot, about to stamp down on her head, but Natalie rushed him, kneeing him hard in the groin. Then she grabbed Tabby off the floor, took her hand, and began to run, knowing it wouldn't be sensible to hang around.

'You fucking cunt!' Ned bellowed.

Natalie stopped, coming to an absolute stand still. She let go of Tabby's hand and turned, walking back over to Ned, who was still bent double coughing.

'No one calls me a cunt – *no one*.' Whereupon she elbowed Ned hard in his face, and then she ran.

'Hey, Nats.' Cookie sat on the couch in Cora's small one-bedroom flat above the betting shop in Wigmore Street. She smiled at Natalie as she hurried into the lounge. 'Now if you're wondering why I'm sitting here,' she continued. 'I'm avoiding Barney – don't ask me why, you seriously don't want to know – but Cora offered to cook me a Sunday roast . . . which I'm still waiting for.' Cookie grinned at Cora, who, having let Natalie in, was now sitting down finishing off the bottle of red she'd opened earlier.

Looking distracted, Natalie nodded. 'Oh yeah, sure, whatever, Cora already told me you were coming round.'

'You OK, babes? What's going on? You look upset,' Cookie asked, worried.

'It's Ned.'

'Ned? What about him, what's happened?'

Natalie glanced at Cora, who gulped down the last of the red, then got to her feet and smiled. 'Don't worry, darlin, I'll leave you to it,' she said, heading for the kitchen. 'There's a chicken in there and it ain't going to cook itself . . . More's the fucking pity.' She laughed and Cookie could hear her singing as she clattered around.

She turned to Natalie. 'What's going on? Is this something to do with Pearl?'

'Pearl?'

Cookie nodded. 'Yeah, she's been taken into hospital.'

'Why? Is she going to be all right?'

'I dunno. I don't know much about it.'

'I was coming to tell you that Ned's on the warpath, he was looking for you.'

Cookie's heart began to race. 'Did he say why?'

'No, and I was too busy having my head slammed against a mirror to ask.'

Cookie's face drained. She stood and walked across to Natalie. 'Oh my God, Nats, are you all right? Look, come and sit down.'

'Don't worry, I'm OK. I've come across enough men like Ned in me life. He tried to scare me, but I don't scare that easily. I think it shook up Tabby a bit though.'

The panic Cookie was beginning to feel was echoed in her voice. 'Don't mess with him, Nats. No matter how tough you think you are, he ain't like most men. If you push him, he'll come after you, and then there's no telling what he'll do.'

Natalie gave the smallest of smiles. 'Thanks for worrying, but you don't have to; I'll be OK. It's *you* that I'm worried about. I've seen him have a pop at anyone who looks at him wrong, and I've seen him get handy with his fists, but I've never seen him this wound up. The way he looked, Cooks – the look in his eyes, it was different.'

'Different *how*?'

Natalie paused to think for a moment. 'You know that saying, "like a man possessed"? That's how he was. And he was all beat up. His face was proper battered and bruised.'

Cookie began to pace the room, her arms wrapped around

herself. 'What else did he say? He must have said something else about why he was looking for me.'

Natalie shook her head. 'He'd taken Jace somewhere without asking his mum, so the minute they got back I had words him about it. That's when he went for me.'

'Jace. What was he doing with Jace?'

'I dunno. When I asked Ned, he got well pissed off. But that's about it . . . No, wait – he said something about Finn. He wanted to know where Finn was.'

'But he didn't say why?'

'Nope, but it didn't look like he wanted to have a cosy chat with him.'

Grabbing her jacket and bag from off the table, Cookie began to get ready to leave. 'I better call Finn, see what's happening, see if he knows anything. He left me a voicemail yesterday asking to meet up; he wanted to talk about something. Maybe this is to do with why he wanted to see me . . . And I need to find Ned as well – not that I'm looking forward to that part.'

'You want me to come with you?'

'No, you better not – but thanks, Nats, thanks for everything. I owe you.' Cookie kissed her on the cheek and Natalie smiled then leaned forward to kiss Cookie on her lips, wrapping her arms around her. 'Take care of yourself, Cooks. If you need me, you've got my number. Call me, and no matter where you are, I'll be there . . . Love you, babe.'

Cookie's tone was full of warmth as Nat released her from the embrace. 'Love you too, darlin . . . Now wish me luck.'

'I wouldn't know what to do if anything happened to you, so please come back safely.'

Cookie didn't answer, she had every *intention* of coming back safely, but the question was, would she?

41

It had grown dark and Cookie had been looking for Finn for the past few hours. She'd searched all the obvious haunts. She'd even phoned some of his friends, as well as Zee and the boys when her calls to Finn had gone straight through to voicemail. But no one had seen or heard from him.

Passing Pizza Express, she glanced at her watch. It was gone six and the likelihood of Ned catching up with Finn before she did was growing with each passing hour – if he hadn't already done so.

The wind was picking up and she shivered, pulling up her collar in an attempt to stop the cold rain dripping down her neck.

'Hey! Hey! *Oi!*'

Hearing a voice, she spun round and saw a black Range Rover speeding towards her. The next moment, before she had a chance to move, the car mounted the pavement, screeching to a halt and blocking her in.

She saw Ned's face – lit up by the car's interior light – the bruises around his eye and his head standing out against his pale skin, but she didn't have time to think about what had happened to him, she just needed to run.

Turning, Cookie started to run the other way, but Ned was too quick. He scrambled across the cream seats to open the passenger door, and before she knew it he'd grabbed her by the hair and slammed her against the car.

'You fucked him, didn't you? You fucked my cousin.'

'Get off me, Ned!'

'Did you really think you'd get away with it, hey? Knocking my mum about to keep her quiet, putting her in hospital, all to stop her spilling your dirty secret.'

'I don't know what you're talking about. Let go of me!'

'Oh come on, you don't fool me, babe . . . Whose idea was that then, Cooks? Yours? Finn's?'

'I said get off. *Stop*, Ned, fucking stop!'

He shook her like a rag doll. 'Well whose ever idea it was, unfortunately you didn't do a good enough job, Cooks. She spilled the beans all right, couldn't bleedin' wait . . . So go on, how many times? How many times did you fuck him?'

'Ned, *please*,' Cookie pleaded.

He twisted her round to face him. 'So that ain't a denial?' His breathing was hard and frantic.

'Get off me!'

'What was he like, Cookie? Did he make you scream? Did he fuck you until you screamed, *did he*? Answer me!' Ned was spitting with rage as he reached his free hand into his pocket and pulled out a gun, jamming it against her temple.

She screamed. Ned gripped her throat then slammed his hand hard over her mouth, but she managed to twist round and bite down on his hand.

Unaccustomed to her fighting back, Ned let go for a second and Cookie seized the opportunity to take off, sprinting towards Soho Square with Ned only a few feet behind her.

'Cookie, come here now! Do as you're fucking told. Don't you run away from me!'

Hoping to cut through to the other side of the square, she rushed for the iron gate of the gardens but it was locked. She rattled it. 'No, no, no.' And glancing over her shoulder, she saw Ned, now almost within reach, so without hesitation Cookie jumped up, pulling herself onto the black wrought-iron railings and straddling the top of the bars.

'Where the fuck are you going?' Ned pulled on her foot, grappling to bring her down, but she kicked back, catching him in the face.

Ned let go. 'Bitch!' He sounded in pain but it only incensed him more. As Cookie landed on the other side of the railings, Ned rushed at them, vaulting up and over easily.

Her heart pounding, Cookie ran across the square, skidding on the muddy, wet grass. She sprinted towards the Tudor hut in the middle of the square, racing to get away from Ned.

'I'll catch you, Cooks, so you might as well give it up now.' In the dark, she heard Ned angrily shouting behind her.

Panting, she dodged behind a tree only for Ned to leap at her, causing her to stumble. She tried to get her balance, but Ned grabbed at her again, and as the rain fell harder, Cookie found herself falling onto the wet earth.

Gripping her by the hair, Ned dragged her off the path and into the bushes by the railings, hidden from view.

Still fighting hard to get away, Cookie felt every cut and graze from the uneven ground, the stones and sticks digging into her as she struggled.

'We'll do it here then, shall we? Cos you ain't going anywhere. You're going to pay for fucking that cunt.'

Standing, he stepped over her, straddling her body. 'Now start fucking talking.'

As Ned began to crouch, Cookie kicked out, catching him right on his knee. Unable to move away quick enough, she felt the power of Ned's fist smash down against her face. She yelled as loud as she could, her mouth filling with blood.

Ned leapt on top of her and, as always when he dished out violence, she felt his erection.

'Get off me! *Get off me!*'

Covered in mud and with her face swelling, Cookie grappled her hand to the side and, feeling a stone, she grabbed it, bringing it up to slam it against the side of Ned's head.

'Fuck! You bitch!' Ned fell off her, holding his head. Cookie pushed him away then scrambled to her feet and scuttled off into the dark as fast as she could without looking back.

42

'Finn? Finn? Oh Jesus, thank God you answered.' Cookie clutched the phone against her cheek. She was in pain, and her clothes were muddy and soaked through. Blood from her mouth stained the front of her jacket. She didn't even want to think about what she looked like as she stood in Tottenham Court Road. 'Where are you? I've been trying to get in touch for ages . . . Finn, I can't hear you . . . Finn?' Cookie's phone cut off and she saw that her battery had gone dead. 'Shit. *Shit.*' Her hands shook, partly from cold and partly from fear.

She had to think. *Think.* She didn't know Finn's number off by heart to call him from another phone, yet she needed to speak to him, she *had* to warn him about Ned.

Her heart pounding, Cookie glanced around the almost empty street, trying to figure out the best thing to do. She was only a ten-minute – seven minutes at a push – jog away from Hanson Street, maybe she could go there? Get his number from one of the kids? Pearl was in hospital, so on that score she was safe. The only problem was Ned: he might be still in the area, looking for Finn. She couldn't risk him seeing her, not before she'd warned Finn, anyway. She didn't want blood on her hands.

With only a slight pause, Cookie began to run, oblivious to the pouring rain. Realizing that her heels were slowing her down, she paused in front of the health shop on Rathbone Place to whip off her shoes, then took off again, clutching her Louboutins in her hand as she dashed along, feet burning, until she reached the bottom end of Hanson Street.

Limping now and slowing down, Cookie stumbled along until she saw a figure she recognized ahead of her. Immediately she yelled and started to wave. 'Finn! Finn! *Finn!*'

He didn't turn, the rain and wind taking away her words. She started to run again, looking around to make sure Ned wasn't about. 'Finn!' He began to stroll into the building and Cookie yelled even louder, desperate to get his attention. '*Finn!*'

This time he heard.

She saw him frown then begin to rush towards her. He spoke as he ran. 'Oh my God, what happened? What the fuck happened to your face?' Finn touched Cookie's mouth, then he shook his head; she winced at the pain from the split lip. 'He did this to you?'

Cookie nodded.

He shook his head angrily. 'Is this because Pearl told him we were having an affair behind his back?'

'What?' she gasped, shocked.

'She knew there was something going on between us and she threatened to tell him. That's why I wanted to meet you, I didn't want to leave any message on your phone though, in case Ned listened.'

'Hold on, hold on.' Cookie sounded confused. 'Threatened to tell him what? There wasn't anything to tell. We haven't done anything.'

'I told her that; I also told her if she even *thought* about telling Ned, I'd have to get someone to deal with her.'

'Jesus Finn, you threatened her? No wonder she's got it in for us. Pearl hates anyone telling her what to do.' She stopped and a thought flitted into her head. 'Did you follow through? Did you *actually* get someone to attack her?'

'Attack her? What you on about?'

'She's in hospital.'

Finn couldn't look any more surprised.

'She's saying it was *me* that put her there. That I knocked her about. That's what she told Ned, that's what he thinks.'

'Fuck, what a mess. Then again, this is Pearl we're talking about, so nothing would surprise me.'

A car went by and Cookie pulled Finn away from the kerbside, ducking behind the parked cars. 'We need to get out of here, Finn. Ned's on the warpath. He won't stop until he kills both of us.'

'Where is he now? Tell me where he is so I can go and blow his fucking head off.' He touched her face again gently.

'And what if he blows yours off first? He's carrying a gun on him; I thought he was going to use it on me earlier.'

Finn shook his head. 'I've let him get away with too much. It's time to put a stop to it once and for all.'

She grabbed his hand. 'Finn, listen to me. This isn't about him or me, it's about you – you need to get out of here.'

Still not looking entirely convinced, he let her lead him into the building and the two of them sprinted up the tiled stone stairs, all the while making sure that Ned wasn't behind them.

When they made it to Finn's room, Cookie's eyes went straight to the suitcase on top of the wardrobe. 'Throw in everything you'll need,' she said, hauling it down. 'Anything important – you know passport, licence . . .'

He looked at her. 'Cookie.'

Busy pulling clothes out of the drawer, she gave him a quick glance. 'What?'

'I love you.'

Cookie blinked, not saying anything. The atmosphere in the room crackled with silent tension as Finn continued to stare at her. She turned away to grab a couple more items out of the drawers. 'Come on, let's go; we don't want to wait around here longer than we have to.'

'Did you hear what I said? *Cookie*, did you hear me? I said I *love* you.'

Cookie gave the tiniest of nods. 'I know . . . Look Finn, I—'

He shook his head. 'You don't need to say anything. It doesn't matter.' The hurt shot through his voice and his eyes. 'You're right, let's go.'

They rushed back out of the building and into the night, checking over their shoulder as they ran through the pouring rain to Finn's car, which was parked around the corner.

Finn opened the boot of his grey Audi and threw his bag inside, then ran round to the driver's door. 'Hurry up, Cooks, we can relax once we're out of here. The further away, the better.' He smiled at her encouragingly, the rain running down his handsome face. 'I'll look after you, Cooks; we'll be OK, we'll sort out all the details later.'

Cookie shook her head. 'You don't understand, I can't come with you.'

Finn stepped away from the car. 'What are you talking about? Let's go.'

'I can't, I'm *sorry*.' She began to back away, fighting the tears, but he grabbed her arm.

'You can't be serious – there's no way you can stay with Ned now. Not after he's done this to you, and not now that he thinks there was something going on between me and you. It ain't safe.'

'It's safer if I stay,' she insisted. 'If I go, he's bound to come after me, Ned's not going to let me disappear, especially with you. He'll make it his mission to hunt me down. Then he'll kill us both. This way you've got a chance of getting away. Who knows, he might not even come after you.'

'If you ain't going, neither am I.'

Wiping the rain from her eyes, Cookie shook her head angrily. 'You are *not* going to do that to me, Finn. I won't be held responsible for your death, cos that's what will happen if you stay – and you know it. It's not like the last time, when Zee and the boys did a runner. Then, he was just pissed off about it. This is different. He won't let you off this time.'

Finn matched her anger. 'Same goes for you, yet you expect *me* to go and leave you with him? Are you for real? What sort of guy would that make me?'

'A sensible one. One who listened. One who says he loves me. If that's true, then you'll do this for me.'

Finn's face flushed. He turned away but immediately spun back to look at her. 'Oh no, no, you don't get to do that,' he shouted. 'You don't get to use the fact that I love you when it suits then the rest of the time you're happy to fucking ignore it.'

'Finn, it's complicated.'

Finn burst into bitter laughter. 'Tell me you didn't just say that!'

'I need to stay for other reasons as well, stuff you don't know about.'

'Then tell me. There's always some sort of secret with you . . . You think I won't look after you, is that it? You think I'll let you down? Cos I won't.'

'Jesus Christ, it ain't all about you.'

'Then *tell* me, fucking tell me what it is! Maybe I can help.'

'I can't.' The tears ran down her face. 'Don't ask me anymore, *please* . . . And now I'm going to go, and you're going to get in your car and drive away.'

'But—'

'*Go.*' Cookie trembled, her eyes brimming with tears. '*Please.*'

Without a word, he nodded then got in his car. But at the last minute, he glanced up at Cookie, who standing under a street-light. 'I am going to see you again, ain't I, Cooks? At least tell me that.'

'Of course.' Though she tried to ignore the feeling in her gut that said different.

Turning on the engine, Finn looked at the road ahead, then suddenly he hit the steering wheel and jumped back out of the car. He grabbed Cookie, drawing her into him, their faces, their lips, inches away from each other.

'I will be back, Cooks. You and me – this isn't over, we haven't even begun,' he whispered. 'And as for you not loving me … well, it don't matter, it won't change the fact that I love you. Don't ever forget that.'

Not saying anything else, Finn stared into her face then stepped away.

'Go, go, before it's too late,' Cookie said, her voice sounding like it was breaking.

Getting back into the car, he gave her a nod. He started the engine, slowly pulling off down the road.

'Wait! Finn!'

The car stopped and she ran after it, leaning in through the open driver's window. She gently kissed Finn on his lips, closing her eyes for a moment. Then she pulled away from him and moved back on the kerb. 'Now go … *Go.*'

But Finn opened the door and stepped out. He grabbed Cookie and pulled her into him, wrapping his arms around her as the rain fell. He kissed her softly, gently, his lips brushing against hers, then harder, his passion pouring out. Then he stared into her eyes. 'I love you, and this ain't over.'

He got back in the car and sped off, the wet from the road spraying up.

She waved as the car lights disappeared into the night. 'I love you too, Finn.' Then she turned and ran . . .

The house was quiet; only the sound of the grandfather clock broke the silence. 'Hello, Ned.' Cookie stepped into the large drawing room, hearing her footsteps echo on the wooden floor. She threw her wet jacket on the side and stared at the back of the winged velvet chair Ned was sitting in.

He didn't turn round, just continued gazing into the fire. 'I would've found you, Cookie. I would've found you and killed you, you know that, don't you?'

'I was never going to leave you, Ned. I was *always* coming back. We've got a deal, ain't we?'

There was a slight pause. 'You know I'm going to kill him, don't you?' Ned prodded the fire, bringing out the glowing red and orange metal poker. 'I'm going to hunt him down and, when I find him, he's a dead man.'

'Nothing happened, Ned.'

'*Liar!*' He threw the poker and it landed on the velvet chair next to him, singing the material. 'Don't fucking lie to me!'

'I'm not, I swear. Ned.'

'Then why did my mum say as much?'

Cookie walked round to look at Ned. She stood in front of the almost shoulder-high original fireplace, the heat from the fire welcoming. 'Cos she's Pearl, and that's the sort of shit she does. She tries to stir up trouble, even if that means setting you and Finn against each other. She doesn't care. She's always hated me, you know that . . . Fact is, I wouldn't do that to you. I would never sleep with anyone, especially not your cousin.'

He looked up at her. 'You're a whore, so of course you would. You'd fuck anything if it meant—'

'Meant what?' she cut him off. 'Meant what, Ned? What is it that Finn could give me? There's *nothing* going on, nothing has *ever* gone on . . . so there's no need to touch him, is there? Look, I'm here now. It's you and me, Ned. That's all that matters, ain't it?'

He didn't answer, only licked his lips. The intensity of his stare made her gaze flicker to the floor. 'Take your clothes off. Let me see you.'

Her shoulders tensed but she nodded and did as she was told.

Ned sat back, looking at her, then he put his foot on her leg, resting it against her thigh. 'One push, that's all it would take, Cooks. One push and you'd be in that fire. You wouldn't be able to whore yourself out so easily then, would you? What do you think?'

Standing naked, Cookie felt slight pressure on her leg pushing her back towards the fire as Ned toyed with her. She tried to steady herself, trying to keep her balance. 'Ned, *please*. I'm begging you, *don't*.' She swallowed down the tears, the terror, knowing that her best chance was to stay calm, like she always did, like she'd learnt to, like she had to.

He began to breathe heavily, deeply, watching. Cookie continued to stay motionless, statue still.

'Go upstairs and wait for me.'

She began to edge away. 'OK . . . OK.' She hurried to go but he grabbed her hand, the roaring fire crackling. 'Say it. Say it.'

'I love you, Ned . . . I love you more than life itself.'

43

Two days later, Natalie and Tabby stood watching Ned as he walked down the stairs of the club accompanied by a boy around the age of sixteen.

'Where's Cookie?' Natalie snapped. 'You better not have done anything to her. I can't get through to her on her mobile.'

'Yeah, we're worried,' Tabby added. 'What have you done to her?'

'Fucking hell, what is it with you two, eh? What are you, Thelma and Louise? Do me a favour! And perhaps you should take it as a hint that she ain't taking your calls. Cookie obviously doesn't want to speak to you, so jog on – unless of course you want me to remember that you guys had a pop at me the other day. You wouldn't want me to start thinking about that, would you?'

'Think about what you like, I don't care.' Natalie glared at him. 'We're worried about Cookie, so tell us where she is.'

'Ain't you got anything better to do than go round chewing blokes ears off? Maybe you need to get yourself a fella, Nat, perhaps then you'll leave me out of it.'

'You really are an arrogant bastard, ain't you? And for your information, I don't do men anymore.'

'Then try fucking a vibrator. I'll get you one; anything to get rid of all that pent-up crap you've got going on.'

'Why do you always have to be such a bully?' Tabby asked.

Ned looked at her scornfully. 'Do you really think I'm going to waste my time talking to you? Some toothless crackhead? Get the fuck out of my way, bitch.'

'I'm clean, if you must know,' Tabby said defensively.

Ned leaned down towards her and sniffed in disgust. 'That's a matter of opinion, ain't it?'

'Ignore him, Tabby,' Natalie said. 'He's one of life's prize wankers.'

'Watch yourself, Nat. The mood I'm in, I'd be happy to see you pushing up daisies.' He barged past them and Natalie and Tabby stomped off through to the back. The few customers who were in the club on a Tuesday lunchtime hurriedly looked away when Ned glared at them.

He turned to the boy, who was dressed in a baggy Nike tracksuit, emphasizing his skinny frame. 'Remember what I said: you play the loving nephew. No fuck-ups, otherwise you'll be back on the streets where you came from, understand?'

The boy nodded, fear glinting in his eyes. 'Yes, Ned.'

Ned gave him a hard prod in the stomach, causing the boy to cough.

'We ain't even started yet and you're messing up. What did I tell you to say?'

'Sorry . . . Yes, *Uncle* Ned.'

'That's better,' Ned growled. 'And don't forget it.'

The boy nodded, bit down on his lip and looked like he was trying to stop the tears.

Before anything else was said, the staff door opened and Lorni and Jace walked through. Ned smiled. 'All right, Lorni? Hi, Jace. Thanks for meeting me.'

'That's OK.' Lorni smiled back, but her smile lacked the enthusiasm of Ned's.

'So listen, I've got a few friends coming round and I need the place spotless. Sorry for the short notice, but I'm a bit stuck. Of course I'll pay you double.'

'I'm just pleased to get the work.'

'And I thought, seeing as you'd be busy, I could take Jace out, you know for a bit of lunch, keep the kid occupied.'

'No, it's fine, he can come with me.' Her tone was sharp.

Ned had to work hard on a smile this time. 'It's no bother . . . oh, this is my nephew, by the way. Sid, this is Lorni. I thought Sid could keep Jace company and Jace could keep Sid company. Seriously, Lorni, you'd be doing me a favour. Sid's into Xbox and all that crap, it's like he's talking another language. Ain't that right, Sid?'

'Yeah, Uncle Ned knows fuc—' Sid stopped as he caught the glare that Ned threw at him. 'I mean, he knows *nothing* about gadgets,' he continued. 'Proper old geezer.'

'Oi, less of the old. I've still got a good few years until I'm fifty, mate . . . Anyway, you ain't said hello to Jace.'

'All right?' Sid smiled at Jace, who grinned, clearly excited at the prospect of an afternoon playing Xbox.

'*Please*, Mum, can I go?'

Lorni's gaze flicked to Sid and then back to Ned, who stood there smiling, waiting for Lorni to bite.

'Think about it this way, you'd be able to get on with the cleaning without him nipping at your feet. The place is empty,' Ned said, thinking about how he'd sent Cookie to the Lanesborough, a spa not far from Buckingham Palace, to get her out of the way. She'd spent most of the last two days in bed . . . *recovering* from her latest punishment, but now she was back on her feet, it wouldn't do him any favours if Lorni saw her looking a bit worse for wear.

'Well . . .' Lorni hesitated.

'Look, what time do you want him back? He'll be fine and, like

I say, you'll be doing me a favour. My brother dumped Sid on me this morning and, much as I might love my nephew, me and teenagers, well . . .' He rolled his eyes and laughed.

'*Mum,* can I?'

'OK, fine. Fine.' Lorni laughed as well. 'But don't give Ned any grief.'

She began to go into her purse. 'Here, get yourself something to eat.'

'Put that away,' Ned said. 'My treat – and I won't take no for an answer . . . Now come on, Jace, let's go. A boys' day out. What d'you reckon?'

'Wicked!'

And as they walked out of the club, Ned felt his phone buzz and he smiled, knowing exactly who it was.

'So listen, we don't have to tell your mum everything, do we? We can have secrets, can't we? Me and Sid have them all the time, don't we, Sid?'

Sid sat in the back with Jace in the front. 'Yeah.'

'They're not bad ones, but boys need to have secrets, don't they?' Ned glanced at Jace as he drove his Bentley Bentayga along Park Lane.

Jace sucked on a bubble gum lollipop and nodded. He glanced back at Ned. He couldn't remember a day as brilliant as this one. They'd driven around and Ned had showed him all the bridges; he'd even promised to take him on the London Eye. It made him wish he was Sid; to have an uncle like Ned would be the best thing ever.

'What sort of secrets?' Jace asked.

'Oh, stuff like . . . I don't know: going to see people and having fun, eating too much ice cream. Like last time I took Sid out we went to see my friends and watched movies, but we didn't tell his mum because he was supposed to be at my house doing his homework.'

Jace giggled.

'And seeing as you were so good at keeping a secret last time – you know, when we went out for a McDonalds without telling your mum – I thought, now we're all mates, it would be fun to share more with you. That's what men do; they don't tell women everything.' Ned winked and took a left into Piccadilly, driving slowly through the traffic.

'I have a secret,' Jace said, smiling and swinging his legs as he watched a couple of mounted police go by.

Indicating to take a right down St James's, Ned frowned. 'Do you, mate?'

Enthusiastically, Jace nodded. 'Yeah.'

'Wanna share?'

Jace took another suck of the lollipop, tasting the strawberry flavour fizz down his throat. He wanted to spend all the time he could with his new friends; Ned made him feel happy and Sid was funny, he liked him as well. If he shared his secret with Ned, then maybe he would think Jace was a big man too. He'd like that. Then they could go out all the time together.

'You won't tell my mum?'

Ned laughed as the Bentley cruised along. 'What did I say, mate? Men stick together, women don't need to know all the ins and outs, do they?'

Jace giggled again. 'My mum's name isn't really Lorni.'

Ned did a double-take. 'What do you mean?' He took another right and slowed down, parking up behind a blue Rolls-Royce.

Jace shrugged shyly. 'My mum, well Lorni, that's not her real name, she keeps changing it every time we move. And . . . and I don't think my real name is Jace, but I dunno . . .' He trailed off and looked out of the window, all of a sudden feeling like he'd done the wrong thing. He felt himself blushing red, thinking about how his mum would be really mad with him if she found out. She might even cry. And now he didn't feel so happy.

'Hey, hey, mate. Look at me,' Ned said, gently putting his finger under Jace's chin and turning his head fully towards him. 'What's with the long face? That was a cool secret, wasn't it, Sid?'

'Yeah, nice one, Jace.'

'Really?' Jace's relief sounded in his voice.

'The best,' Ned said. 'And I've got one for you.'

'Have you?'

Ned nodded, letting go of Jace's chin. 'Yeah, see that man over there, the one coming out of the Rolls-Royce, the blue car in front, why don't you give him a wave? That's my mate.'

Jace waved, watching the man walk towards the car. 'And that's a secret?'

Ned laughed as he pressed the button on the window to open it. 'No, that would be a pretty rubbish secret, wouldn't it? This is Simon, by the way.'

Simon Draper grinned at Jace as he leaned in the window. 'Hiya, mate, you all right?'

Jace blushed, smiling. 'Yeah.'

'No, the secret is,' Ned continued, 'in a couple of weeks we're going to go to a party with Simon to see his friend.'

Jace felt the happiness tickle in his stomach.

'And there might even be more than one party. Would you like that?'

Jace nodded.

'Good, but you mustn't tell your mum, like I won't tell her the secret you told me. OK? We can pretend we're going to the cinema and stuff. Maybe we can persuade her to let you have a sleepover; that way we can stay out as long as we want. Sid can come as well, it'll be fun.'

Holding the lollipop in his mouth, Jace clapped in delight.

Ned turned to Simon. 'What do you think? You reckon he's all right?'

Simon patted Ned on the back. 'You've done well, Ned, and about time too . . . But yeah, I think my client will love him, he's perfect.'

44

It was half past eight Tuesday night and Cookie limped down the stairs of Barney's club – which was closed until ten – looking for Natalie and Tabby. She hadn't returned their calls, mainly because she'd felt too rough after the punishment that Ned had dished out, one of the worst yet; but she'd also been dreading the questions they would ask, questions she couldn't answer. They were good friends, they cared about her, and the feeling was mutual, but she couldn't confide in them. She only hoped that she hadn't hurt their feelings.

'Cookie, please, talk to me,' Barney pleaded, having spotted her the minute she walked in. She turned to face him and Barney let out a gasp. 'Jesus Christ! What happened – need I ask?'

'I'm fine, so don't make a drama out of it, Barney.'

Barney, all dressed up to go out, shrugged off his full-length fur trench coat and threw his beige bag on the bartop. 'You've got to leave him, Cooks. I know what you said to me about Parker and wanting to see through your plan for Jo, but look at your face.'

Cookie stared at Barney. 'Don't say anything else. I don't want to hear it, OK? I know what I'm doing.'

'I don't think you do. I think if you're not careful, he'll kill you before you even get to Jo . . . Finn called me, by the way. He wanted to make sure you're all right. He sounded in a real state, upset, he was worried about you, like we all are, and he wanted me to tell you that he's fine . . . He's given me the address where he's staying for now. I'll give it to you, if you want it.'

Cookie nodded.

Barney looked at her warmly. 'What's going on, Cooks? It feels like it's a dangerous game you're playing, whatever it is. I'm scared for you.'

'I have to go. I want to speak to Natalie and Tabby before the club opens.'

Looking forlorn, Barney nodded. 'They're in the kitchen. I was about to pop out for some biscuits . . . I miss you, Cooks.'

She began to walk away.

'I've spoken to my friend, you know, the one I was telling you about. He says he'll do what he can. Try to get the name. But you're right, Jo is in the area – well, she was. They're not quite sure, because apparently she's being lying low, not checking in with the authorities every year like she's supposed to. Apparently, that's common among people given anonymity. They want to get on with their lives, forget their past. But hopefully I'll be able to get that name.'

Cookie turned to look at him, walking backwards as she spoke. 'I want to thank you, I really do, but I don't know who you are anymore, Barney.'

'And what about Finn – what should I say to him if he calls again?'

But she didn't answer, and Barney stood watching her go. Upset, he turned round to put his coat back on, then jumped at the sight of Ned, steeping out from behind one of the mirrored columns. 'How long have you been there?'

'Long enough.'

'Hasn't anybody told you that you shouldn't go round sneaking up on people?'

Ned sneered and laughed. 'And what are *you* going to do about it?'

Barney flushed with anger. 'This is my club, you know.'

'Oh I know, and if you want me to leave, that's fine. I get it.' Ned grinned. 'Come on then, throw me out . . . No? I didn't think so.'

'One day the way you treat others will catch up with you, Ned, but I'm glad to see that you've got a small bit of payback – your comeuppance?' He pointed to Ned's face and Ned, too quick for Barney, grabbed his finger.

'If you don't want me to break it, snap it right off, then I'd quit the smart remarks, if I were you. Now, what was she saying?'

'Nothing, it was me who was saying; I told her that she needed to leave you, it's one thing your face being battered into a bloody mess but it's quite another seeing my friend – who I love – looking all bruised and swollen.'

Ned tilted his head, bending back Barney's finger until he let out a squeal at the pain. 'And did Cookie tell you that if she tries to leave me, I'll kill her? Just like I'll kill anyone that even thinks about helping her.' He let go of Barney's hand. 'So think on, mate.'

Grabbing his coat, Barney walked off towards the kitchen, leaving Ned standing in the middle of the club.

'Ned!' Ten minutes later, Jace ran up to Ned, throwing his arms around his neck as Ned sat on the bed in Barney's guest room. 'Have you come to see me?'

Ned winked. 'Of course I have. How's it going?'

'What are you doing here?' Lorni walked in behind Jace. She unzipped her jacket, wet from rain, and hung it on the back of the door. 'I'm not being rude, Ned, but this is my private space and I'd rather you didn't come in when you want to. It makes me feel uncomfortable.'

'He came to see me, Mum,' Jace said proudly.

'That's right, mate, I did. Of course I came to see you as well, Lorni . . . I thought I'd pop in for a little chat, see how you're getting along. See if you wanted any more hours, you know, cleaning at my house?'

'What is this?' Lorni asked suspiciously. 'You could've called or seen me tomorrow.'

'I wanted to see you tonight, though.'

As she stared at Ned, Lorni saw what he was holding in his hand. The letters from her bag. She spun around to face Jace. 'Why don't you go and get yourself into the bath?'

'But what about Ned? I wanted to talk to—'

'Just do it!' Lorni snapped.

Ned smiled. 'Do as your mum says, Jace.' He spoke warmly. 'Sometimes we all have to do things we don't want to, so be a man about it, OK?'

Jace beamed. 'Yes, Ned.'

'Good lad.'

Jace grabbed a towel off the side and skipped into the en suite bathroom.

'Look, I know you like it here,' Ned said as he got to his feet, holding Lorni's letters. 'So I don't see there's any need for you to worry about me knowing your little secret. You can carry on working for me, and I'll keep my mouth shut.'

Lorni's heart raced. 'What are you talking about?'

He waved the letters. 'Come on, I've read them, I've seen what they say.'

Lorni's eyes filled with tears. 'You had no right. Just tell me what you want.'

Ned opened his arms wide, then he walked up to her and wiped the tears out of her eyes. 'What I want? I don't want anything. It makes interesting reading, and according to the guy I spoke to—'

'You spoke to someone?' The fear in Lorni's voice was clear.

'Yeah, I rang the number on the letter. He wanted to know where you were.'

Tears ran down Lorni's face. 'What did you tell him?'

'What did I tell him? Nothing. What do you take me for? Jesus, I hate authority as much as you do . . . Look, I wanted to know who you were, that's all. Now you're working for me, I thought I'd see if I could pick up a couple of references.' He grinned.

'What, by going in my bag and looking at my private letters?'

'Calm down, I'm only joking.'

Lorni went to snatch the letters from Ned, but he held them in the air, far too high for her to reach. 'Please, give me them back.'

'Don't look so worried. I ain't going to tell anyone, Lorni . . . Though that ain't even your name, is it?' He waved the letters and winked. 'And it's a good job that I can keep secrets, cos you were supposed to tell the courts where you were. You're not supposed to disappear and go underground.'

Lorni's face was bright red. 'Why are you doing this to me? What do you want? All I'm trying to do is get on with my life.'

'I've told you: I don't *want* anything. I only came for a chat. Look, cards on the table, I needed to know who you were. I like you, Lorni, and if you're going to be in my house, I need to know a bit more about you. You must understand that, right? I mean, you could have been anybody.' He stopped to laugh. 'Well, you are, aren't you? Point is, I like to know who I'm dealing with, especially after what you did to Pete.'

'Pete?'

'Don't look like that; you and me both know it was you who clumped him over the head – well, you or Tabby. I found him in the alleyway that night we first met. Lucky for you he's OK; he ain't dead.' He touched his cheek absent-mindedly. 'Not yet.'

Lorni began to pace. 'I don't know what you're talking about.'

Ned laughed again. 'Calm down, sweetheart, I'm not looking to get you into trouble. Like I say, I like you and I like Jace. He got on great with my nephew, by the way, we'll have to do it again soon . . . Lorni, come on. It's OK. Don't be upset, you want a hug?' He winked and chuckled.

She backed away. 'No thank you.'

'OK, well, we're all good now, aren't we?' He opened the door to leave. 'Say goodbye to Jace for me. He's a good kid, you should be proud of him . . . By the way, I'll need you for some cleaning tomorrow. Oh, and Lorni, your secret's safe with me.'

45

Ned was sitting having coffee on his roof terrace, enjoying a bit of afternoon sun while talking with Simon on the phone. 'The boy's easy, willing to please. It's his mother who's a bit over the top, but don't worry, I've got it sorted. She's working for me at the moment, cleaning. She seems grateful for the job and I put a bit of a fright up her the other day with something I said, but now I'm doing the good cop routine. You know how it is.' He laughed. 'It's like the kids that I pick up, you need to fuck with their head a bit, break them a little. Frighten 'em, then be nice to 'em. Makes them think they can trust you, like you've got a special bond. It works every time.' He took a sip of coffee.

'Well I'm glad you've sorted it, cos I wanted to talk about that. Plans have changed – my client, he's coming across sooner than I thought. He's coming over on Friday sometime. So I'll need the boy for the whole of Friday night and a couple of days next week, though I'll sort that out when I know the details.'

From being relaxed, Ned sat bolt up in his chair. 'Friday? That's tomorrow.'

'What is this, fucking playschool? I know when Friday is and I'm telling you that you need to get it sorted.'

'Si, come on, you were talking ten days before, and even that was a bit of squeeze – these things take time. The mum still needs a bit of working on. It's helped having Sid about, makes me look like the regular family man, but I don't want to push it, Si.'

'You better fucking push it, cos you know exactly what's going to happen to you otherwise,' Simon growled.

'I can't exactly kidnap him, can I?'

'Do what you have to.'

'Jesus Christ, Si.' Ned exhaled, the pressure building up behind his eyes.

'Look, no harm's going to come to the kid; he likes you, trusts you, and if he ain't that sharp he might not even realize what's happening . . . It's not like you're taking him to do a snuff movie, is it? I don't know how many times I told you, this geezer likes to look, that's all, so pull your fucking self together.'

Angrily, Ned threw his coffee over the deep purple Japanese maple tree which was planted in a clay pot next to him. 'Look, I'll do my best. I'm taking Jace and Sid out tomorrow lunchtime to get a bite to eat, I've invited the mum along as well. You know, to work on her, give her a bit of the old charm offensive, but I'm not sure if she'll come.'

'I don't care what you fucking do, Ned, as long as you bring Jace to me on Friday night. You got that?'

Ned hissed down the phone. 'Yeah, loud and fucking clear.'

'Glad to hear it, cos I wouldn't want to have to come to your funeral.'

A couple of hours later, with Simon still playing on his mind, Ned stood over his mother in ICU. They'd told him they were worried about her and the bleeding on her brain had been difficult to stop. And now they'd put her in an induced coma to try to help with the swelling on the brain. But they didn't know when, *if*, she'd recover. Fury shot through Ned and, kissing Pearl on her head, he marched out of the ICU, barging into the nurse as he went.

46

Forty minutes after leaving the hospital, Ned stormed down the stairs of the club in time to see Barney embracing a tall, balding man. He growled at them. 'Hate to break up the love fest, but I want a word with you, Barn.'

Ignoring Ned, Barney nodded to the man as he walked him to the stairs. 'Thanks, I owe you. If there's anything I can to do for you, call me.'

The man glanced at Ned but didn't say anything as he made his way out.

Ned sneered. He sniffed several times – an after-effect of the cocaine he'd taken as soon as he left the hospital – and wiped his nose in the crook of his elbow. 'New boyfriend?'

'Not that it's any of your business, but no.'

Ned began to pace around the club, turning occasionally to glance at Barney. He pointed and wagged his finger. 'I've been thinking, and the more I think, the more I remember – and the more I remember, the more fucking pissed off I get.'

Barney looked nervous but remained silent as he watched Ned prowling round the club.

'You see, Barney, the other day when you were talking to Cookie, when I was standing here, right behind that column, I'm sure I heard you mention the name *Finn*. In fact, I'm not sure, I'm fucking *certain* you did . . . So come on then, tell me, what were you saying? Do you know where he is?'

'We never even mentioned him,' Barney said, looking Ned in the eye.

Ned strolled up to Barney. 'One thing I really hate is when someone lies to me right in my face. I see it as a mug-off, like they must think that I'm stupid. Is that what you think, Barney? Do you think I'm stupid?'

'Ned, I don't know where this is coming from, but you already know what we were talking about. I told her to leave you and, always the gentleman, you nearly broke my finger. So no, we weren't talking about Finn, I swear.'

Ned grinned, feeling the cocaine surge through his body. 'Whose life do you swear on . . . *yours?*' His voice was low and threatening.

'I don't know what you want me to say, Ned. I can't tell you something that isn't true.'

Ned pushed his face into Barney's, so close their noses touched and Ned could feel the warmth from Barney's breath. 'But you're already telling me something that ain't true. You and I both know that you were chatting about Finn, and I want to know what that was and where he is.' Ned grabbed Barney's arm, twisting it behind his back and pushing him down on the table. 'Now we can do this the easy way, or the painful way.' Ned laughed as he twisted Barney's arm even further round.

Barney let out a yell. 'I don't know anything, Ned, we never talked about him.' His words were breathless and full of pain.

Ned raised his knee up and knelt on Barney's cheek, pushing it harder into the table. 'Do yourself a favour and start rabbiting, otherwise this ain't going to turn out well for you . . . *Do you know where Finn is?*'

'No of course not, *no.*'

Ned twisted Barney's arm round that little bit more and

Barney's cry filled the club. 'I'll ask you *again* . . . Do you know where Finn is?'

Barney's tears rolled on the table. '*No.*' The pain almost silenced him.

'OK, well let's see if you know where he is after this . . .' Ned jammed Barney's arm right round and right up, twisting it almost to the point of breaking it. Barney screamed.

'All right, all right, yes, yes, I know where he is.'

Releasing the hold, Ned roared with laughter. 'There you go, that's better. It always makes me laugh when people want to play the hero, though in my experience it never lasts long . . . So come on, give me the address.'

Barney still lying on the table, recited the address: '73 High Bucely Road, Harrow.'

Ned nodded. 'You know, if you're sending me on a goose chase, I'll come after you again . . . Where's your phone?'

'In my coat.'

Ned went into Barney's coat pocket and pulled out his mobile and threw it on the floor, stood on it, smashing it to pieces. 'We don't want you phoning anyone, do we? You know, giving them the heads-up. You wouldn't do that to me, would you? Because if you did, I won't be so nice next time.'

'I promise, I promise I'll keep my mouth shut.'

'That's what I like to hear,' Ned said as he looked at Barney on the table, then he shrugged. 'Oh fuck it, I'm here now, why not.' And with that, Ned pulled back Barney's arm, twisting and breaking his bone with a loud crack.

'Barney! Oh my God, Barney!' Tabby ran down the stairs and rushed over to Barney, who was lying on the floor in agony.

'What happened?' She helped to sit him up, leaning him against the bar side.

'Ned happened.'

'Oh Barney. You need to go to hospital; I'll call an ambulance. Where's your phone?'

Barney struggled to talk, his face deathly pale. 'He smashed it.'

'OK, I'll call them from mine . . . You'll be fine, Barney.' Tears ran down Tabby's face. 'I'll look after you.'

'Thanks, Tabs.'

She pulled out her mobile. 'I'll come to the hospital with you, OK?'

He shook his head, trembling in shock. 'No, I need you to go and do something for me. In my front trouser pocket, there's an envelope. I want you to give it to Cookie.'

Tabby nodded. Careful not to hurt him, she went into Barney's pocket, pulling out the plain white envelope.

'Give that to Cookie, but make sure you let her know I haven't looked in it. Can you also say that I'm sorry . . . Can you do that for me?' Barney's voice was layered with pain.

Tabby looked at the envelope. 'What is it?'

Barney gave her a crooked smile. 'Nothing much . . . Now off you go.'

Tabby looked at him. 'I can't leave you like this, Barn.'

'It's fine, just call an ambulance – and tell them I tripped.'

'Where's Lorni? Is she upstairs? Can she wait with you?'

'No, she went to see Cora.'

Tabby frowned. 'OK, how about I call Natalie and get her to go with you?'

Barney attempted a smile. 'That would be good . . . And Tabby, let Cookie know Ned's after Finn. He knows where he is. And call Finn as well, let him know.'

'Oh my God.'

Exhausted, Barney closed his eyes, but he continued to talk. 'You need to remember this address: *73 High Bucely Road*. Tell her that's where Finn is . . . Tell her that's where Ned's gone, and I think he's going to kill Finn.'

47

An hour and a half later Natalie sat in the ambulance with Barney, who'd been given an injection of painkiller and oxygen. She squeezed his hand and smiled. 'How you feeling now? You look much better; that diamorphine seems to be doing the trick.' She winked at him. 'I wouldn't mind some myself.'

'To tell you the truth, Nats, I feel stupid and angry that I gave him Finn's address.'

'You can't blame yourself, and nobody else will. We all know what Ned's like. If you hadn't have told him, he might have done much worse.'

'Nats?' Barney winced as the ambulance went over a bump. 'Do you think Cookie will forgive me?'

'Forgive you? What has she got to forgive? Cos you gave the address to Ned? Barney, I've already told you, it's not your fault.'

'No, I'm talking about something else – I'm talking about the reason why we fell out.'

'Well, I don't know what you've done but it can't be that bad. Besides, Cookie's got a good heart so, whatever upset her, I'm sure she'll come round. Anyway, if she didn't know it before, she's going to see what an amazing friend you are; you've had her back and you stood up to Ned – that takes bottle.'

He smiled gratefully. 'I'm praying Tabby will be able to contact Finn and Cookie and warn them about Ned . . . And hopefully Tabs won't lose that letter either. Maybe I shouldn't have given it to her, but it felt right in the moment . . . Oh I don't know,' Barney sighed.

'The only problem is Cookie's not answering her phone – well, she wasn't when I tried calling her earlier while the medics were checking you over.' She paused and frowned. 'What letter, by the way?'

Barney stared groggily at her, trying to focus. 'You swear you won't say anything?'

Natalie raised her eyebrows. 'This is me we're talking about! Course I won't.'

'So this doesn't go any further, right?' He brought down his voice, slurring his words a little under the influence of the pain-killers, but still with sufficient wits about him to make sure the paramedic who was sitting near the doors of the ambulance with his headphones on couldn't hear. 'Cookie is looking for Jo Martin. Don't ask me why, cos I can't say, but in the envelope that I gave to Tabby is the name Jo Martin's using now.'

Natalie stared at him and blinked. 'Wow, that's . . . that's . . .'

'. . . a huge deal, isn't it?'

'You could say that. How did you find out? I mean, I thought these things were supposed to be confidential? You know, a secret?'

'There's no such thing as secrets; nothing stays hidden forever. I don't know what's in the letter, I gave it to Tabby – and she has no idea what's in there either. I didn't even tell her what I'm tell-ing you.'

Natalie shook her head. 'I love Tabby, but I'm not sure that was such a good idea, giving it to her. I mean, she's a bit flaky, ain't she? I wouldn't put it past her to lose it or open it – and I'm not saying that to be nasty; that's just Tabs.'

'I know, I know, but I wasn't thinking properly, what with all the pain. And I was afraid Ned might come back and I didn't want him to find it . . . *Shit.*' Barney looked upset. 'I've messed up again, haven't I, Nats?'

'Look, don't worry, I'll sort it. I'll call Tabby and see if she's found Cookie, see what she's done with the letter, but I'll do it discreetly. I don't want her to think that we're checking up on her.'

Barney gave her hand a squeeze. 'Thank you, you're a real friend, Nats.' They arrived at the hospital and the doors of the ambulance were flung open. Barney's stretcher was carried off and Natalie stepped down, following him to the door of A and E.

'Listen, Barney, I'll come and check on you in a minute, but I'd better call Tabby first, make sure she hasn't gone AWOL.' She laughed and smiled at Barney again. 'It's going to be all right, you know. Try not to worry.'

As soon as Barney had been wheeled in, Natalie pulled out her mobile and called Tabby. It rang for a moment, then Natalie heard Tabby's voice.

'Hello? Nats?'

'All right, darlin'? I was only calling to see how it's going.'

'Not great.'

'What's wrong?' Natalie asked as she stepped out of the way of an old lady shuffling along with her four-wheeled Zimmer frame.

'I can't get through to Finn or Cookie. Cookie's phone rings but she ain't answering, and I don't want to leave a message in case Ned picks it up.'

'So you haven't seen Cookie?' Natalie spoke breathlessly.

'No. I don't even know where to look anymore; no one's seen her.'

'Well you need to, Finn's in danger.'

'Do you think Ned is really going to kill him?'

'Yeah, I do, and it's time someone put Ned in his place – he hurts too many people. I think that time should come very soon, don't you?'

'*What do you mean?*'

'Nothing, it's fine . . . but I need you to do me a favour.'

'*It'll cost you.*'

Natalie chewed on the top of her thumb. 'When doesn't it! But you know I'll make it worth your while . . .'

48

Zee yawned. She hadn't been able to sleep for the past few nights, mainly because she'd got used to sleeping next to her boyfriend Stuart, but Finn had treated him, Craig and Matthew to a football weekend away to watch a West Ham game.

She hadn't wanted to go – she actually couldn't think of anything worse – and even though she was now in the house with just Finn for company she didn't regret turning down the chance to go with them, but she was looking forward to Stuart coming back on Sunday.

Opening her bedroom door to go and get herself a drink from the kitchen, Zee heard the sound of breaking glass. She froze and continued to listen, but hearing nothing she began to move again – until the sound of footsteps coming along the hallway caused her to freeze in her tracks.

The footsteps got nearer; they sounded like they were almost outside her room. It was probably only Finn, but she looked through the crack in her bedroom door and let out a gasp, slamming her hand over her own mouth. It was Ned.

Her heart pounded against her chest and her gaze darted around the bedroom. There was no way she could alert Finn; she could hardly shout out a warning to him. Instead she tiptoed across to her bedside table to get her phone, all the time listening out for Ned. She heard the sound of footsteps again, only this time they were coming towards her door.

She threw herself onto the floor, rolled under the bed and lay motionless, listening to Ned walk in. She was so terrified, it felt like her heart was going to explode through her chest, and she held her breath for what seemed like forever, but eventually she heard Ned walk back out.

Still hidden under the bed and with her hands trembling, Zee scrolled through her contacts. She pressed dial, but Finn's phone went straight through to voicemail. She scrolled through some more of her contacts and pressed dial again, hoping this time someone would pick up. Again it went to voicemail. She tried the same number once more. This time it rang then she heard a familiar voice.

'Hello?'

'It's me, Zee . . .' she whispered.

'Hey, Zee, is everything all right? Sorry if you've been trying to call me today but I'm having real problems with my phone. It won't let me answer when people call me, then it goes straight to my voicemail. It seems to have a mind of its own.' She laughed. 'I think I might need a new one.' Cookie's voice sounded loud and chirpy in the silence of the room.

'Ned's here.'

'What?'

'He's in the house and Finn's asleep. I tried calling Finn to wake him up and warn him, but it's off.'

'Oh my God. Where are you?'

'I'm in the house; I've had to hide under the bed. The boys are away so it's just me and Finn here. Please come, Cooks, I don't know what Ned's going to do and I'm scared.'

'OK baby, OK, try not to panic. Text me the address, OK? And Zee, whatever you do, stay safe.'

Zee's fingers fumbled over the keypad as she texted the address to Cookie, then as slowly and as quietly as she could, she began to make her way out from under the bed.

★

In the doorway of the master bedroom, Ned stared at Finn as he lay asleep in his bed. He watched him for a couple of minutes then he walked into the room.

'Hello, sleeping beauty.'

Finn, woken by his cousin's voice and dressed in only boxers, bolted out of the king-size bed.

'Where you going, Finn? Look around, there's no place to hide, and even if you do run, I'll be right behind you.'

Ned brought out a knife from his pocket, the blade shining in the moonlight. 'You ready to die, Finn?' He stared at his cousin and grinned. 'You should never have played around with my whore of a girlfriend; it was *always* going to end in trouble.'

Finn glared at his cousin and then at the knife and he sneered, 'Yeah, but it was worth it.'

Fury shot through Ned. He took a stride towards Finn. 'You've got all the answers, ain't you, but it stops here. Can't say I'm sorry.'

Finn's gaze moved to the knife again. 'So this is how it ends? After all these years together, this is it?'

'You got that right, but you brought this on yourself.' Suddenly Ned swiped at Finn with his fist, catching him square on the jaw. Finn's lip burst open and he dived at Ned, who ducked out of the way, but not before Finn managed to grab hold of his neck and slam him into a headlock. Ned slashed at him with the knife, catching him across the thigh. Seizing the advantage, Ned slammed his cousin into the wall but Finn was too quick and drove his elbow hard into Ned's nose, sending Ned staggering back.

Finn followed up by leaping on him and trying to grapple the knife out of his cousin's hand as he lay sprawled cross the bed, but Ned twisted his arm, slicing at Finn's leg.

The blood seeped out, and as Finn jumped back in pain, Ned

crunched his foot directly onto Finn's kneecap, causing him to bend over and yell out in agony as his knee bone jutted out, dislocated. Before he could move, Ned slammed his fist into Finn's face, breaking his nose.

As blood spurted from Finn's nose, Ned raised the knife to bring it down on his cousin. Somehow Finn managed to bob out of the way, but with his knee dislocated, he lost his balance and immediately Ned threw his body on top of his cousin, pommelling his fists on every part of Finn's face.

Ned felt his knuckle dislodge Finn's front teeth, and he felt the wet blood on his hands as Finn's gums poured with blood. Then he slashed the knife at Finn, slicing at him, his clothes getting covered with blood as the flesh peeled open on Finn's face.

He was about to put an end to his cousin once and for all when something smashed into the back of his head.

'Fuck!' Ned yelled as Zee dropped the wooden chair she'd hit him with. The impact had sent him flying, knocking the knife from his hand and giving Finn the chance to stagger up, though the blood pouring from his wounds was making him weak, and there was so much of the stuff in his eyes he could hardly see.

'You stupid bitch!' Ned yelled at Zee, scrambling for the knife at the same time, but Zee, younger and quicker, was able to get there before him.

'Finn! Finn!' she screamed, wanting him to look her way so she could throw the knife to him, but Ned grabbed her ankles, pulling them forward sharply, which caused Zee to fall backwards and smash her head on the edge of the dresser, knocking her unconscious.

Not wasting any time, Ned took hold of the knife and charged at his cousin, plunging it into Finn's chest.

Finn dropped to the floor in a pool of his own blood, then lay motionless.

Panting, Ned stood above his cousin. Even though Finn wasn't moving, he booted him hard in his side. 'What did I tell you? What did I always promise you, eh? I told you, if you ever went near Cookie you'd be a dead man, and you know I'm a man of my word.'

Then, breathing heavily, Ned wiped down the knife before walking out of the house into the night.

'Ned! Ned!' Cookie banged on the large red front door of the house in Harrow. 'Ned! Ned! Ned! It's me, please don't do anything stupid. Ned! *Please*, listen to me. I love you, Ned, that's all that matters. It's you and me, ain't it? Finn don't matter, he doesn't mean anything to me, you know that, so there's no need to do anything to him, is there? Please, baby, open the door, will you?' There was no reply, the place looked empty.

She looked down the side of the house and saw there was a large garden and the gate leading to it was open. Immediately Cookie sprinted down the path towards it.

As she passed through the gate, Cookie saw that the back door was wide open as well. Her heart began to race and, scared of what she might find, she took a deep breath before dashing inside.

Cookie found herself in the large kitchen, which seemed to be empty. Cautiously, using her phone for a light, she moved through to the next room, which turned out to be the dining room. She glanced around: everything was tidy, nothing out of place. 'Hello? Hello? Zee? Ned? Finn?' There was nothing but silence. She made her way through another door, and this time she found herself in the hallway.

Tiptoeing along, Cookie frowned. She could hear a dripping sound and she glanced around to see what it was, the torch on her phone lighting the hall. She stopped and looked up, pointing the phone to the landing above the stairs; there was water dripping off them, bouncing down onto the polished wooden floor. It was only as she got closer that Cookie saw it wasn't water at all – it was blood.

Terrified, she raced up the stairs and saw a rivulet of red trickling out from the room opposite. 'No, no, no, no, please, please, no.' She switched on the light and ran inside. Shaking uncontrollably, she stared in horror at Finn, who lay in the middle of the room, blood from the stab wounds in his bare chest pooling on the floor.

She screamed and rushed to him, and it was then Cookie caught a glimpse of Zee, who was lying just as still. 'Zee! Zee!' There was no reply from her either.

On her hands and knees, Cookie scrambled over to Zee. She could see that she was breathing. 'Baby, Zee, wake up, darlin'. It's me, Cookie, you're safe now . . . Sweetheart, wake up.'

Behind her, Cookie heard the tiniest of moans and she looked over and saw Finn's eyelids flicker.

'Finn! Finn!' Leaving Zee, she hurried back to him. 'Baby, it's me, it's Cookie.' She stared down at him, his beautiful face slashed to ribbons, then she pulled out her phone, praying it would work, and pressed 999.

'Emergency services which—'

'Ambulance,' she cut in. 'You need to send an ambulance, he's dying, he's dying. You've got to hurry. We're at 73 High Bucely Road. It's the big house right next to the church, please hurry, *please.*'

Cookie clicked off the call and spoke into Finn's ear. 'Finn? Finn? Can you hear me? Baby, if you can hear me, I need you to listen to what I'm going to say . . . I'm *sorry*, I'm so, so sorry.' She wiped away her tears. 'And . . . and I should've told you before,

I should have said this before when I had the chance, but I'm saying it now . . . *I love you.* I love you too. I know I shouldn't have pretended that I didn't, but I was scared, I was scared what that would mean. I was scared of the way it made me feel. But I do, I love you, so you've got to fight, you hear me? Don't you slip away, cos it can't end like this. You were the one who said it hadn't even begun, remember? Finn, I can't lose you as well, so don't you die on me, don't you dare die.'

49

Friday morning came, and Natalie stood in the doorway of the guest room above Barney's club watching Lorni. 'Are you all right, babe? I just gave Jace some toast downstairs; he's on his sixth piece, I hope you don't mind . . . You off to see Barney? They said he's got to be in for another couple of days – he's doing his nut.' She smiled warmly.

Lorni's face was pinched. 'No, I'm moving on.' She sounded upset.

'What? Why? I thought you liked it here.'

She nodded as she threw a towel into the large nylon bag she'd picked up from Poundland. 'I do. But it's not going to work out.'

Natalie walked into the room and sat on the bed. 'What do you mean, it ain't working out? Have you had a row with Barney?'

Lorni gave a small shake of the head, struggling to stop herself from crying.

'Then what? Has someone else upset you? Have I done something? Look, whatever it is, we can sort it out. I know Cookie comes across as a bit of a bitch – don't tell her I said that – when you don't know her, but once you do, she's great, amazing, you'll have a friend for life there. And I know Tabby can blow hot and cold, but that's cos she's a bit jealous, Lorn. We're all she's got, so you coming in, she's sees it as being pushed aside, you're like a rival for our affection. But don't take that personally.'

'Thanks, Nats, but it isn't any of those things.'

'Then what? What can be so bad that you're going to take Jace to God knows where? Have him going from one place to another—'

'Don't judge me!' Lorni snapped. 'I love my son and I'm doing what I think's best.'

'I'm not judging you,' Natalie said kindly. 'I'm only saying that he likes it here and we all love having him. Stick around and we'll spoil him rotten.'

'I wish I could, but I can't.'

'OK, but at least tell me why.'

Lorni threw one of the second-hand T-shirts that Cora had given Jace into the bag. 'It was something Ned said.'

Natalie scoffed. 'Ned? Forget about him. You can't leave cos of what he said.'

Lorni gave Natalie a tight smile. 'I wish it was as easy as that . . . He knows about Pete, by the way, what I did.'

'Pete? Is that why you're going? Believe me, Ned won't give a shit if Pete's six foot under. Ned's got a body count as long as your arm.'

'It's not that – Pete's OK, apparently. It's other stuff. Ned found some letters in my bag, spoke to someone I don't want to find me, and I'd rather not wait around to see what happens . . . Look I don't want to be rude, Nats, but I don't really want to talk about it. Anyway,' she said, trying to shrug it off. 'Sometimes you have to move on – sometimes your past catches up to you.'

'We all have a past, Lorni. We all have our secrets. I reckon Soho is a treasure trove of them.'

'Yeah, some bigger than others. I'm sorry, but I've made up my mind . . . Tell Barney goodbye for me, won't you?'

Natalie sounded shocked. 'You're going without saying good-bye to him? You can't do that, he'll be gutted.'

'Well, I can't take Jace to the hospital.' Lorni zipped up the bag.

'Of course you can.'

Anger flushed Lorni's cheeks and leapt into her eyes. 'OK, the truth is, I don't want to take Jace . . . There are just, there are too many people there, OK? And I'd rather him not be around so many people. It makes me feel uncomfortable.'

Natalie sat in silence for a few seconds, studying her. 'You mean too many cameras?'

Zipping up her bag, Lorni shrugged. 'No, I mean there are too many people, and I don't want to leave Jace here on his own.'

'Look, if you want to see him, if you want to say goodbye to Barney, I can watch Jace for a few hours. I don't have to be anywhere for now.'

'Are you sure?'

'Of course.'

'And if Ned – well, if Ned or anyone else comes, you know . . .' She trailed off.

Natalie took hold of Lorni's hand. 'Don't worry, Lorn. I'll guard Jace with my life.'

50

'Barney? Barney, it's me . . . Hey.' Cookie, carrying an armful of magazines, stood at the door of Barney's room in the hospital and smiled. 'I heard what happened. I'm so sorry.'

'Cookie!' Barney sounded surprised. 'I didn't think you'd come.'

'I'm hardly going to stay away when you're in hospital, am I?' She hurried to his bedside, placing the magazines on the white cabinet. 'Did you hear what happened to Finn?'

Barney nodded. 'Yeah, Natalie brought a few bits for me early this morning and she told me. How are you holding up?'

Cookie looked down, tightly clutching her hands in her lap. 'It's not looking good: he went straight to surgery last night, but they've had to rush him into theatre again this morning. I'm not sure if he'll make it . . .' She stopped and took a deep breath. 'I couldn't handle sitting around waiting for news, so I thought—'

'You'd come and see me?' Barney interrupted. 'And I'm so pleased you did, Cooks, I'm so pleased you're here. Where's Ned now?'

'I don't know. I haven't heard from him.'

'What did the police say?'

Cookie glanced up and tilted her head. 'What is this, a busman's holiday?' She bit her lip. 'Sorry, I shouldn't have said that. I actually spent what seemed like half the night talking to them. Not my choice. I kept Ned's name out of it, of course, and Zee's, but I'm not worried about her – she won't say a word. But I basically told them I'd found Finn there at the house. That's all.' She shrugged. 'You know we don't involve them; it's not the world we come from, and besides, I don't want them sniffing round. The Old Bill would only be too happy to get their teeth into our business, start digging, and before you know it, I'd be doing a ten-stretch along with Ned.' She gave a wry smile. 'I ain't proud of that fact, though.'

'I know, and you ain't a bad person, Cooks, but you need to be careful. Ned's freefalling, and I'm scared you'll be next in line . . . Has Tabby seen you, by the way?'

'No. I got a few missed calls from her last night, but my phone's been playing up. Why?"

'My friend came through.'

Cookie's face drained of colour. She held onto the bedside cabinet; the room felt like it was spinning round. She gasped for breath, feeling like she was being strangled. 'What?'

'That's right, he came through. Tabby's got the envelope for you.'

'Who is she? Who is Jo Martin?' Her words trembled out.

'I don't know, I didn't open it. Look, why don't you go and find Tabby. I hope it brings you what you wanted.'

Cookie nodded and got up unsteadily from the chair. 'I'm glad you're all right, Barn. How long are you going to be in here?'

'I'll be out tomorrow, hopefully. The arm's broken in a couple of places, so they're going to operate this afternoon, pin it back together.'

She smiled. 'I don't know if we'll ever be the same again, but life's too short ain't it, to stay mad at people you care about. And I *do* care.'

Cookie walked to the door.

'I loved him, Cookie.'

Cookie turned around, puzzled. 'Sorry?'

'I fell in love. That's what happened.' Barney's eyes were full of tears, but he wiped them away.

Cookie walked back towards the bed. 'I don't understand.'

Barney fiddled with the crisp starched white sheets. 'I know it might sound like a cliché, but you can't help who you fall in love with,' he said wistfully.

'I'm not following you. Who are you talking about?'

Barney rolled his eyes at himself. 'The only man I've ever loved.'

Full of curiosity, Cookie sat on the bed. 'Go on.'

'Well at the time I was working for the NDIU – the National Drugs Intelligence Unit – gathering evidence about organized crime.' He smiled at her knowingly. 'There's a variety of things that the job involves, but one of those things is undercover work. And yeah, you guessed it, doll, stupid me fell for the guy I was collecting evidence about . . . He was a big name in the drugs game and, as time went on, I couldn't do it anymore, so eventually I ended up confessing all to him, to Aiden.'

'Jesus, Barn, that was a risky thing to do! It's lucky you ain't at the bottom of the Thames.'

'I know, but ironically I didn't want to lie to him. Instead I ended up covering for him, feeding him information. I even took money, helped launder it – how do you think I bought the club? That was when NDIU swooped in; they'd been suspicious for a while.'

'Did you both get caught?'

Barney shook his head. 'No, I'd helped him leave the country a week earlier. He went to Brazil, told me he'd be back, but he never did come back.'

'I'm so sorry.'

Barney shrugged.

'So how long was it going on for?' Cookie asked.

'Just over a year, eighteen months . . . Anyway, I ended up serving time.'

'You?' Cookie said in astonishment.

'Yeah, they threw the book at me because, as you put it, I'm Old Bill and I wouldn't cooperate. I spent sixteen years inside.'

'Oh my God.'

'So you see, Cooks, we all have our secrets. I didn't want anyone to know about my life before – like you say, Soho isn't really made for ex-coppers, but it's where my heart is. It's where me and Aidan used to hang out.'

'Do you regret it? You must do.'

Barney took a deep breath, took hold of Cookie's hands and smiled. 'I lost my career, most of my friends – though not all of them; some stood by me, like the guy who sneaked me the info about Jo Martin.'

'And who said the force didn't have bent coppers?'

'He's not bent. Not really. He's what I'd call a slightly bendy copper. Not everything's black and white. But the point is, he stuck by me when others didn't. Ultimately, I lost my house, my family, I lost everything. So to answer your question: do I regret it? . . . Do I fuck!' He roared with laughter, his eyes lighting up. 'Let me tell you, Cooks, that man, he gave me the best time of my life and, baby, I don't regret a thing.'

Walking through the entrance hall and thinking about Barney as she tried to keep her thoughts from flitting to Finn, Cookie heard her name being called.

'Cooks! Cooks!'

It was Tabby.

'Hey, Tabs, I've been to see Barney. He said you had something for me?'

'I'm going to see him now, but yeah, here . . .' She pulled the envelope from her pocket, and tried to uncrumple it. 'Sorry about that,' she said. 'Is it important?'

Cookie stared at the envelope before taking it. 'Yeah.'

'Well I ain't looked at it.'

Cookie smiled and kissed Tabby on the cheek. 'Thank you. I'll see you later.'

At the door of the hospital, Cookie pulled her collar up and paused a moment, watching the rain. Then she took a deep breath and, her hands shaking, she tore open the envelope and stared at the name written on the single piece of paper. The next thing Cookie did was run.

51

It was almost three o'clock, and driving along in the pouring rain, Cookie saw Lorni. Pulling over the Range Rover in a bus lane, she beeped her horn, lowering the window. 'Do you need a lift? Where are you off to?' she shouted to be heard over the busy traffic.

'I'm going to the hospital to see Barney,' Lorni said, stepping nearer the car.

'I've just come from there, I'll take you if you want?'

'It's OK, I can walk, I don't want you having to go out of your way.'

Cookie looked at her, concerned. 'The weather's shitty, you don't want to be walking in this.'

Lorni squinted at the rain. 'Yep, it's not good.' Then she grinned and nodded. 'So yes, please, I'd love a lift.'

'Then come on, jump in.'

Fifteen minutes later, Cookie had managed to avoid most of the heavy traffic, driving through central London in the direction of the hospital.

'I really appreciate this,' Lorni said.

'No problem. If there's one thing I hate, it's getting wet.'

They fell into silence and Cookie continued to drive, but Lorni sat up in her seat and turned to her. 'You've gone past the hospital. Cookie, the hospital's back there.'

'I know where it is,' Cookie said flatly.

'Then I need to get out. Stop here, it'll be fine.'

Cookie ignored her and carried on driving, though she began to increase her speed when she turned into Southampton Row.

'What the hell are you doing?' There was a tinge of panic in Lorni's voice. 'Has this got something to do with Ned?'

Cookie glanced at her. 'Ned? Oh my God, you're good, I'll say that for you. You're *really* good at this, but then I wouldn't expect anything less from you.'

Driving along Aldwych, Lorni's eyes filled with tears. 'I have no idea what you're talking about.'

'Wow, Lorni, you're such a good liar. Ten out of fucking ten,' Cookie snarled.

'Look, take me back OK? Jace will be wondering where I am. Cookie, please, I don't want him worrying.'

Cookie, red with anger, spat out her words: 'There you go again. You *can't* stop fucking lying, can you?'

'What am I supposed to be lying about?' Lorni sounded desperate.

'I know you must have told him you were going to see Barney, so he ain't going to be worried, is he? Not for a while anyway.'

'Cookie, what have I done to you? Why are you acting like this? Tell me, *please*, what I've done. Whatever it is, can't we sort it out?' Lorni's eyes were wide with fear, but once again Cookie ignored her while she weaved in and out of the traffic, making her way through the backroads and alleyways, heading along the embankment, past East Smithfield and down into the Limehouse link tunnel.

'Let me out, Cookie, stop the car and let me out!' Lorni screamed.

'Shut up, shut up, OK!' With one hand on the wheel, Cookie slid the other down by the side of her seat, bringing out one of the coshes Ned kept in the car. She slammed it against the side of Lorni's head, dazing her into silence.

Shaking, Cookie continued to drive, glancing occasionally at Lorni, thoughts and feelings rushing through her, memories and the pain of *that* day sitting firmly in her heart.

The rain continued to pelt down as she manoeuvred through the traffic on Newham Way. She swiped away her tears, taking deep breaths in an effort to calm herself on the approach to Tilbury Docks.

She heard Lorni groan, then out of the corner of her eye, she saw her sit up in the passenger seat, rubbing her head. 'Where are we?' Lorni looked out into the darkness.

'Didn't I tell you to keep your mouth shut?' Cookie shouted, still driving hard and veering into a small lane which took them past derelict buildings. She skidded the car down an uneven track, not bothering to mind the rain-filled potholes, the Range Rover bouncing along as it hit them at almost eighty miles an hour.

'Cookie! Cookie, *stop!* You're going to kill us!'

Slowing down in the middle of a disused shipping site in front of a derelict warehouse, Cookie stopped the car. 'Well, I'm going to kill one of us, Lorni – or should I call you Jo?'

'I'm not Jo – listen to me, Cookie, I ain't Jo Martin.' Lorni stood terrified by the isolated dockside, the cold, dark Thames below her. 'Please take me back to Jace. *Please.*'

Cookie stood holding a gun that Ned kept hidden in the tube lining of the spare wheel. 'When is it going to dawn on you: you ain't ever going to see Jace again. Like I never saw Parker again.'

'Who's Parker?'

Cookie, overwhelmed with tears and anger, walked up to Lorni and slapped her hard across her face. 'You ain't even got the decency to remember my son's name, have you?'

Lorni held her cheek, which raised into an angry welt. 'Oh my God, Cookie, *please, please.*'

'Don't beg me, it's a bit late for that now, ain't it? Is that what Parker did? Did he beg you and your sick dad to stop hurting him, did he? Did he beg you to take him back to me?' Cookie was crying hard. 'He was my *son.* My son and you took him. You took him and killed him in the worst way possible.'

'Cookie, listen to me, I am *so* sorry about Parker, but that wasn't me.'

'Don't *tell* me you're sorry – and stop lying, stop fucking lying. You owe me that at least,' Cookie screamed, her finger trembling on the trigger.

'Please don't shoot, *please* don't. Oh my God, Cookie, I can't leave Jace, please think of him, please, I'm begging you.' She dropped to her knees.

'Oh, I'm not going to shoot you. You're going to step off that edge over there all by yourself.'

Lorni turned and stared to where Cookie was pointing. 'I can't swim.'

'Then you drown, but if it's any comfort, even if you could swim, you'd drown here. It's dark, cold, the drop to the river is a long way down; there'd be no saving yourself. And it's a slow death, drowning, so while you're dying, I want you to remember what you did. I want you to regret it – and you will, you will, cos when you're under that water, when your lungs feel like they're exploding, when the agony of running out of air hits you, then you'll regret it.'

Still kneeling, Lorni leaned forward, resting her hands on the cold, wet concrete. 'Cookie, how can I prove to you I ain't Jo?'

'You can't, I know it's you; it was *your* name.'

Lorni held her head in despair. 'But it ain't me, that's what I'm trying to tell you.'

'Of course you're going to say that. Deny until you die, though I guess you'll only have to keep that up for the next couple of minutes. And let's be honest, you've never fooled me, not really. Since you arrived there's been something suspect about you, something not quite right. Your story and the reason why you and Jace keep moving from place to place never quite added up.'

'Yeah, but not for the reason you think, not because I'm Jo Martin.' Soaked from the pouring rain, Lorni rushed out her words. 'Cookie, listen to me, give me a chance to tell you the real reason.'

'I'm not interested, you're a born liar. I know all there is to know . . . Now get up and jump off that wall.' She gestured with the gun and Lorni did as she was told; she got up and walked to the edge, looking down to the whirling river below.

'That's it, now take one more step . . . I want to see you die.'

52

Jace sat swinging his legs on the chair in the club with an uneaten packet of crisps in front of him.

'Hey, Jacey, what's with the long face? Why you looking so sad, honey?' Natalie asked, placing the bottles of Perrier water in the fridge behind the bar.

Jace shrugged.

'That's not an answer. Is it because your mum's running a bit late? I'm sure she'll be here shortly. She's probably nattering away to Barney. You know what they're both like.'

'It's not that.'

Natalie frowned. 'Then what, sweetheart? What can be so bad that you ain't eating your crisps?' Natalie said as she walked round the bar to sit next to Jace. 'Come on, tell me, you can trust me.'

He shrugged again.

'Your shoulders will drop off soon, if you ain't careful. Jace, look at me, what is it?'

'It's Ned.'

'What's he done to you?' Natalie's tone was a mixture of worry and anger.

'He hasn't done anything to me, but he said he was going to take me out to lunch and he hasn't come . . . I thought he was my friend.' Tears welled in Jace's eyes. He'd been waiting for Ned and he'd been so excited, but maybe Ned didn't want to be his friend anymore.

'Listen, Jace, Ned … well, how can I put this? Fact is, Ned's not always a nice man.'

'He is to me. We were going to go to lunch and then he said we'd go to a party.'

'A party?' Natalie asked, puzzled.

'Yeah, with his friend Simon, but I'm not supposed to say, it was a secret. Only, if he's not coming, it doesn't matter if I tell you, does it?' Jace said sadly, a big tear running down his face. 'He was my only friend.'

Natalie, looking worried, wiped the tear away. 'Ned's not your only friend, we're your friends here. Me, Barney, Cookie, Cora, Tabby, we're all your mates, Jace.'

'But Mum said we might have to leave again.'

'I know, and that's really tough.'

'And then I'll be lonely again.'

'Oh, Jace.' Natalie gave him a big hug. 'I used to get lonely.'

'Did you?'

Natalie smiled and nodded. 'Yeah, but then things got better. Do you know why?'

Jace shook his head.

'They got better . . .' she went into the inside pocket of her denim jacket, pulling something out. '. . . Because of Grey . . . This is Grey, Jace, and he's my best friend.' She looked at the tatty elephant. 'Say hello to Grey, Jace.' Then she put Grey against Jace's cheek and giggled. 'He's giving you kisses.'

Jace's eyes twinkled. 'Hello, Grey.'

'Here, hold him a minute.' She went to answer her mobile, which was ringing on the bar. 'Hello?'

'Hey Nats, it's me, Tabby.'

'You OK?'

'Yeah, just wanted to let you know that I did what you asked me. I changed the name; I just wrote it on a new piece of paper.'

'Thank you. I knew I could count on you, Tabs.' She talked as she watched Jace play with Grey.

'You never said why, though. Why did you want me to change your name?'

'Oh, it's no big deal. Don't worry about it, but . . . it was . . . it was one of the kids who used to work for her.'

She stepped away from Jace, making sure he couldn't hear and speaking with her back to him.

'She got in a bit of bother, pregnant by one of the clients, and needed some quick money to go to the clinic, you know, to sort it out. She was scared to go to Ned, so I helped. It wasn't a lot of money, a few hundred quid or so, but Cookie recently found out that someone had put their hand in their pocket and, you know Cookie, she's got a good heart and felt responsible, wanted to give the money back to whoever it was . . . I said to the girl it was OK to tell Cookie it was me, but then for some strange reason she wrote it down in a letter. What happened to the digital age, eh?'

She laughed nervously, hoping that she sounded convincing and hoping that Tabby wouldn't start thinking about what she was saying *too* much, otherwise Tabby would easily see through her story. 'She dropped it off with Barney, but I changed my mind at the last minute. I dunno why, but I did . . . So anyway, that's why I said to put any old name in the envelope, that way Cookie won't have a clue who it is.'

'Any name? Like a make-up name?'

'Yeah, that's what I told you to do.'

'I didn't know that's what you meant.' A ripple of panic went through her voice.

'What do you mean, Tabs?'

'I put Lorni's name. I didn't know. I'm sorry I . . .'

'*You fucking idiot*, you fucking idiot! You have no idea what you've done. You stupid, stupid cow!' Natalie screamed down the phone before throwing her mobile against the wall.

'Everything all right? Trouble in paradise?'

She turned round and saw Ned grinning, holding Grey, turning him round and round in his hands.

'Get off him! Get off him! Don't you dare fucking touch Grey!' She leapt forward and snatched the toy elephant from a bemused-looking Ned, then she held Grey tightly, kissing him before putting him back in her pocket.

'Jesus, Nats, you really are loop-the-loop. I reckon you've been sniffing the perks of Soho too much.'

She was breathing hard. 'Go away, Ned, you're not welcome here.'

Ned ruffled Jace's hair. 'I think Jace would say different, wouldn't you, Jace? Where's your mum?'

Jace beamed at Ned. 'She's gone out.'

Natalie took a step forward. 'Go upstairs, Jace.'

Ned shook his head and glanced at Jace. 'You don't have to, mate, we're going for a little boys' night out, see Simon, have some fun, aren't we?'

'I said, *go upstairs*. Now!' The scream, the anger, the mixture of urgency and fury made Jace get up and run out of the club and through the staff door to the upstairs flat.

Ned looked at her. 'There wasn't any need for that,' he said in a mocking tone.

'There was every need to get him away from you.'

'But you're not going to get him away from me. I'm taking him with me.'

She smashed a glass on the side of the bar and pointed the jagged end at Ned. 'You ain't taking him anywhere, cos I'm not going to let you.'

★

'You all right, Tabby? You've been ages; I thought you'd gone to Peru to pick those beans,' Barney said as Tabby brought over a cup of coffee.

'Sorry, I needed to make a phone call.'

'Everything all right, Tabs?'

Tabby nodded. 'I'm fine.'

Barney patted the bed. 'Come and sit down, hon, I've known you long enough to realize when you're lying to me. Now what's happened?

'It's that letter,' Tabby blurted out.

'The one you gave to Cookie?'

'Yeah.' She wiped her nose on her sleeve.

'What about it?'

Tabby's gaze darted around for a moment, and then she looked directly at Barney. 'I did something I shouldn't have done. I opened the letter.'

'Oh my God, Tabs,' Barney said quietly.

'But that's not it, I changed the name inside.'

Barney's face blanched. 'You did what?'

'I'm sorry, I'm sorry, but she made out it wasn't a big deal. Only it must have been, cos just now on the phone she was proper screaming at me. She was so angry, Barney. But earlier when she asked me to change it, she made it sound so casual, so I did it for her, cos she's my friend.'

'Wait, what? *She*? Who's *she*?'

Tabby took a deep breath. 'Natalie. It was Natalie's name in the envelope and I changed it.' She looked down, ashamed. 'Sorry.'

'Oh Jesus.' Barney put his hand over his mouth. 'Why the hell did you do it? Oh, don't tell me: she paid you. Is there nothing you wouldn't do for money?'

Tabby was crying now. 'It wasn't that; I told you, Nats is my friend. She always looks out for me, no matter what. She won't let anyone dog me out. She tears them to strips if they do. But she got so angry with me when I told her I'd put Lorni's name on the letter.'

'What?'

Tabby blinked. 'I changed Natalie's name for Lorni's.'

'Oh my God, quick, call Cookie – and if she doesn't answer, text her, OK? We need to get hold of her.'

Tabby scrambled to get her mobile out of her pocket. 'Sure, but why?'

'Because if we don't, I've got a terrible feeling that Cookie's going to kill Lorni.'

53

Cookie's phone rang as she stood with the gun still pointing directly at Lorni. She ignored it, but it rang again and kept on ringing. Eventually, distracted and annoyed by it in equal measure, she pulled it out from her pocket and saw it was Tabby. Though she didn't bother answering, she kept it in her hand.

'Go on, Lorni, I'm waiting. *Jump.*'

Lorni looked down into the water, tears streaming from her. 'I can't. I can't.'

'Oh I think you can . . . Go on, *do it.*' She flicked off the safety catch on the gun. 'Otherwise, I'm going to start shooting, but I ain't going to kill you. I'll start with your foot first and then with your knee – I hear that's really painful – and I'll work my way up until, before you know it, you'll be jumping just to get away.'

The phone rang again in Cookie's hand, then it beeped as a text message came through.

'I'm going to count to three, and if you haven't jumped I'm going for your foot.' She pointed the gun at Lorni's feet.

Lorni, terrified, nodded, inching her way to the edge and tottering there, the wind buffeting her. 'OK, OK,' she whispered and closed her eyes, stepping one leg out over the edge into nothing but air, at exactly the same time as Cookie glanced at the text.

Jo Martin is Natalie not Lorni.

'Lorni! No! *No!*' Cookie dropped the gun and dived forward, her body slamming to the ground as she tried to grab Lorni and save her from falling, but she only managed to grab Lorni's arms, leaving her dangling dangerously over the edge with the dark waters below.

Making sure she wasn't going to be dragged forward by Lorni pulling on her, Cookie hooked her foot through one of the metal rings fixed in the concrete so that boats could tie up. 'Hold on, Lorni, hold on!' Desperate, Cookie shouted, gritting her teeth and using all her strength to try to drag Lorni back up.

'I'm falling, I'm falling! Help me! Help me!' Terror ran through Lorni's screams.

Cookie held on, but she felt Lorni's hands slipping down her arm. 'Walk up, try to walk up the wall. Push your weight against it . . . But hurry.'

With her foot still secured in the tie ring, Cookie felt Lorni begin to pull towards her, the strain on her arms painful, but a moment later she saw the top of Lorni's body appearing. 'That's it, that's it, Lorni, keep going.'

And with Cookie's help, Lorni scrambled and fought her way up to safety and once on the top she was promptly sick.

Wiping her mouth, Lorni's eyes blazed. 'You crazy fucking bitch, what did you think you were doing?'

Cookie's head was spinning and she stumbled over her words. 'I . . . I thought you were Jo Martin. I thought you were her.'

Shaking, Lorni continued to scream, 'Oh and that makes it all right, does it?'

'Yeah, yeah it does, cos after what she did to Parker, she deserves this and more. Don't tell me you wouldn't do the same for Jace.'

Deathly pale, Lorni shook her head. 'Hold a gun to an innocent person and make them jump in the Thames? No, I wouldn't.

And you know why? Cos I'm not fucking crazy.' Her shriek soared in the air.

Cookie screamed back, 'I didn't know, OK?'

Spitting with anger, Lorni ran up to Cookie and pushed her hard in the chest, causing Cookie to stumble back. 'Then try checking; try fucking checking next time you want to shoot someone.'

Cookie couldn't see through his tears. 'They took him. They took him, Lorni. I watched them take Parker. He was banging on the window of the car and I couldn't get to him. I couldn't get to him, and that's the last image I've got of him. The fear in his eyes, screaming for me, and I couldn't get to him.'

Tears poured from her as she bent over, holding her head. Wailing. Then she dropped to the ground. 'I'm so sorry, Lorni, I'm sorry.' Cookie wrapped her arms around her knees and rocked, her body racked with sobs. 'You have no idea how long I've waited for this moment. Since they killed Parker, it's the only thing that mattered, the only thing. I didn't care about anything else. I didn't care how I was treated, I didn't care what I did, I didn't care about anything apart from waiting for the day I could look Jo Martin in the eyes and kill the person who killed my baby.'

For a while neither of them spoke; the only sounds were the rain and Cookie's sobbing.

'It's OK . . . it's OK. Cookie, it's OK.'

Cookie felt Lorni's hand on her back. She looked up at her. 'It ain't OK, though, is it? I nearly killed you, and that's not OK.'

'Well you didn't kill me, did you? And you're right, I would do the same if it was Jace. At times we all do things for love which we shouldn't. You did this for Parker, I get it. I get it, Cookie.'

Soaking wet, Cookie wiped her face. 'It's Natalie. Jo Martin is Natalie.'

'What? No, she can't be.'

'She is.'

'No, you don't understand.' All the colour drained from Lorni's face. 'She's with Jace. I left her babysitting, Jace is on his own with her.'

Cookie put her foot down, driving at speed back to the West End and as she drove, she listened to Lorni's story.

'I was raped, that's how Jace came about – not that I see him like that. I love Jace, and when I look at him that's all I see. From the moment I found out I was pregnant, I wanted him.'

'I felt the same way about Parker.' Cookie exhaled when she said his name, the familiar pain stabbing in her chest. 'Anyway, go on.'

'I worked for this woman, lovely lady. I cleaned for her but she treated me like her equal, the same way she treated the other partners in her law firm. Growing up in care, I'd never felt respected; it was the first time I had, so it meant a lot. Anyway, she used to invite me to her parties. I'd say I would come, but I felt uncomfortable at the thought of mixing with her friends, like they'd look down their noses at me, and I didn't want to put myself through that. You know how it is.'

Cookie nodded, but she didn't say anything; she just continued driving through the rain, listening to Lorni.

'But she kept asking, and in the end I did go, and I met some bloke. He seemed nice enough. We went on a couple of dates, but I wasn't that into him. I could tell he was pissed off that I wasn't giving out. Then one night he drove me home and I invited him in for coffee, and he took that as a green light for him to do what he liked.' She shrugged.

'I'm sorry, Lorni.'

'Well, I left the job cos I didn't want to run into him – he worked in her law firm – then I found out I was pregnant with Jonathan.'

'Jonathan?'

Lorni nodded. 'Yeah, that's his real name . . . mine's Lorraine.' She smiled shyly.

Cookie gave her a quick glance but then continued concentrating on the road, speeding along in the wet.

'But it's fine, you can keep calling me Lorni. I think I like it more than Lorraine. Anyway, I got on with my life, started training as a nursery nurse and put what happened behind me. I told a couple of people about what happened and somehow I guess it got back to the woman who I used to work for. She must have told Rob about Jace, cos the next thing I knew, he'd tracked me down and was banging on my door demanding to see his son. I refused, of course – by this time Jace was three, almost four years old. So Rob started sending me these letters – the ones Ned read.'

'Ned?' Cookie sounded shocked. 'He knows about this?'

'A bit, not much.'

'Sorry, go on.'

'Rob started to get nasty; he began coming round and threatening me, telling me that he was going to make out that I was a bad mother. He had all these expensive solicitors to back him up. They started harassing me, I got so many phone calls, Cooks. I got scared. I didn't trust the system – I'd been brought up in care so I didn't trust social services either. I didn't trust anyone. And the problem was, I hadn't reported the rape to the police when it happened. I didn't think they'd believe someone like me. He was a bigshot lawyer and I was nothing.'

Turning left into Shaftesbury Avenue, Cookie swerved round a lorry then reached across and touched Lorni's hand. 'You ain't nothing, never think that.'

Lorni gave a sad smile. 'I went to court a few times to fight for custody, but I didn't have a solicitor – I couldn't afford it – and because I couldn't prove any domestic or sexual violence, I didn't receive legal aid. His solicitor ran rings around me, saying stuff that wasn't true. I didn't know how to defend myself, and it looked more and more like they were going to get full custody. Then, with the final hearing coming up, I got scared. I had a feeling I'd lose Jace, so I ran . . . and I've been running ever since, and now I can never go back, not if I want to keep Jace.'

Cookie pulled into a space outside Desires. 'That's why you keep moving?'

'Yeah, it's no life for Jace, but I don't know what else to do. I can't get a proper job and he can't go to school. I've really messed up, Cookie.'

Cookie opened the car door and got out, then leaned in to look at Lorni. 'No, that bastard who raped you messed up, and once this is all over, I'll help you, Lorni. I'll do whatever I can to fix this. Now come on, let's go and find Jace.'

54

'Jo! Jo!' Cookie shouted as she ran down the stairs into the club, thoughts running through her head. She switched the lights on and looked around. The place was a mess, upturned chairs and smashed glasses littered the floor.

'Quick, look upstairs – they might be there,' Cookie said, setting off without waiting for an answer.

They dashed through the staff room and up the stairs into the flat, making their way through the different rooms. 'There's no sign of him. Oh my God, what she's done to him?'

Cookie glanced at Lorni, wanting to reassure her, but she had a terrible feeling in her stomach. 'Lorni, don't panic; we'll find them. I promise we'll find them; they can't have gone far.' Cookie's voice broke, scared for Jace while thoughts of what happened to Parker raced through her mind.

'Let's check downstairs again – who knows, they could be in the kitchen or one of the backrooms. I'll check the kitchen and you check the cellar, OK? Maybe they're there.' Though even as she said it, Cookie didn't hold out much hope.

Rushing through the main club, Cookie continued to call. 'Jo? Jo? Jace?' She ran through the back corridor and dashed into the kitchen, then she froze. Sitting there, bleeding from a wound to her head, was Natalie – Jo Martin, the woman she'd been waiting to speak to all this time, all these years. Only now that she finally knew who she was talking to, she didn't have the words – she

314

couldn't find the right words even though she'd planned what to say, what to do to her when she finally caught up with her. As she stared at the woman sitting there, she wasn't seeing Jo, she was seeing Natalie, her friend.

'Hello, Katherine.'

Cookie took a step back, grabbing the table for support. 'You know my name? You know who I am?'

'I've known since the first day I saw you. You haven't changed, and it's nice to hear that everyone still calls you Cookie, not Katherine . . . That's what your son called you, wasn't it? They talked about that in court; they said Parker was a sweet little boy, funny little boy full of adventure, and his favourite two things were insects and mealtimes, and at one point he called everything and everyone Cookie, because he loved them so much. That's what the Crown Prosecutor said on day two. Everyone laughed on that day, but no one was laughing on day three. Nobody was laughing then.' Cuddling Grey, Jo stared at Cookie.

Cookie's head was spinning; this wasn't how she thought it would go. It wasn't Jo who was supposed to know who she was, it was supposed to be the other way round. She held her head, trying to get her breath. 'How, how do you know? How do you know what I look like?'

'I saw you in the playground that day. I saw you looking for Parker. I watched you for a while and I wanted to speak to you, I wanted to talk to you. I thought you looked nice. I thought you'd make a nice friend.'

Triggered by her words, Cookie dashed over and grabbed hold of Jo's top. 'No, no, you don't get to say that to me.' Tears streamed down Cookie's face. 'You don't tell me that you saw me before you took my son. You don't tell me that I looked nice. You're sick, you're sick.' She banged Jo against the wall and Jo didn't do anything to resist. 'Did you think you could hide forever?'

'No, I'm pleased you know. I wanted to tell you. I've wanted to tell you for so long, but I never could bring myself to, because I enjoyed being your friend. I liked being close to you, and I knew once you realized who I was, you wouldn't want to be my friend anymore.'

'*Friends?* You're sick, you're fucking sick. What is the matter with you? How could you do this to me – because yes, yes, I loved Natalie so much. Natalie was my friend. You made me love her because she was my brilliant friend, the friend that helped me, the friend that I spoke to when I was feeling down, the friend that made me laugh so hard I almost weed myself. But she wasn't real, was she? Because the real Natalie is Jo Martin, the same Jo who took my son. Who *killed* my son.' Cookie's face curled up, tears and snot running into her mouth. 'Oh my God, you kissed me. You sick, sick bitch.' She slammed Jo against the wall again and screamed at her.

Cookie looked down and shook her head, then she whispered, 'Why? Tell me why you hurt him. Why did you take Parker away from me? He was my baby.'

'I didn't mean to. I mean, I didn't know what he was going to do . . . I don't think I did, the truth is I don't know, but I don't think you know what real fear is. I was fourteen and I was scared. I was so scared of him, Katherine. He was like a monster to me, and he's still up here, in my head.'

Cookie pointed to herself. 'Don't tell me I don't know what real fear is – that day when Parker went missing, that was real fear. And Parker – Parker would have had real fear when you took him. And every day being with Ned, trying to stay alive, that's real fear, so don't try to tell me anything about fear, Jo. You aren't the only one who owns it,' Cookie screeched, almost choking on her tears.

'You and me are so similar, Katherine – our lives are very much the same.'

'I am nothing like you. Understand that. I am *nothing* like you. I couldn't do the things you did.' Cookie was weeping, her whole body shaking.

'I didn't let him hurt Parker. I didn't. In court they said because of the fire they couldn't tell if Parker had been touched, abused, but he wasn't. I swear he wasn't. I would never have let that happen. I tried to help him, I really did.'

'You took him away from me, so why would you help him?'

'Because I'm not a monster, no matter what they say about me. It wasn't how everyone thinks it was. I swear I tried to help him . . .

'Parker, come on Parker. Come on, that's it, I'm going to take you home.' Trembling, Jo crept into the bedroom, making sure that her dad didn't wake up, though he'd passed out drunk, which she hoped meant she had a little more time.

Her dad had been celebrating Parker's arrival, drinking more than the ginormous amount he normally did. Then Jo had listened to him call some friends, inviting them to come and have some fun, to party. That's what had made her come to get Parker; that's what had given her the courage to take him home to the girl she'd seen in the play-ground, because Jo knew exactly what her dad's friends were like – she knew what happened at those parties and she didn't want Parker or Grey anywhere near them.

Parker ran towards her, and Jo took his hand and then picked him up, tiptoeing along the landing, desperate for her dad not to hear, hoping he was still asleep on the couch. She was trembling but Parker made her feel better; the way he'd wrapped his arms around her neck to hold on to her was something Grey never did.

At the top of stairs Jo stopped. She could smell smoke, fire, but she continued making her way down the stairs, wanting to get Parker out as soon as she could – but at the bottom, when she opened the door, the heat held her back as if it were her jailer, making sure she didn't escape while her dad slept.

Jo held onto Parker, trying to get through the burning flames, but the smoke was thick and choking, wrapping round them like a snake and making it hard to breathe. 'It's OK, Parker, we've got you. Me and Grey have got you, we'll keep you safe, we won't let him near you, we promise . . . Parker? Parker?'

She coughed and Jo could see the smoke had made Parker sleepy, which she thought was a good thing because now he wouldn't know there wasn't another way out, and at least this way Jo knew for certain that her dad and his friends wouldn't ever be able to be near Parker. And happy with that thought, Jo and Grey slowly walked back up the stairs and she laid a sleeping Parker on the bed and then she waited to burn . . .

'So you see Katherine, Parker wasn't scared, he had me and Grey, and he just fell asleep, he didn't know about the flames, he didn't hear the fire brigade battle to try to get us out, he was asleep.'

Before Cookie could say anything else, Lorni rushed in. 'You're here, you've found her, has she told you? Has she told you where Jace is?'

Cookie shook her head, realizing that she hadn't even asked.

'Cookie? Did she tell you?' Giving up on trying to get an answer from Cookie, Lorni stepped towards Jo and demanded, 'What have you done with him? Jo, what have you done with Jace? I swear, if you've hurt him, if you've done anything to him. I—'

Jo struggled to her feet, bleeding profusely. 'I haven't done anything, I swear . . . Lorni, you've got to believe me. Ned took him.'

'Ned? What would Ned want with him?' Cookie looked at her in disbelief.

'He *did*; it was Ned that knocked me about. I tried to stop him, I swear, Lorni, but in the end I wasn't any match for him. I'm so sorry.'

Cookie blinked and looked at Jo properly. She hadn't even thought about what had happened to her – all she'd been thinking about was Parker. 'But why, why would Ned take him? That's what I don't understand.'

Jo shook her head. 'I dunno. He said something about taking Jace to see his friend Simon. Earlier, before Ned got here, Jace told me that Ned was supposed to be taking him to a party with Simon – he was upset that Ned hadn't showed up.'

Cookie felt her blood running cold. 'Simon Draper?'

'I don't know,' Jo said truthfully.

'Was Sid with him?' Lorni asked.

'Sid? Who's Sid?' Cookie frowned.

'Sid. Ned's nephew.'

Panic surged through Cookie and she shook her head. 'Ned ain't got a nephew.'

'But last week he showed up here with Sid, and I let him take Jace for a "boys' day out",' Lorni said, looking and sounding scared. 'Where do you think he's taken Jace?'

'The only reason Ned would take Jace to Simon would because of the sort of parties he sometimes holds,' Cookie said, trying to hold back her fear.

'What sort of parties?'

Cookie looked at Jo and then at Lorni. 'You don't want to know.'

'Tell me!' Lorni screamed. '*What sort of parties?*'

'They're sick ones, Lorni, sick ones . . .'

★

'Are you sure I shouldn't come?' Lorni stood by Cookie's car as Cookie started the engine.

'No, it's best you don't. I know what Ned's like, I know what Simon's like, and besides, what if I'm wrong? What if Jace comes back and there's nobody here?'

'Are you sure we shouldn't call the police?'

Reversing out of the tight parking spot, Cookie nodded. 'Believe me, this time I'd be only too happy to involve them if we could, but it's too dangerous. Simon's got bent coppers who tip him off, and if he gets word the Old Bill are on the way, you'll never see Jace again. But Lorni, I promise you, I promise that if Jace *is* with Ned and Simon, I'll bring him back to you. I might not have been able to bring my boy back, but I promise I'll bring Jace.'

Lorni nodded.

Revving the engine and about to set off, a thought hit Cookie. 'Where's Jo gone?'

'I don't know. I left her in the kitchen but she's probably gone now. Run off somewhere. Are you all right?'

'I will be once I bring Jace back,' Cookie called back as she set off down the road at top speed.

55

The route to Simon's house in the heart of Kent was one Cookie knew all too well. She'd been taken there on numerous occasions, dozens of times in fact, back when Ned was pimping her out to men. The memory of those parties still gave her nightmares; she'd had things done to her that left her unable to walk for days. And if Simon *had* taken Jace, if Simon really was having a party, Cookie knew there was only one place he was going to host it. And with that in mind, she pressed her foot on the accelerator, pushing the Range Rover to its limit as she sped down the motorway.

A few miles outside the village of Penshurst, Cookie parked the car and turned the lights off. Simon's mock Tudor mansion was no more than a couple of minutes' walk, but that was only if she took the direct approach, walking down his long tree-lined drive-way. Her only hope of getting Jace out alive depended on not being seen. So, pulling up the hood on her jacket, Cookie set out across the fields.

In the back of Cookie's Range Rover, Jo sat up. She watched until Cookie had disappeared into the darkness, then clambered over the back seats and let herself out of the passenger door. As she did, she stepped on something hard lying in the footwell: a gun. Slipping it into her pocket, she took off in the direction Cookie had gone.

★

In the darkness, Cookie dashed through the woods, stopping at any noise while trying to ignore the panic rising inside her. She was drenched from the rain, and the sodden undergrowth kept wrapping itself round her legs, slowing her down, but finally she made it to a wooden fence and beyond it the neatly mowed lawns of Simon's estate. Yelping as a piece of barbed wire tore her trousers and dug into her flesh, she cleared the fence and ran along the overgrown path, sweat trickling down her spine. She didn't stop until she came to a large oak tree. Using the tree for cover, she surveyed the house, all lit up for a party, and the cars parked outside . . . including Ned's Bentley and the distinctive blue Rolls-Royce which she knew belonged to Simon Draper.

Ducking, she ran across to the rose garden wall, pushing herself against it, feeling the cold stones on her back. She looked towards the front door and counted, five, six men, talking, laughing, drinking.

Desperate not to be spotted, Cookie took cover among the thorny rosebushes, making her way on her hands and knees towards the back of the house, where she knew there was another entrance. But her heart sank as she spotted one of Simon's henchmen smoking a cigarette by the back door.

Trying to remember the layout of the mansion, her gaze scanned the house and her stare rested on a ground-floor window that was wide open. She glanced around, listening, making sure no one was coming. Taking a deep breath, she raced across to the window and clambered inside.

The room led into a corridor, and Cookie crept along listening out for voices, her heart pounding. She peeked into the lounge: it was empty. Moving as quickly as she could, Cookie made her way further along the corridor, listening at every door before checking inside.

By the stairwell, Cookie heard voices both in front of her and behind her. Thrown into a panic, she searched for a hiding place, but seeing nowhere she opened the nearest door and slipped inside, finding herself in the large library.

She raced towards the window, but it was locked. She pulled the curtains aside, searching for a key, then turned to look where else it might be hidden. It was then that she saw him. In the corner of the room, sitting in a chair looking dazed and upset, was Jace, bare chested and wearing only boxer shorts.

'Jace!' she gasped. 'Jace, oh thank God.' She rushed to him, kneeling in front of his chair and immediately he flung his arms around her. She felt him shaking and she squeezed her eyes shut to stop her tears. 'Are you all right, Jace? Did someone hurt you, did someone touch you?' she said, taking off her jacket and placing it over his shoulders.

Jace shook his head, but he didn't speak. Anger and hatred for Ned and Simon surged through her. 'I'm going to get you out of here, OK? But we need to hurry.'

She grabbed his hand and ran to the door, listening for sounds of movement. Praying that the coast was clear, she took a deep breath, opened the door and prepared to run.

'Cookie? What the fuck are you doing here?'

Halfway down the corridor she heard her name and she turned and saw Simon Draper standing there. About to run the other way, she heard voices coming from that direction, so her only option was to push Jace, who was crying in terror, back into the library.

She slammed the door pressing her body against it, then her eyes darted around and she ran across to the small table by the bookshelves.

'Jace, help me move this. Grab the other end.'

With Jace's help she picked up the table, carrying it to barricade the door.

'*Cookie, what the fuck do you think you're doing?*' Simon's voice boomed out from the other side. He rattled the handle, trying to barge his way in.

Pressing her body against the door in the hope of holding Simon back, she whispered to the boy, 'Jace, Jace, get that chair! Get the chair and smash the window, smash it, honey, and then you run, you hear me, you run and keep on running. *Do it!*'

As Cookie pushed her weight against the door, Jace grabbed the wooden chair and smashed it against the window, but it didn't break; the chair seemed too heavy for Jace to swing properly and he didn't have the force to do any real damage. 'Try again, Jace! Try again. I can't hold him for much longer. That's it, baby—'

The table they'd used as a barricade crashed to one side and Cookie flung herself out of the way as Simon barged in.

Jace screamed and ran behind Cookie, who stood facing Simon.

'Well, this is a nice surprise; I was telling Ned only the other day that it's been too long since I've seen you. Maybe once you hand me the boy, we can get reacquainted. I'm sure Ned won't mind.' He winked.

'You're not having him. You'll have to kill me first.'

Simon pulled a face. 'Seems a shame, but OK . . . Jace, come here, son. We've got a deal ain't we, mate? Come on.' He held out his hand.

'Don't listen to him, Jace.'

'He ain't got a choice,' Simon snarled. 'Now fucking come here, Jace, stop wasting my time.' Simon raised his voice. '*Now!*'

Jace was shaking, his eyes full of fear. He went to move towards Simon but Cookie grabbed hold of his arm. 'You don't have to do what he says.'

Simon took a step nearer. 'I think he does . . . Come here.'

'Leave him alone, Simon.' Cookie began to back away.

'You heard her.' Jo appeared in the doorway. Glaring at Simon, she nodded to Cookie, who stared back at her wide-eyed with shock, then she gave the briefest of smiles to Jace. She kicked the door closed behind her. 'Now where were we?'

'Who the fuck are you?'

Jo grinned. 'Someone you wish wasn't here.' And before Simon could react, she sprang forward and smashed the butt of the gun in his face, shattering his nose.

'Fuck, you . . .' But Simon's words were cut off as Jo brought the gun down again onto his head, pounding it, once, twice, the gun's cold metal gouging into his flesh, the blood spurting out.

Simon dropped to the floor and Jo, panting with exertion, turned to Cookie, who was holding Jace against her, shielding him from the sight.

'We've got to get out of here. We'll go through the window.' Jo picked up the chair and did what Jace was unable to do, shattering the window into tiny pieces.

'Quick, Jace, you go first,' Cookie urged, and Jace nodded encouragement as he stepped through the jagged glass, followed by Cookie and then Jo.

The cold air hit.

'*Cookie! Cookie! Where the fuck are you!*'

'That's Ned.' Cookie whispered, her voice shaking. 'He must have heard Simon say my name.'

'We've got to go, come on.' Jo pointed to the woods and they took off, running as fast as they could, the angry voice of Ned ringing out in the darkness behind them.

Cookie glanced at Jace, his face full of fear, then turned away, images of Parker's frightened eyes flooding her mind.

'*Cookie!*'

Ned's voice seemed to be getting closer and she pulled Jace along even faster. She looked around her, but it was so dark she could barely see anything. She couldn't even make out where Jo had got to.

'*Cookie! Cookie!*' Ned bellowed out her name again as she and Jace skidded and tripped on the mud. He was definitely getting closer; she could feel him bearing down on her.

'*Come here! Where you going, Cookie? You know you can't get away from me; you know there ain't anywhere you can go that I won't find you.*'

She was too afraid to turn around, but his voice sounded closer than ever and she could hear the sound of his running feet. '*Cookie! Don't you run away from me, don't you fucking do that!*'

Then she felt his hands on her shoulders and she heard Jace scream as she fell face first to the ground.

'Get off, get off!' She fought back, but Ned was too strong. He flipped her over to face him.

'You ungrateful fucking bitch, I gave you everything I could, but it still ain't it enough, is it?' He put his hands round her neck and started to squeeze. 'I told you, didn't I? If you *ever* left me, I'd kill you. I told you, Cookie, you're mine – why couldn't you have just listened?' He squeezed even harder, her eyes bulging as the air was cut off. 'Say you love me, say you love me, Cookie.' But Cookie couldn't say anything as Ned pressed ever harder and she felt herself blacking out, her life slipping away.

'*Get off her!*'

Cookie heard a bang. Then something warm and wet splattered her face and Ned released the pressure on her throat. Coughing and spluttering, she rolled clear of Ned. She could hear him, still lying on the ground, bellowing in agony.

She wiped her eyes and scrambled up, realizing she was covered in blood. Ned's blood. 'You shot him?'

'Right in the balls.' Jo shrugged. 'I reckon it was the perfect place, don't you?'

As Ned continued to roll about on in agony, Jo put her hand on Jace's shoulder and guided him towards Cookie. 'You two need to go. You need to get out of here. The police will be here soon.'

'The police?'

'Yeah, I called them. I told them there was a child in danger, that someone had fired a gun.'

'Why? Why would you do that?'

'This way you won't be a part of it. They'll not be looking anywhere else. They won't be sniffing around. They'll only be too pleased to see me back behind bars . . . It's the least I can do, Katherine. *Please* let me do this. I can't bring Parker back, but I can do this. Now go. Run, run . . . And Katherine, take care of yourself.'

And without saying anything, Cookie nodded and ran into the night with Jace.

Jo heard the sirens before she saw the blue lights coming down the track they were standing on. Eight police cars, and somewhere in the distance she heard a helicopter. She stared down at Ned, who held his hands between his legs, groaning from where he'd been shot. She booted him in his side and crouched next to him, lifting his head up by his hair. 'Look, they're here now. Can you see them?'

Ned could only groan.

Lit up by the headlights of the police cars as they approached, Jo whispered into Ned's ear, 'They'll probably give you eight years, maybe less, and you'll be out in two. And then what, Ned? What will you do? You'll probably go after my Katherine and make her life a living hell. You've done it before, so why wouldn't you do it again? But I don't want you to do that. Me and Grey

327

don't want you to hurt her again. She's been through enough, don't you think?'

Jo stood up, squinting in the lights of the cars. 'And that's why you ain't going to see the inside of any jail cell, Ned, cos you ain't ever going to hurt my Katherine again. She deserves to be free.' She pulled back the trigger, aiming the gun at Ned's head. 'Now fuck off out of here.'

And then she fired.

FIVE MONTHS LATER

Soho stopped. The pavements were lined, and hand in hand in a line they walked behind the white flowers spelling the name PARKER in the glass horse-drawn hearse. Cookie turned to Barney, her whole body shaking.

'That's it, girl, you've got this, you can do this,' Barney nodded to her. Unable to speak through her tears, Cookie mouthed the words *thank you* as she squeezed Tabby's hand on the other side.

They all walked, following the carriage, and she nodded to the Turkish couple from the deli, the waiters from the restaurant, the ladies from the nail bar, the owner of the launderette. They were all out for her . . . for Parker. A memorial for him arranged by Finn after he'd found out she'd never attended Parker's funeral.

At Soho Square, Finn, with his scars still red and angry, leaned over her shoulder and whispered, 'This was Barney's idea. He told me Parker liked insects, so we thought he'd like this.'

And right in front of them, hundreds of butterflies were let out of boxes, flying and soaring into the cloudless sky.

She walked forward, watching, remembering, and for the first time she heard Parker's voice, his laughter in her head, free from anything apart from the love she felt towards him. 'Goodbye, Parker. Goodbye.'

Then she felt arms around her and she turned to smile at Lorni and Tabby, Cora and Finn, Barney, and of course, Jace. Her family. And for the first time in what seemed like forever, Katherine 'Cookie' Mackenzie had finally found peace.

Even though she was locked up again, for the first time in her life Jo felt free. At peace. Her dad no longer lived in her head and she didn't have to pretend anymore; she didn't have to move from one place to another. This cell, like that old box under the bed, was her home, and Jo felt comfortable in it. As long as she had Grey, she knew she'd be fine.

She held on tightly to him, humming away, thinking about everything that had happened.

She'd heard through the grapevine that Simon Draper had got what was coming to him. He'd been picked up by the police and placed on remand in Pentonville. While he was there, a couple of the lags had jumped him, determined to give the nonce what was coming to him. He'd been found the next day with his throat sliced in half. Jo giggled at the thought.

Even that evil old witch Pearl was in no fit state to bother anyone now. In the unlikely event that she ever made it out of hospital, she had nowhere to go now that Ned was pushing up daisies. Though there was always a bed in here for her; Pearl would find it a home from home.

Jo climbed up on the barred window ledge and looked out. 'Goodnight, Tabs. Goodnight, Barney. Goodnight, Cora.' Then she dropped her voice to a whisper. 'Goodnight, Katherine.' Then she laughed and yelled loudly: 'Nearly forgot you: Goodnight, Lorni. Goodnight, Jace.'

'Keep it down in there.'

'Fuck off!' she shouted back at the screw, then began to imagine what they'd all be doing now. Barney fussing over something and nothing, Cora having a natter and a gossip, Tabby trying to stay off the gear, Lorni chasing after Jace, and Katherine . . . well, she hoped Katherine would be being spoilt rotten by Finn. Loved. Happy. Cared for. And even though the outside world wasn't really where she felt she belonged, Jo would miss them all. They were her family. She'd miss the club, the deli, the Turkish couple who always fought, she'd miss the buzz of Soho, but most of all she'd miss the Streets . . .

ACKNOWLEDGEMENTS

A huge thank you goes to Wayne Brookes, my editor, who made me roar with laughter with his emails and helped shape the book with his thoughtful insights. I'd also like to thank Anne for the amazing job she did on the copy-edits, and a big thank you as well to Rebecca Needes for all her helpful input. I'd like to give a big shout out to the rest of the team at Pan Mac; it's very exciting to have this book published by them. As always, a massive thanks goes to Darley, my wonderful agent, and the rest of the team at the agency. Lots of love for my family and friends who give me unwavering support. And of course to you, the reader – a big thank you for the loyalty and support you show.